D0828144

"This is a really intriguing book, a far.
It's beautifully written, and the characters are defined and interesting."
— Elizabeth Bear, author of *Hammered* and *Blood and Iron*

"Welcome to the teradome: an eternal, but decidedly unholy, city with a lav-ishly rendered cast of freaks, a decadent 'City Imperishable' haunted by 'slob-bering monsters from the noumenal world' and threatened with barbarians at the gate."
— Richard Calder, author of *Dead Boys/Girls/Things* and *The Twist*

"The pacing is terrific, the imagery sharp, clear, and very, very weird."
— *SF Site*

"Jay Lake is hot… one of the bright new voices in the field."
— Paul Di Filippo, *SciFi.com*

"Lake is an up-and-coming sf writer to watch."
— *Library Journal*

"…a top-flight talent."
— *Booklist*

Jay Lake lives in Portland, Oregon, with his books and two inept cats, where he works on numerous writing and editing projects, including the World Fantasy Award-nominated *Polyphony* anthology series from Wheatland Press. Recent proj-ects include *Rocket Science* and *TEL : Stories*. His next novel after *Trial of Flowers* is *Mainspring,* coming summer 2007. Jay is the winner of the 2004 John W. Camp-bell Award for Best New Writer, and a multiple nominee for the Hugo and World Fantasy Awards.

TRIAL OF FLOWERS

A NOVEL OF THE CITY IMPERISHABLE

Other books by Jay Lake include:

Novels
Rocket Science
Mainspring (forthcoming)
Madness of Flowers (forthcoming)

Collections
Greetings from Lake Wu
Green Grow the Rushes-Oh
American Sorrows
Dogs in the Moonlight
The River Knows Its Own (forthcoming)

Edited Works
Polyphony, Volumes 1-6 (with Deborah Layne)
All-Star Zeppelin Adventure Stories (with David Moles)
TEL : Stories
Spicy Slipstream Stories (with Nick Mamatas)

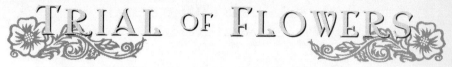

TRIAL OF FLOWERS

A NOVEL OF THE CITY IMPERISHABLE

JAY LAKE

NIGHT SHADE BOOKS
SAN FRANCISCO

First Edition

ISBN-10   1-59780-056-2
ISBN-13   978-1-59780-056-3
Printed in Canada

Night Shade Books
Please visit us on the web at
http://www.nightshadebooks.com

For Gene Wolfe, who first gave me the magic,
Deborah Layne, who helped me rediscover it,
and Tami Gierloff, who has kept it alight.

Acknowledgment:
I would like to thank Forrest Aguirre, whose fault this ultimately is. My thanks also to Jason Williams, Jeremy Lassen and Jennifer Jackson for making this book possible, as well as to readers Sarah Bryant, J. B. Kim and Ruth Nestvold, and especially Daniel Spector and Kelly Beuhler for their work on both book and map. Thanks also to Marty Halpern for the copyediting. Most importantly, Tami Gierloff, who put up with me writing this, and read it back to me line by line when I needed that most.

The City Imperishable

I
AUTUMN OF THE CITY IMPERISHABLE

The lindens along Pondwater Avenue burned, making light and shadows of their own in the moonless night. One by one the trees exploded as the sap within passed the boiling point, the noise spurring the scream of panicked horses in back alley stables. Sharp-scented smoke stung Jason's eyes as bark and woodpunk swirled burning into the dark autumn sky.

No hand had set the fire, no angry curse had driven the blaze. The trees had burst into flame of their own accord. Jason knew he should have been moved to fear by the sight, but the noumenal, or at least the passing strange, had become too commonplace of late.

As the explosions died away, servants and laborers moving in to douse the embers. There was nothing to be learned here. No one knew any more than he did. Jason turned his face back toward the river and home.

Recently everyone had studied caution. Even he, barely thirty, felt the weight of the city on his shoulders. His father had left no legacy save struggle, pain and the soul bottles long scattered throughout the City Imperishable. Instead, Jason had found purpose in committing himself to his master's work of keeping the City Imperishable secured from the secret wars of the noumenal world. This season the task threatened to overwhelm him.

As he walked Jason slipped a silver obol from his pocket and worried it between his fingers. The familiar face his touch found on the coin resembled his master—Ignatius of Redtower, Second Counselor to the Inner Chamber of the Assemblage of Burgesses. While Jason himself was mainly a tradesman, Ignatius was a true initiate of the mysteries of the noumenal world, a philosophick doctor of the Hermetic Orders. The connections between the two of them were deep and tangled, rooted in the fall of Jason's father.

A dwarf awaited Jason where Pondwater Avenue crossed Silver Alley. Lips scarred with old thread holes, fever-eyed, his heavy square body tottered on the stunted legs of his kind. Thousands of dwarfs dwelled, or had dwelt, within the City Imperishable. Raised in confined boxes to shape their legs and torsos, dwarfs were well educated as a result of being a captive audience in the most literal sense. Traditionally they worked as civil servants or in commerce throughout the city.

Jason understood this all too well. After the disastrous collapse of the family fortunes, he had spent the final, most difficult years of his childhood in the care of his father's business manager, one Bijaz the dwarf. Strange times, during which he had learned many of the ways and rituals of the city dwarfs, including fingertalk. He'd paid a high price for his tutelage. Bijaz had sewn Jason's lips shut in a perverse echo of dwarf custom. Somewhere in the endless nights with needle and candle, Jason had discovered a taste for pain in himself, and eventually in others.

In the end he and his father's business manager had parted without the encumbrance of friendship. Jason had gone on his way, weathering the strange affair of the soul bottles that had in turn led him into Ignatius' service and toward a higher sense of purpose than mere finance or dissolute vice. The old dwarf had moved on as well, and now stood high in the councils of his kind, speaking for the Sewn faction to the Inner Chamber and the Burgesses.

Onesiphorous, the dwarf now waiting for him, was a leader opposed to Bijaz and the Sewn. The Slashed were a "free dwarf" movement that had seeped into the city's cobbled streets during the wet, hot days of the recent summer. As that season turned to autumn, the Slashed leader had sought Jason out. Jason felt disposed to favor his cause, just for the sake of the thing.

"Factor," said the dwarf. No fingertalk for the Slashed. It was a point of pride among the rebellious. His voice was different, too, lacking the whistling undertones of a traditional dwarf. The lips of the Sewn were stitched tight around a little opening pursed for nutrition and speech, always as if poised for some pain-barbed kiss.

"Onesiphorous." Jason nodded, drifting to a halt beneath the black iron pole of the gas lamp where the dwarf awaited him. "Out enjoying the arboreal autos-da-fé?"

The dwarf snorted. "No concern of mine what the rich folk up the hills do with their landscaping."

"I suppose not. So what brings you out to the quality districts?" The Slashed had been moving dwarfs and dwarfesses south to Port Defiance and beyond by the bargeload since the end of summer. Fleeing, much like the ruby-coated parrots of Imperatrix Park had fled.

The City was in trouble. Even the dead knew that.

"Have you had word from Ignatius this last day or two?"

Jason was surprised. The Slashed agitator usually wanted to harangue him regarding city policy or pass word about what was taking place belowstairs and behind doors. It was a game of information, rumor traded for wishful thinking. For one, Jason had warned the Slashed about the Fixed Youth Edict. Most of the boxing rooms had been empty when the Provost's bailiffs had shattered their doors.

That had earned Jason the gratitude of many dwarfs both in and out of the movement. In return Onesiphorous kept him well-informed.

But Ignatius was Jason's concern, no matter for the Slashed.

Caution, thought Jason. More was burning here than trees. "Ignatius is at his own works."

"As may be. Still, I would seek him out were I you."

"Indeed, sir dwarf."

Onesiphorous turned and stumped downhill, heading toward the River Saltus. The lights of the gas lamps stitched the darkness ahead. Jason matched the dwarf's pace, waiting to see what else his interlocutor might have to say. His thoughts were awhirl over what might be transpiring with Ignatius.

"This place is still our home," the dwarf muttered. "Even as we're leaving."

"You know the Burgesses have promised to protect your people." Ignatius had extracted that concession from the First Counselor in the wake of the botched Fixed Youth Edict.

Onesiphorous spat. "As if. Too much coming. Everyone knows there's armies on the march, looking to burn us all out. There's been blood in the shadows since long before the Bladed Throne fell empty. That's the way of life here. But now…there'll be snow in the Great Hall of the Assemblage before we see greenleaf on the lindens once more. The protection of the Burgesses doesn't mean a fart in the river."

"The City will stand." Jason wished he believed that himself. Tradition said that the City Imperishable had never been conquered by an outside enemy.

"Walls will stand, maybe. Guarding smoke and ashes." Onesiphorous stopped again, glanced up, catching Jason's eye. "Why are you staying?"

"It's still my home." Ghosts, memories, the only place he knew. His father had died here, Jason lived here. For all that Jason managed a shipping warehouse down along the docks at Sturgeon Quay—when he wasn't skulking about Ignatius' errands—he'd never even passed outside the city walls. "There is nowhere else."

"That's the difference between you and me. I can see somewhere else." The dwarf shook his head and waddled away down an alley.

"Then why are you still here?" Jason asked the empty shadows. Somewhere blocks behind him, a tardy linden exploded with a crack like wooden thunder.

The city is.

Those were the city's words, a motto found on even the oldest coins grubbed from forgotten wood-walled barrows split open during excavations. The same phrase was carved on the lintels of the River Gate and the Sudgate. It was sewn in silk and jeweled banners hanging in the Assemblage of Burgesses, that those worthies might look up from their hard-won graft and consider for a moment whose fortunes they held in their hands.

Jason had recently been considering the merits of "the city was." This morning he walked the eastern wall, where the shift from "is" to "was" seemed all too easy to see. This expanse of ramified and crumbling stonework was the farthest point in the City Imperishable from his usual riverfront haunts. He was here seeing to the city's defenses in lieu of Ignatius of Redtower, who as Onesiphorous had pointed out the preceding night, remained obstinately absent—no response to Jason's letters or increasingly urgent inquiries. Just continued silence.

Or a vanishing.

He would just as soon not have the Slashed dwarf looking after his master's whereabouts. Jason indulged himself in a swell of sweet anger. Since taking up Ignatius' service, Jason had mostly neglected the secret playroom hidden below his warehouse, with its whipping frames and branding braziers. Even so, those arts were never too far from his mind, almost the only remnant of his high birth yet available to him. He still had both the skill and pleasure of pain, at least within the rooms of imagination.

"I will kill that dwarf," he whispered.

His breath puffed into tiny clouds like the ghosts of his words. It was cold, cold far out of season when the fruit of the fall gardens should be setting, and the leaves on the city's trees first veining to silver, red and brown.

It did not help matters that Jason knew no more about military science than he did about transforming gallstones into gemstones. Each artifice had its masters. Jason was skilled at factoring trade, finding profit in the delay of goods upon a dock or the fee split between a bargeman and a port inspector. There were no bills of lading for him this morning, just walls, stones and emplacements. Problems for masons and artillery commanders.

This part of the eastern wall was the highest elevation in the city. To the riverward the City Imperishable stretched to wakefulness. At his feet Wall Street ran amid its rows of ruined houses. Golden corn, ripe for harvest, grew within many of the ancient foundations. Beyond that, spread out across the old Parade Grounds in a confusion of tents and sheds and tailgates, the Green Market was already in chattering session.

Sweeping his gaze west and south Jason could see down Upper Melisande Avenue as it ran through the Temple District to Delator Square. He turned away from memories of his father's bitter end on the punishment platform there, looking farther north across the Little Bull River, where Cork Street rose up from the banks to the crest of Nannyback Hill. The Rugmaker's Cupola loomed with its spiral of red and yellow stonework. It was the tallest building in that end of town and the only structure that rose above the level of his vantage. From there he followed the lines of the city back south past Delator Square and along the slope of the New Hill to the flatlands near the River Saltus where the Limerock Palace glowered in dawn's light. In between and among the landmarks rose a wide forest of towers, rooftops and battlements, chimneys, steam plants and water works, treetops, tentpoles and prayer platforms.

Somewhere out of sight a brass band tootled its way into tune. He heard the laughter of women, the whistles and shouts of the drovers in the market. His nose was assaulted by the smell of cookfires, coal furnaces, horses, oxen, sewage, sweat, even a bit of woodsmoke from the night before, bounded and defined by the inescapable and endless reek of the River Saltus.

This was the City Imperishable.

Home.

Up here it was obvious how the metropolis had over time contracted inward from its defending walls. Crowded and busy as the city was down by the River Saltus, fields of green and gold and brown grew hard by the ancient battlements.

Amid the ruins in the shadow of the eastern wall, "the city is" had already become "the city was."

Jason turned east to look out across the struggling, straggling country that lay beneath the dominion of the City Imperishable and its nonexistent armies. The Rose Downs climbed toward the bright-limned clouds of morning. The lands were divided by the Little Bull River as it meandered from the grasslands beyond the horizon. An invading horde could have followed the watercourse across the ragged farmland, over the tangled woodlots and dark acres of wild rose, along the winding roads and wandering streams. No one would have stood to oppose such a force save for Jason himself and those latecoming farmers still bringing wagonloads of eggs and potatoes and fresh-slaughtered hogs into the city.

"How are these walls to be standing against anything at all without experienced men to be topping them?" asked a soft voice in a strange accent from somewhere along the Sunward Sea.

Jason startled, sliding on crumbled gravel from the wall's eroding top as he stepped. He turned, annoyed at his own surprise. "You are the mercenary?" he snapped. This was not an errand he would have sought, save for the need created by his master's absence.

"Please," said the man. "To be known as a freerider." He was small, smaller even than Jason, who had never attained great height himself. Pale eyes, almost the color of ice chips, set in a pale, clean-shaven face topped with silvered hair more blonde than Jason's own. The freerider wore a nicely tailored frock coat and trousers in a very light blue that set off his eyes. No weapons were in evidence.

"Freerider, then," said Jason. "Of Winter's Company. Your name?"

"I am to be Enero. The Winter Boys, we are to call ourselves. But you are not being Ignatius."

Jason had no great brief for this small man who thought himself so danger-ous and smart. An hour or two in his old playroom and Jason would have the soldier dancing a different measure altogether. Nonetheless, his master had intended to meet the man here this morning. "I am Jason the Factor. His agent. You are most clever to notice."

"Indeed. I am being paid for cleverness. Cleverness or deadness. You are here to be speaking with Ignatius' voice?"

"Yes." It was a lie, bald-faced as beardless Enero himself, but Ignatius had not made contact for three days. Last night's messages after the conversation with Onesiphorous had met with no more success than Jason's previous ef-forts. Which was poor news indeed. His master held great influence in the city, and was perhaps heir as well to the Imperatorial throne so long lost in shadow and dust that most had forgotten its existence.

The man for these times, in other words, when danger threatened on all fronts. The governance of the city was spiraling in on itself like a hawk with a broken wing. The Burgesses paid no mind to anything save who should fall first so that others in power might dance on their bones.

In short, a disaster if Ignatius were well and truly gone. That he would have left without telling Jason or anyone else of his departure—inconceivable. Yet he must have known something might be in the offing, or he would not have arranged for Jason to come out in his stead at this unnatural hour.

So, a lie: "I speak for him." Then, bad bargaining: "He needed you. We need you." Ignatius was convinced, Jason knew, that the rumored armies riding from the Yellow Mountains and the Sand Sea were all too real.

The captain of the Winter Boys scratched his naked chin and stared thought-fully at Jason. "We were to being given quarters for two seasons, for a gross of men and horses, provisioned and victualed, with the services of a good gunsmith and a decent ostler. To be two silver obols per day per man, plus to be a fifty-obol bonus per day for the officers to share."

That would run almost four hundred silver obols per day with expenses, thought Jason. He had no idea what arrangements Ignatius might actually have intended. Armed toughs set to watch dockside cargo of a moonless night cost no more than a silver obol per blade, not accounting for expenses.

Hired swords did not come with a company of their fellows, armed and armored.

"The arrangements are not mine," Jason said, trying to hide his ignorance. "I'll sign a chitty for the provisions and the craftsmen. The good Doctor Ignatius will see to your cash."

Enero seemed unmoved. "To be riding onward into the Jade Coast is a fine thing in the autumn of the year. Our mother the North Wind is to be plucking at our backs."

Damn Ignatius, thought Jason, to leave him so uninformed. A man who did not know the value of what he bought had no way to set the price. "Your demands shall be met for a week, then. When Ignatius returns, you will have to answer to him if you have cozened me." Not that the Inner Chamber was going to be interested in any requests Jason might tender for funds. His loyalty was to Ignatius, not the Assemblage of Burgesses, and that lack of commitment ran in both directions.

Where was Ignatius?

He glanced up to see the Winter Boy studying him closely.

"What are you being in fear of besides the wind?"

So many answers to that, Jason thought. Fires in the night. People dying with words in unknown tongues upon their lips. Panic. These things he did not say. Instead: "You name it. We're going to have a divine autumn here."

"Bullets are not to be stopping nightwalkers, but they are to be working wonders against men on horseback."

"Right."

"To be giving me my chitty?"

"Of course." Jason reached inside his overcoat for his own drafts. He would have to cover the first week's cash out of the company accounts.

Somehow, even with the noumenal attacks and the disappearance of his master, that was the most irritating insult of all.

IMAGO OF LOCKWOOD

"Funds, by the sweet fig of Dorgau, a man needs funds the way a bird needs air!" Imago stalked the low-beamed barroom in the light of stinking oil lamps. His progress was witnessed only by a handful of drooling drunkards and a hulking one-armed Tokhari—a vast brute with the copper skin, autumn brown eyes and black hair of his desert-dwelling folk—who showed no signs of understanding any language he might speak.

Or possibly any language spoken by anyone at all.

Imago wasn't a tall man, but his boot heels were high. The soles within built up higher. He wasn't a large man, but the shoulders of his evening coat were padded. The crown of his hat reached somewhat farther than the norm. His dark curly hair he kept oiled and brushed to stand large and frame his face as if he were a bigger man. In short, Imago took care of his appearance, and always seemed more than he was.

At this moment he was infused with the twin fires of wine and penury. He owed money to the Tribade thanks to his run of ill luck in the gaming parlors of Cork Street, and his latest legal ventures had as yet brought him no coin at all.

"You!" he shouted, whirling to point at the Tokhari. "Would you not have heard the case of three sisters beggared by the wrongful acts of the servants of a great trading house?"

"*Em zhakkal,*" muttered the Tokhari.

"Exactly! He *was* a jackal." Imago turned to stamp through another circuit of the low room. Each pass got him a bit closer to the door without alerting the watchful barman, who wanted paying, as barmen always did. Small-minded bastards. "What kind of world is it when a judge can't stay bought from kippers to chambers?"

Spin and stalk. One more pass and he could step out on the hop.

"I would have paid him," Imago added, "if the judgment had come through."

Stride and stride and turn by the empty gun rack at the far end of the room.

The big tribesman glowered. "*Izh-al madir.*"

"My dear?" said Imago on his last pass by the Tokhari. "A thought not to be borne." His hand was on the handle, the door was open and he was out into the cold rain, stepping twice as fast as the outraged shout behind him.

He had two more suits coming before the bench this week, being heard by a different judge from the thieving coxcomb who'd refused to remain properly dishonest. All he needed to do now was find some way to eat, sleep and remain properly dressed on his remaining assets: a copper orichalk and three stringy carrots.

Well, he always had his sharp looks and his sharper wit.

Meanwhile, the rain was soaking into the padding of his jacket, and neither looks nor wit would keep the drops away.

The fortunes of House Lockwood were brought low indeed, Imago thought. He had awoken painfully stiff, his back and legs a prescient echo of the years of his older age yet to come. His brother Humphrey lived with their Mater in a moldering hovel on the banks of the Eeljaw deep in the dread-infested jungles of the Jade Coast, attended by a few retainers, miserable City dwarfs who had lacked the pride to remain within the purview of civilized life.

Not he. Imago and his pride had spent the night sleeping in a farmer's cart that had recently contained a large quantity of onions. The small scraps that had not been unloaded at market yet stung Imago's belly, but by the same marker, the waxed canvas tarpaulin sheltered him from night's cold rain.

And now to judge by the bright steam that filled his vision, the sun had returned with some modicum of warmth.

Imago rolled off the tailgate before the wagon's owner came to help him on his way. It was a new day, ripe with possibilities for coin, for honor, for a revolution of the soul. The greatest gift the gods had given him was a true appreciation for the potential of each sunrise.

He hit the cobbles to see the potential realized in the form of two Assemblage bailiffs in their red wool tunics, staffs in hand.

"There he is!" shouted one of them.

Imago of Lockwood was off running once more.

It was a hard dodge into the alley at the back of the Root Market, Little Loach Close, then a wild, leaping run through the stacks of baskets stinking with washed horseradish and ginger, around the piles of potatoes and turnips, a drop and scuttle beneath the belly of a draft horse smoking with morning sweat, past the startled shouts of tradesmen and bearers and market idlers.

From the sounds of things behind him, the bailiffs were making slower progress. Imago spun out of the alley mouth onto Upper Filigree Avenue, shrugged free of his dark coat covered with shreds of onion and stepped with purpose into a group of jeweler's boys hurrying riverward from breaking their night's fast.

By the time the bailiffs spilled from the alley in pursuit, cursing and bruised amid one last angry flight of tubers, Imago was just another dark-haired man in a pale, stain-mottled shirt.

Once again a day had dawned with promise. Though whatever writ or warrant the Burgesses had laid against him would make it difficult for him to see to his cases later in the week.

It was time to rethink his approach. Numerous curiosities were buried in the laws of the City Imperishable. With luck and skill, he could leverage one or another of those.

Belisare the dwarf was the Claviger Familias of House Lockwood, steward and holder of the keys to the family's wealth, though that worthy was long fled to the swamps of the Eeljaw with the rest of Imago's cowardly family. Belisare, as it happened, had a brother who remained in the City Imperishable, one Ducôte. Imago felt it was past time to pay his respects to that good dwarf, and call on the last familial connection that had not yet cast him out.

He hurried toward the docks, where Ducôte operated a scriptorium near Softwood Quay. It wouldn't do to be loitering on the streets with the bailiffs out searching for him. That of course would be a point in his favor with Ducôte, who was widely known to work with the Slashed.

Filigree Avenue would take him almost all the way down to the water, debouching into the Spice Market. Following the street along the shoulder of Nannyback Hill and riverward, Imago made sure to stay close to groups of men, never walking alone where he might be spotted. There were only so many bailiffs, and they were preoccupied keeping the restless and the angry away from the walls of the Limerock Palace, yet still someone had seen fit to dispatch the men in red for him.

He needed to find a way out from under whatever paper the Assemblage had issued against him. That alone was sufficient to be disaster to his plans. Even setting aside the suits he had been prosecuting—barratry was less and less a useful profession in these suspicious days—he could scarcely garner coin or place his bets on Cork Street without freedom of movement.

That Ducôte might recommend a trip downriver to Belisare and the exile of House Lockwood was a possibility Imago resolutely discarded from his thoughts. No city-dwelling dwarf who was numbered among the Slashed could possibly be so conventional or narrow in his thinking.

It was not conceivable.

BIJAZ THE DWARF

The dwarf was sweating in the heat and smoke of a brazier set before him. Someone in the shadows above and behind him pounded a drum heartbeat-slow. The traditional muslin wrappings of his station clung to his body like winding sheets on a drowned man. His pulse pounded. The stinking surge of desire rising from his crotch, his armpits, the skin at the yoke of his neck, was almost enough to drive him to rub himself against the nearest doorpost.

Instead, he practiced restraint.

He knew that the fire burned with herbs and resin. It was part of why he came here. Bijaz did not partake directly of the myriad of vices so freely available in the City Imperishable. He mortally feared crawling inside a waterpipe and not coming out until he was carried on a board to a pit in the Potter's Field. All the same, he was not at fault if the very air throbbed with intoxicants. No sin or temptation was appended to the act of breathing itself.

Other furtive shapes sat near him, facing the pit below. Four were obviously boxed dwarfs—all of them Sewn with lips properly sealed. One was perhaps from among the rare cut dwarfs, adult victims trimmed to size by the chirurgeon amid an excess of zeal and funds. There was even a full-man crouched to make himself small in this space where the tall were meant only to be on display. A born dwarfess, almost as rare as a cut dwarf in this city of dwarfs, silently moved from man to man—it was always men who came to these places—offering wine and rainwater in narrow beakers shaped to fit the pursed opening between sewn lips.

Bijaz fingered his own knots. His lips, ever clamped together, were hot to the touch. He would no more have cut them open and joined the Slashed than he would have cut off his pizzle. At that thought, his other hand slipped within the sweat-soaked muslin of his wraps to add to the violent pressure at his groin.

The boy chained in the center of the pit writhed in the blinding glare of a trio of limelights that hissed and flared with the stench of burnt vapor.

Bijaz's hand began to slowly stroke his cock within his robes. The boy below him was tall, a full-man nearly grown, long-limbed and beautiful. The three dwarfesses with their leather straps and their canvas needles had just withdrawn. Blood twitched upon the boy's lips in bright ruby beads. He was now one of the Sewn. For a little while. Promised the gods only knew what and doubtless drugged besides, the boy continued to slide his hips back and forth, his body slicked with rubbed-on oils and the tongue tracings of his recent tormentors.

The boy's moans caught at Bijaz's ears as the lips of a lover would. His hand moved a little faster within his robes, the sweat flowed from him like mist on the riverbanks of the Jade Coast. To be a dwarf was to spend the years of youth boxed in agony, while the full-men walked laughing and free in the sunlight. To be a dwarf was to have your head stuffed with numbers and letters and facts until wax ran from your ears and your eyes bled, while the full-men drank and gambled and whored in the taverns and gaming parlors of the City Imperishable. To be a dwarf was to be sworn to service and a life of staring at cobblestones and twice-counted coins, while the full-men knelt for honors before the high folk of the city and rode fine horses through the bright streets.

Sometimes a dwarf needed to get back something of his own. Sometimes a dwarf needed to see a full-man brought low. Sometimes a dwarf needed to find his pride in blood and sweat. He had once plucked both pleasure and that missing pride from his old master's son Jason when that full-man was young and in dire need, but those days were long past. Those moments of trembling passion and blinding light within his head were long gone.

He could rebuild his pride on another's suffering, for a night or a week or a moon's passing. Ten gold obols and favors owed the Tribade to enter the doorway, with bare swords at his back ready to strike him down even while he brought himself to climax, should his words or deeds pass beyond the rules of this secret place.

A naked dwarf, masked by a rotting horse's head, entered the pit. His distended cock was painted bright blue and he carried three slim rapiers on a belt slung over one shoulder. Bijaz felt the hot rush in his groin at the sight of the blades. His thigh sticky and warm, he slumped a bit in his chair and signaled for more wine.

If the horseman were able to stretch the death out for several hours, as the best of them could with good boys and luck, Bijaz might come twice, even three times more this night, and walk out feeling as if he were a real man.

At least for a while.

What he feared was how often he needed to return. How much the Tribade would ask of him for his secret shaming lust.

What he feared was everything. Bijaz wanted the old days back, as badly as he wanted to walk tall and win the love of bright-thighed women who would tower over him in summer fields.

Bijaz was led into a closed carriage and driven awhile through city streets before being discharged to find his own way—a precaution against him ever revealing the location of the dwarf pit. For his part, Bijaz made no attempt to recognize the turns or the particular pattern in the clatter of the cobbles over which the carriage drove.

He found himself on Melisande Avenue, and began waddling home. The moon was missing, hidden behind clouds barely visible above the rooftops of the City Imperishable. Every shadow was deeper, darker, grimmer.

The evening had been a disappointment. The boy had died long, which was to be desired, but behaved poorly, sobbing and begging for his life. Half-done well, as it were. Bijaz tried not to think who the full-man might have been. Child of a great house, from the look of his nose, sold into darkness to settle a hidden debt or defer a murder already bought and paid for. As for Bijaz, he had only a much lighter purse to show for his night. That and the semen crusted upon his thighs.

Someone screamed a block or two distant. Not an uncommon occurrence of late in the night's small hours in the City Imperishable. Bijaz paid no attention. He knew he would be watched carefully all the way home. He was no safer than now, after an evening in the pit. The Tribade did not like informers.

Another scream, from somewhere above him this time. The rooftops?

A pattering rain began. Bijaz looked up in time to see a pair of legs drop to the street in front of him. Nothing else—shattered, shorn bone gleamed white in hissing light from a gas lamp at the corner ahead, though no blood ran from them.

The blood, in fact, was what was raining down.

A noumenal attack! Like the burning trees, the monster worms tunneling out of wellheads, along with all the other horrors that had bedeviled the city recently.

He began to run, searching for cover. Bijaz would bet brass against gold the legs belonged to one of his Tribade watchers. Whatever rampaged out here would have no brief for him or the dwarf pit, but that would make no difference either way if it caught him. As he raced past the gas lamp, his boots slipping on blood-slicked cobbles, Bijaz glanced up to see ghostly teeth leering down at him from a mouth big as a beer wagon.

He lost his footing, careening into the gutter on his belly in a wave of slops and shit before his chin struck the kerbstone and stars found him.

Morning found him far too slowly. Bijaz opened his eyes to an oddly filtered light, and the pain-wrapped ache that came from spending time unconscious rather than sleeping. Something was wrong with his mouth, and he lay under burlap.

That last was easily remedied. Pushing it aside, Bijaz found himself staring upward at a gas lamp, clouds pearling the sky above. His tongue was reporting in, failing to find certain familiar teeth. His lips were crusted shut.

Pain was an old friend to any boxed dwarf. Bijaz put one hand on the kerbstone and pulled himself to his knees. The burlap fell away—it was the cheap matting used by the bailiffs and the various private night patrols to mark and cover bodies for the morning corpse wagon. Someone either had an unfortunate sense of humor, or had taken him for dead in the night.

He was still where he had fallen, along Melisande Avenue. Down here closer to the river was a neighborhood of tall, narrow homes with stained-glass windows, gilded gargoyles at the cornices, windowboxes dotted with the colors of autumn flowers drowned and cold-bitten by the unseasonal weather. Linden trees already were losing their leaves, bare branches pointing like prayers to the sky.

Melisande was not his neighborhood riverward of Delator Square, not at all. Dwarfs here were expected to use alleyways or side entrances, not be staggering bloody-faced, clothed in filth, past lacquered front doors and iron hitching posts. The people who lived here were great and beautiful, factors and even minor syndics, full-men one and all.

At that thought, Bijaz's memory flashed on an image of last night's boy, eyes bulging as he tried to vomit blood through tight-sewn lips. Some of it had leaked along the blade puncturing both cheeks and the tongue within, but most of it was clearly running down into his lungs. The young full-man had been near the end by then. In that moment Bijaz's sense of his own filth was enough to make him wish for a blade for himself, to slice away his own member as the boy's had been cut free by the horse-headed dwarf.

That was *someone*'s boy. Dead now, for vanity and evil, trembling desire. Filth. He was filth.

On his feet, Bijaz staggered a moment and nearly lurched into a baker's apprentice with a cart of warm, fresh loaves. The scent of yeast and butter drove the shame and blood-lust from him. The guilt remained, an old, familiar friend.

The Assemblage. He was supposed to appear before the Inner Chamber of the Assemblage this morning. The Provost and the Counselors would not take his tardiness well. He could do nothing about the missing teeth save suffer, and avoid foods with salt in them. However, he had no choice but to discard the bloodied, gutter-soaked muslin that wrapped his body.

And here was him without a purse.

Bijaz stalked down the sidewalk, unsteady of stride but firm of purpose, looking for another dwarf, any dwarf, that might yet be loyal to the City Imperishable. He needed one of the Sewn, with their lips still properly shut, not one of those Slashed bastards. He needed help right away, or his months of work on behalf of them all, Sewn and ungrateful Slashed alike, might well come to nothing.

The godmonger that Bijaz found had led him to washing water, then had given him fresh wrappings. Well, mostly fresh, and certainly devoid of the unfortunate stains of the previous night. His benefactor had also supplied him with distilled spirits of uncertain provenance to dull the pain in his teeth and upper jaw.

All good, as far as it went.

Not so good was the damned dwarf's sticking to Bijaz like river muck to a dock ladder. They were past the Sepia Wing, walking down Maldoror Street along the south wall of the Limerock Palace, almost to the Costard Gate. Bijaz had thought to lose the godmonger along Margolin Avenue amid the crowds of clerks and deliveries, but he had not had the luck.

Maybe the little buggerer's tutelary spirits had whispered to him the significance of Bijaz's errands.

Or perhaps, Bijaz had to admit, his own tutelary spirits were speaking. Who or whatever they might be. He wasn't in a mood to listen. Pain from his broken teeth was leaching his patience, and his fears for what might be coming next in the City Imperishable seemed closer to the surface than ever.

He must stop going to the dwarf pits. Someone would find him out. He would be disgraced. Boys aplenty could be hired in the Sudgate, that he might beat bloody for days on end for less than a single silver obol. But Bijaz knew that the clean-limbed young men in the pits would die with or without his presence. They were not killed for him personally. That rationale had kept him returning through the years. He was not responsible.

Still, he wished he could find a different ritual.

"So seek," said the godmonger. He was boxed and Sewn to be sure, dressed in muslin wrappings as the best and most respectful of dwarfs would be. Even so, his skin spoke of a heritage strange to the City Imperishable—a deeper shade of brown than ordinarily seen so far north, with a certain cast to eyes the color of polished oak. The godmonger's fingers flickered with a strange cast as well, making the sign for LILIES ON THE RIVER with an accented motion. That meant to accept one's fate, ride with the current of events rather than fight.

"I did not mean to make my thoughts so plain," muttered Bijaz. "Though I am grateful beyond measure for your assistance, I must soon pass on to errands of my own."

More fingertalk: THE WIND SPEAKS FROM ALL QUARTERS. Meaning there is always more than one voice giving advice. "Open your ears, man, as well as your eyes," the godmonger said. "I found you slicked in filth and heart's blood. This is not how life should be lived in any city. Do you think this is *right*? Those crowds in the plazas? Our people fleeing for the Jade Coast?"

"No. It's *not* right. I know that. That's what my work is about. Moreover, I need to be on my way."

"You're not listening." The slanted eyes seemed sad, distant. The godmonger's fingers began a motion, the radical for MOUNTAIN, then dropped away without finishing the thought.

"I don't have time to listen," said Bijaz. "Come to my offices on Bentpin Alley in the Temple District; I shall repay you tenfold for your services."

The godmonger gave one last try as they trailed to a halt before the red-coated bailiffs guarding the Costard Gate. "No coin is as great as the full measure of your attention."

"As may be," said Bijaz. With his fingers: THE STORM TRAMPLES THE GRAIN.

"Indeed." Giving a grave nod to the scowling bailiffs, the godmonger drifted away.

Bijaz turned to face them. "I am summoned before the Inner Chamber."

"Yes, sir," said the youngest, one Federico known to Bijaz. "We been expecting you. Not like the rest of the trash been begging entry this morning." He handed his staff to one of the other bailiffs, but kept his pepperbox pistol in his hand. "Come with me, please."

JASON THE FACTOR

Jason took a fiacre from his warehouse quarters at Sturgeon Quay to the Limerock Palace. He was done sending messages and lodging inquiries with the liveried bailiffs and black-suited clerks of the Assemblage. They were polite enough, but they answered to different masters from his, and their purposes were their own.

Ignatius of Redtower had been very clear: Jason was never to visit him at the palace. Their association was no great secret—Jason would hardly have been an effective agent of Ignatius' interests if it were—but the Assemblage followed its own protocols and etiquettes, which Ignatius navigated with the purposeful efficiency of a fish seeking its spawning stream.

It was the case that Jason came and went from the Assemblage in pursuit of his business, his nominal employment and true source of funds being warehousing and factoring on the part of an owner long since retired to a Jade Coast plantation. Despite his presence in the halls of government, Jason took pains to meet Ignatius in the tiny, steam-filled cafés of Filigree Avenue, or the waterfront bars, or of an evening walking the iron-bound cobbles of the Metal Districts.

Never in Ignatius' own apartments and offices within the Limerock Palace. Not until now.

Even the trip in the little carriage was difficult. The streets teemed with people. Not refugees—for where was there to flee, except the foetid jungles downriver?—but the dispossessed, the frightened, the unruly. Tokhari drovers wrestled their suspicious camels through herds of children, flocks of goats butted past men carrying their households on their backs, farmers selling illegally on the street called their wares in voices as loud as the godmongers who had thriven uncommon thick of late. The jehu whipped his lithe, skittish horse, but that proved fruitless, for the animal had little choice in the matter, and the wide-axled fiacre even less.

Jason finally gave the driver three copper chalkies for his trouble, and dismounted to push through the crowd, heading up Short Street on his own two feet.

The mass of people had a convection of their own, carrying with them the scents of their native spices, the sour spew of babies, the wet-corn smell of dogs, the fresh-dirt odor of mushrooms. They pushed together in the swirl that had blocked his fiacre, colors and fabrics and sweating, muscled arms in the rising light of the morning. He was no more than a chip tossed into the spin and turn of this river of muddled flesh.

Close in, Jason could tell the overriding emotion was fear. People whispered and chattered and called out to one another, gathered round the godmongers, bet each other lengths of rope and handfuls of ten-to-a-chalkie nails.

He wondered what pushed them out like this, to share a slow-moving panic. Surely not the lindens burning on Pondwater Avenue the night before. There must have been more deaths that he hadn't heard about in his early morning hike up to the eastern wall.

As Ignatius had taught him, Jason opened his ears and listened. Not to any one voice or thread, but letting certain words find him out of the litany of complaints and commerce and the comforting of children. If he tried, he knew how to hear the voice of the many chattering from each of a thousand mouths.

...dead by morning...my sister screamed...bigger than a draft horse, with teeth as long...nothing but water and bones...take my chances with those madmen...dog barked til it drowned in blood...

It was of course rumor that he listened to—that captain of more armies than any commander of men ever led, now running roughshod through these people's lives. Something big and hairy brushed his face, taking his thoughts with it. Jason saw only a great, pale knee with a red-brown blotch. He looked up at a man in mummer's motley riding a canted saddle on the back of a camelopard. The animal's neck craned and it stared down at him with eyes the liquid brown of roaches' wings, two stubby horns of hair above its long, narrow face. The mummer also stared, the mouth painted large and bright upon his visage disguising his true expression. Upon the reins, his hands flickered in the fingertalk sign for WATER UPON THE STEPS, which meant a danger in familiar guise.

Even before Jason could frame an answer, the ridiculous mount and its more ridiculous rider turned away, high-stepping past a brewer's wagon stalled in the press of foot traffic. The drover idled on his bench, not even bothering with the whip, as a gang of children fed oats to his draft horses.

Oats laced, no doubt, with fish oil to make them shit rivers later. That was what children did.

Eventually Jason reached the Limerock Palace. The gateways contained no gates as such—some prior Provost had sold them off long ago for scrap. The city's seat of government, inasmuch as the City Imperishable could be said to have a government, still lurked behind walls. Half a dozen Assemblage bailiffs armed with iron-shod staves and pepperbox pistols stood in the open arch of the Riverward Gate. The crowd was thinner here, once Short Street had opened into Terminus Plaza. With the unspoken good sense the poor and purposeful had left a good-sized lacuna around the bailiffs.

Jason had already decided on the forward approach. "I require admittance in order to wait on Ignatius of Redtower," he said.

The biggest bailiff, a man with a face intelligent as any ox, shifted his weight against his staff and brought his pistol to port arms against the maroon-dyed leather across his chest. "Let's see your silver flower."

Persons with free access to the Limerock Palace carried or wore a small silver nettle as a token. Ignatius had never secured a flower for Jason, as they had kept their business away from the palace.

"I don't have a flower. I need to see Ignatius. He is Second Counselor of the Inner Chamber of the Assemblage of Burgesses."

The ox laughed. "Of course he is. Any idiot knows that." Leaning forward: "Any idiot should know the Provost closed the palace two nights ago. Only them with a flower or a summons dated since the closure is allowed to pass the gates."

Jason's temper slipped away. "I don't have a flower. I don't have a summons. I *do* have an urgent need to see Ignatius, on the business of the defense of the city. Can you send to him, at the least?"

"Don't see why I should."

"Because when he finds out you kept me out here, and him ignorant in there, he'll make you wish you had." Oh, for a razor and a few moments alone with this buffoon, Jason thought. He could make the man sing a completely different tune.

"Imre," said the ox, jerking his chin without taking his eyes off Jason. "Go send to the Second Counselor's steward and tell him that the Honorable has a little birdie singing at the gate."

As one of the other bailiffs trotted off, Jason marked the lead bailiff for future trouble. He wasn't spending his morning talking to mercenaries on crumbling walls just so the servants of the Assemblage could treat him like a half-witted beggar boy.

He also wasn't in a position to stare down or force his way past six of the Provost's finest sworn men. He reminded himself that this insult was properly laid at the door of the Provost, and through the Provost, the Assemblage of Burgesses. The City Imperishable was one thing, bustling with wealth but essentially ungoverned; the Burgesses quite another, governing an empire that no longer existed save for the City Imperishable itself.

Sometimes Jason thought it might have been simpler if the Imperator Terminus had come back from the wars. One sword, one law, one word. Not like the vacant offices and corrupt inefficiencies of today. Regardless, he would be damned if he was going to give way to these ignorant bastards, so he stood his ground, waiting for Imre to return with a response.

The lead bailiff caressed his pistol, rubbing sausage fingers up and down the angles where the barrels joined, watching Jason as a dog watches a dying cat. Jason gave him the razor-eye right back, mapping the holds and pain points he might use to subdue the man if he found him alone. The other four uniformed thugs divided their time between scanning the uneasy crowd that ebbed and flowed through Terminus Plaza and keeping their focus on Jason, the only bona fide threat in sight.

The stink of anger had long mixed with the salt reek of sweat in the bailiff's red woolen coats, Jason and the ox reduced to an interlocked, twitching stare, when Imre returned. The junior bailiff looked pale.

"Respects, sir," he said to his detail commander. "Second Counselor's steward wants to see this man right away."

Good, thought Jason. He and Green Kelly had never held much regard for one another, but they both served Ignatius. He would make it his business to find out why his messages were going astray. It wouldn't do to come to blows with the steward, so he must be certain to hold his temper.

The oxlike bailiff favored Jason with one last stare, then nodded. "Take him in, then. As for you," he added, "it's no matter to me they want you within. You're still trouble. If I catch you again, one of us will be sorry."

"You may take that as read, my good man," Jason replied. He stalked off after Imre. Though he did not visit Ignatius in the Limerock Palace, Jason knew that the philosophick doctor resided in the Acanthus Wing where his master had a gabled turret from which to read the signs in the heavens. At least when he was not conspiring at government.

Jason followed Imre as they passed through the Pilean Gardens, the plaza that lies between the Riverward Gate and the Laurel Wing. The Pilean Gardens were planted with hedge mazes growing only about four feet high, originally designed for dwarf races and tourneys during the rule of the Imperator Marten Blackeyes. Most of the trails and pathways between the hedges had long since been planted with miniature roses and dwarf camellias, so that when seen from the upper levels of the Limerock Palace a river of colors chased itself through the ancient mazes.

Imre led Jason across the Freeway, the marble-slabbed path that ran straight through the Pilean Gardens. Each side of the path was guttered for the blood that was spilled when dwarfs had ridden at the lists on shaggy little ponies from beyond the Yellow Mountains. Today it was simply a walkway with good drainage, used by those who came through the Riverward Gate—servants and residents and officials of the Assemblage. Petitioners and those on formal business called at the Costard Gate, around the south side of the Limerock Palace.

The West Doors led them into the Grand Promenade of the Laurel Wing. From there it was a walk of six or seven minutes to the Acanthus Wing and up to Ignatius' apartments. Fuming in his anger, and worried about Ignatius, Jason stalked past mirrors the size of wagon beds, portrait galleries lined with paintings with a worth beyond price, displays of antique lances and swords and firearms, vases from past the Sunward Sea, the armored skeletons of the Six Chieftains struck down in single combat by the Imperator Maldoror, along with Maldoror himself, slain by the seventh who became in turn the Imperator Septime, first of the Imperators Orogene.

The wealth of nations and the history of an empire: Jason would have set fire to it all with his own hand if that would enable him to find answers to the plagues and nightmares that stalked the City Imperishable, and turn aside whatever force of arms might be coming on the winter wind.

Rumor was an army that could not be defeated, but other armies were on the move just as dangerous, riding with long-barreled jezails and horsetail banners. That and the burning lindens were much on his mind.

Finally Imre brought Jason before the doors to the Second Counselor's apartments. Green Kelly stood there, a small man with a twisted shoulder and mismatched eyes. Eyes favoring Jason with a glare that had blades in it.

"He's yours," said Imre gruffly to the steward. "Anything happens, Serjeant Robichande will have both our heads."

Green Kelly brightened slightly. "Robichande don't like Jason the Factor?"

Imre grunted, then walked away.

"Might be a point in your favor," Green Kelly conceded to Jason. "You'd be looking for Himself, being one of his specials. Ain't you supposed to call elsewhere?"

"Three runners I've sent," Jason said. "I've also left messages via the telelocutor at the palace switchboard. All of which costs money. He's missed appointments, including one this morning I know he had no intention of missing. I need him. The city needs him."

Green Kelly spat on the tiled floor, the gob landing on the upturned fist of some long-dead warrior memorialized in mosaic. "*Need*. Hah. Mice needs cats to teach 'em the error of their ways, but they'll still not be thanking them for the instruction."

"I am not a mouse."

"Nah. None of you specials are."

The stared each other down a few moments, Jason breaking first out of sheer frustration at the time wasted. "So where is he?"

Green Kelly nodded over his shoulder. "Locked himself in three days ago with word he was not to be disturbed for nothing, not even the return of Imperator Terminus."

"He's been in there this whole time? What about food? What has he been doing?"

"Nothing," said Green Kelly. "Never rang my bell, h'ain't asked for nothing."

"Have you checked on him?"

"Seen the Imperator Terminus just lately, have you?"

Jason could have slapped the twisted man down. "I've seen burning trees and frightened people and a mercenary who dressed like a Cork Street dandy. I don't need to see Terminus. I need to see Ignatius."

Green Kelly shrugged. "Have a seat. Wait for the bell."

"No."

"Listen." The steward leaned close. "It ain't just propriety, if you take my meaning. The master has strange snares within."

"I know that." Their initial meeting years earlier at Jason's quarters on Sturgeon Quay, before he and Ignatius had laid down their hatreds and called their enmity over, had skirted the boundaries of those snares. Jason and his master began in hatred only to find their grudging friendship amid the strange magics of his father's soul bottles. "How long will he repair within?"

"He has never gone this long without food." It took great and obvious effort for Green Kelly to admit even this to Jason.

Jason stared at Ignatius' door. It was little different from other doors on this hallway, seven feet tall with three panels, gilded frame with careful paintings of flowers, birds and butterflies on the inner portion of each panel. The door to the master's apartments featured fritillaries among plum blossoms, a close study of rose apples and summer clover painted brilliant green as if seen in the light of a strong sun.

Nothing that hinted at binding spells or hidden blades or something dark that drank men's blood and set trees aflame in the night.

"I will enter," said Jason. "The responsibility is mine."

"He will take badly to you for it." Relief tinged in Green Kelly's voice.

"Sobeit." Jason set one hand on the gilded lever that was the door handle. "Stand here and wait for me."

"Oh, I wouldn't miss this for the world."

IMAGO OF LOCKWOOD

"If you had the sense nature gave a gannet, you'd take ship for the coast," the dwarf muttered. His lips were scarred with old needle holes—he had been masterless or Slashed for a long time.

Imago stood up from before the painfully low desk—dwarf height, of course. "My pardons, I have obviously come to the wrong place."

"Sit, sit." Ducôte waved a knob-knuckled hand, flickering through some fingertalk message that Imago could not interpret. "I'll hear you out. Great fires, man, if *I* had the sense of a seabird I'd have gone a month or more past. Yet here I sit."

Ducôte's scriptorium was a bankrupted brewery just at the foot of Softwood Quay, where barges from upriver had once offloaded hops and grains to feed the vats. The building was three stories tall on the outside, with windows and ornamentation of a commercial sort. Inside were no intermediate floors, only a ceiling warehouse-high and the remains of the scaffolds and walkways that had served the previous owners' needs.

Within were two dozen tall copy desks, peopled by assorted men, women, dwarfs and dwarfesses working at letters with classic quill pens, or the new ball-calligraphs—round-topped mechanisms like brass mushrooms bristling with metal tabs, which impressed characters one at a time on paper like tiny printing engines. Imago wondered if they could be used for divination. A real press, a cast iron beast embedded in belts and springs and massive levers, lurked at the back of the scriptorium. It was currently idle but surrounded by type cases and great stacks of paper that spoke of a volume of work.

All in all, a palace of business already humming at the manufacture of lucre on behalf of its proprietor.

Imago turned from his admiring appraisal to meet the smoked-glass gaze of the dwarf, gray eyes gleaming behind wire-framed lenses. "And well-sat you are, my good sir."

"I am not your good sir," said Ducôte. "I am no friend to my brother either, but for his sake I am seeing you. I would just as soon see you on a boat south."

"The fortunes of House Lockwood were ever the fortunes of the City Imperishable."

"Then pity the city." Ducôte tugged his lenses from his nose and rubbed his eyes. Like all boxed dwarfs and dwarfesses, his head and arms were sized for the man he should have been—a lank gangrel from the look of him, save for the meaty, stubby hands which resembled paws affixed to his wrists. "You have the look of a dandy, and not even an effective one at that judging from the distress of your clothing and the state of your hair. What will you have of me, scion of Lockwood? A few obols to see you on your way? You will forgive me if I do not take your paper."

Imago smiled and made a show of stretching casually. "Do not mistake good looks for poor resolve. I am not a weak man, Ducôte. My father was. He went south seeking fortune and found fever. Mater and my worthless brother hide in the great house he tried to build, holding common cause and petty spite alike with *your* worthless brother. I am here, to make better my name and more. But I have fallen on distress, and thought that you with your work among the Slashed would have at least pity, if not wise counsel for me. I admit that my plans have failed."

"It would perhaps be redundant of me to point out that you yourself are not a dwarf boxed and raised, and thus of little interest to the Slashed."

Imago snorted. "I am no idiot. I know that since the Fixed Youth Edict, the Slashed count the Burgesses among their greatest enemies. Rest assured, having just fled the bailiffs myself to reach you, I count them no less against me than you do. We have common cause."

That actually made Ducôte smile. It wasn't a pleasant expression on his face. "It may be that you have common cause with me. I perceive no return consideration on my part for a penurious idler already at odds with the law."

Imago knew he had the dwarf's interest in that moment, for if Ducôte truly saw no value in his association, the dwarf would have had him thrown out already. Now to parlay that interest into something he could use to advance his own concerns. "My good Ducôte, consider this: I am a free agent, unencumbered by loyalties to fortune, faction or family. I am somewhat trained in the law, literate to a fault, generous of spirit and can argue a soldier out of his steel socks if given the chance to spin my words awhile. No one will look at me and think of the Slashed, or the declining luck of the City Imperishable. In short, I offer you a chance to have eyes and ears and hands and sharp, clever thoughts at your service, that few will recognize as such or remark upon."

"And in return for your generous donation of time and attention, all that falls to me is to resolve your misdeeds before the Burgesses. Not to mention provide you with funds to repair your wardrobe and wine cellar, no doubt?"

"Oh, no." Imago leaned close, laying the palms of his hands on Ducôte's desk. This was the moment to show the strength of his hand. As always, forward momentum would carry the day. "I want much more of you than that. I want you to help make me Lord Mayor of the City Imperishable."

Ducôte made a burbling snort. His chest shuddered, until Imago feared the dwarf might be set to spew, but instead the fit passed into laughter. Nasty, derisive laughter, but laughter all the same.

"Mock if you want," Imago said softly, "but such an agent your folk have never had as the man who holds the reins of power in the city."

The dwarf made as if to wave him away. "Idiot. There hasn't been a Lord Mayor since, well…"

"Since the Imperator Arnulf the Dyspeptic had the last one torn apart by wild dogs in Delator Square and abolished elections some seven centuries past."

"Well, yes. What you do propose to do about it all these years later? I do not see where this leads." The dwarf was fascinated. Imago could see the gleam in Ducôte's eyes. His host had the scent of opportunity.

Imago hurled into the breach with all the persuasion his tongue could summon. "I am a barrator, and sometime champertor. One does not make one's living at such trades in ignorance of the statutes of one's chosen venue."

"Living, hah! You don't have enough orichalks to cover a dead man's eyes."

While that was quite literally—and unfortunately—true, Imago would scarcely allow such a remark to slow him down. "Be that as it may, my good Ducôte, I have read much of the law in this city. Imperator Arnulf abolished elections, but he did not abolish the office of Lord Mayor. You are a man of commerce. How is the City Imperishable governed?"

The dwarf gave Imago a lengthy, narrow-eyed stare. Ducôte was clearly aware of the hook and looking hard for it before he got caught himself. "By the Assemblage of Burgesses, of course," he said slowly. "They appoint the portmaster and the counselors who oversee the necessary functions of the city."

"Law is about nothing if not nuance, my good dwarf. Consider this: the Assemblage has sat *sua sponte* in perpetual session since the Imperator Terminus marched to war six hundred years ago. The Imperator was sovereign ruler of our empire. There is no empire anymore, save leagues of empty, broken lands along the River Saltus and its vassal streams, and the farmlands of the Rose Downs stretching east. Those remnants the Assemblage governs in its own right, as executor for the powers of the vacant throne. But even after Arnulf, the Imperator was executive of the City Imperishable only by proxy for the vacant office of Lord Mayor. The Assemblage governs the city merely as a courtesy of custom, not by statute."

Ducôte laughed, more softly this time. "If the elections were abolished, how do you propose to assume this vacant office? Presuming the Assemblage were disposed to do anything other than have your throat cut before you were fed screaming to the freshwater sharks."

"Ah." Imago grinned. "Codex Civitas, 8 Imperator Chela II has a ruling from the Assizes Bench on the elevation of one Proppolio the Baker to the office of Lord Mayor by acclamation, endorsed by the Imperator himself. The judges stated that non-elective accession to office was legitimate, and suggested specifically the Trial of Flowers as a means of that ascent. That's precedent, Ducôte. Based on the rule of Lord Mayor Margolin the Cooper. Those old fustybuggers in the Burgesses don't shit without precedent."

The dwarf studied Imago carefully. "Making another assumption, which is to say that you didn't just invent all of that, what in the name of the five devils of il-Tokh is the Trial of Flowers?"

"That's the beauty of it. There *is* no definition in the law. All we have to do is make a declaration, call for a Trial of Flowers in some manner sure to engender public enthusiasm, and we shall carry the day. Once I am installed as Lord Mayor, well, things will be very different."

"Do you seriously expect this to succeed?"

"That I cannot tell you. I can only try." Of course, thought Imago, it wouldn't hurt at all that by long-established precedent, if he was contending for the office of Lord Mayor, he would also be immune from prosecution or civil suit. The Burgesses were most careful to keep those protections strong for their own benefit.

"You place great faith in the shield of the law," Ducôte said mildly. "I for one find you utterly mad. It is of little wonder that Humphrey and my fool of a brother cut you off from the family fortunes." As Imago opened his mouth to protest, the dwarf went on forcefully: "That being said, it is obvious to anyone with eyes and ears that the City Imperishable is on the verge of terrible times. The Burgesses are fools and worse, venal and purblind to a man, ignoring eldritch portents, bad harvests and distant armies on the march with equal indifference. I am not certain you could be worse in the role of Lord Mayor. *But,* if we mount this scheme, and if somehow you succeed in your madness, I will own you. Your attention, your priority, your very words and deeds will belong to me. Take that as given now, or go forth and dodge bailiffs til you tire of the game or they split your head."

He would in truth be agent for the Slashed, Imago realized. But then, as Lord Mayor he would have power of his own, eventually enough to shake off the problems if the dwarf proved too restless.

"I will take your terms, my good Ducôte. I have a plan for power, but lack resources. You have resources, but lack a plan for power. It is a fair enough match."

"Possibly." The dwarf stood, extended one blunt hand in order to shake on the bargain. "Do not think you will be shaking me off like a dog with fleas when you wear the gold chain of office. By taking my coin, you put us in this thing together. I have eyes and ears, and sharp blades in silent hands, should I need them."

"Indeed." They shook, mutual distaste set aside for the sake of the prize.

Ducôte stepped to a sideboard, securing a bottle of some southern vintage and two crystal stems from which to drink. "Have you thought on how to bring your plan to the ears of the public without incurring fatal penalties?" he asked, returning to the desk. His lenses flashed opaque in the glare of the lamp over his desk.

Imago glanced at the printing press that hulked at the back of the dwarf's scriptorium. "You have the engine of creation right here, sir. It falls only to us to craft the words that will call the desires of our worried citizens into being."

The Tribade ran many of the rackets in the City Imperishable. No one who worked the docks or the markets for any length of time could remain ignorant of the sisters and their role in the economies both public and private. Unlike the Canvas Brotherhoods of the Jade Coast ports, or their counterparts in the cities of the Sunward Sea, the Tribade preferred to work indirectly. Few would admit to being Tribadist enforcers, for example, yet those who ran seriously afoul of the dark sisters found their shops and warehouses reduced to ashes, or sometimes their knees and elbows reduced to splinters.

In short, it was hard to move silently in the dark pathways and echoing sewers of the City Imperishable without the knowledge and assent, if not cooperation, of the Tribade.

Naturally, Ducôte sent Imago to the Tribade first. They spoke of it on one of the dead-end upper galleries of his scriptorium, a creaking walkway to nowhere that gave them a certain species of privacy surrounded by empty air for yards in all directions. It would be easy to trace the flow of secrets that sprang from a conversation in that high place of dust and the restless susurrus of bats in the rafters above.

"You'll need to speak to Herself," he said, poking Imago in the belly. "The Biggest Sister."

"I've made it my business to stay in the courts, not the docks," Imago complained. "Besides which, the Tribade are no friends of mine. Are you certain?"

"No friends of yours." Ducôte snorted. "More of your creditors, no doubt. You plan to rule a city, when you cannot walk a block down the street in broad daylight? No, you're going to the Tribade, and you'll find a way to make them heed you without taking your thumbs for a welcher.

"We're not going to be able to send out posters and criers without them knowing it. If they don't approve, your message won't last the day. If they do approve, well, you have a chance with the mobs from the docks and the Sudgate. Believe me, if you want a few thousand angry people marching on the Costard Gate shouting your name, it won't happen without the Tribade's help."

The problem was, Imago thought, they *would* take his thumbs for a welcher. "I'll need something to establish good faith," he said. "An offering of funds, for example."

Ducôte was not impressed. "Law and politics run on the fuel of words as much as money. I shall provide coin when it is needed. You are the wellspring of words. Establish good faith with your stock in trade, barrator."

"Indeed," said Imago sourly, images of his probable fate at the hands of the dark sisters flickering in his thoughts like the wine-nightmares of a lost night. For all its subtle and shadowy nature, the Tribade was known for its punishments. Just the previous month one Martin Leone, tincture merchant of Nannyback Hill, had been found bound to the central pillar of the Bloody Bridge. He was nude, his skin dyed purple, his head in the water of the Little Bull River just to the level of his mouth. Whispered word was that Leone had shorted the Tribade on two shipments of orchil dye from Bas Gronegrim on the Sunward Sea, cutting them with plant tints from the meadow flowers of the Rose Downs.

Breathing river water and all that swam, floated or sank in the stuff was not among Imago's plans for that day or any other.

"So you'll be off," said the dwarf. "This'll be a matter for the Biggest Sister. You might want to find her before her enforcers find you."

"My thanks, sir dwarf."

Ducôte nodded. "You could try the Sudgate," he said, then winked and walked away.

Swallowing his displeasure, Imago found his way outside to the alleys of Softwood Quay. They were, as always, crowded with broken fishpots, stacks of algae-clotted wire baskets, long, low-sided lumber carts, the filth and debris of several dozen cookshops, excreta of horses, mules, dogs and people, as well as other, more obscure species—all redolent with the sort of bouquet one normally associated with large dead things stranded on a sandbar in the river.

What they were not crowded with, most unusually, was people.

Late morning by the river, there should have been hundreds thronging the alleys and narrow streets just above the docks. Right now, there was no one at all.

"This is not good," Imago muttered. Though he would be much better served by simply retiring immediately to the scriptorium, the notion of bracing Ducôte for protection from whatever had terrified the street today overwhelmed his pride. He would be quick and clever then, as befit a future Lord Mayor.

Keeping to the shadowed wall he sidled toward the larger expanse of Water Street. It would lead to the Sudgate, and might give him a clue as to where his good fellow citizens had gone.

BIJAZ THE DWARF

The Costard Gate opened to the South Garden, which despite the name was a fairly modest expanse of cobbles surrounding a dry fountain. The fountain had been built, for reasons unknown, without any plumbing as far as modern inspection could determine. It was surmounted by a statue known as Follice—some hirsute yet feminine deity brought (or taken) as tribute from beyond the Yellow Mountains in the glory days of the City Imperishable's lost empire.

There was a moral there, Bijaz supposed, but he had never been able to winkle it out. Perhaps the godmonger would have been able to put it into words.

Ordinarily the South Garden was filled with carriages, fiacres, hansoms—conveyances of all descriptions bringing the Burgesses of the Assemblage and their patrons, courtiers, supplicants and toadies to and from the Limerock Palace on the business of the City Imperishable. Today, as Bijaz trudged after Federico, the space felt much bigger than normal. The only transport in evidence was a high-wheeled steam cart being tended by two solemn young women clad in scarlet leathers. There were no horses, and the stable gates to the east were shut.

"Has the Provost forbidden all traffic?" Bijaz asked. The pain in his teeth was not improved by speech, but he set it aside.

Federico nodded, echoing the motion with a grunt. "There has been trouble at the gates this morning. The Provost and the Third Counselor told everyone the threat was too great." The bailiff glanced at Bijaz. "Your name was on a short list, sir."

"Short, indeed."

The South Doors were meant to impress. This was the entrance of state, where citizens and foreigners alike came to petition the Burgesses, and ambassadors were kept waiting to reinforce their humility. The steps leading upward were overly long on the tread and too shallow on the riser, so that supplicants might know they were ascending to a place of power. The pillars flanking the doors were carved in a relief of the Imperator Septime being eaten by river snakes, that the mighty might know how far they would fall should they overreach.

The doors themselves were slabs of marble, pivoting open on hidden counterweights, rising five yards high. Each was banded with gold, for commerce, and iron, for force of arms, though the iron had been allowed to rust since the Imperator Terminus had marched away. Between the bands more reliefs had been carved, these showing the wealth of empire—fruits and flowers and fish; bullocks and boats and bowmen.

All taken, it wasn't the most tasteless piece of public architecture Bijaz knew of. For his money, that distinction went indisputably to the Temple of Pinea, with its painted caryatids rendered in loving if improbably oversized detail.

Thankfully they passed the over-ornate portal quickly enough, and proceeded through hushed antechambers. The Great Hall where the Assemblage of Burgesses met—once the Imperatorial throne room—was to the right, past a mazy series of sitting rooms and cloaking closets designed to allow great finesse in the separation and staging of supplicants and guests attending the will of the Burgesses.

Judging by the echoes and shadows, the Burgesses were not meeting this day. Bijaz was unsurprised. The true administration of the City fell to the Inner Chamber, which was in session with near daily frequency recently, while the Burgesses panicked, dithering between their deliberative responsibilities and the need most of them appeared to feel to attend first to their estates or syndicates. The Inner Chamber met in the Sapphire Court, at the top of Annalida's Tower overlooking the Hidden Courts where the Ilion Wing met the Laurel Wing.

Federico led Bijaz through another series of hallways and chambers to an echoing hall built against the base of Annalida's Tower, where two more bailiffs stood before a dressed stone wall that curved into the room. They guarded an iron-bound oak door obviously intended to withstand assault.

Like much of the City Imperishable, things were turned around. The outside was in, attackers presumed to be behind the walls rather than at the gates.

"Bijaz, a dwarf, to attend the will of the Inner Chamber," Federico bawled.

They were very much standing on formality and procedure this day. In other times, Bijaz had wandered in and out of a number of such meetings with no more challenge than a wary nod from a charwoman.

The bailiffs opened the iron-bound door and waved Bijaz in. A stair climbed the wall to his right, a spiral within the sixty-foot diameter of Annalida's Tower, though it found the next level of the tower before winding even a quarter way around the perimeter. All else on this level was books. Cases from floor to ceiling were built into the curve of the wall surrounding the room. The shelves were interrupted only by the door through which he had just passed, and the rising of the stairs. More shelves stood a few feet in from the wall-cases, like a temple ring of the ancient men on some distant hilltop. Each of those topped off waist-high to a full-man for easy reading of maps, scrolls or larger volumes. At the center, a pillar stood supporting the floor above, also rounded with cases.

He had lingered a time or two in this lowest room, amid the must of leather and the dust of paper. Most of the books were in languages Bijaz did not recognize, printed or lettered in strange inks that looked as if they might glow by night. A philosophick library, to be sure, literature of the noumenal meant to be read only by lidded eyes.

This day his head hurt from his fall in the street, and the Inner Chamber certainly did not await his pleasure, so Bijaz hurried up the stairs. His big feet thumped from step to step as quickly as his shortened legs could carry him without too much cost to his dignity or pain to his head.

Small as it was, the Inner Chamber sat in rump session when Bijaz emerged from the stairs puffing and soaked once more in his own sweat. The Sapphire Court was fifty feet across, walled all the round in opaque blue glass. The light colored his skin with a terrible pallor, as one dead, and always made him feel as if he traveled underwater here in the high levels of the Limerock Palace. The Provost, the First Counselor and the Third Counselor sat in the large leather chairs that were ever drawn in a circle at the center of the room. As he approached, Bijaz realized that the other three seats were vacant. The Second Counselor, usually his most reliable supporter on the Inner Chamber, was absent, along with the Secretary of the Inner Chamber and the Intendant-General, master of the treasuries.

"My lords counselor, I am here," Bijaz stated. Redundant, but respectful.

The First Counselor favored him with a sour glare. The Honorable Syndic Arran Prothro by name, he was at the business of the Assemblage all his waking hours. Bijaz knew Prothro's affairs of business were tended to by his brother-in-law, who was also known to tend to Prothro's wife, the man's own sister.

Bijaz had always thought the gods had missed an opportunity by not guiding Prothro's steps to the office of Provost, for then he would have been Prothro the Provost.

"Where is he?" demanded the First Counselor.

"Who?" asked Bijaz, seized with a sudden cold terror that he was being called to account for the boy who's life had been spent in the dwarf pit the preceding night.

"Our esteemed Second Counselor. You're one of his little rats, dwarf. Where is he?"

In the bowel-watering flood of his relief, Bijaz in all good spite wished Prothro's wife the joy of her brother in return for frightening him so. "I…I'm sure I don't know, sir."

"Well neither does anybody else," snapped the Provost. "We've got that idiot Almandine out searching for him, and half my bailiffs besides."

That explained where the Secretary was. He wasn't sure of the Intendant-General. "Is the Honorable Syndic Chelattini in health?" Bijaz asked, wondering if some new visitation had taken to killing off the members of the Inner Chamber one by one.

Teeth. Why did he suddenly think of teeth the size of windowpanes? And that thought in turn brought his own aches to the forefront.

Prothro waved the question off. "Is he ever in health? No, the windy bastard is off dealing with the portmaster on some issue that could not await further attention. He has, however, not shown any signs of vanishing as of yet. More's the pity."

"I have heard no word of Ignatius' disappearance, my lords." Of course he hadn't. He'd been spending his lust with bloody coin, then fleeing whatever had attacked him.

Teeth.

Once more Bijaz felt a clenching in his gut, and wished mightily in that moment for a washing closet in which to retire awhile. His churning borborygmi were surely echoing in the ears of the lords counselor.

If only he'd found his way to his offices this morning, instead of dawdling with that idiot godmonger. *Had his rescuer seen the teeth?* If he'd done as he'd intended, Bijaz might have spoken to the earnest young dwarfs and dwarfesses who served as his eyes and ears and been better prepared for this hour.

"No one has," said the Provost, glum. "Dwarfs disappear every day in their dozens, unremarked but witnessed by all as they pass the Sudgate or board ship for the coast. But we mislay a lord counselor of the Assemblage and somehow no one has heard the faintest breath of rumor."

"Counselors are not my business," said Bijaz, seizing on a familiar topic, "but dwarfs most certainly are. The Slashed continue to make inroads where they are not wanted. Could they have conspired against Ignatius?" He had no doubt the idea was silly—the Slashed probably had the least to fear from the missing Second Counselor, but anything that focused official attention on the rebel scum was all to the good in Bijaz's book.

"*Dwarfs*," said the First Counselor, in a tone of voice that made the term a vile imprecation.

Bijaz was accustomed to Prothro's distaste for his people—however necessary the old shit-eater might grudgingly admit their services to be. In this moment he began to realize how dreadfully important the absence of Ignatius of Redtower might prove to his own fortunes.

"You half-men on your stumpy legs are just empty bellies and crying mouths," the First Counselor continued. "Tits on a granny, ugly and useless. If your people carried good matchlock rifles I might rue their departure more. As it is, well…the granaries at Sourapple Roads were fired these two nights past." He leaned forward. "What do you think of that?"

What Bijaz thought was that burning granaries would feed the rumors of war already running ripe through the City Imperishable. What Bijaz was willing to say in this room was something else entirely. He fell back on logistics, the dwarf's stock in trade. When something fails, account for what remains. "I think that if someone is burning granaries it will be a hard winter indeed, my lord counselor."

"You would think right."

Things burned these days for no reason. Trees. Carts. People. Like giant teeth snapping in the dark. Despite himself, he had to ask: "Who set these alight? Raiders?"

"No one saw," the Provost replied, with a careful glance at the First Counselor. Prothro nodded slightly, and the Provost went on. "We believe it was the same provocateurs who have been wreaking havoc in the city during the nights of this miserable autumn. Agents of the Tokhari and their Yellow Mountain allies."

The attackers were not Tokhari unless the desert-dwellers had lately grown teeth the size of chairs, thought Bijaz. He was sufficiently wise not to speak so to these men frightened of force of arms and an unseen enemy they struggled to understand. He tried logic instead. "Winter nears, sirs. This has never been campaign weather, and any raiders from across either the Redrock River or the Yellow Mountains must ride two-score days from their lands to threaten us. I know my lord Second Counselor felt that the night attacks were noumen—"

"Enough!" The First Counselor slapped the leather arm of his chair, an angry flush filling his face, an unnerving purple in the filtered light of the Sapphire

Court. "I have heard far too many spook stories from our friend Ignatius. Never anything but fog and rumor, smoke and fear. We face fire now, little man, fire and sword and the snows of winter. We *know* the armies are coming. Both of them. Scouts and traders alike have reported, and the caravan traffic has dropped off too quickly in advance of the season's end. Noumena indeed. The ranting of doctors and chemicalists and priests. Nursery tales!"

"I believe my lord Second Counselor contracted a free company to stand atop our walls," Bijaz pointed out. "Surely he knew the value of sword and shield."

"The Inner Chamber approved no such expense," said the Third Counselor, intruding on the discussion.

Astaretto always had been an oily bastard. A wrong-side cousin to Chelattini, he lacked the Intendant-General's refreshingly forthright approach to issues of corruption and power. Which was to say, Chelattini took whatever he thought was his rightful share, and dealt honestly enough with the remainder. The Intendant-General's cousin schemed and plotted for much that he could have had simply for the proclaiming.

Bijaz had no use for the thrill of the game. He was far more interested in outcomes. "As may be, sirs. I am not charged with their wages in any case. I merely point out that Ignatius of Redtower was not exclusively obsessed with his nursery tales."

"We *all* recognize that the Second Counselor's concerns were…are…more than nursery tales," said the Provost into the glares that followed. "Philosophick doctors of his ilk have done much to advance and protect the fortunes of the City Imperishable these past centuries. This is the age of powered steam and electrick spark-currents. Noumena are slipping into the past, like the gods themselves. When was there last a theophany on the mosaic walkways of Upper Melisande Avenue? In no one's memory, I tell you."

Teeth, thought Bijaz. Teeth. Time to speak to the point. "Who is it that fires the lindens in the rain, and fills bakers' lungs with water on dry summer nights?" he asked softly. "My people flee because they fear the rumor of war, but they are fleeing *now* because of the noumenal attacks. That's not just fear, that's terror.

"My lord First Counselor does not care a fig for the fortunes of dwarfs and dwarfesses, but even your own syndicate would falter if a dozen of my fellows did not work in your counting house six days out of seven, sir. Likewise the rest of the City Imperishable—who measures the grain and checks the portmaster's manifests and assesses taxes?

"*My* people, my lords counselor. And my people are fleeing. Not from distant swords and barbarian horseman. They are fleeing the tide Ignatius sought to stem."

"You're all fools!" shouted Prothro. "Even if the sabotage is somehow nou-menal, it is still the work of foreign hedge wizards and stonecallers. There is no secret war. That's puffery for the pulpit and the market square. It is a real war we must fear from the armies of those same saboteurs. The City Imper-ishable has never been sacked. I do not intend to be the First Counselor who rules over the unhappy day when that history changes.

"Stay or go, dwarf. It is no mind to me. Others can read and write and count. Mark me...those who flee will not be allowed to return. We sum-moned you today to inform you of an Edict of Attainder that has been drawn up. No dwarf leaving the City Imperishable shall be permitted to take more than two bags and fifty silver obols. Property, funds and chattels left behind for longer than fourteen days will be seized. Those loyal dwarfs who remain shall answer to an assessment of fifty silver obols as well, on behalf of their brethren who have fled.

"I have an army to raise, man. Your people can stay and count pistols and payroll, or they can leave, but either way you will pay what is only fair for your own defense."

In the silence that followed, the wind could be heard worrying at the win-dow frames. Bijaz felt his chest close up as if the great teeth had caught him tight. His head throbbed where the blows to his skull were still soft and sore. The muscles in his legs twitched, as if his own limbs sought to run away and carry him with them.

To take everything from the dwarfs. This was madness. Utter madness. How long before those who stayed were punished further?

Where was Ignatius, who might have talked them around? That the Provost would not meet his eyes was little comfort now. Astaretto just smiled, which told Bijaz all he needed to know about who had the commission to conduct inventories of seized property.

"Will full-men be subject to this Edict?" Bijaz asked softly.

"The loyalty of the *men* of this city is not in question," Prothro said, but even he had the residual grace to look discommoded. Astaretto continued to smile, tapping his fingers together, the pale green silks of his sleeves swinging back and forth. The First Counselor went on: "If there is an exodus among our citizens, they will be dealt with accordingly."

"Dwarfs are citizens."

"Among our *taller* citizens, then. Be careful, dwarf, that I do not place you in charge of levying the assessments. Unless that is what you wish...?"

In that moment Bijaz wished for a dozen tall boys, all of them of Prothro's kith and kin, to put to sword and fire in a dozen inventive ways. This was even greater madness than the Fixed Youth Edict of the previous summer, which had sought to lay claim to the next generation of dwarfs yet in their boxes.

"No, sir. I would not care to have that charge. Though I thank you for your wisdom, which all may agree is beyond doubt." Bijaz bowed. "I believe my work here is completed."

"It is for the sake of the City…" The Provost's voice trailed off as he glanced at the First Counselor.

"Indeed," Bijaz repeated. He turned his back and walked away, wondering what came next. Hopefully not a blade betwixt his ribs.

JASON THE FACTOR

He had never been inside Ignatius' apartments before. His master was as close as one could come to a wizard of myth and legend in these modern times. Jason himself had seen a thing or two pass from the man's fingertips that defied empirical explanation, but the antechamber of the apartment was no more or less than one might expect to find from a senior member of the Assemblage of Burgesses who spent far too much time working on the business of the City Imperishable and its people. There was no sign of noumenal workings. Just paper piled everywhere, old serving dishes crusted with the moldering remains of suppers past, dust, odd articles of clothing and all the instruments of contemplation. The smell of paper was almost overpowering, but no scent of blood or violence lurked behind it. Only old sweat, wine, leather and the acrid scent from the gaslights flickering low.

Green Kelly the steward hovered close behind Jason. "No good will come, I am telling you."

"No good, indeed," Jason said. He paused, Green Kelly bumping into his back, and looked more carefully around the room. The disarray was significant—just accounting for the books alone, he marked at least two dozen volumes standing open, many in stacks, compendia of law and precedent, a treatise on cereal crops and more that he couldn't evaluate from a distance. It was the careful, balanced disarray of a working space, not the chaos left behind as the result of a rapid departure.

Or an assault.

Jason had no doubt that if certain people wished it, an assault could be conducted within the Limerock Palace, and no one would be the wiser. It was the largest building in the City Imperishable, covering what would otherwise be blocks and blocks of ordinary streets. Bailiffs and maids and stewards notwithstanding, the number of hallways and rooms was uncounted and uncountable. There would be little trouble for someone versed in the intestinal architecture of the place to pass unremarked and work what mischief they desired.

Which of course raised the question of concealed entrances in these apartments. The walls were a confusion of paneling obscured by armoires, bookshelves and scroll racks. Though it seemed overmuch like low comedy to suspect doors behind those furnishings, Jason somehow thought that he would be looking before the day was done.

Where *was* Ignatius?

Jason turned on the cowering steward. "He has stairs within somewhere?"

"In…in the next chamber, sir. His workroom."

A workroom sounded more promising. Jason pushed past a tottering pile of leather despatch cases, their flaps dangling down like so many dead tongues, toward the door that stood cracked open between an armoire carved in representation of bountiful harvest and a particularly large and ugly ormolu umbrella stand.

The next room was much the same as the previous, save for the floor-to-ceiling windows looking out over the Pilean Gardens. Sheer curtains clouded the view, with heavier drapes drawn back before them. Anyone could have gained access to the apartments there, Jason realized. Otherwise this room was also cluttered, though the wrack ran more to maps and charts and a drafting table, and the books to tinted prints of trees and rolling countryside. Geography rather than law, then. Ethnography as well, judging from the assorted swords, spears and fetish masks hanging between the crowded shelves and cabinets. It smelled less of food and more of moths and old rot.

The stairs spiraled up through the ceiling, an obvious addition to the original design of the room and not so eptly executed as the architecturally minded might have hoped. They were competent smithwork, banged out by someone obviously more used to crafting ladders or safety rails than anything meant to match up to the ornate gilded-crown molding that ran around the edges of the ceiling and the lintels of the windows and door. From the look of things, someone—Ignatius, presumably—had caused them to be made off-site and brought in for assembly. The final coldwork fastening the frame together was crude at best, suggesting the craftsman had not come into the Limerock Palace with his work.

Again, the disarray was meaningful, not destructive.

"What is above us?" Jason asked, peering up the stairs at the round hole hacked in the ceiling.

"Don't rightly know, sir." Green Kelly sounded nervous to the point of fear. "Himself was never letting me past these two rooms. If he's got him a bed, it'll be above, but he slept in one of the chairs down here often as not."

"No one went up?"

"No."

"What about the doorway on that floor?"

"What doorway?"

"Ah." Jason continued to stare at the hole. It was strangely shadowed, as if black gauze had been draped above. "Ignatius," he called loudly, feeling the fool even as he did so. "Are you well?"

They were answered only by the rattle of wind in the garden.

"*Sir!*" he shouted.

Nothing.

Jason set one hand on the plain iron rail of the spiral stairs. A spark leapt, singeing his palm with a sharp sting as he snapped his arm back. He bit off a curse and sucked on his offended skin for a moment.

"I'm back to the hallway, sir," muttered Green Kelly, who then scuttled off without further ado.

Jason looked up once more, then set his foot on the first iron riser. The noumenal awaited, it seemed.

He needed the man his master more than he needed his fear. With a clenching in his gut, Jason advanced up the stairs.

If the first level had been the ordinary rooms of a man with extraordinary responsibilities, the second level was, well, extraordinary. The darkness into which the stairs spiraled upward remained obstinate and unyielding until it swathed his head like a fuligin cloak. Jason felt the distinct sensation of having to push onward against something that was elastic yet possessing of strength. It was as if he were violating a membrane.

He plunged upward, bowing his head slightly in the vain hope of keeping the unpleasantness from his clenched-tight eyes.

With a noise similar to the pop of a wine cork, he was through. The stair skipped a quarter turn of its spiral, leaving a flat little landing shaped like a fat slice of pie before heading upward. This second floor of Ignatius' apartments appeared larger than the workroom below, presenting an eye-bending insanity of curvilinear shapes barely visible in the dim light. Jason's nose twitched at the musty smell of soil and rotting wood.

He did not care just yet to step away from the cold iron railing clutched firmly within his grip. Instead he stood on the metal plate of the landing and tried to comprehend those things that he saw.

Ignatius appeared to have *grown* the walls of this room. It resembled a giant burl of some dark wood, walnut perhaps, that had somehow been turned inside out. A patch of carpeting existed at Jason's feet, evidence this had once been a normal chamber. The sickly glow of whatever fungus grew amid the deep cracks in the drunken-crazy walls gave light to a rose pattern, with interlaced golden cords, scattered with dirt and bark.

There were objects embedded in the burled walls, gleaming faintly in the fungal light. Jason squinted a little as he tried to focus. A head? And were those hands?

The thought of being trapped within the growing wood, which seemed almost to breathe, sent a shuddering chill through Jason's chest. Ignatius could not have entombed all these people—Jason could see at least a dozen figures, now that his eye had caught the pattern. Possibly quite a few more.

No, Ignatius could not have done such ill work. The nature of his own power was reciprocal. The Hermetic Orders to which Jason's master was sworn and bound channeled its noumenal power so: Each action in that realm carried a corresponding reaction in the phenomenal realm of everyday life. Hatred met with hatred, lust with lust, pain with pain.

Ignatius of Redtower had the means to sear the souls of men within his grasp, but was in turn bound by perfect chains wrought of his own power. Which was, in a material sense, why he had agents such as Jason to do his work on the streets of the City Imperishable.

It was nearly impossible that he would have imprisoned a dozen or more people. These were neither tortured prisoners nor vengeful ghosts. Jason stepped away from the spiral stairs, regretting immediately the loss of the safety of the metal rail.

Iron grounded a man in the face of noumena, everyone knew that. This was lore old as the stone doors in the distant hillsides of the Rose Downs. Released from the protection of some smith's work, he risked losing himself in the forest of Ignatius' upper room.

The world held little enough of what the folk on the street called magic. The gods had worked no miracles for the span of lifetimes. Hedge wizards in the markets of the City Imperishable could sing down a ghost to prickle your hackles and hack at your prick, but if they had any real power they wouldn't be shilling the bumpkins for five chalkies a go. Distance lent power to the stonecallers of the Yellow Mountains and the watermen of the Sunward Sea.

Jason gave that no credence. Distance also made foreign men ten feet tall with their faces between their legs, yet when you found those exotic outlanders ready to trade at the docks, they were very much like other men.

This…this was different. This was power close as his next breath, for all that he understood none of it. Every step he took pushed through air that was too thick, a translucent echo of the dark membrane that had shielded the room from penetration below. Not the blazing magic of nursery stories and minstrel plays. More like the quiet work of stock and stone, the strength that made summer vines pull down bridges, and pushed saplings through cobbles after a season or two unattended.

He came to the first face and stared at it, afraid that it would be staring back.

Wood. Carved from the burl. Or grown. A sculpture or model, nearly perfect, of a familiar man. Jason studied it for a few moments before recognizing the sad-eyed face of the Provost of the Assemblage of Burgesses, Zaharias of Fallen Arch. It was the Provost to the life, such that no artist could have rendered with such fidelity or detail.

He looked onward to find more faces. Green Kelly the steward. Arran Prothro, the First Counselor. Bijaz the dwarf, Jason's own one-time benefactor and long-time unfriend. A few men and women he did not recognize. Somewhere in the middle of the room, Jason found himself.

That gave him pause. His own wooden simulacrum appeared pensive, worried. The fetch was wearing a wide-shouldered coat with a fur collar. Much as Jason himself had been wearing that morning to meet with the captain of the Winter Boys up on the eastern wall.

His mind seized on that, something to consider that was less worrisome than the broader question of how this place had been caused to be. Power, indeed. Applied to divination or possibly scrying.

Ignatius of Redtower looked upon his friends and enemies in the grain of a giant walnut burl.

Somehow stating it so simply did little to settle Jason's thoughts and fears. Enough, he told himself. No one and nothing was here except these wooden fetches of people who walked under the sunlight outside. Feet scuffing in the scattered dirt and rotten bark, he made his way back to the stairs. The act of returning to contact with iron gave him a profound sense of relief, driving back a fear he had not quite acknowledged. This time he felt no inclination whatsoever to call aloud farther up the spiral. Bad enough to see what was next. Why issue warnings?

Another membranous shadow, another forcing of the way, and he was on the third level of Ignatius' apartments. Which, assuming no secret strangeness of architecture, was also the third and uppermost floor of the Acanthus Wing of the Limerock Palace.

The spiral stair ended here, amid sunlit carpet in a rose-and-ropes pattern. This room was far less strange than the one below it, for it was filled with mechanical devices, their parts and the tools for making them. The north-facing windows were uncovered, letting in the late morning light and the racket of birds beyond. Brasswork and copper tubing and bright steel gleamed with the glory of tiny metal suns.

The room was a riot of machinery. Jason knew something of mechanical equipment—cranes and derricks, the steam traction engines that sometimes came to the docks hauling long trains of flat wagons, their waterborne cousins that drove ships up the River Saltus against the current faster than ever sail or oar could hope to do. Even little machines, the clever pulley systems and the mechanical scales filled with springs and counterweights, the clocks that beat out the measure of the hours both paid and unpaid by which the workers of his warehouse set their rhythms.

This was a different class of work entirely. There were several examples of whatever it was Ignatius had been laboring at—open frames filled with rods serving as axles for a whole series of gears and eccentric cams, those rods in turn meeting others, until the whole affair was something like a mechanical loom that had heard the voices of the saints and set out to make itself emperor of the birds.

As he focused on those, Jason realized that much of what surrounded the three large frames consisted of components and parts for their assemblage. He had not the least idea what these were for, possibly divination of another sort, but he knew that he was looking at years of effort and fantastic cost in workmanship.

Why?

He walked across the space, boots sinking slightly into the carpet. The floor was grubby here—Green Kelly did not come up with his sweeper—but this was dust and metal shavings, not the strange embedded filth of the level below. The room, he realized, was lined with counters, somewhat akin to the working benches of a master woodwright. Tiny lathes and little furnaces stood along the bench tops, amid them the filigree brass head of a man mounted on steel shoulders. A mouth, to speak the words of divination? Along with tools galore, to crimp and form and shave and punch metal.

After a moment he realized that this room, like the one below, had no doors.

Nor did it show any evidence of recent occupation by Ignatius. No stink of the noumenal either, not like the oppressive mix of shadow and grime and pressure in the air down the spiral stairs. An ordinary room, belonging to a man obsessed with mechanical output.

There was a smell out of place, though. Jason tilted back his head, closed his eyes and sniffed. Oil. That cold absence of scent that stood in for metal. Moldering carpet. Also something a bit rotten, in a familiar way. Like the faintest whiff of an abattoir brought on the wind from a district or more away. Old blood.

He opened his eyes. Where?

Jason quartered the room, stepping slowly over cracked-open crates and bins of small gears and louche, coiled springs. He kept sniffing, but he also looked. The room was overflowing with clutter, but little of it was big enough to hide an injured man.

Or a body.

Old blood. For whatever that was worth. Three days since Green Kelly had seen Ignatius. A man could bleed a lot in three days.

He finally found a damp stain in the carpet near the south wall. It was a dark patch, which yielded a sludgy maroon-black smear when brushed with his fingers. Jason elected not to taste it. Instead he stared at the wall.

Wood, framed in panels, somewhat resembling the door on the ground floor, or the walls below. The blood was concentrated along the molding where the wall met the floor. He noted that this was one of the few areas of the room's perimeter clear of obstruction—no work bench, no crate or frame stood here.

Jason knocked on the wall. It sounded hollow, as if a space lay behind it larger than the natural gap to be expected between this room and the next. He began to search the edges of the panels, looking for a catch or a hidden mechanism. It was not hard to find a little cover of an irregular shape cut to blend with the wood grain. It opened to reveal a brass handle.

A door, then, with blood running from behind it.

At least he knew where Ignatius was.

Jason took a breath and tugged at the brass handle. The door swung open to reveal a narrow stair that ran flush with the wall of the room. A puddle of blood spread at the landing. Red-brown boot prints led up, but not back down again.

He followed them quickly, worried that he would find Ignatius dead in the attic above, trying not to imagine what this might mean to the city. What he found instead was a tiny room with a tiny window, embedded in what must be a little dormer or cupola overlooking the Pilean Gardens. It was empty, lapped wood over bare beams, save for a single wooden chair and a profusion of large feathers, many of them snapped or broken. Blood smeared the floor as if someone had rolled or been dragged about the room.

But the window was not broken, and no one was there, not in body or spirit.

The appearance of things strongly suggested that Ignatius of Redtower had been attacked or wounded in his workroom, staggered up the stairs, met and fought with a large bird inside an enclosed attic, then vanished.

A noumenal attack, Jason realized. Which in his experience only took place on the streets, under open skies. Not in enclosed rooftop rooms.

He looked around, wondering what might breathe in the shadows of the small space. Though he was able to see every inch of the area at a glance, Jason felt an icy stab in his heart. He was overcome with a profound desire to touch cold iron.

Valor sometimes lay in the retreat. Jason retraced his steps as quickly as he could, shouting for Green Kelly as he skidded down the metal spiral. It was only when he was bursting into the public hallway on the ground floor that he realized he hadn't seen the musty wooden room of faces on his way back down the stairs.

Green Kelly cringed, one arm bent behind his back by Enero the Freerider, who also brandished a knife. Jason wondered briefly what the mercenary was doing here, inside the Limerock Palace, but his attention was captured by the two bailiffs who stood just outside arm's reach, brandishing their pepperbox pistols. Both were red-faced with anger. One of them was bleeding from a slash to the cheek.

Naturally, that would be the oxlike Serjeant Robichande.

IMAGO OF LOCKWOOD

Water Street echoed with the murmur of crowds a few blocks away. In fact, Imago saw them to the south of him, behind a noisily evolving barricade of wagons and crates. He turned and looked to the north. Another hasty barricade in progress, two blocks distant.

He stood alone near the head of the Softwood Quay, surrounded by stacks of raw and milled lumber freshly shipped in from farther up river. A lone dog barked nearby. Wood creaked slightly, the noise of old warehouses settling on their pilings—something that one almost never heard, given the perpetual dockside racket. The air smelled sharply of salt and some compound he could not name, as if he were within an old apothecary shop.

Those were not the scents of the City Imperishable. Neither was silence ever the sound of this city.

Imago did the only sensible thing. He ran as if his heels were aflame—heading south, for though it was the longer way, it took him toward where he most needed to be. Even better, the air felt less oppressive in that direction.

It was the air that slowed him, in fact, snatching at his clothes and arms and legs like a thousand damp hands. He was running, through heavier and heavier fog that slowly turned to mud, even in bright daylight. Oddly, sound began returning. Somewhere a shutter banged. Somewhere a man shouted. Somewhere a ship's bell rang as a steam whistle erupted into a thrice-damned scream. Here, now, Imago was enfolded over and over, tighter and tighter, closer and closer.

His legs moved more slowly with each step, though his muscles worked hard enough to reach a trembling, acid burn. It was as if he had been running for hours, but the cobbles beneath his feet remained stubbornly unchanged. Light at the edges of his vision shifted to red, and the sounds that had found their way to him slowed and blurred to the low-voiced thumpings of frogs in the gutters. His breath came slower, too, as the weight of years settled on his chest and sensation slipped from his legs.

Was this what it felt like to die? That thought filled him mostly with sadness, rather than terror or remorse.

When the river erupted to his right, it was with the deliberate speed of pitch dripping from a roofing brush. The water made a leisurely climb into the sky, moving a bit faster than Imago himself, but still in no great hurry to surrender to the downward pull of the world.

He tried to turn, fighting the slow tug of falling into the still and silent red spaces that called to him. Anything heralding change in the gradual eternity of his dying might also restore him to the moments of his life. Such a change was visible now: bright fire had begun to burn in the air over the river.

Fire on the river. Water in the air. One of the ships moored in midcurrent was discharging a cannon at the docks, Imago realized. Friend, enemy or indifferent meddler, he had no way of knowing, but he could only pray that whatever held him in its grip would be distracted by the bombardments.

His agonizing turn toward the source of the attack became easier. Imago could still see nothing of his own assailant, had no real notion of whatever agent was retarding him, but its attention was shifting away from him.

More water rose, this time mixed with a cloud of splinters, metal and smashed netting from a pile of fish crates that had sustained a mortal blow. He was somehow moving with terrible lassitude, yet at the same time beginning to outrun the explosions striking the shore. The sense of being clutched became tighter, but the effect weaker.

Life!

It didn't like the shooting, then, whatever the thing was that grasped at him. It could be defeated. In the months since the noumenal attacks had begun at midsummer, no one had yet found that to be the case. Imago was proving it now, as befit a future executive of the City Imperishable, with the rightful aid of one of his offshore visitors.

Not that he would normally have run toward firing of any kind. Far from it. All the same, that way lies salvation—air was once more filling his lungs, and he was able to feel his legs properly. He kept moving, pushing through the fading red that yet threatened to fill the world.

The next cannon shot actually reached his ears. He saw the ball spinning past his head. He could have touched it as it flew by. The invisible hands still plucked, but weaker.

Imago hit the descending wall of water, stumbled, felt the peppering of shards and splinters, tumbled over the dock's edge toward the River Saltus. He was released by the invisible grasp to plunge into the green darkness a free man, free to be troubled by water snakes, freshwater sharks, mossy snags, disease, infection and any of the other myriad choices that bedeviled the free.

Above him the silver skin of the surface rippled with the scars of entry, surrounded by the tiny satellites of descending debris. Below him the bile-dark muck of the river opened wide to swallow him up.

He fought for the light.

River water sluiced from Imago's sleeves as he climbed a rotting ladder nailed to a piling. He felt several leeches attached to his calves, beneath his trousers. His suit was ruined, almost certainly beyond salvage for anything more than the grimmest of labor. By Dorgau's sweet fig, he would look a fright.

But he was alive.

Imago pulled himself gasping onto the dock, just south of the Old Lighter Quay. He'd moved down the river a few blocks, then. Carried by the current. The barricade he'd seen was already breaking up amid the noise of splintering wood, nervous laughter and the too-loud chatter of men and women and dwarfs convincing themselves that each of them had not been one of the fools, had only cooperated in making the thing in the first place because it was the civic thing to do.

No one was at fault, no one had panicked.

Were he not soaked with slime and duckweed and leeches, Imago would have been happy to step into the circular delusion and shake off his own sense of folly. Though such an effort would not be so simple for him, with death sitting so close upon his shoulder. Besides, wretched as he appeared in this moment, no one would credit his words.

"You," said a woman. She wasn't part of the melting crowd, though she stood among the people who swarmed away from the last of the frightened mob to rejoin the usual walk of commerce.

Gasping, Imago squatted on the edge of the dock with his trouser legs turned up, plucking at the leeches. "Yes?" She was hard to look up at—too tall, too thin, clad in dark gray leather, with hair the color of rotten iron and a lined face with eyes as gray as her clothing. Though she carried no weapons that he saw, she still seemed dangerous as any bailiff armored for riot. "Tribade?" he asked politely, when she had made no answer. "I am looking for Herself."

"Then I have a coincidence to report." The woman smiled, her lips blade-thin. Her teeth between them were stained dark as her leather. "Though she requires only parts of you, not your self entire."

Dorgau and the nine brass apes take his wretched appearance! He would make no impression of account whatsoever on any of these women draggled and worn as he was. There was nothing for it but to talk his way on through. "I might be of more use to her whole than in part."

"I can take you to her." The knife-smile slipped into a malicious grin. "I make no promises about your return."

"My life is nothing but bad bargains at this moment," said Imago. "I can live without promises."

"If anyone ever lives, little man, it is only without promises." She extended her hand, but he refused it and climbed to his feet, water still dripping off him as he stood.

They headed south down Water Street toward the Sudgate, Imago and the gray woman, moving through the usual crowds. Imago's clothes still dripped, though stinking water no longer splashed from him with each step. Minutes after the attack had dissipated, it was as if nothing had ever taken place. There might have been a slightly higher pitch to the street chatter, perhaps a few more people stepping too quickly and looking past their shoulders.

Imago understood the feeling. But he needed to know more.

"What was that thing that almost got me?"

The Tribadist shrugged. Her stride was longer than his, and so he scurried to keep up. Not that dignity was in much supply for him, wreathed in muck from the River Saltus.

"I don't know enough about the noumenal," he continued.

"You don't know enough about anything," she said.

"Tell me this at least," he asked, "do you know what captain it is to whom I owe my life?"

"No." Another few steps. "The ship was *Lissa Lightfoot*, flying a city flag out of Port Regret. Coastwise trader, from the look of her."

"You saw that much. Did you see what she was firing at?"

"You."

Beyond that, she would tell him nothing as they pushed south.

The Sudgate was an architectural monstrosity. Imago had once been told it was one of the original fortifications of the City Imperishable, dating from even before the city itself. A river-fort, then, from the days when men built with stones the size of houses and worshipped bloody gods by burning one another under a harvest moon.

Whatever its beginning—fort of the hill men, high-walled sheepfold, river bandit's hold—the Sudgate had grown and regrown to follow century upon century of changes in the history of the City. The southbound wagon-road passed through a thick-walled tunnel that ran beneath the middle of the structure, which angled back and forth to bar cavalry charges while still allowing commerce through.

At the water's edge, the Sudgate extended a stone arm into the River Saltus. The jetty projecting directly from the walls of the river-fort had stood in place so long it had built up a neck of land that hosted a collection of struggling trees, lean-tos and illegal fishing tie-ups. A tower loomed at the end, built to hold a winch assembly that could have drawn a boom across the river had the Imperators or the Assemblage of Burgesses ever troubled themselves to build a matching tower on the swampy, uninhabitable western bank. The tower now boasted a dock from which the portmaster launched a customs cutter to inspect cargoes coming upriver.

The true glory, or horror, depending on one's sense of taste, of the Sudgate was the layers of structure that rose above the winding curtain walls of the fortress. After all the centuries, the upper works overhung the walls by a nerve-wracking distance, cantilevered outward on many generations' mixed ideas of engineering. Measured from blank-walled base to corbelled roofline, the Sudgate was the tallest edifice in the city except for the Rugmaker's Cupola. Even so, sitting as it did by the riverbank, there were a number of other buildings, including the eastern wall, that reached higher elevations.

In addition, the Sudgate was second only to the Limerock Palace itself for sheer size. That bulk was dressed in a rococo architecture that violated the eye. Whatever defensive purposes the walls and towers might have once served, they were long subsumed in the innumerable follies that clad the exterior.

For well over a millennium, the Sudgate had been the primary sinkhole in the City Imperishable for construction funding, convict labor, insider contracts and the sheer inertia of public budgets.

Unlike the Limerock Palace, the twisting insanity of the interior stood largely empty. The Sudgate was a monument mostly to the Sudgate. Even the watch posts and murder holes of the road tunnel itself were long vacant. An invading army could camp within the complexity of its walls and levels for weeks, assessing its target city and picking its moment. Nobody but beggars and rats would have known.

The Tribadist led Imago down some nameless alley that ran alongside the cyclopean walls. Other than Water Street itself, and the better-guarded waterfront godowns, the Sudgate Districts were an anonymous haunt of the ragged poor. The people were far more destitute than even the desperate dandies and smiling panhandlers he knew along Cork Street and in the Spice Market. Ordurophages, corpse pickers, child breeders, broken-backed old veterans and one-eyed beggars in semen-stained smocks, the limbless and the luckless.

This was a different world from anything he lived with day to day.

"Disgusting," said the Tribadist, with a glance at him.

"These people?" Imago almost agreed with her, then stopped himself. He took a careful moment's thought. "No. The city is."

"Disgusting?"

"Not disgusting. It just *is*, whatever it is, ma'am. Our words. Who we are. Those words are true. These folk are the City Imperishable as much as the Burgesses in the Limerock Palace. All of us together."

"Hmm."

Half a block later she pushed him into a pot shop where dog haunches and a monkey's head—he hoped to darkness it *was* a monkey's head—hung in the rafters to show the authenticity of the meat in the stew to be had for an orichalk a mug. With another orichalk's mug rental, Imago noted wryly.

"Earwig," the Tribadist said with a nod to the old woman tending the fire.

Toothless and hazy-eyed, the hag simply grunted as she moved through a rippling shrug which stood in place for a wave of the hand. Imago and the Tribadist stepped past her to a stinking little pantry. To no surprise of his, the back of the pantry was a door opening into a narrow, stale tunnel.

"We don't use this entrance often," she said as they stepped into damp, stone-scented shadows. Imago realized it must be cut through the lower skirting walls of the Sudgate. The door closed behind them, leaving no light at all. "When we don't require it, the passage beyond is deadly." He could practically hear her smile in the dark. "Don't bother remembering the way."

Imago shuffled along behind her, subsumed in the chafing, damp river stink of his own attire, shivering already and wondering how a debtor clothed in filth would establish good faith with the Biggest Sister of the Tribade.

After a time they came upon a dim glow reflected down airshafts and lightwells. Enough to remind Imago his eyes had not gone blind in the stone darkness, but barely more. Monsters and gods could have hidden half a dozen steps to either side and been nothing more than shadows. The Tribadist took him through a maze of corridors and stairwells, and twice up ladderways.

Her purpose was clear enough. The place was so vast and complex that even if he did somehow find his way in from the pot shop, he wouldn't be able to follow this path twice.

Unlike almost every other built-up area of the City Imperishable, the fortified bowels of the Sudgate were almost deserted. If this place had been used for anything in the last few centuries, it was as a civic cellar. As the light improved, he saw lumber, pipes, loads of brick and stone deposited and long forgotten in corridors and wider spaces.

Odder things, as well, at the higher levels—barding for something much bigger than a horse, mounted on wooden frames in a room with high slit windows that let in the first direct light he'd seen inside this place. Four sets of it, dark pockmarks showing where the armor had once been bejeweled. Elephants, Imago decided. As if anyone would ride to war on those mad-eyed southern jungle beasts.

He saw six desiccated corpses hanging from whipping frames arranged in a circle, as if they had been meant to die watching one another. Someone had cut off their feet, lest they escape. Or maybe the rats had not bothered to climb for a greater feast.

A room cluttered with candelabras and chandeliers, presumably from a long-forgotten remodeling of the Limerock Palace. A glass bottle taller than he was, top sealed with lead, something swimming within that showed gleaming eyes and webbed hands. A room full of trays on rolling racks, taken from some bakery, each tray filled with dark rocks.

Strange and curious as it was, the bowels of the Sudgate didn't have the heavy, clutching tang of terminal danger he'd felt down by the Softwood Quay. The interior passages of the baroque fortress contained a certain sense of sameness.

The two of them were in a narrow, high-ceilinged corridor, seemingly intended for a servants' or soldiers' passage, next to a great hall. Wide, short windows were let into one side of the room about thirty feet up. They admitted a greasy light through glass clouded and grimed with age. He was certain they'd walked this way at least once already.

"Why are you leading me in circles?"

The Tribadist stopped and turned to face him. She stood in a vaguely brighter block of shadow where that greasy light made its way down, and had her malicious grin once more in place. "What makes you think that?"

"I can be as foolish as the next man," Imago said quietly. "But it does not follow that I am a fool. If you aim to mislead me to my death, kill me now. I am no man of action, surely it will not be troublesome for one such as you. If you aim to confuse me and dump me in the roadway again as some manner of lesson learned, consider me confused and cease wasting my time. If we are truly going to see Herself, the Biggest Sister, then pray take me there now."

She put up one hand, as if to ward off disputation. "What did you mean when you said the folk of the Sudgate alleys were the City Imperishable?"

That was not among the responses he had expected. "Well…I meant what I said. You made as if to sneer at them…no…" Imago paused, thinking carefully. "You invited me to sneer at them. I will not do so. Surely some among the pot shops and rag pickers are sots who walked away from their daily obol. There are wealthier folk who would scorn them, though I mostly pity them. But children born in the gutter did not cause the place they came from. There are levels to the life of a city, just as there are levels to the natural world. As above, so below; as below, so above."

She played with a dagger he had not seen her draw, stropping it against the leather guarding her left forearm. "How unnatural of you to think so."

"I cannot help who I was born to. Why should I condemn them?"

The Tribadist's grin tightened to something that suggested fins knifing through dark water. "Tell me. This wonderful insight, this humane perspective of yours, does it serve well to settle debts you have incurred at the gaming table and in the wine sink?"

Here was the crux and nub of the debate, then. "That is why I need to speak to Herself."

The knife flipped, a rapid, short flight that landed it back in her right hand. "Tell me what you will say. You might consider starting with something on the order of, 'I have the money in my care.'" She made a show of looking up and down his clothing, ruined by water and much. "Or did you lose your purse in the river, my good sir of Lockwood?"

For a brief, mad moment he considered pursuing the fantasy she offered—pretending to have gold now lost at the bottom of the River Saltus and pleading for time to make good what he already intended to settle. Unfortunately, it was all too obvious that the Tribadist enforcer knew perfectly well that he carried no funds. She seemed the sort who would spend a day setting boys to diving the dark river muck, just to lend proof against his lies.

"No, no purse. I bring instead a stake in a much larger game, bought into at the cost of settling my debts."

"And you believe that Biggest Sister will be pleased to trade your assurances concerning the risks of a future venture for hard coin already lost?" The knife was lodged in the soggy mess of his shirtfront, once good silk. She flicked and a button flew off to ricochet against the stone wall like a tiny ivory bullet.

"I believe nothing. I have only an offer to make. However, it is one of substance."

"Lies, little man. Whatever your offer is, it presents nothing except lies. The Tribade knows all men lie. Finding how deep the truth has been buried is one of the secrets of our craft." She poked the skin of his chest, where it was tight across the sternum. Blood that was almost black in the dim light bloomed upon his shirt. He tried not to flinch from the pain. "If I dig, shall I find gold within?"

"Only lungs and heart hard at their labor, and scarcely worth the cost of yours to reach them." He spread his hands, ignoring the burn of the metal point lodged just within the skin of his chest. "Please take me to Herself, or have done with me. I do not wish to game with you further."

The knife slid out, bringing blessed relief. "Tell me now. My ears are hers."

With the iron-colored hair, Imago had no reason to doubt this woman was high in the councils of the Tribade. "There is an old law," he began. "One which gives us a chance to rearrange the seats of power in the City Imperishable…"

Standing in the grimy shadows, he laid out the plan to this most dangerous woman much as he had to Ducôte, believing his words would be enough to talk him past the debt and into the hidden lair of the Biggest Sister of the Tribade. He had to believe that, or he had nothing.

"So," she said after he was done speaking. The Tribadist was obviously framing her thoughts, and she was thus far neither laughing at him nor stabbing him to death.

Imago felt these were good signs.

She continued: "Assume for a moment you sought support for this Trial of Flowers. You would need the street on your side, as well as at least a few of the syndics and factors. The street has voice, but no power. The moneymen have power they wield in silence. Together you might shake up the Burgesses."

She leaned close, continuing: "A pretty plan indeed. For a man. But tell me this. Why you? Why now? I could take this to the streets myself. Your gaming debts are worth more than some alleged future in power."

"Excellent questions, ma'am," said Imago, who wished he knew the answers. "Have I persuaded you to permit me audience with Biggest Sister?"

"You've had your audience."

Imago stared at her a moment. The meaning was clear, though he could scarce credit it. "You are a woman, walking the streets alone, without pomp or escort."

The grin again: this time the cutting one, not the malicious. "Yes, I am a woman alone. As is every woman of the Tribade, from the youngest courier scurrying through the Spice Market to the crones older than memory who tend the stills and vats in hypogeal chambers. Who did you think Biggest Sister was? Some large-bellied woman on a golden throne, attended by dancing maidens and men with ivory phalluses hanging from their belts? You'd have to apply to the Temple District for that ilk."

He couldn't decide whether to bow or browbeat her. The knife kept him from the latter, his dignity from the former. "You tricked me."

"I will not bother to respond to that," she said. "You have bought a temporary remission of your debt with pretty words. Now tell me why I or anyone else should care that it be you who pursues this course of action."

"Because I have no interests in the City Imperishable." Imago leapt to his argument, trusting the words to come as they always did—this was the moment, even more than when he had spoken before to Ducôte. Her question would never have occurred to the dwarf, and Ducôte himself would not be one to stand in public for a high office above taller men. "I am of this place, I know our streets and people, where our money comes from and where it goes. My own family has departed for the Jade Coast and the salubrious swamps of the Eeljaw River. I owe nothing to anyone, present company excepted, and will stand strong in the arguing. This moment goes to the bold. I propose to be bold, and present my case well and quickly."

"Before the Debtor's Court catches you, for one," she said. "I happen to know that a bench warrant was sworn out against you this morning."

"I owe nothing to the courts!"

"As may be. I am not a judge, though I hear your name is known to them from their dockets. You are bold." She laughed. "I'll give you that." He saw decision cross her face, like watching wind change upon the water. "I wish to show you something. Then I will render judgment on behalf of the Tribade."

"I am yours, milady," Imago said with a bow.

"Hardly. That would presume I wanted you for something."

She led him then on an upward climb, ascending for a while more within the warren-walls of the Sudgate.

They eventually emerged on a narrow ledge just below the roofline of the High Hall—the most elevated point in the Sudgate complex. Even the defensive towers on the curtain were below them here. Imago could see rounded rooftop gardens, thick little circular forests of canyamo ready to harvest and dry for the pipe.

The city rose to his north and east, the great ranging complex of the Limerock Palace in the middle distance the most obvious structure. Gilded and tiled domes of the Temple District drew the eye to proclaim themselves. The Rugmaker's Cupola on Nannyback Hill punctuated the skyline at the north horizon. Smokestacks and factories and mansions and commercial buildings stood all across the City Imperishable, the modern world slowly colonizing all the traditional districts, save those so rich or so poor as to be untouchable.

A wind plucked at his shirt and hair in unpleasant reminder of the invisible hands grasping him at the docks. The foreshortened view at his feet both attracted and repelled him—he wished to jump and run screaming in the same motion. There was no railing here, only stone and empty space.

Biggest Sister took his arm in a grip as iron as her hair. Imago had no doubt in that moment she could cast him from the roof and no one would be the wiser. Instead she gave him a gentle shake, as if to wake him.

"What do you see out there, you who would rule?"

Buildings. Smoke. Steam. Streams of people and carts and the odd traction engine climbing the slopes on the other side of the Little Bull River. The clangor and clamor of a city slipping away from greatness and into the future. But that wasn't what she meant.

"People," he said, thinking back on their brief conversation before they reached the pot shop. "I see people in their thousands. Every building was raised by people's hands. Every coin earned, every thing created by people."

"Every single person out there was born of a woman," said Biggest Sister. She continued almost absently, though her grip upon his arm did not loosen. "I have killed seventeen men and eight women in my years. I have ordered the death of over three score more. A number soon to include yours if events had followed their usual pattern. I bore three children of my own before entering the Tribade, and one after. No one among the sisterhood who would have the power to kill may do so until she has brought life from between her legs. Have you brought life from between your legs, Imago of Lockwood?"

"You know the answer," he said quietly.

"Yes, I do. Yet I also know that the street, men and women alike, will not accept a woman to rule over them. For good or ill, it is the way of things here in our City Imperishable. That is part of why the Tribade bides so deep in shadow, sir. Your scheme is mad, the desperate hope of a foolish man too far gone in debt. But you swing meat between your legs, which is the first requirement for bearing a chain of office in this city. You survived a daylight attack from our noumenal enemies, which may become another requirement if our troubles keep going the way they have been, despite the denials of the Burgesses. You have the gift for words. Most of all, you have timing on your side."

"How is that?"

"We need change here in the City Imperishable. That would mean we might bend instead of breaking before the coming threats. Armies march, and our best people flee before the storm. Go, Imago, play at your Trial of Flowers. The Tribade will aid you, from the shadows."

"If I fail?"

"If you fail, I don't imagine I will have the privilege of killing you." That malicious grin again. "If you succeed, well, we will talk about the value of your debts when that happy moment occurs." She released his arm, stepped back to the little skylight through which they had climbed, and vanished into the roof.

Imago stood on the ledge a moment, unsure as to the meaning of all that had just happened.

BIJAZ THE DWARF

He emerged from the ground floor of Annalida's Tower to find the room beyond crowded, much against his expectations. A half-dozen bailiffs restrained two men, while several shouting clerks harangued them. Head down, Bijaz moved to avoid the affray when one of the prisoners began violently protesting his treatment.

The words caught at the dwarf's ear. He knew that voice. Bijaz looked up to see a man of medium height with blonde hair and brown eyes, dressed in an evening suit that had the look of long wear.

It was Jason the Factor, son of his old master Faneuil.

Bijaz had taken custody of Jason when Faneuil was executed for debt fifteen years earlier, and raised the boy as his own for some years before finding him work as a factor on behalf of Bijaz's full-man brother, Tomb. He was a man now, this boy that had once been under the dwarf's control, but still as instantly recognizable to the dwarf as one of his own children. Including the scars where Bijaz had drawn the needle tight through Jason's lips.

Their relationship had been…complex. Bijaz had stoked his own inner fires on Jason's powerlessness in those years. For some very good reasons, the sight of Jason brought the boy dying in the dwarf pit to mind all over again.

His former ward was in custody along with another man, a slightly built, silver-haired gentleman in a pale blue coat with the look that bespoke tailoring. There were bloodstains on the coat. Bijaz noted that the stranger did not bother struggling as Jason was.

"Those men are my responsibility," Bijaz shouted. He had a booming voice when need required, but still he was shocked at himself for just blurting the words without consideration.

The largest bailiff, a huge fellow with a fresh-clotted slash upon his cheek, whirled on Bijaz. The man was easily twice the height of the dwarf, with serjeant's tabs upon his red wool tunic. "You want to be part of this as well?" He was a very angry man. "I can march you up to the Sapphire Court right alongside these two fools."

"More fool *you*, Serjeant." Bijaz pitched his voice as if haranguing a crowd in Imperatrix Park, making sure the other bailiffs and indeed anyone coming down the corridor could hear him. "I have just come from the Inner Chamber, sent by them on an errand of urgency." In a sense, that last was true. "I require the services of Jason and his bodyguard to carry out their will. Would you prefer to argue with the First Counselor?"

The serjeant backed down, but not far. "This man defied lawful orders. After that he assaulted me."

"Swear out a complaint and have it served. You are a bailiff, surely you know the particulars of that process. In the meantime, unless you plan to disturb the Inner Chamber at their deliberations to seek summary judgment, I suggest you release these men to me." Bijaz leered, a deliberate provocation. "I will sign for them if you wish."

Some of the bailiffs looked relieved, one even hiding a smile. Not the serjeant. "I know you, dwarf," he said, stabbing a finger. "You'll be in more trouble than a fishmonger at a temple fry if I don't see satisfaction. I'll be speaking to the Provost later, when they close their session up there."

"Speak away. He knows what manner of dwarf I am." Bijaz jerked his head. "Jason, bring your man and come with me."

Jason shrugged free from the grip of the bailiffs, and towing his bloody-coated companion, hurried after Bijaz.

"What in Dorgau's nine brass hells was that?" the young man hissed as they made their way quickly toward the South Doors, leaving a knot of disputative bailiffs behind them.

"An exercise in authority," said Bijaz. His fingers flickered in the signs for ICE THAWING ON THE RIVER, meaning, wait for another time.

Jason nodded slightly, crooking his left little finger to indicate unquestioning acknowledgment.

They retraced his steps, a route as familiar to Bijaz as the path from his favored eating house to the offices and quarters he kept in Bentpin Alley. They hurried, anticipating the emergence of cogent thought from the knot of bailiffs yet puzzling behind them as they made their way to the South Doors and across the garden to the Costard Gate. Federico was still on guard and waved Bijaz out into the street without question, though he looked hard at the stains on the coat of Jason's companion.

Maldoror Street was more crowded than it had been earlier, mostly drovers cutting down toward Water Street and the Sudgate with cargo for outside the city. Two men passed atop camelopards. The riders were dressed as mummers, their mounts picking paths slowly through the crowd. Jason stared at them longer than he probably should have, then turned to Bijaz as the three of them passed between a pair of papermaker's stinking carts.

"I must thank you for the rescue. That fool Green Kelly shouted for the guards at the wrong time, I think." He sighed, then added, "We have not been friends for a while, have we?"

"Indeed." Bijaz tugged at his beard, unsettled and nervous now that the deed was done. "I have no love for the Inner Chamber, not anymore, if ever I did. Taking you from them was a thing of the moment. It was done to spit in their eyes, not honor you."

"I am to be honored by your spittle, little man," said the stranger. "We are to be having troubles and more being within that rotten palace."

"We all are." Bijaz led them across the road to a row of stalls, which clung to the fronts of the various inns and shops that existed to serve the extensive staff of the Limerock Palace. The stalls tended toward cheaper food that could be eaten while walking, and the kinds of souvenirs bought by sailors on a day's leave. The usual crowd swirled close, and they mingled. "The whole city has troubles," the dwarf added. "You may be on your way, gentlemen."

"Ignatius has vanished," said Jason, ignoring Bijaz's dismissal.

"I know that. His absence is a fire to the sticks of my troubles."

"No. Vanished. As in gone, probably dead."

Bijaz stopped, causing two men behind him with a large basket of live chickens to nearly run him down. Amid cursing and clucking, he stared at Jason. "What? How? Who knows of this?"

"Gone. I do not understand myself. We know of this, and Green Kelly I suppose."

"He was not to be telling the bailiffs any or all," said the stranger happily.

"And who the hells are you?" Bijaz demanded.

"The man who might save every one of us soon," said Jason.

"What, from an invasion of tailors?"

"How many troops are you to be in command of?" The stranger's voice was hard now.

"Less than you, it seems." Bijaz reined in his frustrated sarcasm. A bodyguard or mercenary, then, attached to Jason somehow. "My apologies, sir. The tide of politics runs hard against me, and your friend Jason and I have long since lost favor with one another."

"*Here* you are," said the godmonger from behind him.

"Things are now worse," he added.

Bijaz, Jason and the bodyguard hurried away from the Limerock Palace, to be out of the bailiffs' reach in the event that the serjeant and the Inner Chamber consulted amongst themselves and realized that Bijaz had played them all for fools in his own small way. The godmonger attached himself as an unwelcome fourth to their little group, tagging along even as the others walked in silence. Talking on the public street seemed less and less to be a reasonable idea.

Bijaz led them toward the Temple District, to be close to his offices in Bent-pin Alley. He didn't feel prepared to evade official detection; it was enough to put distance between him and the serjeant's anger. Jason and his dangerous friend could damned well take care of themselves.

Passing up Melisande Avenue and through Delator Square the four of them saw yet another pair of mummers mounted on camelopards. One of the men in whiteface carried a long silver lance with an ice blue pennon at the tip. Bijaz glanced suspiciously at the pale blue of the bodyguard's stained coat, but could not make up his mind if he saw a connection. For one, no signal or recognition that he could detect passed between the riders and the man.

At the far side of Delator Square, they pushed through a crowd gathered around the rusting iron posts marking the boundary of the Temple District. People were looking up, pointing. Bijaz stopped and looked. Something circled high above. It was of substantial size, to be so visible at such a distance. Jason and the other two companions took note, but they pushed on.

Bijaz did not want to think about teeth, about the noumenal, about anything but a few moments of quiet and safety before he set to the serious plotting of how to maintain the fortunes, both literal and metaphorical, of his people. The aspect of the Inner Chamber's actions that stung him like a nettle whip was this: Bijaz had long worked assiduously to keep the dwarfs of the City Imperishable safe within the city. He served the Sewn, the loyal dwarfs. Those whom the Inner Chamber would now punish, perhaps through the instrument of his personal attention as overseer of the levy, as answer to the fleeing rebels.

He wanted very badly to find that idiot Onesiphorous the Slashed and beat him senseless. The man had no morals! He had sold away the birthrights and best interests of every one of the boxed.

Bijaz led them to their destination, two streets down from Bentpin Alley and a block north of Upper Melisande Avenue on Randebar Street. Auntie One Shoe's Finer Chicken Pot, it was called, a place habituated mostly by priests and their catamites, mouse-faced women of the holy orders and that special species of melancholy servant one found working in the temples and abbeys of the district.

A quiet crowd, in other words, save for the mutter of thanksgiving prayers over the food. Which truly was excellent, at least to Bijaz's taste. Nothing like the fine fare favored by Burgesses and syndics and white-faced women hiding their tattooed mouths behind fans made from fingerbones, of course. He was far happier with a rich red wine and food that came in bowls with slabs of bread than he would be eating tiny colored bits crafted to look like plants or rocks off dishes painted to look like food—a recent craze in the crystal-goblet restaurants of the New Hill and the like.

"Here," Bijaz said, pushing the foursome into a table at the back of Auntie One Shoe's dining room. A bald priest in stained orange robes gave him a sour look from the next table, but Bijaz returned the expression with a cold intensity. The priest found something else to focus on.

The restaurant was as plain as its food. Pressed tin ceiling, much like any of the mercantiles about the city. Narrow windows set close together, easily shuttered in times of storm or trouble. The tables were mismatched, brought in one at a time as need dictated, and likewise the chairs, and even the wine glasses and coffee mugs.

It was good enough for him.

"Nice place," said Jason, once they'd settled into their seats. There had been a slight scuffle for the best view of the door, which the bodyguard had won.

Bijaz had less care for his back, and so took the worst seat without argument. "It does not matter what you think, my onetime friend. We are here, we will sup together for old times' sake, then we will be on our respective ways."

Jason blinked. "Why did you even trouble to bring us here, then?"

"To walk you safely away from the view of the bailiffs, and ensure no one was on our trail." Bijaz drummed his fingers on the table. "Make nothing more of it, sir."

"I must," Jason protested. "Affairs in the City Imperishable are too grievous for us to let this chance meeting come to nothing."

"Did you not see the angel flying over the city?" asked the godmonger, toying with a leather bag hung from a thong about his neck. A silly fetish, Bijaz thought, kidney stones of some saint or prophet.

"No angel," spat the bodyguard. "An Alate, it was being."

Bijaz shrugged. "I saw something distant that might have been large. My problems are close by and larger. You—all three of you—have joined them temporarily."

"Don't tell me about your problems," said the godmonger. "I fished you out of a gutter this morning, bloody to the ankles and half out of your wits. If that did not prepare you to open your eyes and ears to what comes, you are beyond help."

"What comes is disaster for us, Sewn and Slashed alike." Bijaz nodded to the waiter who hovered nearby. "Four of my usual, Sammael." He turned his attention back to his companions. "The Inner Chamber would raise an army to fight the warriors that come, and they will do it by breaking the backs of dwarfs, both Sewn and Slashed. Our possessions are forfeit should we leave the city, and they also move against the goods and coin of loyal folk who have stayed true to the City Imperishable. Dwarfs only, mind you, none of this applies to full-men."

"Idiots," said Jason.

"And more," agreed the godmonger.

The bodyguard shrugged. "Not for me to be taking issue with the payment of armies."

"Our problems are not military," said Jason. "An army may well come upon us, and it may be that the City Imperishable must meet them in the field, but the way things are progressing at the moment, any invader is likely to find the city already defeated. Ignatius of Redtower could not have been lightly taken. He is the most powerful of our philosophick doctors."

"The noumenal world is intended by nature and divine design to remain separate from our phenomenal world," said the godmonger, "but things from the other side walk our streets almost constantly now. When I listen at the darkness, the chattering has grown loud, and nearly comprehensible." The other three just stared blankly at him, so he added, "This is not as things should be."

"Noumenal attack, is that what happened to him?" Jason asked the godmonger, with a nod at Bijaz.

The godmonger favored the other dwarf with a long, slow look. "I don't know. He babbled about teeth, and was covered in blood. Most of it not his own, to his own good fortune."

"Yes," said Bijaz. He did not want to have to explain. "I was walking along Melisande Avenue last night when it happened." He wanted to think on what course he might take, how to oppose the will of the Inner Chamber. Learn what might be learned from this collection of intruders. Not engage in this…pointless…discussion about him. "It slew at least one man, and would have slain me save for chance."

The godmonger reached out, gently touching Bijaz's forehead. "But it did not. You were favored by that chance. You must take that favor and make something of it, reach for the good."

"Good, my sweet pickle," muttered Bijaz. He was lost to good. All he could do was try to help his people while he yet could.

"How did it come to not be killing you?" asked the bodyguard gently.

"I don't know," Bijaz admitted. He thought back on the teeth leering out of the night sky. The memory made him shudder. "I ran. I slipped and fell. Whatever was next was beyond me, as I lay insensate."

"You were not to be fighting with magic or special power?"

"I was not to be anything."

"Bijaz," said Jason. "Look. We do have common cause here, whatever our history. I must find Ignatius. Or at the very least, determine what has become of him. I know he did not intend to meet the threats to this city by raising an army. That's idiotic. We are being attacked from the noumenal world. You do not want the armies raised either, at least not on the backs and purses of your people. The politics of the Inner Chamber are affecting them. The least we can do is work together for the sake of the City."

"Perhaps," Bijaz admitted. "I do not know one way or the other what should be, not right now. We have nothing to set in opposition to the Assemblage, neither as a whole nor as the Inner Chamber."

"That may be changing," said the godmonger. "There is a rumor that the Lord Mayor is returning."

Bijaz felt a surge of irritation. "What Lord Mayor? We don't have any Lord Mayor. I could understand people praying for the return of the Imperator, though that would do us little enough good. But a Lord Mayor?"

"That actually makes a bit of sense," said Jason. "Someone who could oppose the Burgesses, set us on a better course. Though I don't see how it could be done. What rumors, sir priest?"

"Oh, not a priest." The other dwarf smiled, rolling his fetish bag between his fingers. "Surely you know that I am a godmonger. My kind offer spiritual surcease by the variety and kind. You might think of it as faith by subscription, with the right of approval."

Jason nodded. "I suppose I have heard of the difference, though it's never mattered much to me. What rumors, sir godmonger?"

The godmonger shrugged. "People talking in the street outside the Limerock Palace. The Tribade has found someone with the stomach to stand for the office."

"The stomach and an iron overcoat, I should hope," said Bijaz. "Elections are banned in the City Imperishable. That's why there has been no Lord Mayor for generations upon generations."

The waiter brought wine, and a few moments' silence in the conversation as he served it. The wine was a full red, as Bijaz favored his vintages, thick nearly as the grape that birthed it and almost sweet. The alcohol stung his damaged teeth, but soothed the pain a bit.

The bodyguard spoke over the rim of his glass. "Your politics are not being of interest to me. I am being captain of a force to watch your walls. These noumenals are to be concerning me more. As well as whatever army is to be coming soon, of course, but hungry monsters today are to be more frightening than swords in the winter."

"I do not know much," said the godmonger. "However, one way we differ from priests is this—they listen to a single voice with their heads bowed in prayer. My sort hears a crowd. When the voices agree, when the words come out, there is a truth walking behind the darkness. This is a rare thing. I have never heard it before, and never thought to hear it in my time. One of the old wonders, miracles magnified by the lens of years from events just one remove from commonplace. Except this is not commonplace, nor do we live in older times."

"Your monsters are to be gods?"

"Or maybe the other way around," said the godmonger with a smile. "Nothing makes a skeptic of a man faster than reading the words of too many revelations."

That was enough for Bijaz. "Revelations? Then reveal me this. How am I, or *we,* to set aside the will of the Inner Chamber? I will not have my people turned out, their homes and accounts plundered."

"If you are not to be leaving the city, you are to be fighting for your homes. Everyone is knowing this to be true always. Your misfortune that the fight is to be great at this time."

"Get them in the streets," said Jason. His fingers flickered into the sign for SUNRISE COMES, meaning he swore to the inevitable truthfulness of his words. "Have the Sewn and Slashed marching together in protest against the actions of the Inner Chamber. We must find a way to prove that these noumenal attacks are the true menace in their own right, and not the harbinger of imagined invasion."

"How?" Bijaz asked.

The godmonger set his wine down with a noisy gasp and wiped his lips, rubbing fingers across the knots that bound them. "We listen at the darkness."

Bijaz glanced at Jason. "Isn't that what the Second Counselor was doing?"

Jason looked sour. "Unfortunately, I rather imagine so."

The godmonger smiled again. "Heeding the noumenal world is not simple work. That is why you have come into it, friend Bijaz. It is not simple, but people listen to you. If you know the truth, you can tell it to them."

"I don't want noumena, I don't want armies, I want a return to the way things were."

"That you will not be getting."

"I know," muttered Bijaz.

The chicken stew arrived—a meal fit for the narrow mouths of the Sewn, with the meat shredded to small chunks and such vegetables as had survived the kitchen, diced fine. They fell to their meal as men starved.

When they were done, the godmonger was wiping his bowl clean with the last of his bread. He looked up bright-eyed and smiling once more. "Will you listen at the darkness with me?"

"I have absolutely no desire to do any such thing," replied Bijaz.

"They found you once. They will find you again."

"I know, I know."

Jason spoke up. "I for one am interested in this rumor of the Lord Mayor's return. A rebellion against authority would go much better if we had our own authority to show for it."

"We are still to be having the problem for which I am coming to you of this morning," said the bodyguard.

Jason glared at him. "Which is…?"

"Winter Boys are to be killing two Tokhari scouts being on the Rose Downs. Straw Eye men, who are to be running with fire in their souls. This is to be a problem. Your noumenals are to be monsters in your night, but Straw Eye men are someday to be guiding armies before your gates at dawn."

"What do you want me to do about it?"

The soldier—for of course that's what he was, Bijaz realized, despite the cut of his gentleman's clothes—shrugged. "Your Ignatius was to be telling me. Now you are to be telling me. Fight monsters, you are saying, we will to be fighting monsters. Fight Tokhari, we will to be fighting Tokhari. But we are wishing not to die stupidly."

"None of us wish to die stupidly," said Bijaz.

"We may all get the chance," the godmonger replied, far too cheerfully for Bijaz's taste.

Bijaz wound up in his offices with the godmonger, who exhibited the persistence of a blood fly on a dead-calm day. Offices, as such, was almost overstating the case. He rented two rooms above a cobbler specializing in footwear for Temple District priests, laity and staff. The trade mostly ran to quiet-soled slippers or boots insulated with gutta-percha for those sects with too much spark in their services. Bijaz paid his rent and met his expenses from the modest incomes of his own investments, and donations from those among the Sewn with sufficient interest in the political process.

"At least you're a Sewn dwarf," he said to the godmonger. He couldn't just shake the little bastard off, and though he had a sick feeling at the very thought of whatever *listening at the darkness* might entail, Bijaz realized he would probably need to follow that path. Too much was at stake. He finally asked the question he'd been avoiding much of the day. "What is your name, anyway?"

The godmonger's slanted eyes crinkled with his smile even as his fingers slipped into signing. FISH SELL BEST ON THE MARKET BLOCK, he signaled. Everything must happen when its time comes.

Meaning, Bijaz supposed, they should have a detailed discussion of what his involuntary companion had been hinting at. He felt too tired for games. FOLLOW THE RIVER, he signed back. Let it happen when it happens.

"Archer," said the godmonger with a shrug. "My name is Archer. I will force nothing upon you, but neither will I just slip away. You have been marked."

"The whole city has been marked, Archer."

"As may be. You are the goat, though."

Bijaz stared into the other's deep brown eyes. "I am a man among my people, trying to keep them safe. The Slashed flee, and the Sewn are blamed. I work with the Burgesses and the Inner Chamber, and am insulted for my troubles. I walk about my own errands and am struck down by noumena in the night. It would seem that I am the goat."

"What were you doing out at that hour?"

Bijaz had a flash of memory: Pale skin, blood on cheeks and chest, the horse-headed dwarf laughing like a Tokhari demon. Hot semen pouring down his thighs. For the tip of a few coppers the born dwarfess had touched his head and called him vile filth.

"I was listening to my darkness, friend Archer. Listening to my darkness."

The godmonger's face filled with a certain distant pity. "May I offer you a choice of prayers and sacrifices?"

"No. Just tell me when and where we go to listen."

"Two nights hence," said Archer. "When the moon is halved. Darkness and light will be balanced in those hours, neither one ascendant. By the River Saltus, which runs thick with the blood and shit of our beloved City Imperishable. Meet me on the Sudgate jetty. Fast a day that your body might be cleansed, and come to me with a pure heart if you can."

"Pure as ever I am." Bijaz pulled paper and fountain pen from his desk. He owned a ball-calligraph, but it was too much trouble for him. "Now I must compose letters to certain of the Sewn."

"I myself have wonders to attend to." Archer rose and bowed. "Please, do not lose your way."

"If I do I'm sure you will be able to find me," said Bijaz dryly.

JASON THE FACTOR

Enero trailed him through the city. Jason was making for the waterfront—his own warehouse at Sturgeon Quay would serve him well if he had no better thoughts. It was equally true that everyone and everything in the city came from the docks and returned to the docks. Much like men who spring wailing from a woman's womb, then spend their lives trying to return.

Somehow the idea of the River Saltus as civic cloaca appealed to him.

Where in the nine brass hells of Dorgau the Munificent was Ignatius of Redtower? Something wingéd and noumenal had taken him. At the very least, this was what Jason was meant to think from the evidence in his master's apartments. Wherever he had gone, if anyone could win their way back, it would be Ignatius. By the gods, the City needed his master to return.

Everything stank.

He spent a few moments indulging himself in the privilege of simply watching his step.

"You are to be looking for this Lord Mayor who is not existing?" asked Enero, after they'd dodged traffic on leaf-slick cobbles awhile.

"It's just a whisper," said Jason. "I want to think on how this thing could be done. Or at least brought to further force as a full-blown rumor. The idea of a Lord Mayor may be more powerful than the man himself in office." Ignatius of Redtower had shown him that, time and again. Word of deeds both great and foul often carried far more weight from a distance. "The Inner Chamber leads poorly now, especially without my master, and the Assemblage as a whole is a debating party, not an executive. A Lord Mayor ascending could either force them to abandon their petty politics in favor of worthwhile action, which would be to the good, or even force a broader transformation altogether."

"There is not being a Lord Mayor. Not for the centuries, yes?"

"Someone knows how to bring that office back." He dodged a tall, knob-kneed leg that stretched over him. "That has to be what drives the rumors. I want to listen to the city awhile."

"And the Winter Boys are to be watching the walls for scouts?"

"Monsters, my good man. I am far more concerned with monsters."

"You are to be making your own monsters here in the City Imperishable.

It is to be no small wonder that your greatness has long since departed south to other lands."

"As may be." Jason gave him a sidelong glance. "You stormed into the Limerock Palace to tell me that your men had killed two scouts?"

"True enough, but that is also being a story I am to be telling for those two half-men to be hearing."

"So…?" They'd reached Water Street, and Jason wanted to go to ground awhile and listen, without this bloody dandy of Ignatius' choosing at his side. He might hear of his master, and he'd certainly hear of the supposed return of the Lord Mayor.

"The Alate was to be coming to me, to be speaking of your danger."

"Alate?" Jason didn't know the term.

"Wingéd man. A race of the uttermost east, some are to be saying, from high in the Shattercliff Mountains. I am being told they are noumenal, but I am knowing these flyers to be the Alate. A creature which eats and shits and bleeds and is crying pain." Enero flexed his fists and smiled. "I am to have killed them before. They are dying simple as pigeons, but with having more of the fuss about them."

"So you killed this one?"

"No." Enero sounded surprised. "He was to be warning me you were to be losing your way before your master, and I was to be going to the chamber where you were being found."

Once he untangled it, Jason found this statement somewhat curious. "What made you believe him?"

Enero reached into his coat and pulled out a small square of wax paper, such as a lunch might have come in. He handed it to Jason, who stopped in the shade of a stack of baled cotton to open the package.

A human ear lay within, shriveled and sad on the wax paper. The flesh was bloody, torn free by main force apparently. It was a left ear. The lobe sported a tiny iron stud much like those often favored by Ignatius of Redtower.

"The Alate brought you this?"

"I was to be finding this convincing."

Feathers, thought Jason. The little room at the top of Ignatius' apartment had been full of feathers. He felt a rush of sick horror. "The Alate killed Ignatius."

Enero studied the ear a moment. "I am not to be thinking that. The Alate was to be filled with dread, not to be triumphant. Nor to be shivering with battle lust."

"May I keep it?"

"Of course."

That was generous of Enero. If this was indeed Ignatius' ear—which would

account for the blood Jason found—it would be an article of significant noumenal power. Enero was giving him advantage without recompense, an act
that carried a strange echo of the ethos of Ignatius' own Hermetic Order of
Philosophick Doctors, which held that each magical action carried its own opposite within, like a seed inside a fruit. Jason glanced briefly at the mercenary
captain, then folded the wax paper, the ear within, and pocketed the package.
He would seek the needed assistance later in tracking down his missing master
by this noumenal thread, but for the moment he wanted to understand more
of what was happening now. "This Alate mentioned me by name?"

"Not to be speaking of the person Jason the Factor of the City Imperishable, no. To be speaking of danger to my paymaster, chains of coin which are
binding my Winter Boys to the city. I am knowing this to be you. There is
to be no other, no?"

"No, I suppose not. Are you back to the walls now?" It was an ill-concealed
hint.

"First I am to be having my suit cleansed." With a sharp nod, Enero walked
away.

Jason wondered how many of the Winter Boys had been in the crowd following along with them from the first.

The ear would have to wait until he had the time and resources to follow the
trail it represented—such noumenal searching was completely outside his own
abilities. Instead, Jason began his search for rumor at the Teakwood Scow. It
was a dockside tavern that had allegedly begun life as a lumber barge bringing
hardwoods up from the swamps and forests of the Jade Coast. If there was
a hull to be seen under the lapboard walls, it was beyond him, and the Scow
rose tall as any of the other buildings on its stretch of Water Street.

His warehousemen drank there, and some of the dockside idlers known
to Jason from around Sturgeon Quay. Though he did not spend overmuch
time in the Scow, preferring to avoid fraternizing, Jason was familiar enough
with the place. Far too often he had roused men from there, or on the reverse,
slipped funds to Old Jack Capp to keep his crews from wandering farther
astray.

Inside was much like any other dockside tavern. None of the nets-and-buoys
décor favored by fish-houses catering to the quality trade from up the city's
hills. The Teakwood Scow was dedicated to serious drinking, with long trestle
tables beneath a high, smoky ceiling stained by the pipes of generations of
longshoremen. Sailors drank somewhere else where they were welcome—this
place belonged to the City Imperishable and its dockmen.

Jason returned the nods of those who knew him, then took a stool at the
bar and slipped a handful of chalkies to the tired woman pouring out the

drinks—funds enough to keep a man in drink for hours. "Ale in a small pot, with boiled water to follow," he said.

He had no intention of getting drunk.

Ceramic in hand, the taste of the place on his lips—it was a bitter brown ale like the liquid stepbrother of peasant bread—he closed his eyes and listened as Ignatius had taught him.

A dozen conversations filled the room, along with snores, moans, slurps and burps. With his eyes shut, he became more conscious of the smells. Blood sausage in a pan of hot water. The reek of spilled beer going bad on the floor. A veritable symphony of flatulence. Someone drinking acrid wine. The strange, dank scent of a kitchen at work.

And the people. Grumbling about certain labor jobbers. Mocking a man for his wife playing the harlot while he worked evenings down the docks. "Not worth the chalkie, neither, save for to stick an oar in old Steffan's pond," a middle-aged man cackled. Other voices:

…bloody snake it was, made of water and duckweed with eyes of guttering mud…aunt's gone back upriver to gran's place, said she's had enough…Burgesses! Tits on a fish, I'm telling…Tribade said it, so it must be true…then he killed his horse…

Jason slipped into the rhythms of the speech for a while, but he couldn't tease more out than the usual dissatisfactions. Some of that matched his own undercurrent of worry about Ignatius, but he also realized that it had been a mistake to come here. He was known at the Teakwood Scow. His employees drank here. Everyone guarded their words, a little.

He opened his eyes, nodded to the barwoman and slipped back into the street. It was time to move three or four quays upriver and find a new tavern.

It took Jason three bars and more ale than he'd meant to drink before he picked up the thread of rumor which he sought.

"Old laws. Like as not they'll tell us we can't be wearing our shoes on Wednesdays or summat, they start digging into those books."

"Ain't been a public vote in this city since long 'fore anyone cares to remember. How else you going to have a mayor?"

That got Jason's attention. He turned, leaning on his elbow to look over this establishment with a little more care. It was neither a sailor's bar nor a shoreman's. Rather, this place was mostly filled with carters and drovers and draymen, their big, huffing teams idling outside under the watchful eyes of bribed and bribable boys while the men brought the hard sweat of horses in with them.

The place reeked of leather and lather and rotten straw. Two bruisers, men big enough to haul beer barrels off the back of a cart single-handed, sat close to him talking the politics of the day.

"...fecking bailiffs can lick my big bay's arse til it bleeds," said the one with short red hair that looked as if it had been cut with a flensing knife. "Limerock Palace could sink up to the weathervane, none of our'n would miss a thing of it."

"If they could get that fellow to put that chain of office 'round his neck without his head being shortened first, there might be summat for the working man." That from the dark-haired drinker with a lazy eye.

"Old laws or no?" Redhead guffawed.

Jason took the bull by the pizzle and dragged a chair to their table. Sullen silence welled over him, until he dropped two silver obols onto the scarred wood. The quiet transformed from sullen to attentive.

"Man throws coin like 'at 'round, might find hisself short a purse," observed Lazy Eye.

"Might at that," said Jason. "But not in a drover's bar. Man hauls goods, collects on deliveries, he's an honest man. Whether or not he has any use for pretty strangers."

"Ain't that pretty," said Redhead.

"See. We're not so different." He nodded at the bar, signaling the squat man there for another round.

"Man who throws coin 'round generally wants summat."

"Of course," said Jason. "I'm looking for our next Lord Mayor."

The redhead began laughing. "If you're a killer, I'm a gray goose," he managed to choke out.

Jason hadn't expected that. "Who's killing?"

"Anyone." Lazy Eye grinned. "Stands to reason. Him changes the powers what be, somebody be having less power. Big people don't like little people coming along, cutting into the rackets."

"The new Lord Mayor is a little person?" A dwarf, he wondered? Not possible. These men would have looked at that in a whole different light.

"Like us," said Redhead. "From the street. Done gone declared himself to Biggest Sister. Tribade's already whispering, let him pass, give him a ride, soup, a half-chalkie if he needs it."

It wasn't the worst place to start a political campaign, Jason reflected, with the Tribade. Though he still didn't see how anyone would hope to take power away from the Assemblage of Burgesses. "No elections here. Unions vote, guilds vote, Burgesses vote amongst themselves. Who's to vote for a Lord Mayor?"

"He'll vote hisself in."

"Yeah."

"Well," said Jason. "Add my whisper to the Tribade's, if anyone speaks of it. I've coin and more for the man who would be mayor. Tell him to ask after the factor on Sturgeon Quay."

The silver obols disappeared. "Aye, sir."

"As your worship says."

"Right. Drink in good health, gentlemen." Jason stepped over to the bar and settled the entire tab for the two carters, then headed back for his warehouse.

He had first met Ignatius of Redtower over the curious matter of the soul bottles—the last investment of Jason's father, which had driven the family to penury and his father to a debtor's death. Up until that time Jason had never thought much of magic. The contest of wills between him and Ignatius, and the cooperation that followed, had thoroughly convinced him of the noumenal.

For one, they had found the voice of Ignatius' late father among the breath of the trapped souls.

That episode had been a nine-day wonder along the docks, and even spoken of up the hills, but eventually folk turned to other stories—rapes and murders and robberies and clever smuggling, the daily fare of waterfront chatter. It was nothing to the rest of the City Imperishable, in the end, but the whole business had turned Jason's life in a new direction.

Ignatius was a central figure in a generations-long war of dust and shadows. The Second Counselor was even said to be heir to the Imperator Terminus, and his profile certainly matched that which yet graced the city coins. Jason doubted the putative line of descent signified much of anything in these late days.

As for the hidden war, he had only seen the very edges of that struggle. He knew the conflict long predated the current threat of invasion that so preoccupied the First Counselor's imagination. In the years since the affair of the soul bottles, Jason had stood with Ignatius in alleys and upon rooftops, down sewers and atop the city walls. For the most part they had argued with, cajoled and occasionally fought other men. A few times he had seen shapes in the night the memory of which could still afflict him with cold sweats.

These last few months, with the burnings and the dryland drownings and the savage deaths across the City Imperishable, represented altogether another war. Where the danger had always stalked just beyond the reach of the eye, just past the outstretched fingertip, now it walked bold as brass down the city's streets, slaying as it went. Though no two noumenal attacks were identical, and no two witnesses ever agreed on what they might have seen, it was clear to Jason the agency arose from Ignatius' ancient adversaries.

Some great curse or spell or long ago geas upon the City Imperishable was taking life now. If anything, he thought the rumors of war were a result of the noumenal assault, rather than the other way around.

The Inner Chamber had it wrong, deadly wrong. He needed Ignatius—Jason was no more prepared to fight toothed shadows on his own than he was ready to flap his arms and fly to the top of the Rugmaker's Cupola.

If Ignatius did not come back, it would take a serious rallying of the City to do something. They would need to shake out quite a few philosophick doctors, priests with miracles extending beyond a silver tongue and a quick hand, or strange-eyed foreigners of a mystical bent to stand before the attacks.

He would have set fire to the Limerock Palace himself, were that likely to serve any purpose at all in distracting the Assemblage from their venality and the Inner Chamber from their fears. A Lord Mayor would serve as that fire, in a way.

Action, instead of reaction and reliance on half a thousand years of stability, bought in part by the secret blood of Ignatius and his ilk.

Meanwhile, Jason thought he would have to go to the Tribade himself, seek out this candidate they were advancing. His purposes and theirs generally did not cross, but neither did they often align.

At least he was not enemies with the dark sisters.

Back in his own quarters, Jason put the ear on ice and tried to attend to business—both that of the warehouse, which had not stopped its traffic for the current crisis, as well as the process of thinking more on the matter of the Lord Mayor. That afternoon a boy brought in a sheaf of handbills. Jason gave him a chalkie and sent the lad on his way. He then sat in his windowed office at one corner of the open space and looked through the papers. The late sun made the yellow stock look almost gold, and the flyers crinkled warm in his hands. The scent of ink and oil from the press met his nose like the aroma from a bundle of flowers.

The City Imperishable Languishes Under the Despotic Rule of the Burgesses, read one headline. A modest rant expanding on the topic followed.

Hope Is Needed When Our Lost Crown's Legacy Has Failed
Nights Are Unsafe While Fools Rule the Day

Somebody was certainly working to prepare the sentiment on the street for the coming of a new Lord Mayor. Jason examined the handbills more closely. All had the little sigil of two doves centered in the lower margin of the page, the symbol of work done at Ducôte's scriptorium.

It was bold of that good dwarf to sign his work, Jason thought. That meant the canny old bastard felt safe. The Tribade indeed. If the Provost became angry enough to send bailiffs to close down the press, they would probably succeed. Few in the city had a taste for blood on the cobbles. Furthermore, the Tribade's involvement would make old Zaharias think twice about placing such pressure on civic commerce. Especially when the working public might take note and object. The Limerock Palace needed food delivered to its kitchens as much or more than any other establishment in the City Imperishable.

That idiot Prothro, on the other hand… Were Ignatius here, and still active on the Inner Chamber, he would redirect the First Counselor's frequently misplaced fears. On his own, Prothro was capable of all manner of stupidity. Dorgau take Ignatius for vanishing so.

Enough. He could not allow himself to sink into uncontrolled regret. Business attended. Jason forced his thoughts back to the matter at hand.

Ducôte obviously knew something about what was coming. That dwarf wouldn't have written a doctor's note for his own grandmother without someone paying for ink and paper.

"I'm going out again," he bellowed to Two-Thumbs, his lead daytime gang boss, then headed up Water Street for Ducôte's.

One of the dark sisters fell into step beside Jason half a block from his own warehouse. She was tall, with gray hair and gray eyes, not ill-favored but far beyond the years he preferred in his women. Overly sized for his taste as well. Jason had always required his procurer to bring him boxed dwarfesses. He'd tried a born dwarfess once, but her privates were not shaped well for him.

"Sister," he said, nodding slightly without breaking stride. No one ran business on the docks without reaching an understanding with the Tribade. They didn't ask for money, not usually, but sometimes cargoes came and went without being noted on manifests. People, too, less often, though almost always women.

"My good factor," she said. "You are missing a master, I believe."

While Ignatius' disappearance wasn't precisely a secret, Jason found it more than frustrating that so many people seemed to know of it. "And so?" he said, restraining his temper for the sake of diplomacy.

"The City Imperishable would be missing a master as well. I believe you've taken an interest in that problem."

He slowed his steps. "A rumor or two may have reached my ears, yes."

"More like your ears found their way to the country of rumor, sir." She chuckled. "That's fair enough. There is a man you should meet. Don't bother with that dove Ducôte."

"Is this gentleman available to me?" Jason asked cautiously.

"He is above ground, and in health last I saw him. Imago of Lockwood. Perhaps you know the man?"

Jason felt a pressure in his chest, a surge from his heart. The name similar enough to Ignatius of Redtower that he wondered if it might be a guise. But no, the Tribade knew perfectly well who Ignatius was. They would not be gulled, nor likely see a reason to cozen Jason in this matter either.

"No," he said, regretting this flash of false hope, "I do not know him."

"A fool," said the Tribadist, "with a strange combination of need and ambition. Still, his heart is good despite his lies. He may be what the City Imperishable is crying out for even now."

"Ah." Jason slowed to a halt. "Is he with Ducôte?"

"He was for a brief while. I believe he is moving about the City, building crowds to his name and finding those among the moneyed classes who would support a rising against the Assemblage."

Jason glanced quickly around. It was strange to hear sedition spoken so openly. Most people who thought on those lines feared too much to simply state their intentions in public.

When he looked back, the Tribadist was gone, blending in with the busy crowds.

"Imago of Lockwood," Jason said, setting the name within his mind. "Where shall I find you, sir? Can I serve you, and can you serve me?"

IMAGO OF LOCKWOOD

He walked along Maldoror Street, past the south wall of the Limerock Palace. The roadway was the usual brawl of commerce and traffic, a nearly overwhelming mess that moved only by a combination of miracle and remarkable forbearance. Preoccupied with his experiences at the Sudgate, Imago let his feet set their own path. As a result he occasionally slipped in the ever-present horse droppings and ox pies. Water Street was the shortest way back to Ducôte's scriptorium—for he had nowhere else to go—but given his earlier experiences down by the Softwood Quay, he had no taste for being so close to the River Saltus.

Trapped in the taffy-stretched moment of the noumenal attack, he'd barely heard the reports of the cannonfire that had freed him. He owed *Lissa Lightfoot*'s captain his finest regards, once he had the resources to be more than thankful.

Biggest Sister also. And what had she been to him? A woman, almost as old as his own safely distant Mater. Comparing Biggest Sister with the Dame of Lockwood was much the same as setting a pardine limer from some great hunting lodge in the old hill kingdoms against one of the common mongrels that rooted garbage from the gutters of the City Imperishable.

He was tired. He was sore. He was damp. Imago wished mightily for a safe haven to which he could repair to amend his appearance and change into clothes that did not resemble the bottom of the river. No one, least of all himself, would believe in him, not as he was now looking so like a late-drowned corpse. With that cheerful thought, he bumped into a man smelling of gin, blood and damp wool. Looking up to apologize, the words died in Imago's mouth.

It was a very large bailiff with bandages on his cheek where some scoundrel had done him a bad turn. Rumbling irritation: "You are one Imago of Lockwood."

"Why…no…" He vaguely recognized the huge bailiff from his own courtroom appearances in the Limerock Palace. By Dorgau's sweet fig, it was not like him to be so careless. A lie would not do now, not at all. "I mean, yes, my mind was set on other things, sir…Serjeant, is it?"

"That's no concern of yours." The serjeant scowled, then flipped his staff up with a quick motion of his forearm to tap Imago squarely in the chest. "I got a warrant for your arrest, however, sir. And here I've gone and taken you." He leaned close, displaying a set of teeth in an astonishing array of colors, textures and advancing states of decay, with breath to match. "My day has gone right poor so far. Feel free to run, little man. It'd be my pleasure to beat you down."

"Not at all, Serjeant." Imago's brain finally re-engaged. This was a different manner of difficulty than he navigated in the world of Ducôte and Biggest Sister, frankly his more usual. "No trouble at all."

"Shame." The bailiff grabbed his shoulder with a grip that would leave marks and propelled Imago directly toward the Costard Gate.

"I suppose I was easily taken," Imago said as they walked. "Since I fairly much presented myself. More the fool me. May I inquire as to the charges that have been sworn against me?"

"Debtor's Court warrant. You've pissed away too many obols of the bench's time and treasure, I expect." The bailiff snickered. "Or one of the posher nobs in the Assemblage has got tired of your petty suits and decided to put an end to you."

What in the brass hells had he been thinking, to walk so close to the Limerock Palace? The river would have been safer, noumena or no. His fatigue and distraction were about to cost him dearly.

Imago was perfectly clear on what was done to debtors here in the City Imperishable. If a man was in default for up to a thousand silver obols after his assets had been forfeited, he could expect five lashes in Delator Square, and sometimes be required to drag a door from there back to his dwellings to show his public shame. Ten thousand obols earned twenty-five lashes. In earlier days, there had also been time on display in a cage, though that was mostly waived now. More than ten thousand obols and a man could find his thighs broken in front of a waiting crowd. Though it was not considered a capital sentence, few people survived that experience.

The nature of bankruptcy laws in the City Imperishable lent a certain elegant panic to the practice of securing lines of credit and outright loans. Both of which he had outstanding on Cork Street, unfortunately.

It wasn't like the Numbers Men to bring suit before any bench of the Assemblage, however. Their justice ran to men with names like Black Chalkie and Three-Widows, who carried blunt admonishments in special pockets sewn within the lining of their coats. Imago had no doubt that the fact that he had often drank with those two gentlemen in particular would have no bearing on the beating they would give him, save they'd greet him by name first, and possibly help him to a chirurgeon afterward.

He glanced up at the big serjeant. It was obvious enough that the man wouldn't listen to financial reasoning. Which would be moot anyway, since those arrangements were always for cash in hand. Imago's current treasury of a single copper orichalk wouldn't buy off anyone with the resources of a one-legged beggar's boy.

Soon enough they were inside the warren of the Palace itself.

Imago made a point of never approaching the Debtor's Court. He neither wanted to see nor be seen about those precincts, for Imago firmly believed in the power of images set in one's mind. Unfortunately, his image was at hand.

Where was Biggest Sister when he needed her? She could have extracted him from this unpleasantness. No, he was forced to walk across deep, plush Tokhari carpets worn into pathways by the tread of thousands before him. He was forced to pass tall oak doors with the instruments of question painted on their panels in flaking colors that smelled faintly of oil and soap. He was forced to sit quietly on an unpadded pew in the tiered gallery, firmly in the grip of that bastard serjeant, looking downward while three Burgesses sitting as judges-financial heard some poor bugger of a baker or a miller—Imago couldn't be bothered to listen closely—plead a case of short supply and wages owed and carters being ordered to hold back his payments by the syndicate for whom they worked. He vaguely recognized all three judges, but did not know any of them personally.

After the man was led out red-faced and shaking, Imago was summarily dragged before the bench. This was not one of his courtrooms—his barratry and champerty were brought in the Civil Courts, which heard cases in the Chalcedony Suites—but it had many of the same fixtures and traditions. The judges were dressed in black cassocks buttoned high at the throat, with red cowls draping their shoulders, to be pulled up in order to hide their faces when pronouncing death or banishment as a sentence. Two of the three seated today wore the traditional bear-fur wigs, symbolizing the fearsome might of the law. The third was bald as a marble statue, with flinty eyes that roamed much further than the bored stares of his fellow judges.

Around them were arrayed the clerk of the court, the bailiff of the court, the witness box and cage, the implements of the question and the high water-tank. The walls were lined with half-pillars, the vaulted ceiling painted with a version of the story of Balnea meeting the False Riders. The courtroom itself had seats for several dozen spectators, though only a few young men were present today, busy fellows in neatly pressed suits with an air about them of taking notes on behalf of absent masters. None of them were dwarfs, Imago saw. The Assemblage and its functionaries had succeeded in driving those old servants out one by one in the past few years.

It was no wonder the Slashed and the Sewn alike were so stirred up of late, he thought.

The bald judge gaveled the hearing into session with the most classic implement available—the thighbone of a traitor, wrapped in silver chains. That was not encouraging. They were going to hold strictly to tradition today. Traditional charges, traditional processes of law, traditional punishments.

In the City Imperishable, tradition was often a poor indicator of success, especially for a defendant.

"Who appears before this court?" bawled the clerk as he popped up from his little desk.

"One Imago of Lockwood," shouted the giant bailiff who'd arrested Imago, dragging his charge forward.

Toward the witness cage, Imago noted glumly. Rarely used anymore, the primary purpose of confinement was to allow the implements of the question to be most conveniently put to their purpose.

"Why does this man appear?" The clerk's face was getting red already. Imago wished him the joy of palpitations of the heart.

The serjeant rushed through the answer by rote, blurring the words into something on the order of a legal sneeze. "To answer the warrant sworn by this bench of yesterday, nine Octobres, *anno* 617 Imperator Terminus, the authority of his rein being lawfully subrogated to the Assemblage of Burgesses until the day of his return."

The bald judge banged the gavel again. The other two simply glared at Imago. "The accused will be placed in the cage," he ordered.

Imago did not fight his jailor, even though that was clearly what the big serjeant wanted. Instead he slipped through the open door ahead of the man's shove, and clung to his dignity as the cage bars were slammed closed.

Another bang of the gavel: "The clerk will recount the charges."

"Imago of Lockwood, known to this court as a barrator and a champertor, sometime habitué of the chance houses of Cork Street, of a broken family living in penurious exile on the Jade Coast, you are hereby brought before the judges-financial to answer to the following charges. One, that you have conspired to bring false suits without merits before the judges-civil of this august Assemblage of Burgesses, incurring costs to the treasury of the courts for the hearing of those cases. Two, that in bringing those false suits you presented evidence that was fabricated or misleading, incurring further costs to the treasury of the courts for the hearing of those cases. Three, that in seeking awards of financial or other substantive natures, you intended to incur costs to the treasury of the courts as well as to citizens and licensed syndicates of the City Imperishable.

"It being found *prima facie* that you lack assets, expedited charges were preferred in order to bring you before the judges-financial as quickly as possible to stay further damages to the courts or the City as a whole."

"Thank you," said the bald judge. He leaned forward. "Before we pass sentence, do you have any statement you may wish to make? Bear in mind any words of yours will affect your fate, my good man of Lockwood."

"Well," said Imago. He had been thinking with furious speed and intensity about how to answer the court without incurring some overarching penalty that would impair his further purposes. "First of all there is the little matter of my trial. According to the customs and laws of the City Imperishable, only the Imperator himself can pass a sentence without a due hearing."

"Oh, we will hear you, you may be certain of it," said one of the other judges, a sallow-faced man with a small circle tattooed just beside his right eye. "After that we will find you guilty, then we will sentence you. My good fellow jurist was merely speaking to the inevitability of the process. Did you have a second point before we proceed?"

"I thank the court for its courtesy." Imago tried to bow, but succeeded mostly in banging his head against the bars of the witness cage. "My second point is thus: I claim immunity from prosecution."

In the moments following that statement Imago could have heard a headsman's axe drop. Standing just on the other side of the cage bars, the big serjeant sucked his breath in and held it. The clerk of the court looked up from his ball-calligraph and stared at Imago. The bailiff of the court set one hand on his staff, which had been leaning against the wall. Two of the judges shook their heads, but the bald judge raised a hand to quiet them. He leaned forward, pointing the silver-wrapped thighbone at Imago.

"You are out of order, my gentleman of Lockwood. The bailiff of the court will now bind and gag you."

Here was his moment. He would get two or three sentences out before he was silenced. Imago spoke quickly. "My lords judges, this is solemn precedent and settled law within our city. I am declaring myself a candidate for Lord Mayor, and as such I am granted cer—"

He stopped with a grunt and a rush of breath as the court bailiff's staff prodded him in the gut. With help from the big serjeant, the man reached through the bars with a leather gag and tied it on to Imago while he was bent over trying to suck air into his tortured lungs. Each hand was quickly manacled to the bars. The doors creaked at the back of the courtroom as someone left.

"I am not in the mood for japes," said the bald judge. "Your sauce will do you no good before this court, sir."

One of the suited young men from the gallery approached the bench, stopping about six paces away to bow. "Your honors," he said. "May I beg a word?"

The three jurists exchanged a series of glances before the bald one nodded. "You may come forward and speak."

A whispered consultation began. The sallow judge leaned over and began talking urgently. The third judge, a round-faced, pale man who had kept his silence thus far, was whispering. After a few moments' hushed and hurried huddle, the bald judge banged the thighbone gavel. "This court will take a ten minute recess for consultation."

A few minutes later one of the thin-faced young men who had been watching the trial and been swept up into the recess re-emerged from the judges' chambers. A clerk from another judge's courtroom, or possibly one of the Assemblage's various secretariats, Imago presumed. The young man was still neatly pressed, but had something of an air of distraction about him. His lips were pressed tight as a money lender's fist. He first whispered some dismissal to the arresting serjeant. Once the big man had departed, the clerk approached the cage. With Imago watching him, the man banged on the bars.

That was idiotic. Even more idiotic, Imago found himself startled by the noise. He wanted to speak, but that effort was fruitless with the gag still jammed into place.

With an exasperated sigh, the clerk nodded for the bailiff of the court to remove the leather from Imago's mouth.

Spitting and gasping for free air, Imago managed to choke out a question. "What will you, sir?" He had not expected accolades and smiles in reaction to the presentation of his defense, but this stir was something else entirely. His mood was not improved by the clatter.

"Nothing of my own choosing, you fool," snapped the clerk. "Nonetheless, the court wishes to know precisely what, if any, precedent you have found for declaring yourself a candidate for Lord Mayor in light of the long standing ban on elections *pace* the edicts dating from 42 Imperator Arnulf."

Imago gave him a long, blank stare. "Am I to be beaten for stating my position?"

"You could be beaten regardless," snapped the clerk.

The only way out of this cage and the financial troubles that brought him here in the first place was to run hard toward the golden chain of the Lord Mayor. The day he reached that high estate, this man could trouble him no more.

"As you wish, sir," Imago said sweetly. "Through the precipitate action of the arresting bailiff, I was brought before the court without my notes, but I believe that if you look in 8 Imperator Chela II, you will find a ruling in the case of one Proppolio the Baker. The good citizen became Lord Mayor by acclamation, not election. Imperator Chela II himself endorsed Proppolio's ascension. As Arnulf the Dyspeptic banned elections rather than the office itself, it would seem that this precedent yet stands."

Imago could see a smile flicker on the clerk's set face. He knew the man appreciated the boldness of the effort, if not the legitimacy or purpose.

"Have you declared yourself in the City yet?" the clerk asked slowly.

"Oh, yes." Imago returned the smile to his best effect. "Hundreds know, soon thousands will." Or would once Ducôte got the handbills printed and on the streets. Not to mention the Tribade's help.

"Wait here." The clerk turned away and scuttled back into chambers.

Imago was hardly going anywhere from inside the witness cage but did not feel the need to point that out. Instead he set his back against the bars and awaited, if not an apology, at least a righting of the mess currently being visited upon him.

Soon enough he'd be back on the street, free, his candidacy declared in open court. He had precedent on his side.

Imago was slumped against the bottom of the cage. The crown of his head pressed forward against the bars. The manacles on his wrists had slid down to the point where his arms were folded against his ears. He badly needed to urinate. From the stains on the cage floor and the stink of it, prior witnesses had surrendered to that need.

He'd spent the first hour standing defiantly, watching the business of the court come and go. The clerk had emerged from the judges' chambers behind the bench after a while and told the bailiff to postpone the day's docket. The young men—note-takers and assistants to various personages of the Assemblage and the courts—came and went at a rapid pace. People muttered by the doors to the hall, people muttered by the doors to chambers, but every one of them was silent as they passed the cage.

Imago eventually ceased trying to catch their eyes. Shortly thereafter, he stopped bothering to stand proudly, and instead tried to bend to rest his knees and back. The witness cage was large enough to stand in, but the only other position he could take without exercising skin-shivering muscle control was slumped to the floor.

Slumped he was, aching with the pressure in his bladder, nose burning from the scents of iron and urine; Imago wondered how his proclamation of candidacy had turned a vengeful but essentially petty court hearing into something with the hallmarks of a judicial crisis in the making. It was not as if he had traduced the court with his statements.

After quite some time they brought him a pot to piss in and a bowl of lentil stew.

BIJAZ THE DWARF

He sent his letters, and more. The afternoon melted away in a cycle of shadow painting the hours of the day on the wall of his office. Bijaz felt as if he were laboring against time itself, though no immediate deadline had been presented. Prothro's Edict of Attainder had not yet passed the Assemblage, and likely wouldn't for days yet. The ill was already done—if it were somehow held in abeyance that miracle would be by no agency of Bijaz's, whatever his desires. In the meantime, he sucked at the pain in his teeth and worked as best he could.

Bentpin Alley rumbled and grumbled below his windows. His inner office had two. The quiet cobbler below, who was truly more of a tailor of the feet, after all, possessed with his property a generous street-facing, that Bijaz occupying the second floor naturally shared. The Temple District didn't run toward the raucous commerce of so much of the rest of the City Imperishable, but a sufficiency of draymen and carters still passed through in noisy service of the provisionary requirements of the temples, abbeys, manteions, shrines and seminaries of the district.

Not to mention the bawling and braying herds of sacrifices that seemed destined by both natural law and practical custom to pass through the district several times each day.

Evening descended on the Temple District in an echoing shimmer of sound. The three iron bells on the Rugmaker's Cupola always rang when the sun dropped below the western horizon. Hard after them, the carillon at the Bluewater Temple would ring out the first eight bars of the Sailor's Hymn. By the second bar, the carillon's tones were lost in the cacophony of sacred sound propelling prayers to whichever of heaven's parts might be prepared to hear them.

Bijaz stood by his window, watching the gaslights in the alley spit to life as a lamplighter and his boy made their way along the grubby, shit-stained cobbles. The noise of evening washed over him like a bath from loving hands. Though his wife had long retreated into violet smoke and the false passion of wormwood, the old dwarf yet remembered. The immanence of the present moment brought him back. From the smell of things, somebody close by was frying onions in a hot pan, and a cold breeze moved across the city. If he were patient, he would soon see the first bats of evening flitting across the rooftops, but one of Bijaz's letters had been written so as to secure an appointment. Perhaps it would be his last good deed. Some instinct had propelled him to seek out Onesiphorous the Slashed before he met Archer the night following for the wretched little godmonger's attempt to listen at the darkness.

Otherwise he would have put the Slashed rat off a few more days, to strengthen his resolve. As best as he could determine, they were all stabbed and slabbed, the dwarfs of the City Imperishable, no matter what passed next. Still he had to try.

Whatever sort of moron Onesiphorous might be, that idiot still spoke for many dwarfs in and out of the city. More was the pity.

Bijaz closed and latched his window, donned his leather evening coat and made his way down the stairs into the hissing gaslight of Bentpin Alley.

Onesiphorous' response to Bijaz's letter had come that afternoon via a rather strange messenger boy, a sullen albino mute who had thrust the dwarf's own letter right back into his hands. A response was scrawled on the reverse of the envelope in splattered ink.

Cork Street car line. No. 14. After dark.

Bijaz made his way over to Cork Street, and waited on a bench until the number 14 streetcar came by, moving slowly behind eight mules that whuffled quiet complaints about the load but were stolid amid the traffic.

Cork Street was one of only two car lines in the City Imperishable. The more ambitious expansion of that project had been abandoned in face of the difficulties presented by the hilly terrain and the interruption of the Little Bull River. None of the bridges seemed suitable for hosting the tracks of the car lines, in addition to such loads as they already carried. It pleased the Numbers Men to have their gaming parlors serviced by such a simple and commodious transport, so the streetcars ran on Cork Street north of the Little Bull and along Filigree Avenue to its terminus in the Spice Market. The lines had never spread farther, and so the cars had little effect on how most people of the City lived their lives.

Bijaz sat on a wicker bench and studied the street outside, waiting for the traitor dwarf to find him. Cork Street was by far the best-lit avenue in the city, including the streets and squares around the Limerock Palace. The rare and rather dangerous electricks even illuminated certain buildings, along with a profusion of limelights, gaslights and oil lamps. A narrow strip of park ran down the center of the cobbles, wide enough for a few benches and a double row of oak trees that served as a shadowed punctuation to the night's brilliance. To each side, the gaming parlors varied from blank-doored stairwells entering into dim basements where people lived and died—literally—by their reputations, to gleaming marble edifices that would have fit in among the greater buildings of the Temple District.

Betting halls for betting men of all classes, of course. Though in the case of the truly wealthy, Bijaz knew the Numbers Men were willing to send the games to them. He'd overheard enough of those sorts of salons in his days with Faneuil, Jason the Factor's late, unlamented father.

The City Imperishable made book and held markers for people a thousand leagues distant, it was said. He didn't know the truth of that—Bijaz, like most of his kind, was too concerned with the logic and logistics of business to care about games of chance and bets against a house that made its own odds.

Onesiphorous sat down next to him on the bench. Bijaz hadn't even noticed the other dwarf boarding the streetcar. He gave a grudging nod, then signed LILIES ON THE RIVER in the fingertalk of their kind. A fate was coming, which they did not accept. The fingertalk was a bit of an insult, a nod to the traditions that the Slashed rejected.

The other dwarf shrugged. He was as ungraceful as ever, squat-bodied even by the standards of boxed dwarfs, and this evening he reeked of smoke, as if he'd spent the day in some den. Much to Bijaz's surprise, Onesiphorous' fingers responded. THE CORD THAT BINDS THE GRAIN. This will be held together.

Bijaz presumed the metaphorical cord in question was Onesiphorous. "Thank you for the response," he said with grudging courtesy.

"Your sort rarely exert grace for my benefit." Fingers: FROGS SWIM IN SHIT. Meaning: everyone does what they have to.

It was Bijaz's turn to shrug. "As may be. The pond has gotten much deeper of a sudden. I felt it important we simply talk without argument for a while."

Onesiphorous made a show of glancing around the streetcar. There were six more people on board, two dwarfs and four full-men. They all had the look of gamblers, bent on another sure thing that would lose their last obols no matter what their prayers or their luck had told them. He stood, straining to reach the bell cord, which rang for the streetcar's next stop.

"Let us step into the wider world."

"Indeed," Bijaz said.

Together they found themselves on the cobbles. Onesiphorous led Bijaz around behind the streetcar and across to the narrow park in the middle of the road. People came and went there just as they did everywhere, but in far fewer numbers than those who crowded both sides of Cork Street. They tended to move faster as well—nothing much kept them in the shadowed greenway save certain perversions that were much more readily pursued in other quarters of the city.

The two dwarfs found a quiet bench atop a reviewing stand not much larger than a good-sized dining table.

"Not like one of the Slashed to use your fingers," Bijaz said quietly. "The old ways don't sit with you and yours so well, as I recall."

Onesiphorous took out a tobacco pouch and set to rolling a thin cigarette. "Not like you high and mighty types to seek out the new dwarf, as I recall."

"Fair enough," said Bijaz. He watched the shadows play above him as the city's bats hunted the beetles and nightflyers that lived in the trees. The rich, almost chocolate aroma of Onesiphorous' tobacco filled his nostrils.

A flicker of flame, then the Slashed dwarf took a deep draw. The smoke almost glowed in the darkness. "Tell me," he finally said.

Bijaz had wondered how to approach this. "We're done for. Though it wounds me to say this, you have been right since the beginning."

Another draw, another cloud of luminous smoke. To his credit, and to Bijaz's gratitude, Onesiphorous did not take time to gloat. "Ignatius of Redtower didn't turn up, did he?"

"In fact, no." Bijaz was slightly surprised at that bent in the conversation, though he knew he shouldn't be. He had no reason to believe that Onesiphorous was any less well-provided with sources of information than he was, after all. "Though the issue is more specific than that."

"Hmm?"

On the point of admitting that the end, or at least an end, had come, Bijaz found himself possessed of a surprising reluctance. "I…I have long thought you a fool. A traitor, to boot. I wish to apologize."

Onesiphorous laughed. It was a short, bitter bark. "Well, I have long thought *you* a fool as well, at the very least. I, however, do not wish to apologize."

"Indeed." Bijaz closed his eyes, took a breath. "Just hear me out. The Inner Chamber has drawn up an Edict of Attainder, specifically against the dwarfs and dwarf families of the City Imperishable." He went on to tell Onesiphorous of his meeting that day and what was said about the Edict, including the First Counselor's threat to make Bijaz himself the assessor.

Where in all the hells had Ignatius of Redtower gone?

Onesiphorous rolled another cigarette. The night had grown a bit older in the telling of Bijaz's tale, though the traffic on Cork Street did not seem to have slowed. They'd been accosted twice by harlots and once by a mime, but otherwise continued to have the darkness to themselves.

"It might have gone better if you had joined us some time past," the Slashed dwarf finally said.

Bijaz felt his familiar frustration returning in a hot, breath-stealing rush. "It might have gone better if the dwarfs of the City Imperishable had stayed united in their purposes," he snapped.

"Perhaps." Another draw, another smoke cloud rising pale to trouble the swooping bats. "You think a week, for this thing?"

"They will have to vote it out of the Inner Chamber. I doubt that happened today. Then it will need to be read before the Assemblage. You can be certain they will go into Privy Session for a matter of this nature, to keep the various petitioners and pages from spreading the story back among the streets even before the voting has been tallied. Privy Session in turn requires a larger quorum than Open Session. Figure the bailiffs to take two or three days to roust them all out of their love nests and clubroom bars."

"That's your world. Traditional. Conservative. Playing along." Onesiphorous leaned forward, a small, tired man on stumpy legs. "My world has been trying to convince dwarfs to stand against these changes, stand for themselves and to ship out if they cannot do those things."

"We are an old and honorable race within this city," said Bijaz distantly.

"We are not a *race*. Our children are not born like us." The venom in Onesiphorous' voice was almost startling. "We are a freak, a curiosity, slaves to our upbringing and the monies we need to support ourselves. You raised your daughters in boxes. I would sooner cut off my pizzle and fry it for breakfast than father children to live as we have lived. Nevertheless, for the sake of those who have children, or even only themselves, I have pushed to get us out from under these oppressions. Now your idiots on the Inner Chamber want to tax us for leaving, and tax us for staying. All to fight a war that might never come. How soon before they tax us for just staying alive?"

"I don't know. Dorgau take the man's fingers for a plaything, but Ignatius wouldn't have permitted this madness. He would have played Prothro against Zaharias, kept them focused on our true risks."

Another bitter, barking laugh. "Our true risks are Prothro and Zaharias."

"You and I, maybe," said Bijaz. "But the City Imperishable crumbles before powers far older and darker than some venal full-men."

"I've seen the lindens burn," Onesiphorous answered. "I've heard the screams of men and women dying of terror. The noumenal attacks are a curse, a terrible curse, but they're much like the weather. Our people can move away from this city and its ancient stones and leave the bloody nights far behind. The Inner Chamber has done nothing more with this Edict of Attainder than make the daylight almost as frightening."

"I will not be leaving." Bijaz spread his hands, examining his short, blunt fingers in the reflected light of the verges of Cork Street. "This is my home, accurséd stones and all."

"More's the pity you." Onesiphorous stood. "Stay and fight the ghosts, eh? Ignatius ever tell you *why* the City Imperishable has been dogged with such madness?"

"Why do the winds blow?" asked Bijaz, who felt himself slipping into a dark fog of indifference now that he had passed the burden on.

"Somebody ought to know." Onesiphorous sounded farther away. "Then they might set their minds to stopping it."

"Ignatius knows."

"Where is the man?" The Slashed dwarf flicked the butt end of his most recent cigarette into the air as he walked away. Something large and dark swooped out of the night to grab the gleaming mote.

Archer probably knew, Bijaz thought. The darkness the godmonger listened at doubtless whispered to him of all manner of secret things. Bijaz did not feel moved to bestir himself right at that moment and pursue the truth.

Like those great, bloody teeth in the night, he was afraid that the truth would find him, will he or nil he.

JASON THE FACTOR

His first effort after the brief encounter with the Tribadist had been of small use.

"Man's a fool and more than," growled the dwarf Ducôte when Jason had diffidently mentioned the name Imago of Lockwood. Neither of them was able to be particularly quiet due to the mechanical racket from the back of the scriptorium. The dwarf finger-signed, APPLES FALL FROM THE TREE, BIRDS FALL FROM THE SKY. Meaning, opportunity presents itself. Ducôte nodded and turned away. Jason followed him through the narrow busy desks of the establishment and up a spiral iron stair that reminded him most uncomfortably of Ignatius' apartments in the Limerock Palace.

The two of them came to a stop on a shivering catwalk above the working floor. The great press at the back was hissing and chuffing, motive power for the rollers and plates provided by a steam engine that appeared to be something of an end in itself. The black iron, boiler-bellied monster was being swarmed over by a team of lithe and ragged boys working under the continual harassment of a red-faced dwarfess.

Were he not engaged in securing the future of the City Imperishable, Jason might have lingered to watch the show. He would lay money someone was going to lose a set of fingers before they were done driving a half-ton or so of paper through the maw of the press itself. The dance around the steam engine was another dark comedy entirely.

Ducôte could have sold tickets, had he been so inclined.

"You can't find him such a fool," Jason said bluntly. "Otherwise you would not be running hot plates with such abandon back there."

"Even fools have their uses." Ducôte turned to stare at his operation, to all visible evidence supremely unconcerned with the imminent risk of fatality around the great compound mechanism of steam engine and printing press. "I mislike the way the winter winds are blowing. He had a novel approach to dealing with them."

"Where is this fool, then? I would speak to him."

Ducôte matched bluntness for bluntness. "What is your interest, sir?"

"Much the same as yours, truth be told. The winter winds you so mislike bring more than a chill for ageing bones. The noumenal attacks carry on almost unremarked, and most certainly unanswered. War threatens, which distracts the powerful from those other matters to which they should be attending. Good dwarfs flee the city in numbers unseen since…well, ever. By the spring, we will be as nothing, even if no further ill comes to pass. Done in by our fear. There is power to position. We've not had a man at the head of anything for centuries. Just committees, councils and chambers. I want the man who would be Lord Mayor."

"So you can have him for your own?" Behind his lenses, the dwarf's eyes narrowed with calculation.

"You know me, Ducôte. I control no one but myself. I labor on behalf of others, as a factor for Tomb the Warehouseman, as an agent of Ignatius of Redtower. Tomb will have no warehouse should the City Imperishable collapse. Ignatius will have no place to return to. Do you like the night killings and the dark things that walk in our river fog?"

"No. I am not a fool."

"Well, neither am I. The Inner Chamber will not listen. Prothro and Zaharias fight for power in the quiet manner of their kind. The Assemblage is no more than fish-tits. A Lord Mayor could rally the city, repair walls, roust out the hedge wizards and miracle workers and lead us against our enemies, be they noumenal or armored in old-fashioned steel and leather."

"All the better if he belongs to you?"

"All the better if he belongs to everyone," Jason snapped. "I have my sins, but venality is not usually numbered among them. As for you and your chattering press over there, do not tell me you work from the goodness of your dark heart, friend."

"Peace," said the dwarf. His fingers flickered: STILL WATER BEHIND A STRONG DAM. Then, aloud, "I only seek to understand. I have my interests in our gentleman of Lockwood, to be sure. He has gone to seek a remission of debt from the Tribade, and their blessing."

"I spoke to one of the Tribadists on my way to see you. She said he was about town."

"Perhaps you might look for him about town." Ducôte pushed past Jason, heading for the stairwell. "I shall be here if you need me," he said over his shoulder.

"My joy is as boundless as your generosity," muttered Jason.

He walked the streets well into the evening. Imago of Lockwood's rumor was everywhere, and his name spreading rapidly, but the man himself had thus far proven elusive. This was in contrast to the absent Ignatius of Redtower, whose disappearance haunted Jason like a missing tooth, though few in the City Imperishable seemed to care. The movements of the people carried a new energy. Ducôte's handbills were having their effect. Jason was handed broadsheets from another scriptorium, a garbled rehash of the original work, but the message was much the same.

More to the point, people were talking. He gave up his inquiries soon enough and instead wandered, listening for names, looking for signs of action among the citizens.

At this season it was dark by the sixth hour. The evening bell rang from the Rugmaker's Cupola, perfectly audible along the waterfront, followed by the clangor of the Temple District. The hours were rung shortly after that in the gathering gloom, a time when most of the day laborers were heading for pot shops or their rented rooms—wherever they found food and sleep.

Not this night, though. The streets stayed busy, mostly working men with broad shoulders and sweaty arms even in the evening cool as the fog curled off the River Saltus. The little stalls and carts that normally closed up were still out, their charcoal flames making a constellation of waist-high red galaxies as the smell of rice, wheat cakes, roasted pigeon, seared fish and a hundred other flavors motivated the crowd.

A crowd it certainly was, congealing in little knots around the food stalls, or the barrels of ale rolled out into the street and tapped. That was very much against the law, but law didn't seem to be on the wind tonight.

Jason had managed a warehouse full of longshoremen and drovers these past years. He could read a crowd by the set of shoulders, the quiet muttering, the sharp glances. If these were his men, he'd be paying them off early and sending them on to drink themselves out of whatever mischief was bedeviling them.

The nascent mobs were fixated on the rabble-rousing in the handbills. That and an unusual number of women and children moving from group to group, working the streets.

The Tribade, of course. Inciting. Like crystals in a bowl of saltwater, the pent-up fears and angers of the ordinarily peaceful people of the City Imperishable required only a seed to bring them into a sharp reality.

He smiled. All Jason needed to do now was follow the lines of frustration to their grounding—Imago of Lockwood. Jason spoke for Ignatius, he would be heard.

Jason was near Terminus Plaza as the chimes on the Limerock Palace rang the ninth hour. People had been drifting that way since dusk, moving along in the clusters and eddies that had first formed around food and ale. The night was chill; the gaslights pale, stinking blots in the lowering fog. Workmen brought the implements of their professions—sledge hammers, boathooks, cleavers, thick staves and heavy chains. Such a collection of tools carried openly on the streets hinted at jacquerie in the making. Though there was always fear of the night itself, the flames and drownings and slobbering monsters from the noumenal world.

The nervous energy that had emerged at the beginning of the evening only intensified as the fog thickened. Jason ran into several impromptu patrols, wagons full of rough-voiced young men watching for strangeness. No bailiffs were to be found at all, and the guards paid by the various syndicates and associations had also wisely retired from the streets. It was clear enough this lot didn't intend violence upon the private institutions of the City Imperishable.

Public institutions were another matter entirely. A season's worth of fear and neglect was finally finding focus.

Shortly after the ninth-hour chimes died, a rumor ran through the idlers along Short Street. "Our Lord Mayor's been taken to the Palace," said one man who wore a stained apron and carried two long boning knives. "They're branding him for a traitor even now," shouted a woman in dark brown leathers. "People are being pulled in off the streets," called another faceless voice.

Jason knew these people didn't give a fig for Imago the man. No one here could even identify the aspiring Lord Mayor. Rather, Imago of Lockwood was the first person to stand forth and offer any alternative to the increasingly malign neglect of the Burgesses. He hoped the man was prepared for the weight of the job.

He joined as the knots and streams of men surged into Terminus Plaza and past, along Maldoror Street to the Costard Gate. There the crowd turned into a mob, focused by the relatively narrow expanse of the road itself and the line of buildings opposite the south wall of the Limerock Palace. Had he been inside the Limerock Palace he might have drawn their attention to the

Riverward Gate, where the wide expanse of Terminus Plaza would have made the crowd less fearsome, less aware of its own size and power.

Here in front of the Costard Gate even the noise of breathing and shuffling feet seemed magnified by the stone before and behind them. The fog, which settled thicker and thicker, only made that sense of concentration more intense. He smelled the sharp sweat of those around him, the pitch of torches, the oil from lanterns, the shit and straw and blood scents of clothes worn too long after a day's work. A double line of bailiffs stood before the gate, with two great hay wagons behind them, drawn up to provide a wall at their backs and to slow any breakthrough by the mob.

Everyone was breathing, waiting, an animal with a thousand feet and shared intent, claws at the ready.

Waiting, but for how long?

Ignatius would not have wanted the riot that was sure to follow. Jason could not even say when the last such uprising against authority had taken place—certainly so long ago it was lost to casual memory.

He pushed himself forward into the open circle in front of the bailiffs. They might know him, might listen to him. He recognized a few of them. Some were obviously frightened servants crammed into the red wool. That was a surprise.

Jason raised his voice so that his words rang out and the crowd could hear and know that no trickery was afoot. "Good evening, Serjeant," he said to the huge, familiar bailiff in charge of the detail. If they came to the fight, he was between the two sides. His earlier vows of vengeance against the man were small comfort now. "It might be to our benefit if we discussed the petition the good citizens of the City Imperishable bring to the Limerock Palace this fine night."

Somebody banged metal on metal behind him, calling out sharply: "H'ain't no petition, 'tis a demand!"

Jason ignored the heckler. "The people want to see their future Lord Mayor," he declared loudly.

That brought a cheer behind him, and a clatter of implements-turned-weapons. The front line of bailiffs recoiled slightly into their fellows standing behind them. Except for Robichande—the big serjeant looked sour as an early apple while he stood his ground. He had his answer ready. "In accordance with the Gatherings and Disturbances Act of 1 Imperator Portolo, I order you to disperse to your homes or workplaces on pain of fine and imprisonment."

"Hell no, redskin bastard!" shouted someone. This launched an inarticulate roar and another clattering of weapons from the crowd.

Jason turned, spread his hands. "First we ask nicely!" When he turned back, the bailiffs had drawn their pepperbox pistols. He glanced upward. Men stood upon the walls carrying longarms, probably the new rifled muskets that the gunsmiths of the Metal Districts had been making and selling down to the Sunward Sea. It would be no surprise at all that a few crates of those weapons were in the bailiffs' armory.

"Do they teach you counting skills in the service of the Burgesses?" he asked the big serjeant. "Because there are twenty men behind me for every man behind you. It is a bad bargain you are set to make."

"My words are backed by solid lead and good powder." The serjeant leered at him. "Yours are backed by rabble who will melt like sand in a glass."

"Your words are backed by a hay wain. Guns or no guns, you face too many hands to frighten us off." Jason tried for a softer tone. "Send first for the Provost, see what he will say."

"No need," called a man from atop the gate. Jason looked up to see the Provost himself standing there, Zaharias of Fallen Arch. "Are you not Ignatius' man?"

That stung. "This night I am a city man," Jason shouted back. "Here to seek Imago of Lockwood." Another shout behind him, this time with a surge forward. He almost lost his footing as he stumbled ahead of the men at his back.

They began to chant, and Jason knew that he had lost whatever illusion of control he thought he'd held.

"Im–a–go...Im–a–go...Im–a–go..."

The serjeant bawled out a call to arms that Jason could not distinguish even though he was standing almost immediately in front of the man. He was shoved hard into the red wool of the bailiff's chest as the first cracks echoed from the rifled muskets on the walls. People screamed, their voices strangely muffled in the fog. The serjeant shoved his pepperbox pistol into Jason's gut and tried to shout another order. A pruner's hook slid past Jason's shoulder in that same moment. The sharp edge laid his coat and shirt open, as well as slashing the skin beneath, before it stabbed the big man in the roof of his mouth.

The wielder of the polearm levered off Jason's wounded shoulder, driving him to his knees just as the bailiff's pistol went off. The firearm had been dragged downward with his own collapse, and so the shot tore through Jason's clothes and stung under the already wounded joint. He didn't feel it strike his flesh. Blood gushed from the serjeant's mouth onto Jason's face, a drenching flood colored nearly black by the indistinct gaslight and flickering torches. The screaming and shouting and clash of weapons around him faded to a distant rumble that was drowned out by something plucking once, twice, three times at his face.

He reached up and found a shattered tooth clinging to his cheek. The serjeant toppled, so Jason scrambled for the pistol as someone else fell on him from behind. He grabbed it out of the big man's hand amid the stink of bowels loosening in death and shrugged himself to his feet into the tide of riot.

Someone came at him with a pry bar—a working man, not a bailiff—but Jason had no choice save to discharge the pepperbox into his attacker's face. He turned toward the gate and stepped over the serjeant, pushing between two clumps of struggling men. His foot slipped on something round, but Jason did not look to see if it was a finger or worse. The serjeant's tongue, maybe.

He rolled beneath one of the hay wagons even as someone shoved a pitch torch after him.

"Fire it, brother!" shouted the torch carrier. Jason scuttled away, trying to outrun whatever flame might be set, even on this damp night.

Inside the courtyard was an eerie vacancy. The stable gates were shut, the cobbles empty. The Limerock Palace had not had guards as such in generations, and the greater part of the Provost's force of bailiffs were on the walls or dying in the gate arch. Jason crouched at the end of the second wagon, away from the happy arsonist, and looked up at the gunmen atop the battlements.

The Provost was atop there somewhere. If Jason could only reach Zaharias, convince him to stop the firing—then he realized he was drenched in blood and carrying the bailiff's pistol. They would kill him before he got a word out.

He slid the weapon under the wagon and shrugged out of his coat and shirts until he was naked from the waist up. He was still slick with blood, but much of this was his own. Jason took a moment to worry free the torn sleeve from his cotton chemise and tried to make a bandage for the wound on his left shoulder. It hurt like fire, and was bleeding profusely. He quickly realized he could not do the job one-handed and gave it up, heading for the South Doors instead.

As he scurried across the courtyard, Jason kept expecting a bullet in the back, but the riot broke through the barriers quickly enough to keep the defenders' attention away from a lone man running within the Palace grounds. He made it to the steps in front of the South Doors to find four servants with pepperbox pistols watching in wide-eyed fear.

"They're breaking in, man," Jason gasped with desperation. "I've got to get word to Prothro."

The servants waved him past, then broke their formation to follow him through the South Doors and into the Limerock Palace. As they slipped and slid into the receiving room, the fog-damp marble floors like ice beneath their feet, Jason turned to the man closest to his size. "I need your coat. I can't go before the First Counselor like this."

The servant, a bluff-faced fellow slightly more narrow of build than Jason, shrugged out of his clawhammer coat and handed it over. Jason slid it on, grateful for the binding pressure at the shoulder that would help hold his wound. The coat was black as well, which meant the bloodstains would be less obvious. He could do little about his sticky, naked chest, but the coat would make his state less apparent.

"Which way?" he gasped.

"Anthracite Ballroom," said the largest of the servants, who began making a show of checking his pistol.

Jason fled down the nearest hallway. He had no clue where the Anthracite Ballroom was, but he needed to get away before they asked questions of the more obvious kind—like of his appearance, for one.

Another string of gunfire rattled somewhere outside the open doors. The mob was not far behind him.

First he'd lost Ignatius, now Imago. Jason damned all the gods he'd never held faith in and slowed his pace so as not to look the fugitive.

IMAGO OF LOCKWOOD

Sometime well into the evening, he estimated, the bald judge returned. The courtroom was empty except for Imago, the judge and the two flint-eyed bailiffs who had been watching him occupy his cage. Whatever was about to be said, or done, it was clear that the court wanted no more witnesses than was absolutely necessary.

"My gentleman of Lockwood," said the judge. "You may refer to me as Syndic Wedgeburr."

All judges were Burgesses, and many Burgesses were syndics. And so the power went round in tight circles, and each man maintained his own favor. Imago's sin had been to try to take part of the money from that tight, neat cycle for himself.

He raised his head. He was drenched in sweat, though it was not hot in the room. Trapped in the witness cage, any of several implements of the question would kill him quick as a coney in the huntsman's hands. "Does it matter what I call you?" he asked. He was exhausted.

Wedgeburr studied Imago a moment. "It might," the judge admitted slowly. He turned his glare on the bailiffs. "Attend my judges-financial Southlake and Erascus in chambers, please."

One of them glared mulish and resentful, but the other nudged his colleague. With hard looks at Imago, the two bailiffs slipped out the exit at the back of the courtroom.

"There," said Wedgeburr. "You shan't be killed just now."

"Joy." Imago sat up, ran fingers through his hair, the only gesture he could make to restoring his looks, and what dignity remained. Some game was afoot, else they would have just ruled against him and set him to his sentence. He certainly would not be bailed—everyone knew that no reasonable surety could be set against his reappearance, save denial of his liberty.

But games were winnable. By definition. No one bothered to set stakes in play, who already held all the cards. Certainly not in law or politics.

"What price?" the judge asked, so quietly Imago had to strain to hear.

He was pleased to see the pain the words caused the man.

"Price for what? Not expressing my displeasure with this court and all its officers should I come to wear the Lord Mayor's chain?"

Wedgeburr looked as if he had swallowed a lemon. Whole. "Do not sport with me. You are the one in the cage, my gentleman of Lockwood."

"You are the one asking favors of the man in the cage," Imago said. The words came more easily now, flowing from him as if he were arguing a suit before a more sympathetic bench.

The bald man picked his words with care. "I ask your price for withdrawing this ridiculous claim and taking leave of the City Imperishable."

"I presume you do not intend me to simply picnic outside our tumbledown walls and return in time for drinks at the club."

"You would presume correctly."

"It is clear to me, my lord judge, that my claim is not so ridiculous. Or you would have already found me out of order and I would be enjoying the company of rats in some small cell awaiting the court's future pleasure." Which he nearly was now.

A heavy sigh. "I shall stipulate that what you have asserted regarding a certain long-vacant office would lead to disruption that the Assemblage cannot tolerate in the City Imperishable at this time. Do not think this grants you power. Only, at best, a bargaining position."

"This is my bargain: release me and permit me to walk free in the streets. Hold the claims against me in abeyance until the matter of my possible accession to the office of Lord Mayor is settled. If I fail in my efforts, I will come before you with my wrists together, ready for the chains. If I succeed, I shall endeavor to forget the harsh treatment I have received this day at the hands of those who might soon find themselves heeding my words and writ."

"Here is my bargain, you sweet fool," snapped Wedgeburr, all efforts at judicial restraint lost in the heat of his already-frayed temper. "Leave off your claim, renounce your analysis of the precedent as flawed—for I know you are quite the cunning arguer and could overrule yourself most effectively—and quit the City Imperishable for good. I will personally see you onto a southbound ship with a hundred gold obols in a strongbox. That is a better deal than any you might hope for elsewhere in this city."

"A hundred gold obols?" Despite himself, Imago was impressed. That was many years' wages for a working man, a fair and worthy sum even for a gentleman's endowment. "A fair bribe indeed, and now I know the price of your desperation. I understand that you could never silence me through overruling. All would think it conspiracy, and look for the plots behind the plot. Fair enough. Riddle me this, my lord judge. Why not just have my throat slit and be done with me?"

"Would that I could." From the look in Wedgeburr's eyes, Imago had no doubt the old judge would do the deed personally should he be given a reasonable chance. "If I'd had the wit to silence you one phrase earlier in the course of your pleading, that might have been a reasonable course of action. As it happens, the court would have to obtain the permanent and total confidence of at least seventeen persons to keep your words secret. Too many. Far too many.

"My second mistake was sending Maxwell to ask you the basis of your pleading. Every clerk in the Limerock Palace has been to look at the case of Lord Mayor Proppolio. You have let the spirit out of the bottle, and the hoary engines of precedence have coughed their way into motion. Even if I disposed of you now, the problem remains. If you renounce your claim and quit this madness, there may yet be salvage to be had."

Imago relaxed into the patter of the deal. As long as he did not raise the judge's desperation to fatally vicious heights, all might yet be well. It was a truism of his trade: when the other party came to talk, they always wanted something.

"It seems we have a pretty pass. It is too late for you to drop me down a hole, and to sentence me now for the charges already sworn against me would violate law and precedent in the light of my claim to office. Yet I can take no action while bound by these bars of rusted steel and the edged glares of your bailiffs. It seems to me that all I need do is wait here in patience. Eventually those engines of precedence will drive their cart to my release." Imago smiled. "I see no need to bargain further."

"Accidents can befall a man in a cage."

"Is that precedent?"

"No." Despite his anger, a narrow smile cracked the judge's face. "Would that it were. Sometimes precedence can be overruled by practicality. Allow me to appeal to your sensible nature, my gentleman of Lockwood. The City Imperishable is nearly under siege even now. Armies ride from the Sand Sea and the Yellow Mountains, intent on investing us before the winter snows. Fires burn in the night from their wizards' arts. Any fool can see the unease in the streets, the overloaded boats heading south on the River Saltus." Passion filtered into his voice. "We are a populace ill at ease and toppling into war. Here you propose to launch some bizarre quest for an office vacant so long that it is nothing more than a name out of history. This will distract the City Imperishable from our defense. You would divide us, sir, when we most need union. Precedence be swallowed by Dorgau, we will not allow our laws to lead us into ruin."

"If you would speak sensibly," said Imago with care, "then listen. Siege or no siege, we are already divided. The Burgesses have no idea what goes on in the City. The streets are frightened, the Tribade and the petty businessmen hate you. Have you even spoken to a dwarf of late? Where are the Sewn clerks who used to fill these halls? I do not know what good I can do if I es-say to lead the City Imperishable, but I can hardly do much worse than the Burgesses already have."

"Fool." Wedgeburr shook his head. "Southlake and Erascus wanted you stripped, whipped and slit out of hand, but I argued to save precedent through a withdrawal of your plea."

Making a show of unfelt bravery, Imago laughed. "Unless you plan to torture me at the bottom of a well, I do not think my lords judges will find their plan to be of much use. Even dungeons have keepers with eyes and ears."

"True as may be, but it will do your cooling corpse little good if that turns out to be the case."

Imago tapped the bars of his cage. "My career options have become some-what limited of late, I am afraid to say. My offer still stands—release me and I will say no more of the foolishness that has taken place here this day."

"Unfortunately, my offer will not stand long," warned Wedgeburr. "My fellow judges are feeling a marked lack of patience. You are a venal man, sir. Your record speaks for itself. I shall even double the size of the strongbox if you give me your word now."

Two hundred gold obols. Imago had never imagined having such a wealth of funds. He could set himself in style in Bas Gronegrim or one of the other Sunward cities for quite a time, or bankroll any number of clever ventures sure to pay off.

He didn't need the City Imperishable that much, did he?

A tiny fraction of that money would buy him a cut throat and a long swim an hour downstream. If they were nigh willing to torture him to death right now, the bribe of a ship's captain would be simple insurance against a change of heart on Imago's part.

He regretfully released dreams of avarice. "No, sir. Free me or have done."

He could bet no higher stakes, but Imago was certain the hand was his.

Almost certain.

Mostly.

As Wedgeburr retreated into the judges' chambers, Imago felt a black tarball in the pit of his stomach, like a cancer erupting full blown from the terror of the moment.

He very badly did not want to die in this cage.

Twenty minutes later, the two hard-eyed bailiffs emerged from the chambers. One walked quickly over to the racked instruments of question and made a show of studying several long, narrow blades. The other approached the prisoner with a contemplative look in his eye.

Imago felt a surge of mixed terror and hope. They seemed set to slay him now, and damnation to precedence or opinion either one. This bailiff had something on his mind.

"What will you of me?" Imago asked, hating the crack in his voice brought on by fear. He reeked of his own musk, and his bowels gurgled and burned as if boiled on a stove.

"Was wondering if it would be worth my trouble to strip your clothes first," said the bailiff with a hard and narrow smile. "It seems you've been in filth, my man. I won't bother to wash a corpse's trousers, not for what the ragman pays on my street."

The other bailiff was in front of him. Imago had not even seen him move. The bailiff carried a flatsword, a weapon that resembled a radically oversized butcher's cleaver. Its judicial purpose was for beating legs and backs, but the blade also had a rough, serrated edge on one side.

Wedgeburr was just playing for time, trying to scare him into agreeing. The judge had to be. He'd already said they couldn't just kill Imago now.

Well, if this was a play for his fear, it was working.

"I...I..." He struggled for words.

"Ssh," said the bailiff who'd wanted his trousers. "Judge said no more bargains. You don't have to die quietly if you don't want. They've all left the back way and there's no one in the halls this late of an evening."

The other bailiff raised the flatsword. "For an obol I'll do your throat first."

"I don't have an obol," squeaked Imago. Hot piss ran down his leg. He cherished the strange tickling, the sharp, shameful odor. If this was the last of his life, he would savor it. He began to weep.

"Too bad," said the bailiff, and set the blade against the bars.

BIJAZ THE DWARF

He finally roused himself from the bench in the Cork Street park, swimming upward through the inner fog of his sheer exhaustion. The wicker was cutting into his back and neck, and his teeth continued to insult his skull with a dull ache. Bijaz stood and looked around.

Cork Street was as quiet as he'd ever seen it. That was odd. Tendrils of fog rose up from the Little Bull, unusual this high on Nannyback Hill.

Bijaz had trouble finding it in himself to be concerned. A flickering voice within cursed him onward. Conscience, that was it. What use did he have for conscience? All was lost. He had surrendered to the traitor Onesiphorous, handed over whatever remnant of authority had yet clung to him as a leader in the dwarf community.

He might as well throw himself over the city wall, or take a boat south to work the indigo plantations. He would fry in Dorgau's last hell before he applied to his brother for aid.

The street truly was quiet, though the lights of the gaming parlors still gleamed bright as ever. People scurried furtively, as if afraid of one another, or bothered by the brilliance. Where had everyone gone?

He hated this feeling. Like swimming through treacle, or being caught in a sump in some dark basement of his soul. Bijaz needed something.

A lift.

He needed a night in the dwarf pits.

It had been only a single day. He'd always been able to wait weeks, a month or more between visits.

Filth. He was filth, a turd floating in the gutter. He needed a full-man writhing before him.

Bijaz wondered what it cost for a dwarf to be able to wear the horse's head, to slide steel under skin down in the pit. He would pay anything to dance naked in a man's blood. Anything that lifted him up and made him more than the scum he had become.

He looked up as he walked. Certainly there were women for hire here on Cork Street. Perhaps he could find a man, a boy, and…and…

What?

No full-man whore would allow a dwarf to hurt him, draw his blood, dance on his body. He would gain only a beating for his trouble.

His contacts in the Tribade would be unavailable for weeks.

It seemed that hurling himself into the river might be the best answer.

Soon Bijaz found himself following a young full-man in tight leather pants and very short velvet jacket. The man's legs scissored like a lover's hand clasp. Bijaz could see the faintest roll of his arse. He'd never wanted to use a man so, like a woman, but still his cock stirred beneath his suit.

He quickened his pace, wanting to keep the man in sight.

As they walked, crossing an alley, then a side street, he imagined what could be. A chance meeting at a corner, an invitation to tea. Touching fingers. Back to this man's rented room above a little shop conveniently empty of listening ears by night. There to cuddle close, the fumbling kisses of men unused to loving one another, until Bijaz could find himself atop the other. Then a chokehold, not to kill, just to render into unconsciousness. Surely such a dandy would have a sewing kit?

Needles. Thread. Scissors. A knife, maybe.

He would make his own pit, if he were so lucky.

Caught up in the image of the pale arse spread wide before his sweat-covered blade, Bijaz bumped right into the object of his desire.

The man turned, and she was a woman dressed in male clothing. Her smile broke as she looked down and saw that he was a dwarf. Someone grabbed his shoulder from behind, spun him, slugged him hard across the face before he realized quite what was happening.

"Don't let that freak touch me again!" she screamed.

Bijaz toppled to the sidewalk in time to catch a boot to the ribs.

"Gonna sell you to the Grease Boys," whispered a giant of a man dressed in old robes, like a monk gone so bad he'd become rancid. He straightened up, kicked Bijaz again. "Everything's fine, sweetling," he told the woman, "we'll find you a good trick. Not one of these little monkeys. Just you let me get rid of this one, all right?"

With that, the man picked Bijaz up, hoisted him over one shoulder and yanked his pants down with his free hand. "That better not be your pecker I feel hard up against me," he growled, "or I'll be tearing it off by the roots." He pitched his voice up once more. "Back in a couple of minutes, sweetling."

Arse naked in the chill night air, Bijaz watched a gaslight bob past, then another, before he was floating through darker shadows. He was stunned, his ribs aching, and something made him want to vomit. Spewing down this man's back seemed a supremely poor idea, even at the end of an evening redolent with poor ideas.

"Spudmouth, got fresh meat for you," growled his captor. It took Bijaz a moment to realize the big man was speaking to someone unseen somewhere in front of them. Well in front of Bijaz's behind. "Virgin bunghole if I'm any judge."

Something unintelligible was said in response. A moment more, then a clink of coin, then Bijaz was hurled upon his back onto a pile of burlap sacking in near total darkness. The impact sent a shock of pain through his damaged teeth.

"Roll over unless you want me to cut my way in," snapped a voice made of gravel and pain.

Several other voices snickered. All Bijaz could see were shapes. He started to draw himself into a ball, retreating into a sick, horrible fear, when a knife poked him in the belly.

"No jokes here, little man."

Bijaz rolled. Someone grabbed his ankles and yanked them so far apart the pain in his groin made him gasp. He threw up into the sacking. A hand pressed down hard on the back of his head, shoving his face into his own stinking bile. He tried to scream as something forced its way into his arse, but his voice was cut off by burlap and barf. The penetration was hard and thick as it tore into him. Then a glooping sound and the meaty scent of lard told him he was being lubricated.

After that the real agony began.

When he found a way once more outside the haze of terror and red-forked lightning in his head, Bijaz was surprised to discover it was still nighttime. Or at least dark, here where he was. Had not days passed?

He wondered if the young man dying in the dwarf pit had felt this same sick terror. He wasn't dead yet, but he wasn't sure he didn't prefer to be.

Bijaz tried to draw his legs together, but the abused joints in his groin and the screaming pain in his bunghole stopped him. He realized that an inert mass rested between his thighs, though he felt no weight upon his back.

It took him quite a bit of time to work his way forward, inching his arms, dragging his face then his chest through the crusted, drying bile, before the thing between his thighs fell away. Bijaz rested awhile, wondering why he had been permitted to live. Whoever it was that dwelled in shadows and bought dwarfs to rape didn't seem likely to be concerned with the state of their victims.

Had he ever been?

Slowly he rolled onto his side. His legs started to close, but he was forced to prop one foot on the other calf to hold them open against the pain. He didn't want to think about what oozed down his arse and thigh.

A little light leaked around corners from some distant source. Just enough to make out shapes and shadows. He realized he smelled blood. A lot of blood. No one seemed to be breathing besides himself.

He rested quite a while, his thoughts blank, until his legs were able to close up a bit further; Bijaz reluctantly took the terrible step of turning himself on his hip, so he faced whatever had been between his legs. He reached in the darkness, groping for it, til he found what felt like a knob. It was slimy. He felt around it, quickly found something much slimier, with a hollow center.

It was a neck, Bijaz realized. A neck and a spine.

The teeth had come again.

This time he screamed for real. Not simply the pain, or the fear of what had been done to him. He was past that, past humiliation or even, truly, caring.

He screamed terror raw and naked as he was.

Eventually someone came.

Onesiphorous paid the two porters and sent them on their way. After they were gone, he wrinkled his nose and lit another candle.

"You have any incense here?"

Bijaz lay on the floor, wrapped in a tarpaulin that was already stuck to his body by the drying blood and other, well, fluids. "I…no…"

"I'm going to boil water and fill your tub over here," said the other dwarf, his voice quiet and slow. "Can you stay there til I have that ready?"

"Not too hot," Bijaz whimpered. He was ready to die now, but his heart stubbornly insisted on continuing to beat. "Drown me, please."

"No, sir." Onesiphorous lit the little gas burner and filled the kettle from the cold water tap. "If you didn't get killed by whatever happened to you down there, it won't be me that sees you dead."

"I am dead. My body doesn't know it. I have failed everything. I deserve no more."

"Would you shut up?" Onesiphorous looked down at him with something close to fondness. "I'd like to say this is what becomes of the Sewn, but I don't suppose your politics have much to do with rape and murder."

"Oh, you don't even know—"

Onesiphorous raised one hand. "I don't want to. You don't know either. There's big things on the prowl tonight in the city. We might all need you tomorrow. No rolling off to drown in pity or sorrow or penance. I don't care if you've been masturbating in the dwarf pits, Bijaz. I came back to find you when I heard about the riot."

"Riot?"

"A huge mob stormed the Limerock Palace this evening. So much for your Edict of Attainder."

Bijaz tried to sit up and immediately regretted it most profoundly. "The Lord Mayor!"

"Maybe. See why I need you?"

He didn't even want to think about how badly his arse hurt right now. "I'm done," he said, slumping back down. "Filth, used as filth." Gods, the pain radiated like a bonfire in his colon. "Let me die quietly. You can have whatever you want."

"I want you alive and thinking," said Onesiphorous. "No one else is going to watch our folk. Slashed and Sewn together, we might save ourselves and even regain some of what we have lost. Your backers, your people, they won't listen to me."

"I am nothing. Worse than nothing." Bijaz moaned. "I don't deserve to live."

"Take it up with that godmonger of yours. Don't you have an appointment tomorrow?"

Bijaz lay quietly awhile, testing the muscles of his legs very carefully. "I think I need a doctor."

"I might be able to arrange that, but only if you promise to stop trying to die."

The doctor came later, though it was still night.

"Fog like a serpent's breath," he said as he took Bijaz's hip and made the dwarf roll over on the bed. The doctor was a full-man, which had surprised that small part of Bijaz that still had feelings. He hadn't imagined Onesiphorous sending for one of them.

"Did you no favors, did they?" The doctor's fingers felt along Bijaz's thigh. "Broke your teeth for you, tore your sphincter good. I can sew it up, but you won't enjoy that one bit."

"Yes?"

"Or I can do nothing and you can leave a trail wherever you go."

"Ah."

Onesiphorous actually laughed. "Sounds like nothing but soup and tea for a while."

"You bastard."

The Slashed dwarf leaned close. "So you do care about something. Maybe you'll be useful tomorrow after all."

"Gentlemen," said the doctor. "Your argument does not concern me. My rather large fee *should* concern you, however. Please be silent while I attend to my patient."

A drenching with hot wine, followed by needlework, taught Bijaz new lessons in pain. He bit through two different slats Onesiphorous broke off the back of one of his chairs, but he did not cry out.

When the doctor left, he lay on his bed and sobbed.

Onesiphorous took the padded chair at the desk, levered it high enough to prop his feet and fell asleep while Bijaz tried to find a way to cope with what he had become.

JASON THE FACTOR

He'd had dreams much like the progress of this night's work, especially in the years after the death of his father. Jason ran down empty corridors, through doors that stood both open and shut, only to find more corridors, or sometimes rooms that dead-ended. He knew he didn't have much time, but he needed to find someone who could tell him what it was he wished to know.

Twice he saw maids, but they fled before him. He passed empty desks where night guards should have been. He found himself in a familiar hallway, black and white marble diamonds set in the floor—somewhere very close to the Assemblage's Great Hall, but he wasn't sure where.

Where was Imago? This was as bad as Ignatius, without even the ear to hold on to. Jason's gut twisted as he kept running.

He cannoned through another set of double doors and knocked down a man running the other way. Jason recovered first, and knelt on the man's chest.

"Where's the prisoner?" he shouted. "Imago of Lockwood!" His hands went around the other's neck, just as he recognized his captive.

Imre the bailiff.

"It's you…" Imre said as he choked.

Jason released the bailiff's neck but kept his knees firmly on the man's chest. "Where's the prisoner?"

"They've set fire to the Ilion Wing," gasped Imre, his eyes wide with panic.

"We're in the Ilion Wing, you idiot." Jason took a deep breath. "Where's Imago, damn you for a fool?"

Imre looked baffled, distracted for a moment from his fear. "The one who said he was the Imperator?"

"Lord Mayor."

"Whatever. In the Debtor's Court, I think."

"Take me there," said Jason. "Right now. I don't know where that is."

"Get off me, by Dorgau's sweet pits."

"Parole?"

Imre shuddered. "You work for the Second Counselor. Yes, I can give you my parole."

They both stood, Jason shivering now with a surging combination of panic, fear and frustration. Imre was a good deal larger than he was—had the bailiff not been badly rattled, he would have fought Jason off handily.

"Give me your pistol," Jason said.

"Why?"

"I don't know. Because I might need it." Not to mention that Jason didn't want Imre coming to his senses now without him having some method of regaining the upper hand.

Imre handed Jason the pepperbox pistol. "It's loaded," he warned.

"I should certainly hope so. Now where's the damned courtroom?"

"Back to the Orogene Hall, three archways down on your—"

"Just show me."

"All right." Imre started walking back the way Jason had come. "Can you please tell me what's happening?"

"I have no idea," Jason answered as he caught up to the bailiff. "Except that maybe the war started without an invading army to help it along."

They walked for several minutes. He heard the roar of a crowd through one archway, along with shattering glass and the rending of wood, but they did not catch sight of the actual rioting. Nonetheless, they both picked up their pace. At the third archway, Imre led him to the right, into a hallway lined with statues of old mountain gods—Jason could tell by their pointed beards and strangely shaped eyes. Each idol was three feet tall, though proportioned to suggest the originals were enormous.

"Here," said Imre suddenly, stopping in front of an imposing set of doors, tall with old paintings of unpleasant devices slowly flaking from their panels. They heard the mutter of voices within. "There is usually no one around at this time of night." The bailiff sounded confused.

"Just the occasional rampaging mob," said Jason. "You may consider me a mob of one. Remember, I'm about to do good for the City Imperishable." He hoped. He whacked Imre as hard as he could on the side of the head to keep the bailiff from having to think too hard about his loyalties. Jason threw open the door and dashed inward, brandishing the pepperbox pistol.

The well of the courtroom lay in front of and below him, with spectators' benches arrayed on wide, shallow steps of the gallery descending from the door where Jason entered. Two bailiffs standing beside a tall, narrow, iron cage stared up at him. One of them held a huge sword, the other had one hand on the bars.

Someone huddled low in the cage, as low as the proportions of the cage would permit him to get.

"Stand away from that man!" shouted Jason.

The bailiff with the sword began to laugh. The other let go of the cage, crossed the open space in front of the judge's bench and advanced up the steps.

They were about to kill Imago!

Jason raised the pistol, hoping to stand the bailiff down. The man smiled and kept coming. Jason was too tired to fight, so he pulled the trigger. The pepperbox pistol kicked up, and the man collapsed.

The other bailiff tried to move, but stopped short with a loud groan. Jason raced down the steps, leaping over the fallen man and nearly slipping in the blood flowing back from the body toward the main floor.

The remaining bailiff was trying to regain his balance when the sword handle popped out between the cage bars and caught him in the head. He yelped and clawed for his own pistol, so Jason charged at him and tried to shoot again.

Unfortunately, he didn't know how to advance the action on Imre's pistol. He settled for a sharp kick in the kneecap. When the bailiff collapsed, Jason kicked him in the side of the head for good measure.

"I'd be obliged if you'd run him through with this damned sword," said the man in the cage, who looked to be in a very bad way indeed—hollow-eyed and coated in filth.

Jason realized the prisoner was holding the huge flatsword by the top of the blade. "I hope for your sake that's not double-edged. Imago of Lockwood, I presume."

"The same," said Imago weakly. He stank, Jason realized, but then they both stank.

"I'm looking for a Lord Mayor," Jason said. "So are several thousand other very angry people currently roaming the palace."

"At your service. But if you're not going to stab him, could you at the least release me?"

It took a few minutes of scrambling, and another sharp kick to keep the second bailiff down and groaning, but Jason found the cage keys on the belt of the man he'd shot. Evidence suggested the bullet had shattered the late bailiff's groin. Jason didn't want to know more.

As he let Imago out, he asked, "Were they really about to kill you?"

"Oh, yes. Can I have his pants?"

They avoided the dead man, but stripped the other bailiff. Jason judged it a bad idea to be wearing red wool in the Limerock Palace this night, but the man had a decent linen shirt beneath the tunic. Imago was happy to make do with the shirt and pants to replace his ruined attire. Jason had no intention of taking his own coat off until he was with someone who could attend to the shoulder wound, which continued to burn.

"You look like nine brass hells, sir," Imago said more cheerfully once he was wearing clean trousers and a bandage on his wounded right hand. He now worked some of the grime from his dark, curly hair with his fingertips as he spoke. "I do not believe we've had the pleasure."

"Jason the Factor. Associate of Ignatius of Redtower, and sent on to you by one Ducôte when I went looking for our new Lord Mayor. If we can successfully make an exit from the Limerock Palace with our lives and liberty intact, you and I have much to discuss."

Imago glanced at the dead man on the steps. "You seem to be doing your best to ensure future problems."

"It's a bloody night's work, my good man," said Jason sadly. "I tried very hard to stop it. Many people saw me outside in the forefront of the riot." He shrugged. "In here, there's just us."

"And him," said Imago with a hard look back at the injured bailiff now sprawled on the floor in his smallclothes.

"No," said Jason. "They already know who you are. Me, too, for that matter. I've done my share of things I should not have, but I don't fancy taking another man's life tonight. Especially for no reason other than spite."

"Let us be away, then," said Imago. "As it happens, I am somewhat familiar with the courts wing. We may be able to use the private exits."

After locking and barring the main doors at the head of the spectators' gallery, they departed through the judges' chambers.

Jason and Imago found their way to the Inner Gardens without encountering so much as a rat, let alone bailiff, servant or Burgess. Roughly square, the Inner Gardens were completely surrounded by the various wings of the Limerock Palace. At the least they were far away from the rampaging mobs besetting the Ilion Wing, and whatever response the Provost was mounting.

Assuming the Provost yet lived.

"The main kitchens are at the back of the Inner Gardens, in the Sepia Wing facing Margolin Avenue," said Imago. "We'll stay to the center of the gardens, avoid the windows and doors until we cross over there and can make our way out."

Jason saw the point of this. On that side, the eastern edge of the Limerock Palace, there was no outer wall. The structure simply faced the street. Easier from which to exit quietly, with no constrained, overwatched space to cross.

The two of them walked quickly through double rows of elms planted in a pattern doubtless intended to be pleasing to someone viewing from above. Jason's shoulder pained him dreadfully.

Imago's stride indicated that he, too, had suffered much. "Tell me," he said softly. "What drove you to come storming to my rescue?"

Jason had already risked all for this man. He saw no point in concealing more. "Are you familiar with Ignatius of Redtower?"

"No."

That was disappointing. It seemed terribly unlikely that this compactly built man was Ignatius somehow hiding under a glamour, but he had nourished a certain hope nonetheless. "Second Counselor to the Inner Chamber. My master, who has worked very hard to keep the City Imperishable safe and well."

"And…?"

"He is missing. The Inner Chamber is seriously misdirected in their efforts to fight the noumenal attacks. The dwarfs are ready to rebel in mass, or simply flee. We need someone to take my master's place, somehow lead the noumenal fight, and restore confidence to our citizens."

"You credit me with far more than is wise."

"As may be. But you have declared for Lord Mayor. From what I just saw, the Burgesses took you seriously enough to try to kill you. The mob took you seriously enough to storm the Limerock Palace to free you. While you and I may both know those events owe far more to Ducôte's printing press and the good offices of the Tribade than they do to any innate talent of yours, well, here you are. A name, known to the street and feared by the Assemblage."

Imago began to laugh. "I just wanted to clear some debt."

"Empires have been built on less."

"A city could hardly be lost for more."

Having found Imago of Lockwood, Jason was not the least bit prepared to lose him again. The night had turned even stranger than was normal of late. The kitchens were deserted, fires untended, cats pawing through food spread on countertops. Everyone had fled, presumably into the streets as they had encountered no departing cooks or pantry maids on their way across the Inner Gardens.

Margolin Avenue was wrapped in a heavy fog that had failed to settle over the enclosed space within the Limerock Palace. People shouted here and there, voices muffled by distance and moisture, and most of those who they encountered closer up were running. Though they could not see the flames, the unmistakable stench of a major fire filled the air.

Jason walked quickly but without any hint of panic to lead Imago away from the palace and its bailiffs as rapidly as possible. Wherever the mobs were, it would do no good for them to find Imago just now. The man needed rest and medical care before he could take to the streets as a public figure.

He would also require guards. Jason tried not to think of the size of the draw that the Winter Boys were going to place on his accounts. It didn't seem likely the First Counselor would meet the cost of mercenaries. Not at this point.

They made it to Pritchart Street, which paralleled Melisande Avenue but was less traveled, especially by night. The gaslights were on the corners here, leaving the mid-blocks in deep shadow, which the mist rendered into a species of damp, dark misery. Jason wanted to head up past Delator Square to the Temple District in order to hide Imago at Bijaz's offices.

He didn't care for the dwarf at all, but they were locked into this together, for now. The alternative, to go to his own warehouse, seemed beyond foolish. It would place them close to the River Saltus, apparent wellspring of so many of the noumenal attacks. Water Street would also put them in the center of the working men's mob that had erupted so violently today.

Jason had to admire the way Ducôte channeled the undercurrents of fear that had recently infused the folk of the City Imperishable. Too many had died, to be sure, but at least the City's fighting spirit was roused from its traditional torpor.

Pritchart Street this close to the Limerock Palace consisted of town homes and the odd larger manse, residences to the moneyed classes but not so grand or prestigious as the older homes along the little crescent streets of Heliograph Hill. These were built of quarried stone and Jade Coast hardwoods, product of the last few generations of the builder's art. A few windows even boasted the flickering golden glow of electrics.

Money, indeed, thought Jason, who as a boy had lived in a home not unlike these, and had once resolved on his blood's name to move back up the hill someday. There were other battles now.

Elms rising out of the slate sidewalks pulled water from the fog on the edges of their dying leaves, only to release it in large, cold drops on Jason and Imago. The stones of the walkways were slick, almost ice. The street here was paved with glazed brick that gleamed prettily on sunny days but made for black treachery of a wet night. He could smell smoke from the fireplaces and kitchens of the houses. Someone was playing a harmonium loudly enough to be heard on the street as faint music. A cat cried lust on a rooftop.

Walking up this street, one might never know blood and fire were loose in the City Imperishable. Jason felt a hot tide of envy and longing. This could have been his life, if his father had not been so foolish. At times like this, his hatred knew no bounds. There was no point in reproaching the dead, however. That had been one of the hard lessons of his existence.

"You're slowing," said Imago, tugging Jason to a halt. He touched the shoulder of the borrowed coat. Jason winced, gritting his teeth into silence as a damp smell greeted his nostrils.

Wool rot, he told himself. Nothing to do with the cut on his shoulder. Nothing at all.

Imago went on: "This thing is stiff with blood. You're not long for staying on your feet with that wound. Let's cut over to Melisande Avenue and see if we can hail a cab. I believe we're near the Hotel Septime. There will be a stand there."

"Not tonight," Jason said. He wasn't moving now, which made it harder to stay on his feet. "With riots down along the river, anyone who isn't out swinging a torch is hiding in a cellar somewhere. They'll have bravos at the door and boards up over the plate glass at the Septime, I promise." By all the hells, he had a desperate need to lie down. He didn't know anyone on Pritchart Street, though.

"Bravos or no, you're not going to make it," said Imago.

"Brave words from a man in a cage."

Imago spread his hands. "Look. No bars."

Half a dozen paces later, Jason's legs turned to rubber. In his precipitous collapse he nearly pulled them both to the ground. Imago got Jason's good arm over his shoulder and lifted, trying to make them both walk.

It was slow going, but there was a cross-street ahead, one that should put them close to the hotel. It wasn't a plan Jason had much use for, but his thoughts were too muddy to improve on it.

"I hope you are in funds, sir," whispered Imago.

"Tonight, money will either be too much or not enough," Jason slurred.

A rider approached them through the fog, on a tall, unshod animal so quiet as to whisper in its passing. Jason felt Imago drag them toward the kerb. How had they gotten into the street, he wondered? Something hissed in the air above his head.

Behind them, someone cried out, then gargled to silence. A different voice gave abortive shout, "Hey—" cut off quickly by another hiss. Jason found himself lying at the base of one of the dripping elms, Imago standing over him waving a bread knife he must have stolen from the palace kitchens.

Slick little bugger, Jason thought with admiration.

A massive head, more ox than horse for all its narrow shape, appeared before him. It had fuzzy horns. That made no sense. A man in mummer's motley was scratching between the horns, a crossbow in his hand.

"Bowstrings are quieter than gunpowder," Imago said in a hushed voice.

The mummer grinned. His teeth were either missing or tinted black within his dark-painted mouth. "Indeed, to be sure of it being true."

Jason rallied enough to find his voice. "Who died?"

"Men who were being of bad will. I am thinking them to be footpads in lieu of assassins. You are to be going now."

Lucidity remained a moment longer. "Give my regards to Enero," Jason managed to say before something hot and terrible grabbed his throat from within.

IMAGO OF LOCKWOOD

Whatever his benefactor had intended, the man had not confided sufficiently in Imago. The improbable mummer on the even more improbable camelopard drifted off into the fog. He'd seen a few of those creatures around town lately, but had not stopped to think exactly how many or to what purpose. The idea of heavily armed clowns surveying the city from their long-necked mounts amused him, even in this straitened moment. Imago could recognize a tinge of self-distracting hysteria when it overtook him.

Jason, unfortunately, was also overtaken. The man was dead weight.

"Who needs a Trial of Flowers," Imago grumbled in a low voice, "when I can have a trial of rescuers instead?" The idea of picking up the man by his wrists or armpits and dragging him along seemed not likely to serve, given the shoulder wound.

The Tribade. He would need to find the Tribade. What to do with Jason?

Imago walked over to the two dead footpads and studied them. A crossbow quarrel quivered in each throat, their respective life's blood congealing black in the fog-addled gaslight. Both were, or had been, wearing cloaks. Good boots, as well, he noted. A man didn't come by a good pair of boots every day.

Unfortunately this was not the evening for indulging in freelance cord-wainery. He could use the cloaks, for all that the clasps and collars were blood-soaked. Imago bent and worked them free. Neither man carried a wallet, but he did manage to collect a handful of chalkies and orichalks from their pockets.

Not enough coin to buy them a room at the Hotel Septime, but the funds might serve to hire a cab, or even a cart, if he could find one.

He took the cloaks, wrapped Jason in both of them, then dragged the man bodily back up the kerb and about halfway up the block, away from the bodies. Once he'd gained a little distance, he rolled Jason into the dripping shelter of an ornamental boxwood hedge, then spent time massaging his injured hand, which burned mightily from the effort.

It was work well done. In this muck, no one would find Jason unless they accidentally kicked him while walking by.

Imago left Jason where he lay and went looking for light and noise and maybe some crime—there he would find the Tribade. Hopefully they were already searching for him.

He had to go all the way to Delator Square before he found what he was looking for. As Jason had predicted, the Hotel Septime was boarded up. Most of the rest of Melisande Avenue was quiet as well, with a sense of huddled fear. Imago could almost hear the landlords and proprietors praying to their various gods that the riot would stay down by the river.

He headed uphill, searching for someone smoking a cigarette in a doorway, or sitting on a stoop. Lookouts. He *wanted* to be found, so of course that was proving to be an inordinate challenge.

Delator Square, normally the haunt of beggars and the desperate, played host to something of a counterdemonstration. Old fat men surrounded by sons, nephews and servants strutted nervously with hunter's guns or heirloom swords in their hands. Others talked urgently. A few wagons had been driven in. All of this activity was reduced to a chiaroscuro of light and shadow by the fog, which had climbed to even this elevation above the river.

He still hadn't seen any sign of the Tribade, but Imago thought he might possibly secure one of those wagons before someone decided to fill them with virtuous young men of high birth and head down to the palace to teach the rabble a lesson. That much of the mood of this genteel crowd was easy to pick up.

Idiots. No amount of riding academy swordsmanship was going to stand up to an angry longshoreman.

The rich were truly worthless, Imago thought. Saving of course their use as a source of funds for the clever or light-fingered. He approached a boy holding the horses' reins in front of one of the wagons.

"Need to hire transport for half an hour," he said quietly. "You taking money for these?" Never hurt to pretend to mistake servants for a master, he knew.

"Uh-uh." The boy shook his head. "Pa'd kill me deader'n stink."

"Where's your pa, then? My need is urgent, and my gratitude boundless."

"Huh?"

"I'll pay good."

"Over there." The kid pointed toward one of the earnestly whispering circles of men.

"Thank you," said Imago, and moved off at an angle to try his luck with one of the other carts.

The next one he approached seemed unattended. The horses whickered in the cold, their breath steaming. They smelled of straw and shit, fresh from the stables they were doubtless longing for even now. He walked casually around the back of the wagon to see if anyone was there. Taking the conveyance on his own might risk one of those old fools with the fowling pieces actually hitting something for a change: him.

On the other hand—

His thoughts were interrupted rather violently by a hand on his arm. Imago jumped, suppressing a yelp as his heart hammered in his chest. He turned to find himself looking at the iron-gray eyes of Biggest Sister. Strangely, she was dressed as a maidservant.

"We've got Jason the Factor," she said in a low voice. "The mummer told us where to look. My people took the corpses, too, to cut down on questions. No time to scrub the bricks, but there's not much we can do about that."

"By all the hells, you frightened me." Imago was having trouble getting back his breath, so the words came out in a compressed rush. "He needs a doctor."

"He'll have one. Walk with me, sir, and let us leave this square full of blo-viating fools."

He followed Biggest Sister away from the horse cart, toward Upper Melisande Avenue.

They wound up in a quiet booth at the back of a quiet bar in an alley of the Temple District. It was the kind of place priests came to drink and forgot how to pray. The keep obviously knew Biggest Sister, because as soon as Imago had followed her in, two cups of coffee appeared on the table, along with two shots of brandy.

"You remain unkilled, I see," she said after taking her first sip of the hot, spiked drink.

Imago followed her example. He hadn't realized how much of his warmth the fog had sapped away from him. "We are in the Temple District. Do you perchance have a golden throne hereabouts?"

Biggest Sister laughed. "Unkilled and unrepentant. Those are good signs in a man. You may yet breathe more tomorrow."

"Plenty enough have died tonight," Imago said somberly. "Jason told me something of the riot at the Costard Gate."

Biggest Sister sighed. "They've fired the Ilion Wing, and slain bailiffs and Burgesses and servants alike. I had hoped for change, not rebellion. This is bad for business, and the city."

"Nonetheless, the hand is played. Though I would not be at this table if Jason had not found me when he did."

"I sent him to you."

"My thanks to you as well." Imago dipped his head and tugged at the damp-curled hair with his unhurt left hand.

"Hmm." She drank again, studying him over the rim of her mug. "Now what? Do you still see a city full of people? Or have you come to your senses?"

"In the Limerock Palace, earlier…" He shuddered a moment at the memory of the great flatsword in the hands of the dead-eyed bailiff. "I was offered a considerable sum to announce my error and make a permanent departure."

"How considerable?"

"Two hundred gold obols."

She nodded in appreciation. "They could have you tortured for a dozen years on that kind of money."

"I felt the pull, but I did not accept. If money would not tempt me away, fear will not drive me away."

"Do you mean to say you believe in this mission of yours?"

"Whether I wished to or no, the mission is mine now. I've been threatened personally by three judges. The Burgesses will not let this go. Yes, I believe."

"The next thing we need to do is arrange your Trial of Flowers." Her smile flickered across her face, not the hard-edged killing grin he'd seen on their first meeting, but something approaching genuine amusement. "To satisfy precedent and give the people a reason to acclaim your accession."

"And maybe to stop the madness," he said quietly.

"Oh, no, the madness runs far too deep to be stopped now. You will have to ride that water tiger all the way back to its nest, if you would rule."

"Indeed. Perhaps we can fold riot away and replace it with spectacle."

"A good enough instinct. The greater the spectacle, the more challenging the Burgesses will find any interference in your affairs." Biggest Sister studied him a little longer. "Do not forget who your friends are."

"Ma'am, a clown with a crossbow bought this drink, by providing me with coins from a dead man's pocket. I know my debts."

"These are new ones," she warned. "Not in remission under our agreement. You will pay us every day, with your attention and your thought."

"Ma'am." There was little else he could say.

"As for now," she leaned forward. "Despite what I said today, it seems I do want you for something after all."

Rooms lined a hallway behind the bar. Imago followed her back, dreading what seemed likely to come next but also fascinated.

She locked the door, closing them inside a little bedroom with a large armoire, a big bed covered with a flowered duvet, and almost nothing else save a small side table. A candle flickered by the bed, but Biggest Sister took a moment to trim the wick on an oil lamp, and light it from the taper.

"Now," she said. "Let me see you. Every bit of you."

Imago hesitated. "I...I have been ill used this day."

"Consider that part of your charm."

He pulled himself with some pain out of the stolen linen shirt. Imago's chest was not wide like a laborer's, but it was muscled enough, and he had little rounding in his belly. He went to more than a little trouble to keep his looks in good order, for all the recent chaos had worn his elegance down.

She nodded, then looked pointedly at the bailiff's trousers. Imago sat against the edge of the bed and slipped off his boots, then undid the trousers and tugged them away, too. Despite himself, he was growing hard inside the stained cotton drawers he wore beneath the pants—those, along with his boots, all that remained of the clothes in which he had begun the day. He tugged the drawers loose, and his cock sprung free. A little bead of clear fluid, slightly cloudy, slid down the rounded tip.

"You were cut as a boy," she said. Biggest Sister reached out and took his shaft in her fingers, almost clinically. "Not overlong, but wide enough. You'll do." She released him and began unbuttoning her servant's apron.

He watched, waiting. Imago had a weakness for the taste and feel of new flesh, and the roll of a nipple in his mouth was one of life's more sublime pleasures. When Biggest Sister shrugged out of her blouse, he saw much to his surprise that the small breasts he'd thought to see were in fact sandbags sewn into the bodice of her chemise.

She pulled the garment over her head to show two huge star-shaped scars on a chest flat as his and devoid of even the hint of a nipple. A pair of tattoos spiraled across the scars, one where each breast had been. The spirals faced inward, turning toward one another. Without intending to, Imago found himself staring.

They were snakes, double-headed snakes, limned in black and green and a numinous purple that looked as if it might glow under the right illumination, or lack thereof.

Her voice was hard: "Don't look so surprised, man. We make sacrifices for our power in the Tribade as well." When she slipped out of her own drawers, he saw her cunt was clean shaven. She bore no tattoos down there.

Somehow, it all made him the harder, his cock quivering.

"Here are the rules," she said, twining one hand in his hair. "You will address me as Mother at all times while we are in this room." She was certainly old enough to be his mother. Fit as she was, the fine wrinkles on her skin gave truth to her age, just as the iron-gray hair did. Biggest Sister continued: "You will do nothing without my express order. Especially you will not spill your seed at all. Not in me, not on my skin, nowhere in my presence." She twisted, tugging at his scalp. "If you do so, I will hurt you. Do you think I can hurt you, little man?"

"Oh, yes," he whispered.

Biggest Sister twisted harder, drawing a hissing groan from Imago. "Yes, *Mother*."

"Yes, Mother," he said.

"Better. Now, I want you on your knees. First we will discuss what a bad man you have been."

Cock still straining, he practically fell to the floor as she released his hair. At the last moment, he remembered to say, "Yes, Mother."

Biggest Sister straddled him from behind, pushing the dampness of her cunt lips into the base of his spine as her nails dug into his back. Imago shuddered, with passion, with terror, with the profound glory of being alive.

The night had a few hours to go. He was certain she meant to spend what remained.

Come morning his cock ached as badly as if it had been chewed by ferrets. The rest of his body was not much better, and his injured hand was stiff as old wood. Imago was fully sated as if he had spent an evening among the fricatrices of the Tokhari, yet he never had spilled his seed. Biggest Sister, however, had certainly twisted and writhed through both their portions of orgasmic pleasure.

He looked over at her. She was drawing on the last of her leathers.

"You're marked now," she said. "The Tribade uses men, of course. In time I may send certain of the younger women to you for their children. If you prove yourself."

"Thank you," he said. "I think…Mother."

"We are done with the night rules. We will not play that game again." She stared down at him. "Cover yourself, rest awhile. I'll send someone up with hot water and a bandage for that hand. I think this might be a good day to let the city quiet down a bit. Your name is already on everyone's lips."

"Of course." He hoped that there might be other games for them to play. Even in the absence of nipples, something in his complete surrender of control to Biggest Sister had resonated for Imago. He would follow her out the door and anywhere, should she require it of him.

But what she required of him was not further bedsports, but rather that he finish the battle to find his way to the Lord Mayor's chain. "I shall think on the Trial of Flowers."

"Seek out Ducôte," she advised. "That dwarf knows what the people want. He will help you make a show. But wait awhile. The Assemblage will have bailiffs out looking for you today. I shall send a coach at nightfall."

Imago tested the soreness in his joints. Lack of sleep combined with over-exertion. He would welcome a quiet day. He needed to consider what had happened, both yesterday, and overnight with Mother—Biggest Sister. One question remained: "What about Jason?"

"He will not die."

"Where is he now?"

She laughed softly. "You were not so eager to know last night. Safe enough, and he'll be around to find you when he can, I have no doubt. Once he's healed sufficiently to get up and chase after you. He sees you as the key to locating his missing Ignatius."

"I knew he was safe," Imago said, peeved. "I just wondered where I might find him."

"You did not know he was safe. You had only my word for it."

Imago shrugged. "How else should I know?"

"Trust well, you may come to rule well. Trust badly, you will be feeding the sharks from the bottom of the river. He will find you. Meanwhile, rest. Good day, Imago."

She left him alone with his thoughts and his bruises. Both occupied Imago for some time to follow.

BIJAZ THE DWARF

He woke to a dull pain that initially puzzled him. Someone was frying pig fat nearby, the smell combining with the spit and sizzle of the pan was enough to make Bijaz's mouth water.

He remembered the reason for the pain and opened his eyes.

Onesiphorous stood, cooking at the little gas burner.

"I do not recall buying pig fat," said Bijaz.

"Not unless it was you donned my shoes and walked down to the market at sunrise today. Amazingly, the farmers made their way in from the Rose Downs and the southern extents despite the trouble. Last night the world might have been ending, but the City Imperishable still needed eggs this morning."

"What word this morning, at that?"

"Of you, nothing." Onesiphorous gave him a sour glance. "Another victim in a city filled with victims, I fear. There are handbills aplenty accounting for last night's riot and the burning of the Limerock Palace."

"They burned the entire palace?"

"I seriously doubt that. Though it's what certain of the morning broadsheets claim. Of course, no two of them agree on much of anything. I for one do not propose to head down there and look, not this morning. The bailiffs are bound to be in a sour mood today."

When Bijaz tried to sit up, the pain in his bunghole nearly made him pass out.

"Oh, you're getting fruit squeezings," said Onesiphorous. "The pig fat's for me. I'm afraid it would ruin your digestion."

Bijaz lay still awhile and groaned, wishing he had a pistol so he could shoot himself.

Eventually even the self-pity was wearing. Bijaz found that if he was very careful and kept his weight to one buttock or the other, he could make it to his feet, where the discomfort increased but the pain was lessened. Compared to that, his broken teeth were nothing.

He even drank his fruit squeezings, damning the Slashed dwarf's eyes the whole time. "What do we face today?" Bijaz finally asked.

"A quiet city. If I didn't know any better, I'd say our good working men were ashamed of their outburst. I don't doubt that if the Burgesses had any kind of a militia, they'd send the troops out to the docks just to hang a few unlucky souls, but it could take weeks to hire a free company to do that sort of work here."

"What of our people?"

"No Edict of Attainder read out, but the docks aren't moving. Neither cargo nor passengers. No one's getting on boats to head south."

"Your great project," Bijaz said bitterly.

"My great project has been keeping the good dwarfs of this city alive. Apparently including you this last night, so I shouldn't complain, sir. I may be about to fail in my task, but I for one have not given up."

Thinking about the business of the City Imperishable was better than thinking about the pains in his arse. Bijaz turned it over in his head. "If the docks are sealed, an Edict of Attainder will not matter. There is no way to leave in good order. The road south presents too much distance and danger for any but a well-armed caravan. So instead we...what?"

"Find that miserable Lord Mayor of yours."

"Well, yes," said Bijaz. "The Inner Chamber might well have been silenced, either by the mob or their own fear, but even with the Limerock Palace in flames the Burgesses are hardly overthrown. Some authority in place on our side would do a great deal toward stopping whatever rounds of fire and sword are likely to come next."

"Speaking of fire and sword, or at least sword, what do you know of the mummers riding those ridiculous long-necked beasts? There are more and more of them around the city, and they seem to be unusually well-armed."

"Are they working for the Burgesses?" Gods on thrones, the bureaucrats at the Limerock Palace couldn't have gotten a free company in place already.

Onesiphorous shook his head. "I don't know. But I saw them three times while I was out. Strange, even for our city."

"Where's the Lord Mayor? For that matter, where's that fool Jason?"

"I have no idea where either of them are. Nevertheless, we should find them."

"I have an appointment with the godmonger tonight," Bijaz added distantly. Listening at the darkness had developed a whole new lack of appeal.

"Haven't you had enough of going around at night?"

"Sadly, no."

The day passed slowly, but Bijaz could not move overmuch. He spent the hours in mortal fear of a bowel movement impacting the sutures in his sphincter. Onesiphorous came and went, bringing back handbills and broadsheets and reports of rumor, but they kept the offices closed against callers—Bijaz was in no mood or state to manage himself in front of casual visitors. He did dress, though, in his most formal muslin wraps, with practical shoes on his feet and a purse beneath his layers.

He had an appointment later, after all, though he did not know if he had the stomach to keep it.

The streets remained quiet. Though provisions moved through the city, the usual thrum of commerce had halted as thoroughly as for any public festival. Only this day no merrymakers thronged the squares. It was a time for barred doors.

Bijaz undid the catches at his window and stared moodily at the spires and minarets of the Temple District. His rooms had no great advantage of height, so he could not see toward the river or indeed any great distance at all, but still it was his view. Birds circled, cats prowled the rooftops, a line of acolytes roped together polished the copper dome on the Temple of Arran.

The reek from last night's fires hung over the City Imperishable, almost defining the silence. The sky was clear, the thin, pale blue of winter though the season was not that far advanced, niggardly clouds wisping the heavens high above like frost's breath on windowpanes. He caught a heaviness in the air, as if a storm were coming. Snow to hide the blood and bones of the rioters, to cover sins and virtues alike in a redeeming wrap of crystalline white innocence. Though with the ill luck that had plagued the City Imperishable of late, any such weather would be more likely to torment than to cleanse—rain to fill the gutters and wash roof tiles away and make both rivers jump their banks in foaming brown froth.

In either case, nature's hand could hardly be more destructive than men themselves.

He stared for a while at the close urban horizon, thoughts wandering through fantasies of natural destruction, until he realized the hawk circling overhead was an Alate. Bird men and dead bailiffs. They were all doomed, whether it was the vaporous armies of the noumenal or the very real armies riding hard from both desert and mountain who would do the deed.

Onesiphorous found him still at the window near dusk, as the other dwarf returned yet again from several hours of foraging for information.

"Someone will see you there," he said to Bijaz.

"This is where I live."

"Actually, you live in a house over in the North Wall District. Or at the least your wife does."

Bijaz sighed. Another scab, another scar. "She is long lost to violet smoke and dreams of long-limbed lovers." It was the angry departure of their daughters four years past that had sent his wife retiring to her rooms for good.

"Well, the bailiffs were over on Fireside Street looking for you at that address. So I'm told."

"Me?"

"Business is underway once more down at the Limerock Palace, apparently. Someone has a warrant out for your arrest." Onesiphorous grinned. "I heard it from a baker's boy with an empty bread cart and a bit of a thirst."

"Did they break my doors?" Bijaz asked. Much to his surprise, he found himself anxious.

The other dwarf shrugged. "If you wish to go look, do not allow me to detain you. I'm sure the bailiffs would be happy to perform that function. However, you have a meeting shortly with the godmonger."

"Well, yes. All I've had today is fruit squeezings, so I suppose I have fasted as he required. I must make my slow way to the Sudgate and the jetty."

"You're going to limp all the way down there? Right past the Limerock Palace? You are a fool. At least hire a cab. A brougham instead of an open fiacre, that your passing might not be so easily marked."

"Fair enough." Bijaz paced slowly around the room, testing the limits of his pain. He hurt, tremendously, but no longer felt as if his guts were set to tumble from his body.

The dwarfing box had been worse, in his childhood.

"What of this Imago of Lockwood? Or that fool Jason?"

"Both gone to ground safe as coneys in their holes." Onesiphorous shrugged. "Or dead in the riots, though I imagine the Inner Chamber would have that news shouted from the rooftops were it to be the case. I have seen bills advertising a hundred gold obols for Lockwood's head. Neck optional, apparently."

"I wouldn't care to be a man with his cast of face or hair this night," said Bijaz. "I assume you have searched for him."

"Runners out across town. The Slashed have many friends. Rumors and more, and a few bodies, but no one who can say with certainty where either man might be. I am fairly certain they left the Limerock Palace alive—two men much of their description were seen fleeing along Margolin Avenue during the later stages of the riot."

"Just east of the palace, then. Through the kitchens."

"Yes."

He thought that over a few moments. "Wherever they are, they have to come back out soon enough. Like many of the rest of us, perhaps they took some time to breathe. Or have hidden to lick their wounds. In either case, there is little I can do for them. As you have reminded me, I have business tonight. Will you help me summon this cab?"

"Yes." Onesiphorous favored him with a close look. "But let me say this first. You and I have long thought one another utter fools. Perhaps we were both right. Be that as it may, my most fervent hope is for you to learn something useful from your godmonger this night. Whatever has been held back today here in the city will break tomorrow, or the next day at the latest. We shall both need to rally around the Lord Mayor when he appears, or we are dead dwarfs who have simply neglected to stop breathing yet. There will be no mercy from the Burgesses. Not after last night's riot."

"How many of our dwarfen folk stormed the Costard Gate last night, do you suppose?" Bijaz asked with a smile that crooked his face.

"It will be said that all of us did, should the Burgesses wish that to be so."

An hour after the city's evening bells had racketed their way through the telling of dusk and night's welcome, he was in the cab, a brougham as Onesiphorous had suggested. Bijaz retrieved a few silver obols and a double handful of chalkies from his strongbox, to pay the fare and have a sufficiency for a late trip home even should he be overcharged.

The Sudgate Districts in the middle hours of the night were no good places for an honest man of any means. Even now, the driver had balked at the destination until Bijaz had doubled, then tripled the fare.

He slumped on the diamond-tucked upholstery of the cab's passenger box, breathing in traces of the saddle soap and oils someone had used to clean the leather. Bijaz propped himself on one hip, to keep his weight off his sutures, though he had refused to carry any cane or staff. His pride was stiff enough as it was. The jostling of the cab sent jolts of fire through his wounded arse, while the buttons sewn into the upholstery of the seat pressed hard against him.

Trying to distract himself, he listened as the wheels rattled over cobbles, bricks, flagstones, pavers—all the different street surfaces in the City Imperishable. A man could know where he was by the varying echo of iron-shod wheels on old stone, though Bijaz never traveled enough by cab to learn the noises. He was of no mind to ask the driver, but he kept guessing, without looking up and out of the windows, just to occupy himself.

Bijaz knew from the initial argument with the driver that they would detour around the Limerock Palace, passing farther to the south to avoid the damaged area around Maldoror Street. Rumor reported that the streets between the palace and the river were blockaded and the bailiffs had hard words for anyone pushing too close to the burned walls of the Ilion Wing or the bloodstained cobbles beneath the Costard Gate.

Once beyond the Limerock Palace, the cabbie would have to turn riverward quickly, along Forth Street or Hammer Lane either one, before he strayed too far into the festering slums around the Sudgate. Only on Water Street itself, the highway that led to and through the gate, would the brougham remain in even nominal safety.

Bijaz lay braced against the seat, swallowing his pain as the cab swayed and jolted.

The conveyance finally shuddered to a halt. The driver banged on the passenger box and opened the trap. "Far as we go, tonight," he shouted, voice muffled.

There was nothing for it but to get out and see where he was. Bijaz tugged at the door handle and stepped out into something much like hell.

Dogs the size of horses glimmered in the flare of torchlight, while giants stumbled with stuttering steps past children hung by chains from tall poles. He saw a silver-scaled fish push upward, then drop down again into a mass of ragged, stinking people. All of the strangeness was silent, save for the shuffling of steps and the crackling of flame.

With a whipcrack, the brougham turned behind him, pointed toward the higher, richer and safer districts of the city. As his transport departed, Bijaz realized he saw not a parade of monsters but a procession. The fish was made of chains and wire and cable, a chimera built of cast-offs from ships and armor and the workshops of the Metal Districts. Likewise the great dogs—no more than pairs of men in costumes of fur and felt, with heads constructed of scrapwood and leather.

The silence was strange, eerie, and the children hanging over the heads of the marching men and women were real enough. They were not dead, he saw, for some kicked or swung their hips. All were naked, none were bloody, though their poverty was clear enough. He could count the ribs on most, and almost all had the swollen bellies of the very hungry. None were fledged with their pubic hair yet, either.

Bijaz did not want to know what rite awaited the end of this shuffling mass. Perhaps it was a perverse answer to the bacchanal festivals that marched from time to time elsewhere in the City Imperishable.

Did they celebrate the previous night's rioting, he wondered?

The Sudgate itself loomed nearby, the high walls and upper windows catching some of the light. The architectural horror would be hard to miss. He knew he was north and west of the main mass of it, so he needed to move parallel to the parade's route, then cut south to the base of the jetty in order to find Archer.

This was not his part of the city, these were not his people, but Bijaz had ceased caring overmuch. He simply stepped to the edge of the crowd and walked with them, trusting these folk not to march into the waiting waters of the River Saltus in a single mass.

As they walked, approaching the docks, he realized what this had to be. The fish, the dogs, even the chained children—these people were appealing to the noumenal predators that lately stalked the City. The monsters represented the attackers themselves. God knew he'd seen enough of the teeth. Bijaz shuddered with memory. The children, then, were the victims. Or bait to distract whatever came next.

At least there wasn't that same thick fog tonight. As the procession turned north at the dockside, he slid across the crowd, making his way with difficulty to the water's edge and so a few dozen yards from the base of the Sudgate jetty. Out on the river the wisps danced as the current steamed in the evening chill. The half-moon was high overhead, clearly visible in the reflecting waters. No ships were tied up this far south—they had either fled or avoided this quarter by night.

He would do much the same if he were a vessel's master. Depart, and seek some other river on which to ply his trade.

Even as he left the shuffling torches of the procession behind him, no one said a word. No one paid him any mind. It was the strange equality of the bereft, which he had sometimes found in his work at keeping tradition alive for the city dwarfs. People with nothing to save or lose saw the world differently. He was just another unfortunate in the darkness.

Which, sadly, was true enough.

He reached a muddy little scrub break where the cobbles of Hammer Lane gave out like an old woman's teeth. Several hovels were shoved among the reedy tree trunks, but their inhabitants were absent. Or sleeping within. Bijaz did not care to investigate.

The jetty itself emerged from the walls of the Sudgate, sheer stone obviously not originally designed to be climbed from the side. The scrub break stood on land that had accreted from the flow and flood of the river, and that was host to more hovels and a few ramshackle docks. He picked his way along a beach of rounded, mossy stones and shattered timber baulks that threatened to overthrow him at every step.

Where was that Archer, then? The godmonger's instructions had been clear enough, but Bijaz was no scryer to find a path to a man well-hidden.

"Idiot," he told himself. "Fool."

"Human," said the godmonger from a perch atop a good-sized boulder. Bijaz would have walked right past him without seeing had Archer not spoken.

"I would say good evening," he told the godmonger, "but I do not wish to tell lies in the presence of whatever holiness you might bear this night."

"Indeed." Archer tucked away his little leather fetish bag. "The poor of the Sudgate have taken their fright to the streets, hoping to drive the noumenal to follow the fires of yesterday. Standards seem to be slipping in our city." With an agility uncharacteristic of boxed dwarfs, who almost always struggled with joint problems and weak leg muscles, Archer climbed down off his boulder. "Are you ready for me?"

"I am ready for nothing," Bijaz said. "The last day or so has been unkind to me on a scale I had never hoped to see."

The godmonger's teeth gleamed in the moonlight. "Then you approach the holy with a fitting humility."

"The holy can have my stinking humility," Bijaz muttered.

"Come. We must make our way to the winch tower. It stands between land and water, you know. Like the half-moon, it is balanced between two states."

"I am overjoyed."

He followed the godmonger, picking his way along the treacherous beach and profoundly glad no fog curdled this night. Soon enough he cast away pride and found himself a stick with which to balance. As horrid as the previous night had been, Bijaz was not certain this evening would be any improvement.

He felt sick as well, ready to spew in his trepidation.

JASON THE FACTOR

He'd spent the daylight hours wandering in and out of sleep and talking to earless clowns. Which made no sense, even then, and less now that he'd awoken to an evening fire and the scent of alcohol and old sweat.

A woman he didn't recognize sat in a chair next to his bed, reading a book. She looked up at his movement and smiled. "Do you know who you are?"

"Jason the Factor. Of Tomb's Shipping and Storage at Sturgeon Quay."

"Do you know me?"

"I am afraid you have the advantage of me, ma'am."

She was aging but not old, her face lined, her eyes glittering behind the lenses of small spectacles. She carried herself with the set of someone used to authority, or at least autonomy—not a servant, then. The room was strange. Good wood paneling, a few forgettable paintings of a certain quality on the walls, but nothing to mark the space as being the residence or office of anyone in particular. Just a bed, a chair, two small cabinets and a fireplace.

"It is just as well you do not know me," she said. "I have tended you this day. Though you would not have died, your journey to health might have gone much slower without my type of care."

He reached up to touch his shoulder. The skin seamed over his wound, tender to the touch, but nowhere near the raw violence of the flesh he'd expected.

The woman smiled. "Poultices. Certain prophylactics. And chantry."

"Magic and medicine," he said quietly.

"I am a physician, sir."

Jason swallowed his laugh. Women were not doctors, but then, what did he know? In the Tribade, women were everything, after all. Since Ignatius had vanished, his entire life had turned slantwise.

"I see your thoughts," she added. "You will need to go soon. We do not have the use of this room much longer, not without increasing risk of your discovery. Certain people in this city want you very badly."

He could only imagine. Jason vaguely remembered shooting a bailiff in the groin, though recent events seemed a bit misty in his mind. "Is there someone to whom I should address my gratitude?"

"For your life, you might apply to your friend Enero. For your overly rapid recovery to health, Biggest Sister has the most to answer." She gave him a fast, tiny smile, like a bird flying past a window. "I am no one, a woman of shadows."

"Of course," said Jason. He realized he was naked under the bed covers. "Am I to be clothed?"

She nodded toward one of the cabinets. "Apparel has been fetched in for you. You arrived arrayed in clothing so ruined that I would not have used it to dress a corpse."

The fog on his memories lifted. With their passing came a hot rush of urgency. "Where is Imago? Imago of Lockwood?"

"I cannot say. Again, you might ask Biggest Sister." She rose, set down her book, bowed and left the room without another word.

After a few moments Jason slid from between the sheets—cotton, he realized, but of a smooth, tight weave more luxurious than he was accustomed to. Percale, then, from one of the Sunward cities where the newest looms were in use. He'd always thought the costly fabric a waste of money, though his skin had lain marvelously against it. The textiles and materials produced within the City Imperishable ran far more to woolens and leather, given the temperate summers and chill winters of this latitude. He sometimes transshipped cotton bales, but they were destined for far more coarse a weave than this.

Though someone had bathed him, the sheets on which he rested still reeked of his own sweat and suffering. They were stained as well. He had no wish to consider those dark blotches more closely. Pain in the pursuit of pleasure was one thing—consensual, controlled, contrived—but the agony of a wound was another matter altogether.

On curious impulse, he picked up the book she had been reading. The printing within was Tokhari, a curled alphabet like vines that he could decipher enough to read numbers and shipper names on bills of lading. But this book was something else entirely.

How many women of the City Imperishable read Tokhari, he wondered? Who had she been? A Tribadist, to be sure. But more than just another woman of the dark sisterhood. A hedge wizard in her own right, to have healed him so quickly and thoroughly—for he had no doubt this healing was done overquick.

One cabinet was filled with clean bandages, bottles of medicines, philters and prophylactics. Her tools for treating him. He also found the scales and mirrors of a wizard, along with powders in tiny muslin packets likely cut from the winding sheet of a corpse. The other cabinet was empty save for a set of smallclothes, a pair of brown trousers and a coarse linen shirt folded beneath them. He found his boots next to that cabinet.

Someone had cleaned them and applied a new shine.

Jason dressed, increasingly concerned for the hour, or even indeed the day. The room's sole window was covered by the fall of a heavy velvet drape, but no daylight sent bright fingers around the edges of the curtain. He was hungry, his stomach gurgling like a drunken goat and his bowels aching from a surfeit of wind.

It was time to go. He only wished he still had his coat. Or indeed, any coat.

The hallway reminded him of the interior of the Limerock Palace—wide, high-ceilinged, with a strangely luxurious carpet. A very small woman waited there—born dwarf, he realized. Her kind were vanishingly rare.

Unsmiling she handed him a silk hood. He knew what was expected, had even wondered how he would leave this secret place. Jason slipped the silk over his face, hiding his eyes.

She took his hand without any friendship in her grip at all, and led him away. They turned to one side, through a door and down a narrow servant's stair. More halls, where his boots rang on wood or stone. Turns, stops and once a long pause. He kept silent. Questions would be of no use.

Finally he heard the whicker of a horse, along with the shit and leather scent of a stable. His guide placed his hand against a vertical surface with the smooth finish of lacquer. A coach, then. He felt for the doorsill, lifted his foot with care and climbed in. The door slammed behind him and the coach lurched into motion.

Jason sat with the silk sack upon his head, feeling the idiot and wondering if he should take it off. He was fairly sure no one was in the coach with him—he heard no breathing, felt no solid, body-warm presence nearby, did not smell sweat or perfume or clothing. He compromised by waiting til the coach had turned thrice, then tugged the hood free of his face.

There were no windows.

They drove a few minutes more, then stopped. The door opened, and he stepped out, but the driver or footman had retreated and he saw no one before him. Deliberately, Jason did not look back, but instead stepped up onto the sidewalk and studied the building in front of where he stood.

The Rhodaline Abbey, on Upper Melisande Avenue in the Temple District. If he was not wrong, at the corner of Bentpin Alley, near the home of Bijaz the Sewn.

Behind him, the coach moved off in a clatter of hooves and wheels on the cobbles.

The message was clear enough, but he was not ready to brace Bijaz. The dwarf would be in his offices plotting, or out among the clubs and meeting houses of his kind raising support for his cause. Hopefully, the ascension of the new Lord Mayor.

He needed to go down to the docks, to check his offices and make sure Two-Thumbs had not accidentally sold off the entire business in his absence. After that he would call on Ducôte. The old dwarf seemed a positive genius at keeping track of Imago of Lockwood, and his scriptorium would be at the heart of all the best rumors.

Jason had to laugh at himself. One dwarf was much the same as another, after all, if every third coarse joke ever told in the City Imperishable was to be believed.

He set his feet for Delator Square and the downhill journey riverward from there. The night was cold, and he needed a coat, but a brisk walk would keep him some way ahead of the chills.

The streets were quiet, with a curious undertone to the silence, but not the strange aura of impending violence. More like watchfulness. He made his way easily enough.

Down on the Sturgeon Quay, Tomb's warehouse in fact still stood, though from the look of things nothing much had happened that day anywhere along the docks. Presumably the portmaster had closed the riverfront because of the rioting. Fewer ships were anchored on the river though. Cautious or canny captains were slipping away, dropping cargoes and breaking contracts.

Even if war or revolution didn't come, the underwriters would be months untangling the mess. The very thought brought a smile to Jason's lips. It would not be hard to get the shippers and their clients to lay an accounting before the Assemblage of Burgesses. Chelattini the Intendant-General was not a popular man.

Jason thought to let himself into his warehouse, where his small apartment was located above the offices. He found that he had no keys—had lost them somewhere in the riot or after, but Old Jack Capp kept a set in the strongbox at the Teakwood Scow. When he entered the bar, Capp frowned at him and waved Jason into the kitchen.

"Before they all see you," the keep grumbled.

"All see me what?" As he followed Capp into the kitchen, Jason eyed the man's leather coat enviously. It was considerably colder here right by the river, though the kitchen steamed with the warmth of bubbling stew and spilled beer.

A boy scrubbing pots gave Jason an incurious glare. No one else was present but him and Old Jack.

"Are you daft? Bailiffs came by today, offering obols for your whereabouts. Gold ones to boot. There's enough out there that would sell each other's mothers for drinking money."

Of course the bailiffs were looking for him. He'd shot one. There was no shortage of witnesses to his place at the head of the incipient riot last night. That Jason had not personally put anything to the torch was moot, as would be his reason for pulling the trigger on the pistol belonging to that poor idiot Imre.

Here he'd just strolled through the middle of town as if he owned no cares at all. So rapid a return to health had apparently addled his brains for a time.

"I wanted my keys, but that won't do," he said. "Can't go back to the warehouse right now." Which was a damned shame, since his only path to Ignatius was iced down inside the offices there. He'd send someone to fetch the ear later. Someone he trusted. "I'm going to make for Ducôte's. I need to find the Lord Mayor. Might I borrow your leather?"

Old Jack looked horrified. "Me coat? Never in life, friend. This is a bar, though. I've a room full of other men's coats. Wait a moment."

A few moments later he was out the back and into the network of alleys that ran behind Water Street and the dockside. This time of night, they were the domain of rats, for the most part. Even the desperate didn't sleep in the back ways. Not this close to the river, in this season of strange deaths.

He only hoped nothing noumenal would come sliming out of the water to get him. That was no more to his taste than a gang of Assemblage Bailiffs looking for his blood to pay them back with interest. If *they* caught him, Jason knew he wouldn't survive the trip back to the Limerock Palace.

Instead he concentrated on his path through the alleys.

The bricks, where they existed, were slick with mold. The rutted mud was mixed with rot. Garbage glistened in the moonlight. Things rustled in the deeper shadows, and rats chittered along window ledges and in the overhanging eaves. It was nighttime in the City Imperishable.

He was forced once onto Water Street proper, to cross the Little Bull on Two Rivers Bridge. A wide boulevard in ancient times, it had over the centuries been compressed to the width of two carts by an accretion of shacks, shanties and houses that overhung the Little Bull on both sides while leaning inward to nearly shut off the sky above.

There was nothing for it there save to walk quickly as he might without drawing trouble with the appearance of panic.

Once beyond the bridge he slipped back into the alleys. With a few false turns, for he was less familiar with the byways north of the Little Bull, Jason made his way to Ducôte's scriptorium. The windows were brightly lit, and he could hear the steam engine groaning within, counterpointed by the hammer blows of the press chunking along.

No bailiffs in evidence, either. He figured that he would have spotted them readily enough—surely bailiffs would shut the place down.

Jason moved along the wall to the front door. Risky as stepping out onto Water Street might be, he didn't fancy being taken for a breaker and conked by some overeager pressman. As he reached the corner, a great, furred face bent down out of the air above to meet him.

He jumped back, more angry than startled, then realized he was looking at the head of a camelopard.

It stepped out in front of him on knob-kneed, spindly legs taller than he was. A mummer sat in the too-high saddle, crossbow in one hand.

"You are being well and safe?" he asked Jason in a familiar accent.

Different voice, but this was one of Enero's Winter Boys.

"Yes, I believe so."

"To be watching is a great concern." The crossbow waved in the air. "All is being in wait."

"Indeed," said Jason. He paid this man's coin, at least for now, he didn't need the damned mercenaries sneaking up on him from the shelter of the shadows. "I need to go inside now."

"Of course," replied the clown. He looked down the street, southward. "To be going soon, I am thinking."

Jason went, scuttling past the camelopard and along the front wall of Ducôte's scriptorium to the doors. The great animal clopped away from him, occupying the center of the street and doubtless drawing the attention of anyone approaching.

Grateful, Jason ducked inside.

"I don't know," growled Ducôte. "What in the nine hells did you do with him?"

"I lost track," Jason admitted uncomfortably. "I had been hurt rather badly in the riots. Somewhere up around Pritchart Street, behind the Hotel Septime, I passed out. Haven't seen Imago since."

"You don't look hurt badly."

"No." Jason didn't feel inclined to explain himself. "I experienced a rather sudden recovery."

"Wonders and miracles." The dwarf spat on his own floor. This time they were at Ducôte's desk—the need for secrecy didn't seem to outweigh the inconvenience of climbing to the catwalk for privacy. Most of the City Imperishable knew who Imago of Lockwood was by now, or at least had heard his name. "That man melts away faster than a pocket of coin on payday. Assuming we get him his gold chain, how are we going to hold him still long enough to do anything worth Dorgau's blue damn?"

"He's not dead, is he?"

"Not unless he got eaten bodily by some grue out of the noumenal world. If he lay slain in the streets, we'd know. Every corpse in town's getting the thrice-over, I can tell you. Especially with the price on certain people's heads." Ducôte gave Jason a long stare made all the more blank and lifeless by his lenses.

The look reminded Jason of a number of flounder he'd eaten over the years. "We play a bigger game than a few obols, sir."

"Don't tell me how to pluck chickens, boy. If the Burgesses restore their power now without any changes made, everyone among us will spend time rotting behind stone walls."

"Everybody's got to live in the world."

The dwarf gave his short, sharp bark of a laugh. "There's also some's got to be helped on their way out of it, I'm afraid."

"I don't suppose you have an idea where I'll find Imago?"

"Boy's smart enough to come here, once he crawls out from whatever woman or bottle he's found himself under. What would you do if you were him?"

"Run like the water demons were after me?" Jason asked reflectively.

"No you wouldn't." Another bark. "Any more than me. Or we'd already be long gone to the Jade Coast and beyond. They pay good money for boxed dwarfs down in the cities of the Sunward Sea. We make the best factors, coin masters, what have you. No interest in their family quarrels, and better numbers learning than any of their stupid fops. You, too, Jason. You're no dwarf, but you might could have been."

Coming from this tough old bastard, that was actually a compliment.

"Thank you, sir."

"Go to the back of the hall and get some coffee and something to eat, son. Imago turns up, I'll find you. You get bored, you can write headlines for broadsheets announcing the Trial of Flowers three days hence."

"What would that be?"

"That would be Imago's problem, that's what." The dwarf grinned, evil and humorless.

Everything he did seemed farther and farther away from Ignatius of Redtower. Dorgau take his master and all the rest of them—now he was to craft headlines? He knew even less of headlines than he knew of magic.

Coffee though, that might be worth the trouble. He was near ready to eat the table, food be damned.

IMAGO OF LOCKWOOD

The windowless coach deposited him by the Softwood Quay, near Ducôte's scriptorium. Flexing his stiff hand, he stepped into the evening. The River Saltus was ghosted over with drifting ribbons of fog. Large things moved in the black water. An expectancy hung in the air.

Something screamed close by, a sound louder by far than any mouth had a right to give. The screech stirred the hairs on Imago's neck and arms, and gave him a sharp twist of fear in his gut. It was bad enough being assaulted the previous morning, nearly dragged into the river. This was a shriek of pained hunger and angry need.

All this, to avoid Debtor's Court. What had he been thinking? It would have been so much easier to take a boat when the docks had still been running. Two hundred gold obols...

The thing was done now. He already rode the wolf, or perhaps the wolf rode him. Imago certainly felt hunted, at least judging by the racing of his heart. He nearly slammed himself into the door of the scriptorium, yanked it open in his haste. It creaked on rusting hinges to release a bright bar of light and warmth and the nose-tingling odor of ink. Two women in wool dresses worked standing behind one of the high desks, which had been placed just inside the door. Beyond them, the place seemed as busy as it had ever been, people working at copy desks, the press shuddering and clattering. No shutting down for the night now, even in the absence of further rioting.

They glanced at him, obviously worried, then broke into smiles. One turned and ran toward the back shouting for Ducôte, while the other extended her hands to take his. "Imago of Lockwood, welcome! We had feared for you."

"Out there…" he gasped, flinching from her grip though he was glad to be among friends. Or at least the friendly. "Don't go…"

A swirl of excited folk surrounded him, a chatter of dwarfs and men, followed by Jason the Factor wiping crumbs from his chin. Imago's warnings were lost in the racket, but he backed against the door to block unexpected exit. "You live," he said as Jason approached. The scream outside still echoed within him.

"And you are safe," Jason replied. "We must talk."

"Indeed. Life for life. I owe you much. But for now, where's Ducôte? Tell him to set a guard on this door, and let no one out for a while."

Imago scanned the rafters above and the floor below. No new strangeness seemed set to encroach. "I don't suppose we could be any more committed." They were up on Ducôte's catwalk, just him, Jason and the dwarf, though his much-abused joints had protested at the climb. "Or at least not me."

"After the riot yesterday, all our necks will stretch if the Burgesses regain the upper hand," muttered Ducôte.

Yes, thought Imago, it was far too late to step off the wolf's back. Every moment carried him farther in. "So we go on."

"You are certainly declared," said Jason. "In court, then on the streets. Else we would not have had the fracas at the palace."

Imago nodded. "Correct. As the statute says, I must seek acclamation. We need to make the Trial of Flowers happen. I need to win. As Lord Mayor I'll have legitimacy to set against the Burgesses."

Jason glowered at him. "If we don't find Ignatius, we're all undone."

"Don't even start that right now," said Ducôte. "We arrange Imago's ascension to office first, then we can parcel out the gains and losses. First we win the stakes, eh? Or die trying."

Both men murmured their agreement.

"So…" Jason searched slowly for words, apparently seeking civility. "What precisely *is* the Trial of Flowers?"

Imago shrugged. "On that matter the Codex Civitas is silent. The judges recommended the procedure, they didn't define it."

"It's public." Ducôte lifted a hand, counted off one finger. "It's adversarial, or risky, or both." Another finger. "It's unequivocal." Three. "It's entertaining." Four. "We require legitimacy and clarity. Those four points will need to be met."

"We're not talking about a street festival here," said Jason. He looked thoughtful.

Imago almost laughed. Jason the Factor was not half so grim as he liked to pretend. "No. I have spent much of today considering this. The Assizes Bench ruled on the case of a baker. Not a class of men noted for extreme bravery or skill with weapons. If old Lord Mayor Proppolio had been a butcher, I might believe this involved knives, but what would a baker fight with? Paddles?

"No, the Trial of Flowers was something showier. A mummer's play, or a gifting. A man could, for example, drive a cart through the city handing out a hundred thousand blossoms so that every man, woman, dwarf, dwarfess, dog and monkey in the place wore his colors. His acclamation would be visible behind the ears and on the lapels of all."

"Where are you going to get a cartload of blossoms in this dreadful cold season?" asked Ducôte.

"I'm simply making a point."

"Mummers…" Jason said. "We have mummers. Certain of Winter Boys ride dressed as mummers on their camelopards. Can we bring some cleverness to bear with their arms?"

"Like a tourney?" Ducôte snorted. "Who knows how many would die when the lances went astray? Since the gun came into use, the value has eroded from the armed melee. No one would pay to see men dance to bullets, and we'll need every able body soon enough, so we can't afford to allow them to be killed off."

"Not a tourney. Just something spectacular enough to catch and hold attention. They're *ready* for him. The City Imperishable is aching."

"A processional," said Imago. "I pass through the city, escorted by your mummers. I lead, or ride one of their mounts." Ducôte snorted at that, but said nothing. Imago went on: "We have to make it striking somehow. A mock battle, the daisy and the orchid, sun and moon fighting. Bring the noumenal attacks to everyone's mind, then dispel them."

"Theatre," said the dwarf. "You want bloody theatre."

Imago became excited. "Exactly. It's no different from the courtroom. Anyone can fit the facts to their pleading, it's making sense of the thing and winning the judges' hearts that matters. The man who tells the best story carries the day. That's what we'll do. We'll tell the best story. We shall put on a dumb show; our people will see a leader riding to take up the chain of office, where he will prevail with the aid of their will strengthening his arm."

"You're no soldier nor sword-bearing hero."

He tapped his forehead. "Some men fight with this."

Ducôte looked thoughtful. "Thus acclamation without election. So long as we are very public about it, the Burgesses must needs slay a third of the City Imperishable to reach us. Where are these Winter Boys of yours, Jason, with their camelopards and their capering clowns? They can serve as guards and props both in this show."

"I do not know that Enero would mean for his men to make a display of themselves."

"They dress like fools and ride ridiculous chimeras," snapped the dwarf. "Of course they mean to make a display."

"As may be," Jason replied. "Enero answers to Ignatius. That means he answers to me for now. Especially as I am his paymaster of the moment, sadly enough. I can ask it of him, but I do not believe I can order it of him."

"It will be brilliant," said Imago. "People have seen them in the city the last few days without quite knowing why. They ride high and laughable, yet they are also seen, correctly, as dangerous."

Ducôte knuckled his chin as he thought on the situation, setting wispy gray hairs twining around one another. "What do we do if we cannot secure cooperation from these mummers and their curious mounts?"

"We make some other piece of drama work to our advantage," said Imago. "We still find a way to give the people a show, get them to raise their voices and toss their hats. They want to love someone, something. They want a man that heeds them rather than retreating behind a wall of bailiffs. All we have to do is make it possible for the people to open their hearts."

"I shall seek Enero," said Jason. "But what about the flowers? This is not a Trial of Mummers, after all. We are well past the season for most blossoms."

Imago laughed. "There are flowers and there are flowers. Even when the plants are folded tight with prayers to winter's coming cold, flowers are all around us. Women in the bloom of their youth. Steaming honey cakes from the bakery. Flowing silks from off the Sunward Sea. We will make them believe in flowers, make it sensible and right."

Ducôte snorted. "Mummers on camelopards, each with a dozen yards of silk trailing behind them. Does anyone know how much a camelopard craps, and whether it stinks like pigshit or worse?"

"As it may be," said Imago calmly. Within his heart and head, he felt the hot excitement of a settlement coming together. This was like prevailing in the courtroom, only better. "It's a show, that's all. Like one of the bacchanal festivals. Only instead of following tradition, we're calling ourselves into be-ing. Calling the City Imperishable into being."

"After that happy event," the dwarf said, "a stop to the nonsense. Real patrols upon the walls, respect for Sewn and Slashed alike, someone dealing with the noumenal attacks. Those bastards who rule over us sleep inside the Limerock Palace, or their great houses. You, you walk the streets at night. You've felt the fear."

"Even now, friend Ducôte, even now." Imago sighed. "In the street outside as I arrived, something screamed. Like a giant mouth from one of Dorgau's brass hells."

"Let us hope that miserable bastard Bijaz learns something of the noumenal on his night journey with the little godbuggerer," said Jason. "Ignatius' disap-pearance is closely tied to these assaults. We have a long battle there, I'm afraid, even if we do call out every hedge wizard and miracle worker this side of the Yellow Mountains. Not to mention the priests in the Temple Quarter."

"Most of them are fakes," Imago said.

"Most. Not all, though."

"Indeed," replied Imago. "Indeed."

"Headlines," Ducôte announced. "I need to set up the new handbills for the morning. Lord Mayor to ride triumphant through the streets, that sort of thing."

"I'm not the Lord Mayor yet," said Imago mildly.

"No, but you will be. Else we're all acting out of foolish hope."

"That has never stopped a man," Jason said.

The dwarf looked him over. "Are you going for the Winter Boys now?"

"With what Imago said waits out there? I have no interest in becoming a pile of bloody bones."

"You should go below to the paper room and borrow a cot from the boys. You'll need to sleep some."

Jason shrugged. "I have been sleeping. Drugs and pain kept me out most of last night and today."

"I am also rested," Imago announced. "I shall help you write the hand-bills."

"You will need something of a mock joust," said Jason. "To make the idea of the trial make sense."

"If it's mock, then I shall simply fight flowers."

Jason's face lit up. "The bacchanals! The krewe houses are off of Fishtrap Lane, near the Green Quay, just below the River Gate. They have those great costumes and the horse-drawn fancies. I have seen lilies and orchids alike in the processionals."

"Oh, excellent." Imago was delighted. "I shall mount a camelopard and slay the inconstant lily that represents the moon."

"They will like that," Ducôte said. "The people need something to lift them. Then you and your camelopard clowns can storm the Limerock Palace with lily petals."

"Lily petals and firearms," said Jason. "I will have Enero leave off his walls and patrols and back us against the bailiffs if they do not acknowledge the authority of the Lord Mayor."

The dwarf gave another of his angry, mirthless barks. "Careful, Imago, that the flower does not slay you."

Imago could only think of Biggest Sister with the snake tattoos where her breasts had once been. She was an old flower, but a flower still, his tongue having dipped the honey of her pink orchid a dozen times in the night. She could have slain him. Her words had owned him.

Too many people owned him. When he held the Lord Mayor's chain, he would make all right and well. Something had to change.

"Let us get to work, then," he said. "We do this at noon tomorrow, to rush the Burgesses at their deliberations. Handbills tonight, and building our best rumors to spread by day. At dawn, Jason will seek out Enero and arrange our mounts. I will bother the krewes to find the flower to stand against us."

"A Trial of Flowers, indeed," said Ducôte. "Might this not have all been simpler if you were just a baker like old Proppolio?"

Imago laughed. "You want me to overthrow the Burgesses, raise an army against invaders, battle off incursions from the noumenal world, rescue our lamented Second Counselor from whatever hell he has conjured himself into, and now you wish me to do that all in *baker's whites?*"

"Flowers it is," said Jason. "I will think on how to best make our case to Captain Enero and his Winter Boys."

Ducôte gave him a strange glance. "Money often speaks with the sweetest voice. That is your language, Sir Factor."

BIJAZ THE DWARF

The first rule of magic, of working the noumenal world, was apparently to have endless patience and iron pants. They had been standing atop the winch tower for several hours, motionless save for their breathing.

Bijaz had expected some ceremony: casting leaves and lighting herbs to smoke and working with old brass like the hedge wizards did. Archer the godmonger had simply climbed up the ladders, past the huddled beggar children who hid in the tower by night, and then, well, stopped.

The children had bothered Bijaz, with their large, watery eyes glinting in the shadows. They were silent, too, as if their tongues had been cut out, though they breathed as loud as a hundred-mouthed beast. He feared for them, but turned the thought away. Too much sympathy would get a man killed in the City Imperishable. He had to shake these dark moods, or he was done.

Standing in the cold over the river—and it was much chillier out here on the water—did nothing to lift his spirits. His arse burned from the recent insults of assault and surgery, and his legs quivered with fatigue that worked its way upward in acid inches. His broken teeth stung with the coolth, and his nose itched from the scent of crowded bodies from below and the mossy, dockside reek of the pilings around the base of the winch tower. A little breeze worried at his clothes and multiplied the riparian chill.

That Archer had offered no direction or commentary did not help either. They remained silent for hours. The moon traveled west and the hard lights of distant stars gleamed as they trailed their mistress. Things moved in the river water, but they always did. Bijaz grew colder and sorer.

Finally he stirred. "For what are we waiting?"

"For you to ask," said the godmonger. "This listening is for you."

Bijaz suppressed a frustrated retort, then an equally wretched sigh. "And so I ask. For what are we waiting?"

"What do you seek?"

A prickle ran down Bijaz's scalp and shivered his back. He realized something was different in Archer's voice, changed. The other dwarf's lips were not moving quite to the measure of his words.

"To whom am I speaking?" Bijaz asked.

The river chuckled, and all the children in the tower below stopped breathing at once—that silence thundered in Bijaz's ears. "Us," said the voice, barely bothering with its puppet Archer. It seemed to issue from a dozen distant mouths, multiplied by water and stone, before wrapping him in oily fingers. The wind ran hot, foetid, an echo of the Jade Coast swamps infecting the autumn air. "Do you wish to know more?"

Bijaz summoned his courage. That stout emotion did not heed his call, but his fatigue and fear substituted well enough. He thought of teeth, and bloody rags that had once been men in the city's night. He was a ruined dwarf, but he was here for a purpose. Somehow, his words came strongly despite his fears. "The godmonger...Archer...he spoke of listening at the darkness. But he never told me what I was listening for."

"What do you seek?"

Each time the voice spoke, it gathered strength. The stinking, warm wind felt something closer to solid now.

"A path," Bijaz said. "I seek a path away from the burnings and the drownings and the deaths, that the City Imperishable might last another thousand years. I seek peace in the night."

"Paths are given to those who pay their way."

Bijaz was almost lifted off his feet now, not by a buffeting as if in a storm, but by the solidity of the rank air. It was another noumenal attack, then, but this one was taking time to tell him of his fate. Archer, he saw out of a corner of his blooming panic, hung vertical as a puppet might, though he could not tell what suspended the godmonger in his place.

The very air, perhaps.

"I do not know what price to pay," Bijaz cried out. "Tell me and I will pay it."

"Will you…?"

The wind vanished. Instead he was trapped within a coalescing mass of sticky, thick water. All he could think of was the clear fluid that wept off the burns of dying men. Was this how those dryland drownings happened, people found far from either river with their lungs filled with water?

"I do not want to die," he whimpered.

"Your first mistake." The voice had become a whisper now, tiny and tickling like a spider in his ear. "Everything and everyone dies. The time is coming for the City Imperishable to surrender her stones to crows and dogs."

Bijaz saw thousands of dwarfs lying dead on the cobbles of the City. Short, thick bodies wrapped in bloody muslin, while beggar children wandered among them picking away what they wished.

He would not have this. "What price, then? Paid to whom?"

"To close the gates for another generation or two, you must pay a life, a limb and a love." There was a sense of vast amusement, the River Saltus and the land itself moving with a ripple of deadly glee, then Bijaz fell to the flagstones of the tower's top.

Archer collapsed next to him, drooling blood. The air was cold once more, clammy even. Bijaz's head ached. His arse did, too, all hot and painful once more because of the tumble he'd just taken to the stones. Once more he felt like spewing, but he held himself quiet a moment and the quivering in his gut passed. His need to urinate had not abated, though, and so Bijaz pulled himself to his feet with care for his wounds and stumbled to the rampart of the winch tower to piss into the river.

There were eyes in the water below him, dim and glowing beneath the murk. His cock shriveled at the sight, then sagged.

He could not think on the fear. He must needs do this, for fear of the pain in his bladder. Then he would attend to Archer and think on what the words meant…a life, a limb, a love.

It took more time than Bijaz might have wished to rouse the godmonger. "Archer," he kept whispering, wishing he had water to splash on the dwarf. Perhaps he should have saved his piss for this, he thought. Whatever the voice in the darkness had done to him, it appeared to have done worse to his companion.

Archer's breathing was fast, shallow and out of rhythm. It was hard to be sure by moonlight but he looked pale. Sweat beaded the godmonger's face.

Bijaz wondered if he should leave the other dwarf here and go for help, but he knew no one in the Sudgate Districts. The beggar children below would be just as likely to finish the abuse and rob their bodies. With his injuries Bijaz could scarcely carry Archer down the ladders of the winch tower, let alone across the mossy stones and little brush breaks along the base of the jetty.

Now, if he could fly. Or find some of those men belonging to Jason's bodyguard.

He continued to prod and poke at Archer, trying to awaken the godmonger, huddling close to the other dwarf for warmth as he did so. After quite some time Archer groaned muzzily.

"Can you rise to your feet?' Bijaz asked urgently. "We should get back to our own precincts before dawn finds us here."

"We have not yet..." Archer gasped. "Have I been beaten? We never prayed."

Bijaz felt the chill return a moment. "Later, later. For now, we must go." He knew how Onesiphorous must have felt trying to cajole and jolly him into continuing to live, this previous night. It was as if there was some chain of succor, handing off from unfriend to unfriend. Tomorrow night Archer might rescue yet another fool from mortal pain.

Archer managed to get to his feet with Bijaz's help, but balked at descending the ladder.

"Unless you plan to dive into the river, this is our only path home."

"I know," sighed the godmonger. "I may slip on the rungs and tumble to my death."

"Should I leave you then?"

"No...no..." Archer seemed ready to cry, for a moment, but he mounted his resolve and with shaking limbs found the ladder.

Limbs, and lives, thought Bijaz, he could find in abundance. He had four of the first and one of the latter for his very own. What did it mean to sacrifice love to whatever forces had spoken to him?

He followed Archer downward into the darkness. The beggar children were sleeping—he did not see the glint of eyes in the first faint gray of dawn's approach that seeped in from the open trap above.

As he descended, Bijaz realized he did not hear them breathing, either. He paused, studying the huddled bodies in the shadow. Some were close enough to the vague light from outside for him to see details.

They were still, death-still. Each face had two bloody sockets where vision had been plucked forth. Bijaz knew in that moment where the gleaming eyes he had seen in the River Saltus were from. Taken, along with the lives of these children, that the noumenal might come to him once more.

This time he did spew, clinging to the ladder, heaving terror and exhaustion to angry protests from Archer below him.

"You damned fool of a dwarf," the godmonger screeched.

"Look," said Bijaz in a ragged voice. "Look."

Archer was silent quickly enough once he'd seen for himself.

The two of them found their way through the Sudgate Districts, still soaked in sweat and mess, which made them all but invisible. Just more of the wretched people out in the last hour of the night. Already drovers and carters were making their way up Water Street with the day's goods bound for market. The two found a little fountain on Hammer Lane and bathed in it, transforming themselves from wretched dwarfs to wet dwarfs. Still not ready for presentation to anyone of substance, but now they looked more like victims of too much sport than survivors of a disease ward.

"Coffee," muttered Archer, the first word either of them had spoken since leaving the tower. Bijaz nodded, not yet trusting his own voice, and they wandered east and north until they found a tiny café on an alley branching off of Margolin Avenue, just short of the yellow-painted walls and kitchen loading docks of the Sepia Wing.

Behind a tiny tiled counter, a dark-skinned woman from somewhere along the Sunward Sea worked wreathed in steam. She was huge and muscular, with hair braided tight against her scalp and small spirals tattooed on her cheeks just over the bone. The woman barely glanced at them, switching trays in and out of ovens that smelled of coalfire. Three petite tables stood within, and six more stacked out on the alley cobbles—no sidewalks here, just take one's ease amongst the traffic.

Bijaz still had his purse, with two silver obols and a pile of chalkies. He fished out a handful of brass and passed it over. "Coffee, please, and some of whatever cakes might be hottest from your tray."

She grunted, then said something in a language he did not understand, but her smile was clear enough.

The two of them sat and stared at the steam awhile. Eventually the woman brought cheap mugs of coffee, thick-sided to cut the café's costs, Bijaz supposed, and a little basket with several kinds of pastries inside. He poked the grubby napkin covering the baked goods, saw mostly seeds and nuts embedded in the breads. His own taste ran more to fruit, but he supposed it would not matter too much. The coffee was black, and she had not offered cream or sugar like a civil hostess, but rather honey and cinnamon. Clearly the people who normally came to this place had a different—

"How many?" said Archer, interrupting the manic trivia of Bijaz's thoughts.

Bijaz knew what he meant. "I could not count. In the dozens, I think."

The godmonger toyed with his fetish bag, as if enlightenment lurked in the folds of the leather. "How did it come to pass?"

He gave Archer a sidelong glance over the rim of his mug. "You were there." The first hot sip burned his wounded teeth too much and he set the coffee back down.

"I...I don't remember." Archer trembled, and for a moment Bijaz saw a different fear from the one that yet gripped him.

"Do you imagine you did that thing?" he asked softly.

Archer's eyes glistened. "Yes. Did I call some demon?"

"No." Bijaz tried to find that wave of sympathy he had felt the night before, but the weakness had passed. He had thought to find a certain wisdom in this dwarf, but instead only encountered fear. Like any man. Still, he made his voice a little warmer. "I cannot say for sure how it happened, but I do not think you were the agency of all those deaths."

Archer shuddered. "Their eyes..."

Bijaz leaned forward. "You are a godmonger. Surely you are used to signs and wonders."

"Signs and wonders?" Another shudder, and bitterness in his voice now, Bijaz saw. Bitterness was better than abject despair. The godmonger went on: "That would be a white rabbit appearing in the breaking of a whole melon. A sick woman rising to her feet without her canes. The blessing of the dead. Not those...those...gaping faces."

"What did you mean for me to hear, in your listening at the darkness?"

"Voices in the noumenal world. The chatter of the lately departed finding their way, the grumbling of old places that have grown their own spirits. It is a form of spying. Nothing more, nothing less, and certainly not something that draws power from the deaths of children."

"Their eyes were in the river," Bijaz said quietly. "I saw them, before I woke you, though I did not understand in that moment what they meant."

Archer shuddered again. "You are not a godly dwarf, are you?"

"No," said Bijaz, glad in that moment to be talking of something other than slaughtered children. "No more than most of our kind. You know the boxed are too well-read, too numbered, to take mysteries with the proper seriousness. Sewn and Slashed, we have that much in common."

"But you...you know the gods have power in the world?"

"Only a fool would think otherwise. Yet no god has ever knocked down my door, or changed one of my contracts, or saved a life or brought a death for which I might have prayed. Gods work within the minds of their believers, save for occasional rabbits springing from melons."

"Parlor tricks," said Archer. "Even so, there is a good reason for those parlor tricks. They stand in place of far worse. The world has seen other times in the course of history. The City Imperishable has seen other times. Have you ever wondered why the Imperator Terminus never returned?"

Bijaz shrugged. "He fell in battle, and lost our army. His defeat marked a change in our city's fortunes. Everyone with learning knows that much."

"His name means 'the last ruler.' Why would any monarch call himself that? Terminus intended to leave without returning. He took our Old Gods with him, so that we might live in peace. That is where our power went, with our gods. Bloody great killers that they were." Archer gripped the edge of the table so hard his knuckles turned white. "Believe me, we are better off in these days. Rabbits from melons are infinitely preferable to dead children with their eyes plucked out."

Burning trees, thought Bijaz. Great teeth in the night, walkers out of the river. "The noumenal attacks…these are our Old Gods returning?"

"Or being summoned," said Archer darkly. "By those who wish the renaissance of the days before."

"The Burgesses do nothing to stop them because they stand to gain." He was horrified, absolutely stricken. Prothro and old Zaharias and all the rest. What did they seek in this madness? "The tribes," Bijaz blurted.

"What?" Archer seemed caught cold by that statement.

Words tumbled out of Bijaz in a panicked rush of thinking. "The rumored war coming. People say there've been scouts killed here in the City. From the Tokhari, so I've heard. The Inner Chamber claims the noumenal attacks are the vanguard of invasion, that we must mount resistance and build an army to stop them. The Edict of Attainder raises funds toward that end, and makes ready the dwarfs to be accused as traitors if things go awry. It sets the blame upon us."

Bijaz paused for breath, trying to organize the ideas before they become too jumbled. He continued: "Why are they coming? We have not warred with the northern folk since the days of the Orogene Imperators. If what you say is true, about the Old Gods, then I think the tribes must be coming because their stonecallers see those horrors returning. They want to stop the gods before the City Imperishable rises to some bloody, ancient greatness and tramples everyone." The enormity of the idea caught him with a sick fascination. "They want to save us from ourselves."

"Mercy," said Archer in a breathless voice. He gripped his bag tight. "What is this city doing? Calling the Old Gods back."

"We must find the Lord Mayor. To stop whatever it is that we are becoming."

The godmonger stared at Bijaz a moment. "It will take more than finding him. Things have been unsettled that were much better left sleeping. It is no coincidence that the Old Gods seem drawn to you."

"Not just drawn to me," Bijaz answered slowly. "They told me how to stop them. Though I do not yet fully understand the words. Why would the Old Gods do *that*?"

"Some magics can call forth the voices of the dead. Have you ever thought the dead might not want to be called forth?"

JASON THE FACTOR

Morning found him once more facing the trip to the eastern wall. In order to avoid the bailiffs or other, quieter agents of the Burgesses, Jason sent a boy for a cab.

"Imago," he said as they sat on the iron stairs to nowhere and sipped coffee together—black and stinking, for Ducôte was out of cream. "It's time for me to seek out Enero. Are you going to find the flower?"

"Of course." Imago yawned. "Morning of the day and all that."

Jason stifled an answering yawn. "We must consider where to meet. This affair would be best gathered in Terminus Plaza, but that would be nettling a bull. Long before we were ready, every bailiff in the Limerock Palace would descend upon us like leeches on a marshman's daughter. Let us gather at Delator Square."

That was, after all, where he had witnessed the death of his father these fifteen years gone, and begun the journey from nasty, callow boy to whomever he was today.

"Fair enough," said Imago. "It is a traditional place of punishment."

"Indeed." Jason took a breath, to let pass the surge of irritation that Imago's remark had engendered. "I will arrange for Enero's men to be there in the hour before noon that we might make ready and begin our procession."

Imago laughed, though with a ragged edge of exhaustion to his voice. "And once we have passed through the streets in our noble array, I shall fight the flower in Terminus Plaza. With half the city surrounding us, we shall trample the red-coated bastards to death under the feet of our crowd if they move to stop us."

Bullets, thought Jason. The Provost had rifled muskets, which even a competent servant could make good use of, and a rooftop to fire them from. He would not trample Imago's enthusiasm right now. Energy mattered more than sense at this stage. Surely the Burgesses would be upon them soon if they did nothing but wait.

The lad he'd sent brought a light fiacre an hour after the morning bells. It would have been better for him to ride in something closed, but Jason figured he could sit back beneath the canvas and turn his face. Besides which, at this season there would be a lap robe that he could use to further obscure his appearance.

The small man driving the cab whipped his horse into motion. As the fiacre found its path to Melisande Avenue and up the hills toward the eastern wall, Jason watched from his shaded seat to see who was out in public. The weather was glorious, a cold, clear autumn day with a sky like glazed pottery and pale sun the color of a white gas flame.

Jason tried to catch up to the mood of the populace. He had slept through almost all of yesterday, though he had only an ache in his shoulder to show for it instead of the raging hot wound he by rights should be suffering from. He sent a silent thanks to the woman doctor and whoever of the Tribade stood behind her.

Whatever their exact reasons had been.

Everyone wanted something. He needed Ignatius of Redtower back, to fight the noumenal attacks. The Tribade needed him to bring Ignatius back, to restore the city to normalcy, whether through the agency of Imago of Lockwood as Lord Mayor, or otherwise. Jason suspected that the Inner Chamber and the Burgesses as a whole were too angry to be negotiated away from whatever they planned next. Even so, surely Ignatius was the one to try that, also.

Get this mummery of a Trial out of the way, and he would harass Imago mercilessly until they could find the right philosophick practitioners to follow the trail laid by the bloody ear.

Though he still had not puzzled how the Alates fit into it all—Enero said one of the bird-men had brought him the torn scrap of flesh.

People were on the streets now in close to their normal numbers. He was given to understand that the City Imperishable had been eerily quiet the day before, in the wake of the riot at the Limerock Palace. Today looked almost ordinary save for the large number of weapons in evidence. Swords, staves, pistols, muskets, blunderbusses, polearms.

This was fear, but an angry fear.

Even some of the mummers appeared worried as their camelopards picked their way through the crowds. Though Enero's lot seemed to favor crossbows over firearms. Sacrificing range for silence. Subtlety was not the strongest suit of a clown.

Where had Ignatius found the Winter Boys?

He would know more soon enough.

Upper Melisande Avenue led into the Green Market on the old Parade Grounds. It looked more sparsely attended than was ordinarily the case, as if the farmers from the Rose Downs held back some of their goods in hopes of prices rising further amid hard times.

Though the cost of food was becoming dear, he still hoped that was true. It meant people still looked to the future, instead of fleeing or barricading themselves in to wait out the worst.

The reduced population in the market meant the fiacre pushed through without trouble, into the net of little rubbled streets among ruined walls that led to the edge of the city. Jason supposed each of these had a name on some map in some room deep within the Limerock Palace, but except for Wall Street and the Sunrise Road, no one knew them anymore. Why bother? These days the area was nothing but a maze for children and dogs to romp in.

The City Imperishable had been so much more, once. He wondered if the confused and violent circumstances of the day were the best the City would ever see again.

The fiacre pulled up at Wall Street. The driver leaned around. "You are wanting to be here, my good sir, or are to be desiring to be elsewhere?"

Enero. Jason had not given him a second look down at Ducôte's scriptorium when boarding the cab.

"Dorgau take you, man, you could have said."

"I am to be watching your safety. You are not to be watching mine." Enero jumped down off the board with a grin. "You are to be owing me five chalkies for the ride as well."

"Surely that's not your cab," Jason argued.

"But of course it is being my cab. How else is a man to be going unnoticed about this great city which is to be filled with eyes? All are to be watching for mummers on strange stilt-legged beasts. None is to be watching a little man behind a horse, yes?"

Jason shook seven chalkies out of his purse. It was an overpayment for a cab ride, even of this distance. Enero certainly seemed to be enjoying his own joke. "There you go. Am I to suppose you know why I am looking for you now?"

"You are to be seeking solutions. Winter Boys are making problems to happen or we are making problems to be gone. It is why we are to be existing, yes?"

"The Trial of Flowers is scheduled for noon today," said Jason. "Imago of Lockwood will make a processional and fight a ritual battle in Terminus Plaza. I wish to borrow or hire some of your camelopards so that he might ride high and in view. I wish the rest of your men deployed to protect him, especially from musketeers the Burgesses might place on walls or rooftops as they did during the recent rioting. It wouldn't do to show Imago as the new Lord Mayor and then have him struck down."

Enero studied Jason for a moment. He turned, unlooped a lead from his horse's harness to place it beneath a rock and patted the creature. It lowered its head and began cropping at some grass straggling at the verge of Wall Street. "To be walking with me a moment, please."

Jason fell into step beside the mercenary captain. After a few paces in silence, he asked, "What is the source of your reluctance?"

"I am being hired by Ignatius of Redtower to be holding walls against an army which might never come. I am being told he is missing, being given a severed ear by flying men, being given orders and pay by you, who is to be something of a clerk or agent to my employer. Please not to be taking offense, merely this is how I am seeing things to be."

"No offense," said Jason, who was in fact feeling another hot rush of annoyance.

"Indeed. You are to be having a very poor little civil war in this fine city, which is not being fought well at all I am to be saying. It is to be one thing, to be watching over you and certain other fools on the quiet, yes? But now you are wishing me to be following your new leader through streets of danger, all in the public eye, my poor freeriders who are being fighting men of field and forest to be exposed so amid your stone walls."

"You ride amid the walls now. Your men have been in the city for some days. Imago tells me one of them saved my life."

"The mummers? They are to be Winter Boys, one little squad of our free company. Have you been seeing my other men?"

"No."

"This is to be the point." Enero stopped, whistled sharply. Two soldiers emerged from the rocky top of the eastern wall, where they must have been the whole time, though Jason had not seen them. One waved a crossbow at them. The other carried a rifled musket. Enero waved, and they sagged back into the crenellations. Even though Jason now knew to look for them, he could still barely spot them.

"You are to be wanting watchmen, not soldiers, good sir. It was not to be mummers astride camelopards who were killing those Tokhari scouts I am telling you of before."

"At least lend me your clowns. I'll find some other mount for Imago, show him to the people on the street, but your men will keep the malcontents quiet and make the bailiffs' work more difficult when they come for us." Jason realized as he said those words that he might well die this day. It had certainly been true at the gates of the Limerock Palace two nights ago, but he hadn't had time to think it through and find the fear within himself. Today was different.

"If you are losing all, I am being paid no more, yes?"

"I do not imagine the Burgesses will care to favor you with funds, no," said Jason dryly.

"Hmm. Where at noon shall we be bringing ourselves to this silly plot?"

"The hour before. In Delator Square."

"Mummers you will be having then, yes. Though I am to be telling you that an extra silver obol per man for the day's work would be the best."

It took Jason a moment to sort through that. "So you will be there. My thanks. Are you providing a mount for the Lord Mayor?"

"I am to be thinking the Lord Mayor and yourself." Enero grinned. "You are to be sharing the danger, yes?"

"Of course." He had heard the weapons crack that night. Would it be justice, for his shooting of the bailiff at the Debtor's Court, if he caught a bullet this day? "Thank you."

"Now you are to be needing a ride back to my good Ducôte?"

"No…I think I'll walk. I am heading for Delator Square, and the bailiffs will not likely be looking for me at this end of town, far from my usual places."

"Brave man." Enero smiled. "We will be to your side in a few hours."

Jason stuck out his hand to shake with the captain of the Winter Boys. "This will be your greatest service to the City Imperishable."

Enero shook. "Then it will to be your greatest gratitude, yes?"

"Yes."

He walked along one of the nameless ruined streets. The wildflowers had gone to seed, petals in faded colors barely clinging to tiny stalks. He saw little vines, and trails of ants, a few bees flying yet, though he could not imagine what the bumblers were after. The clear, cold day had brought a wind out of the east that smelled of distant hayfields. Summer's last breath, as it were.

It was the possible last breath of Ignatius of Redtower that was Jason's biggest problem, unfortunately. His little group of uneasy allies were doing better than he expected at opposing the Burgesses, but even if they were successful in elevating Imago, they would not accomplish all that was needful. They would be far better holding some of the power in the Limerock Palace, one of the seats on the Inner Chamber ideally. In times past, the Burgesses had answered to the Imperator as they governed the City Imperishable's wider territories. Tradition held that the Lord Mayor attended to the city proper. Sharing power was an idea that had precedent, and indeed was still enshrined in statute. For all that it was forgotten today.

Precedent and statute, the twinned idols of the Burgesses. He'd worked with the Assemblage for years, not as Ignatius' agent, but in his own right as a factor on the docks, seeking monopolies, preferences, contracts. The Burgesses did nothing that had not been done before, and were conservative as grave dust.

If that damnable riot had not happened, Imago might have found an office in the Limerock Palace. They might have found cooperation in the

Lord Mayor's accession.

Though from what Bijaz told him, the Inner Chamber was set on another course. Maybe not in unanimity, certainly not while Ignatius had sat as Second Counselor. Was it Prothro or Zaharias who had disposed of their inconvenient colleague? Or had they simply plotted while leaving him out of the circle?

"You."

Jason looked up, startled. Green Kelly, Ignatius' steward and palace lackey, stepped out of an alley just ahead. Two ragged but well-fed men loomed behind him.

"What of me?" Jason asked, hoping against hope one of Enero's freeriders was close by, and wondering why he had not taken the cab to Delator Square as the Winter Boy suggested.

Because he'd wanted to listen to the streets, of course. Well, here they were, talking loud and clear.

"Are you any closer to him?"

Ignatius of Redtower, naturally. "I think so." He wasn't about to mention the ear, though Green Kelly was one of the few people likely to actually recognize the pathetic bit of flesh.

Green Kelly came up close, the two big men behind him. "Your highest effort seems to be working at treason against the Inner Chamber."

"It would be treason against the Burgesses, actually," Jason said mildly. He would skin the steward in his playroom, breaking bleeding fingers one by one. "The Inner Chamber is just a committee."

"Where is he?"

"Did you go up the stairs after I was arrested?"

"I…I tried."

The little buggerer was scared. Well, good, Jason thought. Let him wonder. It was Green Kelly who'd brought toughs with him, after all. Both of them were watching Jason with lazy indifference, but he was not fooled. Where was one of those damned mummers when you needed them?

Jason felt he should reveal what he had found. Green Kelly might know more, something they could trade off. "I found blood at the very top, in a hidden attic room. A dormer, if you will. Feathers around. Something took him from there."

An Alate, presumably, but that was more than he was willing to tell Green Kelly. Besides, the window had been latched from within, which argued for the noumenal rather than the aerial as a mode of attack.

"Then you can't get him back," said Green Kelly with a rather nasty note of satisfaction. "You're no philosophick doctor, nor hedge wizard either."

"No," said Jason, marking the tone of the steward's voice. "I'm also not a fool. Everyone knows I'm working to place the gold chain around Imago of

Lockwood's neck. There is no one now with authority or funds to call together those with noumenal powers save the Inner Chamber, and in Ignatius' absence they will not be persuaded. With the standing of the Lord Mayor we can make that call, and track Ignatius."

Green Kelly glanced over his left shoulder at one of the men. "Master had his irregulars. You weren't the only one."

"There's other powers," said the big man. "Some of us walk different paths. You find a thread, we'll pull him in." His fellow bruiser nodded.

"You're hedge wizards?" Jason asked, speaking right over Green Kelly. "Or something noumenal."

Green Kelly ignored the insult. "You're a political. Master fought other battles, too."

"Indeed. I shall keep you in mind."

"We shall keep you in sight," the big man responded. "You get close, we'll know. Watch for us then."

"I am thrilled at your offer of assistance."

"Mind your manners," snapped Green Kelly. "For better or ill, changes are afoot. You come out on the wrong side, you'll wish you was floating face-down in the river. It'd be a damned sight more comfortable than some of the things that could happen to a man."

Green Kelly was most certainly going to find himself in serious trouble once Imago was in office, Jason decided. Here was one he could safely drive his anger toward, after all. "Good day, gentlemen."

"Good day," said Green Kelly. The irregulars nodded.

Jason was forced to step around them in order to resume walking. He was nearly to the edge of the living city, about to catch Randebar Street where it met the ruins, and follow it parallel to Upper Melisande Avenue down to Delator Square to await the noon hour. There would be people along Randebar, not so many this far east, but enough to insulate him from the mischief of these idiots.

IMAGO OF LOCKWOOD

He'd finally pried funds out of Ducôte, but not to settle his debts or create new ones. No, Imago's prideful spending days were behind him. It would be unseemly for a Lord Mayor to have markers being carried by the Numbers Men of Cork Street.

While fantasies of using his power to influence their affairs danced at the edge of Imago's imagination, he'd applied his rhetorical skills, and more than a few of Ducôte's obols, to the problem of gaining access to the krewe houses near the River Gate.

"After all," he'd said, "we can scarcely burgle our way to control of the city."

"Instead you'll bribe your way," the old dwarf had complained.

"Well, that is more in the natural order of things." Imago's last comment set off a round of laughter from the exhausted scriveners and printers who had worked two days straight, and so settled the argument.

Imago stood behind a shabby old man in an ancient bailiff's coat faded to pale pink as he undid a padlock bigger than Imago's hand. Gordo, the watchman's name was. He'd once been a solidly built man of some stature, though now he was bent over. Great flaps of skin dangled from his chin and neck like wattles on some backyard tom.

"I got the crab disease," Gordo said as he looked up from the lock. "I ain't takin' your money for politics nor loyalty. Can't get my daughter married off afore I die without more'n I have."

"Your need is great," said Imago smoothly. As was his own, but he would not explain that to this man. "Though I can do nothing to ease the suffering of your illness, you are not required to attend your own death in financial misery." This was little different than arguing a suit before a judge. "Your aid now is essential to bringing a new change to the City Imperishable."

"Him that tried to burn down the Limerock? I worked seventeen years as a bailiff afore that ass of a Provost paid me off. Let it burn. Even so, methinks a dab hand with a torch scarce marks a man fit for great office, neither."

"Indeed not." Imago had scarcely wielded a torch that night, and was caged during the storming of the Costard Gate, but he felt no need to set the record straight. He couldn't resist adding: "One must not judge by rumor alone."

Gordo tugged the lock open finally, and gave Imago a blank look. "How else is a man to judge? Everybody lies about the truth. Rumor is honest in its intentions. Here, help me with this."

It was a massive sliding door, intended to let huge wains in and out of the building. This particular krewe house belonged to the Krewe of Balnea, which Imago found strangely apropos. Their parades ran to nature themes—bowers, jungles, natural women sometimes, much to the glee of onlookers. They also had flowers.

Though the effort hurt his healing hand, Imago tugged with Gordo to open the door just wide enough to admit the two of them. Inside was dusty to the point of unbreathable, motes swirling like a plague of insects in the occasional blades of pale light cutting through holes in the roof. The place smelled of old leather and dry rot and paint stored too long.

It was clear that the krewe house was originally built as a wheelwright's workshop, or something of that nature. There were still great winches up in the rafters within, originally intended to lift and move the wagon bodies as needed. The krewe presumably used them to assemble and disassemble floats.

Gordo shuffled along, bent low to the left by the pain that was eating away his life. He didn't bother with the lantern—there was light enough to see the giant faces of beasts gleaming down from atop wagon bodies, the ranks of false trees leaning against storage frames, glass eyes bigger than Imago's head glittering on a rack halfway up a wall. It was like a conjuration interrupted half-done, as if some minor god had meant to create a menagerie in the wilderness and gotten no further than the component parts before losing interest.

Imago was fascinated.

He walked beneath the wing of some great bird, a mountain teratornis perhaps. The beak curved down, sharp and hard, looking for all the world as if it were made of silver.

"Flowers near the back," Gordo called from the other side of a great bear with no head. "There's a wider bit over here where they hauls 'em for'ard."

Imago threaded his way to the back, stepping around the pale shafts of light for no good reason. He looked up to see things moving in the rafters behind the winches. Bats, or nightbirds roosting. The holes in the roof would let them out. That would be a sight to see, around the time of the evening bell, though there couldn't be too many of them or the place would have reeked of their scat.

He found the flowers. There were several rolling gardens, filled with silk and paper flowers, and a jungle bower he remembered seeing from bacchanal festivals in the past, mostly because of the natural women who frolicked behind one or two more palm fronds than was strictly necessary. A set of large stalks dangled from a beam, each topped by a different bloom, meant to be worn by a mounted man.

He'd seen that in better days—the tulip jousting with the iris, the daisy contending with the rose. Did it matter which one he used?

Imago chose the rose because it was nigh red as blood. He liked the color. He thought he might take crimson for the color of his office. Crimson and cream. They would make fine robes.

"Would you please go find a boy to fetch a carter?" he asked Gordo. He should have thought to bring one from the dockside, but he'd come down here on his own this morning, while others worked the streets and spread the word. "I shall need this taken away. Preferably by someone who can keep their mouth shut, at least for a few hours."

Gordo stuck out his hand. "Two orichalks for the boy, four chalkies for the carter and another obol for me."

"An obol? To fetch a boy? I could hire one for days on that money."

"An obol for my daughter, while you steal on my watch. They'll sack me for this, but they're like to sack me anyway before much longer, for moving too slow."

Imago gave him three obols, and set about figuring how to lower the rose without damaging it overmuch.

He would need a horseman, too, to wear the thing. Someone not afraid of looking silly who could play the part. Jason, if no one else would serve, though surely some strapping lad from Ducôte's could ride and would be willing to have their name in history.

Somewhere near the hour before noon, Delator Square was terribly crowded. People had come from all over the city—the beggars and stranger folk who often haunted this square were mixed with dockmen, servants in townhouse finery, clerks from the syndicates, shopkeepers, harlots, housewives, nannies, children, dwarfs and dwarfesses, along with the usual followers of any crowd, selling chestnuts and carrots and oiled corn and fried fishtails out of carts and trays.

It looked as if everyone in the City Imperishable had turned out.

Imago sat on the board next to his hired carter and pointed toward the punishment platform, where he meant to find Jason and set up the whole business.

"Not no way we're moving across this'n," said the man. He glanced back at the load, the ridiculous rose costume wrapped in a tarp and tied in place. "It ain't dead heavy, two men could carry it there. But my wagon ain't going through."

"I understand." Imago stood, looked around. To no surprise of his, he saw several camelopards towering above the crowd, their mummers turning back and forth to watch the crowd. He waited until one faced him, then waved his arms wide.

The clown raised his crossbow in acknowledgement, then its mount began to stalk across Delator Square. People moved away from those great legs, with haste if not panic. Three other camelopards lurched into motion to follow.

"We will be helped soon," Imago told the carter.

Sure enough, when the camelopards formed around the wagon and headed toward the platform, a lane formed for them that the carter could never have made on his own. He clucked his team along, as the horses rolled their eyes at the towering camelopards.

"Strange friends you got, sir."

"Strange and stranger. If things go well, find me a few days hence. I'll tip you more for your help."

"I ain't sure I'll want to know you a few days hence," said the carter. Despite his words, there was cheer in his voice. There ought to be, Imago thought, he'd been paid well. Imago had tripled what Gordo gave the man for his hire.

Jason stood with some serious-looking men in gray cloaks and gray leather armor just by the platform. "I've got the flower," said Imago, jumping off the wagon. "We'll need a horseman to carry it off. Not one of those stilt-legged monsters, either, but an honest horse."

"Not difficult," said Jason. He nodded to the carter, then went to the back board of the wagon to check the cargo. "Let's get this business moving. If we're going to do it, we should do it well and soon. Word is the bailiffs have formed marching ranks at the Costard Gate."

"Have you seen Bijaz?" Imago asked.

"Not yet." Jason glanced around, then lowered his voice. "Something's happened down by the Sudgate. The district's buzzing. It might be him, or his doing, but I've no way of knowing. Let's hope he hasn't fallen into the river."

Fifteen minutes later Imago was on the punishment platform being helped into one of the mummer's saddles atop a camelopard. The animal did not like him, an unfamiliar rider, but its clown had his arm around the big skull and was talking low into its ear.

"He'll walk close with you," shouted Jason, who was being pulled away to mount another camelopard much against the creature's wishes.

It was a strange saddle, Imago thought, but the animal was strange. The backbone sloped like a house roof, as if he might pitch off at any time. A complex many-strapped harness put much of the weight against the animal's chest, and also secured the affair into place. The seat was built up past level, til the backside rose higher than the front, presumably to help the rider keep from tumbling to the ground should the animal dip or bend.

Another mummer strapped Imago's legs into stirrups that were so deep as to almost be boots. One of the gray-armored men slipped a lance into a brace on the camelopard's saddle. Imago had asked that it be rigged to the left, so he would not drop the thing when taking it into his wounded right hand. "You are to be doing nothing save to be waving at the crowds!" the freerider screamed over the racket of the square.

Imago certainly wasn't going to steer the damned thing. The view was disconcerting enough this high up. Besides which, one of the items they'd worked out overnight was the route for this processional. Much like the bacchanals, the idea was to show off to as many citizens as possible. They would leave Delator Square and move through the Temple District first, along Upper Melisande Avenue, before turning north over the Little Bull across the Bloody Bridge to the far end of the City Imperishable. After circling that quarter of the city, they planned to come back south on Cork Street to cross the Little Bull River at the Bridge of Chances, up past the elegant trading halls and syndics' mansions on the New Hill, back down Sorrow Avenue to Hammer Lane close to the Sudgate, then crook around to Terminus Plaza via Water Street and

Short Street if possible, else directly onto Orogene Avenue. They very much wanted to avoid Maldoror Avenue and the Costard Gate.

Jason had argued against Terminus Plaza, on some very good grounds, but Imago knew that no matter the route this must be done in sight of the Limerock Palace. Ducôte had backed him, for the sheer public effrontery of the thing.

They would contend with the rifled muskets somehow. Jason's appeal to the Winter Boys appeared to have met with success. Imago rather imagined Biggest Sister would have the rooftops covered in her own way.

He would live, and triumph. Then the real fight would begin.

A racket of whistles, drums and shouting arose. The mummer holding his camelopard's lead line tugged it into motion. The animal, still obviously resenting Imago, followed its usual master. He set one hand on his pennoned lance and began to wave madly.

"I am come," he shouted. "Take me for your Lord Mayor and I will make you safe."

They cheered, though it was clear no one had the least idea what he was saying. As they proceeded along Upper Melisande Avenue, he began to vary his promises. "Carmel swords for each household!" "Redheads in every bed, man or woman as it pleases you!" "Showers of gold at midnight!"

It did not matter. They all cheered him like a savior come from heaven, and the cold light of autumn made Imago feel as if he were gleaming silver-bright.

Though they meant to be there before the next bell rang, the procession took closer to two hours. Crowds thronged the streets, and they were slowed by a terrible bottleneck at the Bridge of Chances. Imago had hoped to ride alongside Jason, but they were put to enough trouble just staying within what would be shouting distance on an ordinary day. As it was, while he could see his colleague, the man might as well have been outside the city walls for all that they could talk.

A dozen other mummers on camelopards were their outriders, but even those men, expert with their creatures, were at the mercy of the rush of the crowds. The mounted Rose, worn by another of the Winter Boys, managed to stay fairly close behind Imago, mostly because of a walking guard of men with drawn swords and pistols who kept a clear space. The costume would not have survived being mobbed.

Somewhere in the middle of it all, the city bells began to toll. It was the same cacophony as the evening bell, but spread out, ringing and rolling across the City. Ships on the water took up the call, firing their guns, though half the captains could not have known what was truly afoot. Boys ran along the rooftops with streamers of silk, while women tossed greenhouse flowers and food from upper windows as they passed.

It was as bad as the most crowded of the bacchanal processions, and all the thousands were screaming his name.

"Im–a–go…Im–a–go…Im–a–go…"

The sounds soon lost their meaning and became a rolling noise, like a storm coming across the Rose Downs.

Him. They were crying for him.

Imago looked up to see Alates circling overhead. Not one or two, but dozens. When he signaled to Jason and pointed up high, the other man just shrugged.

All they could do was march.

The worst of it was that the crowd wanted to move on the Costard Gate, site of their recent unanswered act of rebellion. None of them planning the Trial of Flowers had thought that route safe or wise. Nonetheless, the procession bent unstoppable as a river in flood to turn down Maldoror Street to march triumphant past the site of their recent triumph.

From his high perch, Imago could see what they had feared—bailiffs on the walls around the Costard Gate with rifled muskets in their hands. The people were packed so close, so thick, that they simply kept moving. The gate itself was blocked with a wooden wall, so the river of flesh didn't spill into the South Garden. The Provost, Zaharias of Fallen Arch, stood atop the Costard Gate. He gave Imago a slow salute over a narrow grin.

Keeping his face bright as he could, Imago smiled back, and waved.

They were in Terminus Plaza, the largest open space within the main part of the City Imperishable save for the ruins along the eastern wall. The plaza was a mass of people. More than half the population was here to acclaim him. Bells still rang, cannon still boomed and great banners had risen on poles, slogans painted upon them with indifferent spelling but fervent passion.

IMAGEO FOR US!

ASSEMBLAGE RESING

NEW DAYS FOR THE CITY

BURGESSESE OUT

The Winter Boys cleared a space before the Riverward Gate, prodding with swords and staves and pistols in waving hands. Imago saw a small fellow, Jason's man Enero, madly directing from the center. The mummer at Imago's stirrup shouted something he could not hear, then released the lead lines.

Enero's turn. He took the reins, directed the camelopard toward the clear cobbles. It was eager enough to go there, out of the press, especially with its usual master walking behind it, slapping the animal's flanks to keep it moving.

He was in the open space, facing the mounted Rose with the gate to their right. Jason's camelopard was there as well, facing the gate. Imago glanced over to see the First Counselor and many of the Burgesses atop the Riverward Gate battlements, or along the walls, though the gateway itself had also been blocked. More armed bailiffs mixed in among them, but the redcoats had not settled their weapons to aim.

This was it. Play the part. The Trial of Flowers was about to begin, for all that it was a mummers' farce at heart.

He set his good left hand upon the lance, stood in the stirrups and shouted, *"People of the City Imperishable!"*

In the brilliant light of afternoon, he was met by a roar that would have deafened the distant sea.

BIJAZ THE DWARF

Bijaz and Archer sat in the café for some hours, Bijaz perched on the edge of his chair to avoid irritating his arse further. Most of the people who came and went were dark-skinned as the proprietress and chattered like magpies in some Sunward tongue. They seemed for the most part to be cleaners and lower servants from the Limerock Palace, to judge from their dress.

It made a perfect place to talk quietly. No dwarfs came at all, while the few non-southerners who entered the place looked right past the two of them as full-men so often tended to do. They slipped in and out of fingertalk whenever someone happened by who seemed like they might understand.

Their recent experiences were not a subject fit for sharing, but they were both exhausted and Bijaz didn't fancy a daylight stroll through the streets right now. Not with the bailiffs after him. It had been sheer lunacy to find a resting place this close to the Limerock Palace as it was, but they had been tired beyond measure and fogged with both injury and horror. This place seemed safe enough in its back-alley foreign anonymity.

The empty eye sockets of the dead children particularly haunted Bijaz. Every time the woman behind the counter let coffee drip into a mug, he could only think of the blood pooling on their faces in the half-light of the winch tower. As for what the eyes were doing gleaming in the river, he shuddered even to go near that idea.

They talked about what might lie behind the return of the Old Gods, and the rumors of war that seemed inextricably linked.

"The godmongers practice a trade designed to keep worship, well, at a certain level," said Archer.

"I'd always thought of you as a sort of collective priest. Agents."

"You never spent time in the temples."

"Too close, I suppose. For one, gods have never appealed to me. Besides which, in my experience priests are just people, no more or less holy or sacred than any farmer."

Archer seemed faintly amused, somewhere beneath the layers of fatigue and dread which had settled on him. "How else should they be? Priests are born of women. Sacredness is an aspect of the divine. Consider this: Why should there be dozens and dozens of temples in this city?"

"One hundred seventy-eight, actually," Bijaz said absently. "There's a circular that goes around the district periodically, full of useful information. In the nature of a community improvement effort, I suppose."

"Well, yes." Archer went on to answer his own question. "With that many gods, no single deity accrues too much worship. Sacrifices are spread across that many altars. Prayer and worship and sheer desperation are dissipated. Divinity is, well, about power. What Terminus sought to undercut."

Bijaz had lately seen enough power to last himself a lifetime and more. "Believe me, I take the point of that."

"As does everyone, at some level. What do you think the bacchanal processions are for? The monstrous figures paraded through the streets are meant to mock the Old Gods. It's a perverted summoning. Close enough to the real thing."

A metal fish flashed in Bijaz's memory. "What I saw last night, on the way to meet with you. A bacchanal of the desperate, so to speak, in the Sudgate Districts."

"Precisely. They call the Old Gods in order to send them away again. Afterward some make their way to the Temple District, or to godmongers like me, and draw their gods onward. Then another bacchanal."

It all made sense in a weird way, thought Bijaz—an economy of spiritual power that operated like the check valve on a steam engine. Build up too much pressure in the houses of worship, dance it back to level in the streets. "But the noumenal attacks are frightening people, upsetting the balance."

"Well, yes. The state of affairs here in the City Imperishable is not helping at all. Which may be what has frightened our friends coming from the northwest. It all feeds itself—fear breeds worship, worship invites attack under threat of the old days returning, attack makes for fear. The Tokhari remember our history better than we do."

"Speaking of history," Bijaz said, "there's one thing I don't—" He stopped as two court clerks bustled in. Both carried epees at their belt, which was unusual.

Archer's eyes tracked the clerks as his fingers flickered in the sign for LIGHTNING ON THE ROOFTOPS. Danger all around.

Bijaz answered with WISE MEN PLOW LONG AND PLANT DEEP. Take measures and be patient.

They both sipped at their coffees and sat quietly until the clerks left with a sack of cardamom rolls.

"I believe what you've told me, as far as it goes," Bijaz said, resuming the conversation. "You and your ilk are custodians of history. Fine. You're both more and less than priests. Tell me this. Why did Terminus not arrange his own succession when he left? He marched off to war with the Old Gods in his train and dropped the whole lot of them down some deep hole, but so what here?"

Archer answered the question with another question. "What's the biggest problem we all have with the Burgesses?"

Bijaz had to laugh at that. With his chuckle, the blank-eyed children slipped just a little further away. He found some small relief in finding his distance from the dripping horror in his memory, but that relief was also stained with guilt. "Where should I start? Taxes? Their idiocy about the dwarf community? The way nothing meaningful ever happens?"

"That last. Ships have a single captain. One bee leads the hive. None of the syndicates are governed by committee. Why would anyone choose to run an entire city, not to mention the remains of an empire, that way?"

Bijaz turned that over in his head. The notion had a horrifying logic. "So you godmongers work to keep people spread among all the temples and gods of the City Imperishable, to keep the Old Gods dead and the new ones from becoming too great and terrible. Terminus…he took the Old Gods away, and emptied the seats of power. Because power concentrates."

"Right. This is claimed to be the oldest city in the world. There are streets below our streets, and caves below them. Temples down deep where it is said that goatherds sacrificed their children to jealous gods at the morning of time. The City Imperishable knows itself. There is blood beneath all our stones and soil. Anyone who sits on the Bladed Throne will collect the power of place, of obedience and subservience, of swords bent to their will. In this city, that draws gods the way shit draws flies. This is why Terminus deliberately arranged a lack of succession."

To keep the eyeless dead from clogging the river, for one. "No wonder they'd gone out and wrought empire on the lands of the world. If they stayed home, life became hell."

"Yes."

"So…" Bijaz was pursuing this thought toward a very unpleasant conclusion. "Tell me this, godmonger. What will happen if we elevate Imago to the office of Lord Mayor? Will that reopen the lures of power in this place?"

Archer shrugged. "Neither the office nor that man is in the line of Imperatorial succession. If he's chief among bureaucrats, not much to the ill should take place. If he has the worship of the people, if the walls and cobbles of the city echo with his name…well."

"The riot two nights ago was over his imprisonment. Handbills everywhere. You were present at our dinner. It's all being done for him. The printers and the Tribade are stirring people in Imago's name. His name, most literally. They're aiming for a coronation, to have enough legitimacy to fight the Burgesses."

Archer looked sick. "We need to get to one of them—that Jason of yours, Imago himself, and stop the Trial of Flowers. They're on a road to bringing back…that…"

Bijaz slid back into the horrors of the previous night. "It's what we're trying to avoid. Organize well enough to roll back the noumenal attacks—more to the point, the return of the Old Gods. If centralizing power draws the gods, and not centralizing power allows someone else to work at drawing the gods, what do we do?"

"We start by reaching your friends and stopping this idiocy. Don't let him ascend by acclamation. That would be as bad as half the city worshipping at one temple."

"They're not my friends," muttered Bijaz. "Nonetheless, we must get across town, to my brother's warehouse. Jason will be there." He said that last with more certitude than he felt.

"How?"

"Quietly, I suppose."

Anything to avoid descending into the depths of the City looking for some ancient blood-soaked goatherder's cave, which was where he was afraid this might all wind up at the end of things. He'd seen far too much horror already. He'd created it as well, in the dwarf pits, whispered a voice deep in his head. He was no better than any of them.

Quiet was strangely hard to come by on the streets. Bells pealed across the city, though neither Bijaz nor Archer could think why. A clatter of bailiffs and armed servants swarmed Margolin Avenue, so the two dwarfs doubled back to Forth Street to head west toward the River Saltus. Water Street might get them past the Limerock Palace. Failing that, Bijaz thought he should be able to hire a man to row them up along the dockside.

As they walked, they found themselves alternately facing and crossing a stream of people heading toward the Limerock Palace.

"Is it another riot?" Bijaz wondered aloud.

"There's no smell of smoke," said Archer. "Nothing's been set alight. These folk do not seem so angry. Those bells are ringing from all over the city. They'd hardly be sounding out in the Temple District for an uprising at the palace."

"We've got to get to Jason." As they crossed Orogene Avenue near the docks, Bijaz pushed through a knot of ragged women bearing something on their shoulders. "Keep him out of it this time."

One of the giant dogs from last night moved by, hurrying quickly on the shoulders of two men. Bijaz paused and turned to look. "A bacchanal? There's no festival today."

He realized a stream of women was heading toward the palace, bearing small body after small body. With a sick lurch in his stomach, the dwarf knew these were eyeless beggar children, the dead from the winch tower.

"They mourn," said Archer quietly.

Bijaz felt his anger roiling. "And in mourning they only feed its power all the more." How were they to stop this?

"We should follow these people. I am afraid your Imago will be at the center of things."

"He couldn't have already declared the Trial of Flowers!"

"Acting on the heels of the riots," Archer said. "It makes sense. They want to make their move on the office of Lord Mayor before the Inner Chamber creates some new mischief. Who knows what sacrifices they're attempting inside the Limerock Palace right now?"

"Not that the Inner Chamber has the least idea about how the gods have figured into this. To make matters worse, our idiots are likely staging the greatest bacchanal we've ever had."

"The greatest summoning..."

The dwarfs began running with the crowd, rather than through it, dodging legs and pushing past as many people as they could. Bijaz never hated his size so much as now, when the stumpy, stunted legs of the boxed slowed them in their race to save the City.

Whatever warrants the courts of the Assemblage had out for Bijaz would not have mattered amid the crowd in Terminus Plaza. An army of bailiffs could not have winkled him out of the mass of shouting, shrieking people. Half the city must have turned out there. He'd never seen anything of the sort.

Here being small was an advantage. Both Bijaz and Archer, like almost all boxed dwarfs, had nearly the upper body strength of the full-men they would have been in other circumstances. This meant they could both throw a wicked elbow into an unsuspecting gut or kidney, and plow forward by main force where possible.

The problem was they couldn't see anything. They were forced to follow the direction the full-men and -women were facing. They had no other way to set their course, save by the swell of the noise.

Somehow Bijaz made it to the edge of the crowd, to a point where he could see open cobbles. The Riverward Gate stood across the clear ground, boarded up from within by some wooden barrier. He could make out the

First Counselor Arran Prothro atop the gate, along with a number of other Burgesses and their bailiffs.

Imago rode into the circle mounted on a camelopard, followed by Jason and some idiot wearing a bacchanal flower costume. The crowd shrieked, a roar loud enough to overwhelm Bijaz's hearing.

"Stop it," he screamed. "Stop it now!" Bijaz broke through the first rank to race onto the cobbles, and was struck down by an armed man in gray leather. He got a boot to the ribs as the guard shouted something the dwarf couldn't hear.

One of the Winter Boys, protecting the new Lord Mayor.

"Im–a–go…Im–a–go…Im–a–go…" the crowd screamed.

On his camelopard, facing the Rose ahorse, Imago of Lockwood raised his lance and answered them.

Groaning on the ground, Bijaz knew what must come next.

JASON THE FACTOR

Imago shouted his words of challenge. Beneath Jason's seat the camelopard danced nervously. Like Imago, he'd lost his handler stepping into the open space. He'd also lost the vertigo that had first seized him on mounting the overtall creature—too much was demanded of his attention right now. Jason glanced up at the gatehouse and the wall stretching in each direction. Arms and armor up there, but they were waiting, too. The First Counselor looked directly at him.

Of course the man was. Jason was one of two figures identifiable in a crowd of tens upon tens of thousands. He nodded at Prothro, who nodded back.

Imago was still shouting. A ripple of silence spread away from him as people strained to hear the new Lord Mayor. Nothing was so pregnant with power as a hundred thousand people holding their breath, Jason realized.

"I come to challenge," Imago shouted. His voice boomed. How was he doing that? Even Jason shouldn't be able to hear the man clearly from ten yards away, but the noise of his words was growing like thunder. Jason turned, watching the crowd. Had Ducôte planted some priest or hedge wizard with the power of sound?

What he saw was Bijaz struggling under the boot of one of the Winter Boys. The dwarf's face was twisted, flushed with some effort.

"By the Trial of Flowers, I shall prevail upon you to acclaim me Lord Mayor."

Bijaz caught Jason's gaze. The dwarf was shivering, shaking his head, the sutures of his mouth twitching as he shouted something. Jason tried to turn his camelopard toward Bijaz, but he was caught in place. A noumenal attack, here?

"Come, Sir Rose." Imago's voice echoed like a storm moving across the downlands. "I call you out for the Trial of Flowers."

Jason could read the movement of Bijaz's lips now. "*No!*" He turned his head, which was still his to control, wondering if the pressure on him would stop his breath next. Or worse, burst him into flames.

Imago dropped his lance, the tip pointing toward the mounted Rose. Sir Rose in turn drew a sword like a great, black thorn. Where had he gotten that, Jason wondered? The air around him was almost gelid.

Something dreadful was happening. This was not what they had meant to do, call forth terrible magic.

The Rose charged Imago. Imago whipped his camelopard into motion to meet the oncoming horse, with a strange look upon his face. Jason stretched his hand, as if he could somehow push through the solid air to stop them. The world was running too slowly, off time, the entire City Imperishable under noumenal influence.

"No," he whispered, echoing Bijaz.

"*Yes,*" roared the crowd, thousands of mouths speaking the word at the same time, the sound rippling with the distance of the far corners of the plaza.

Imago's lance met the Rose's thorn and shattered it. The Rose tried to turn away from the point, but the camelopard was moving too fast for the flower knight. The lance entered the flower's face, a point in the tall costume far above the rider's head, Jason knew, but still the blossom exploded in a spray of blood.

In that moment, the pressure on him was released, as people began to shriek. The Rose collapsed into a blizzard of blood-red petals as the horse turned from its charge to avoid ramming into the boarded-up Riverward Gate. Jason wheeled his own mount, heading for Bijaz. Somewhat to his surprise, the camelopard responded to the rein.

In the massed expanse of citizens filling Terminus Plaza, horrid things were breaking loose. Great dogs leapt snarling and snapping, throwing bodies from their jaws. A brilliant silver fish pushed through the crowd with razored fins. People were surging in any direction, falling beneath the pressure of their fellows. Enormous roses showing teeth within their petals exploded upward in a shower of paving stones and torn limbs.

The camelopard nearly ran down the Winter Boy standing over Bijaz. Jason leaned as far as he dared, calling, "Give him to me."

The Winter Boy hauled the dwarf to his feet, then shook his head. Jason understood. Bijaz weighed far too much to be lifted like a child. "Under me, then," he shouted. The camelopard might protect him from some of the riot that was spreading.

Bijaz and another dwarf—the godmonger, Jason realized—scuttled into the cage of the camelopard's legs even as several other Winter Boys converged on the animal as a rallying point. The value of these ridiculous mounts was becoming more apparent to him. Unfortunately, he was not trained to ride to war, or really to ride at all.

The Winter Boys knew their business, though. They formed a circle of swords and pistols, even as the bailiffs on the walls began firing at the noumenal monsters ravaging through the crowds.

When the rifled muskets erupted, the people crowded in the plaza lost what little organization remained to them and dissolved into a mob united by blood and terror. It was all Jason could do to hold his reins tight and pray that one of those great, black dogs did not come for him.

He sat with his back to the wall of the Limerock Palace, watching the shadows of late afternoon stretch across Terminus Plaza. Smoke rose from many of the buildings on the far side of the open space. Hundreds of bodies were scattered across the pavers, and far too many body parts.

Someone handed Jason a tight-rolled cigarette. He shook his head—he did not smoke—but obscurely now wished that he did. Though no blow had landed directly upon him, the rush of panicked people that had finally toppled his mount had also of necessity brought Jason hard to the ground. He and the two dwarfs had continued to hide against the great corpse while the Winter Boys fought, mostly to keep the rush of panic from trampling them.

Eventually the noise and crush had lessened, then in the space of a few moments, they were alone save for the dead and wounded. The noumenal monsters were vanished. He looked up as someone stood over him.

Imago.

The new Lord Mayor, his title bought on the blood of the City, extended a hand. "Come," Imago said. Jason could see that he was exhausted, too. "We must speak with the First Counselor."

Jason took the hand and allowed himself to be levered to his feet. He looked around. Bijaz lay on his back, but still breathing. Archer was propped next to Bijaz, the godmonger leaning against the shoulder of a Winter Boy who was covered in blood.

"You knew, didn't you?" Jason asked. He could barely recognize his own voice.

Bijaz opened one bruised eye. "I tried. I was too late."

"Tell me another time."

The dwarf nodded as Jason followed Imago to the gate. The barrier was gone, though whether torn down in the rioting or removed afterward by the defenders Jason had no way to tell.

Prothro stood flanked by two bailiffs. "My Lord Mayor," he said, with a sharp nod.

"You do not dispute my accession, then, my lord counselor?"

"I fear the point may have been rendered moot. There have been…changes…within the Limerock Palace. This has been a busy day."

"What sort of changes, if I may be so bold?"

The First Counselor smiled, a quirk of the lips that was gone so fast Jason was not sure it had ever been there. "Boldness hardly enters into it, sir. Humility might be more to the point."

"I'm tired of games," said Jason. "Do not play us further, Prothro."

"Then show your obeisance to the Imperator Ignatius. Our ruler has returned to his city." Prothro dropped to his knee, half-turning to face back into the Pilean Gardens.

Jason stared. Ignatius of Redtower stood beyond, left ear torn to a stump, wearing a maroon robe trimmed with fur. He stared back at Jason with a blank expression, then nodded once. "I am returned," he announced, speaking to no one in particular. "Let all who are loyal citizens of the City Imperishable bend their knees to their rightful Imperator."

Beside Jason, Imago dropped to one knee. "Sire, as Lord Mayor I welcome your return to the City."

It could not be. Ignatius never wanted power, had struggled valiantly to keep it spread among many men. Jason had not understood his reasons, but the noumenal wars Ignatius and his family line fought for generations rested on that premise—this much he knew. Just as he knew that Ignatius was heir to the Imperator Terminus. The ruler's face was on the coin, almost a ringer for the Second Counselor.

Terminus was the last ruler. But Ignatius was Jason's master. Was his duty to his master's life work, or to the words this man spoke now? For Jason was nowhere near certain this was his Ignatius. Some fetch or possession from the noumenal world seemed far more likely.

Still, he slowly bent his knee and dropped to the stones. "Master, I welcome your return," he said.

"Indeed." Imperator Ignatius' voice sounded as if it echoed from a distance. "We accept your pledge of faith." He turned and walked away.

After a few moments, Prothro stood. "Several people tried to stop him when he entered the Great Hall," he said almost casually. "They thought it was some trick of yours. He slew six men with fingertips and words. After that they let him find the Bladed Throne on his own."

"That's not Ignatius," said Jason firmly. "His order of philosophick doctors practices a sort of, well, balance of action. Were he to kill, he would take a mortal wound. That's why he has always used agents."

"I know you do not care for me," Prothro retorted, "but grant me credit for some wit. I've worked with him daily for years, which is far more than a dock rat such as yourself can claim. I know that's not Ignatius. Or if it is he, he's so changed as to be a different man. Still, he has long been widely rumored as the heir. He does seem to kill with a word. What do you propose to do to unseat him?"

"Nothing." Imago said, his voice sharp and tired. "Let him sit, see what he does. The whole point of these last few days was to temper the power of the Assemblage so that we might better meet the threats to the City than you have done. He seems to have accomplished that tempering all on his own."

"Certainly, your honor." Prothro's tone made the title a condemnation. "Sit he shall. Sit you shall, for I do not care to have the Limerock Palace torn down around my ears by your mobs." The First Counselor reached within the brocade of his robes and brought out a golden chain, with bright jewels glittering in every second link. "Here. Your chain of office, retrieved from the vaults where it has sat safe all these centuries. I wish you the joy of it."

Imago took the chain, turned it over in his hand. "Why?" he asked after a brief inspection.

"That the thing may be done right," Prothro said. "None may say later I stood in your way. You see, Lord Mayor, I shall grant you this scrying, from nothing more than my own good sense. You won't rule two weeks, and will fall of no deed of mine. His Magnificence won't long outlast you. There's more afoot than you know, and dangers coming you cannot imagine."

"I watched those black dogs tearing at the people of this city," said Imago. "I can imagine much."

"Not enough." Prothro stalked away with his escort.

"I think," Jason said to Imago in a quiet voice, "that you might consider making your offices somewhere outside the Limerock Palace for the nonce."

The two of them turned to find Bijaz leaning against the gate arch. "It's...it's worse than you know," the dwarf stammered. "I have seen what is coming. Archer—the godmonger—showed me too much."

"Let you go elsewhere and make plans to stem the coming tide," Jason said. "Do not linger here."

He watched Imago and Bijaz make their way across Terminus Plaza, past torn and trampled bodies, heading slowly for some assumed place of safety by the river, he supposed. Jason turned to follow his master, with a last long glance at his former, if not friends, at least allies. There were no more words, just smoke and the stench of death and the dying of the day to see them on their way.

II
OLD GODS DANCE IN WINTER

IMAGO OF LOCKWOOD

The foretellings of early autumn had born their frosty fruit: winter's hard hand was set early upon the City Imperishable, even before the Festival of Winter Drownings, which normally played harbinger to the first hard freeze. The Lord Mayor sat in his office midway up the Rugmaker's Cupola and stared out a frost-rimed window at the landscape of stone and snow that stretched before him. He'd chosen a room that afforded a view to the south and west, keeping the Limerock Palace and the ugly pile of the Sudgate beyond in view at all times.

Sometimes he thought that might have been a mistake, though he took petty pleasure from the burn scars and charred beams poking through the roof of the Ilion Wing, visible even from this distance.

However, the location itself was not a mistake. It was quite clear from the first that he wouldn't take up his gold chain of authority inside the palace. Out of practical necessity he'd first officed out of Ducôte's scriptorium. Then the Worshipful Guild of Rugmakers offered him the use of their tower atop Nannyback Hill. The chance to legitimately get away from the old dwarf, who'd continued to treat Imago like a dull-witted servant even after his elevation to office, was too good to pass up.

Once he'd moved into the Rugmaker's Cupola, Imago took an immediate liking to the high place—it lent him status without claiming overmuch ostentation. The spacious office was carpeted with hand-woven rugs from all across the lands which had encompassed the old empire. The rugs he'd kept, though he'd removed the antiques and their display cases and replaced them with drafting tables and maps upon the walls, along with more modern accessories such as the ball-calligraph and, somewhat to his amazement, a functional telelocutor. Though there was no one to ring up on that device save the Limerock Palace. Imago seriously doubted whether anyone there had interest in speaking with him.

The tower gave the room a truncated wedge shape, which had taken some getting used to. The biggest problem here was the unholy racket when the iron bells tolled at evening and morning. The great virtue of the room was that he possessed a view like no one else in the City Imperishable except for the steeplejacks and bell ringers. A view which held more advantages than simply being an overwatch on the beating heart of power. For one, he could see the River Saltus, and a good third or more of the docks, which told him much about who was tied up there and how the business of the city was flowing. It did not take Imago long to learn how to distinguish the classes of merchantmen who came up the river.

There were the low-riding plantation lighters bringing cotton, hardwood and oils from the Jade Coast. Thralls sculled those ships up the river, crews who never touched shore because slavery was banned within the City Imperishable itself, although not in the territories around. He'd seen fewer and fewer of these vessels as the season chilled. Onesiphorous had told him that was normal for this point in the progress of the year.

He could also spot the high-masted ocean traders, great tall clippers that came from the Sunward Sea and sometimes beyond. Often those ships sailed under loans and papers from the City Imperishable, which explained why they called here at the most inconvenient port of their run. Lately their crosstrees and lines glittered with ice often as not, something that the foreign masters and their dark-skinned crews hated bitterly. Hate set sailors to drinking hard, Young Morgan Smithsson the Portmaster told him, and drunken sailors spent their coin ashore. Imago had directed Smithsson to delay the paperwork and dock assignments of the southern ships to keep them idle an extra day or three. This led to a few more brawls and murders than might otherwise be expected, but money was money.

The others were a little more challenging for him to distinguish. To his eye everything that floated in the water had always been much the same, from turds to logs to boats, but he was learning. Cattleboats and softwood lumber scows from upriver looked much the same to him, but he could separate them from the tramp traders that worked the downstream course of the River Saltus and the meandering snake-filled greenways of the Jade Coast. Of course, there were the all-important coal barges, without which the City Imperishable would lack for heat, and steam.

And so forth and so forth, ship after barge after boat in a profusion of types, each with its own significance.

The docks were the life of the City, he was told time and again by earnest elderly guildsmen, and those few proud syndics willing to risk the wrath of the Limerock Palace to meet with him. At least the regular people of the city still shouted his name, though the crowds around him grew ever smaller.

Fewer ships were there each day. Much fewer than the reduced traffic of the season should account for. The blood of the City Imperishable flowed in those hulls of wood and iron.

"What's this?" Imago asked, jolted from his reverie by Onesiphorous handing him another sheet of paper. Possibly the hundredth of the day, he'd lost track long since. Who had performed the duties of this miserable job in the days when the Assemblage of Burgesses held all power? It was no help at all that the Tribade sent him little notes with polite reminders of matters that needed attending to. Ducôte in his turn seemed further alienated each day from Imago, willfully ignorant of the minutiae of running an entire city. The old bastard chose to express himself through increasingly angry circulars demanding ever faster progress on behalf of the city's dwarfs.

"Petition from the freeriders for winter space for their camelopards. It's too late to send them south, Enero's master of mounts claims they won't survive the voyage."

Ah, some new irritation, Imago thought. "And let me guess. We can't stable them because they're taller than a building…"

"Exactly."

Onesiphorous looked miserable, haggard, beaten down by the never-ending flow of detail this office required. Imago knew exactly how the dwarf felt. He had taken the Slashed leader on as his First Counselor a day following the Trial of Flowers on Bijaz's recommendation after Jason twice refused to leave the Limerock Palace and take the job. Having another dwarf working closely with him had also helped to get the increasingly peevish Ducôte out of his affairs.

In the weeks since, they had been buried in paper, rumor and fear. After the massacre in Terminus Plaza, the noumenal attacks all but ceased; the Assemblage had canceled all outside hearings and audiences while the Burgesses writhed under the slow but crushing thumb of the restored Imperator. The city was quieter than it had been since the beginning of the summer, but a Tokhari force was closing in, with their Yellow Mountain allies. Worse, anyone with any sense of the noumenal world was issuing dire warnings of disaster, some of them on the street corners in loud voices. That the attacks were lessened so much only made people avoid the barkers all the more.

"Camelopards…" The idiot detail of the decisions required of him continued to amaze. "I have no idea. What am I supposed to do with camelopards?"

"We can refuse the petition, sir," said Onesiphorous in a tone of voice that made it clear he thought that a dreadful idea.

"No, we cannot. The Winter Boys are the only forces I have that are both loyal and competent. We will need them badly on the walls all too soon, I fear. And besides, I owe them everything including my life from the day of the

Trial." He thought about how tall the damned camelopards were. "I know. Put them in one of the krewe houses off Fishtrap Lane. The one where I got the flower. If that old watchman is still alive…Gordo. If Gordo is still alive, make him the stablemaster. He could use the wage."

"I believe that house belongs to the Krewe of Balnea. What shall I tell them about their costumes and materials, sir?"

"Tell them it's an honor to serve the City, by Dorgau's fig. Grant them a monopoly on a processional route or something. That will shut them up."

"Mmm." Onesiphorous nodded, then left, mumbling further.

At least there had been no need to sign that one. His hand still hurt from the cut of the bailiff's sword, back in the courtroom the night of the riot, while demand for his signature burgeoned daily.

Imago turned his attention to the window once more. The snowfall had resumed without. Which, in a sense, was the worst problem of all. The Little Bull River was low and muddy from some ice dam blocking the flow up beyond the Rose Downs. An ice dam! This early, before the Festival of Winter Drownings. They should only see one of these every ten years, and not til Duodecembres at the earliest. Many in the city drew their water from the Little Bull, as did the municipal pumps. Who knew there were municipal pumps? He did, now, and he also knew their intakes were fouled with mud and sitting right at the water line, instead of a comfortable fathom or more below the surface of a free-running current.

To further complicate matters, wells all over the city—especially south of the Little Bull—were going bad. The water came up black and sulfurous. The continuous freezing was damaging pipes all over town. Only a fool or a desperate man would drink from the River Saltus no matter what the season.

A city which sat at the confluence of two rivers was running out of water. That idiot First Counselor had made it abundantly clear that the Imperator's will was for the Lord Mayor to handle matters that fell within the walls of the City Imperishable. Prothro was also kind enough to remind him that the Limerock Palace had always enjoyed water and sewers as a gift from a grateful city.

The whole while, the Restorationists and the Lord Mayor's men were brawling and sometimes killing each other in the streets, contending for control of the districts and key locales in a very slow form of civil war. For all the good they were doing the city, the Inner Chamber apparently sat in the Sapphire Court and laughed.

Debtor's prison would have been easier. Far, far easier.

His door creaked open again. "My lord Second Counselor is here to see you," said Marelle, one of Onesiphorous' small battalion of dwarfesses who kept his offices running. She was small, even for a dwarfess, and pale as snow with flaxen hair. Something had gone wrong in the boxing of her, he supposed, though she would have been pretty in a fragile way as a full-woman.

Imago nodded. "Very well." The sting of Jason's defection from his cause on the day of the Trial of Flowers was somewhat abated. The crush of city business was sufficient anodyne for almost any hurt. They had not been friends, truly, more allies of convenience. Though he'd owed Jason a greater debt than either Ducôte or the dark sisters, his very life in fact, Jason also held fewer commitments from Imago.

Such calculations. He rubbed a sting of dust from his eyes. This office took the heart from everything.

In any event, he hadn't seen or heard from Jason in weeks. News was not absent—shortly after the Trial of Flowers, the Limerock Palace had sent criers and handbills all over the city proclaiming that the people's favorite had been elevated to the Inner Chamber to advise the restored Imperator.

That day had seen the first significant drop in his own support. Imago fingered the gold chain of his office where it lay upon his desk, wondering if it was meant to remind him of his burden, or more properly broadcast his servitude to the rest of the City Imperishable. Like the office it symbolized, the jeweled gaud was a pretty trap, given to him by Arran Prothro with open malice. Imago had been none the wiser until it was far too late.

Jason looked, if anything, worse than Onesiphorous. And so, by extension, probably also looked worse than Imago himself. Well-dressed, to the new standards of the new court, but eyes like pissholes in old mud and hair brittle as its straw color. The Second Counselor had been a handsome enough man until recently.

Imago rose to embrace his visitor, but Jason waved him off. "Please, no, do not…touch…me."

The Lord Mayor leaned back against the edge of his desk. "What does that mean?"

Jason threw off a stained greatcloak as he sank into a chair and stared upward at Imago. "It means that in the Great Hall we are sometimes sniffed."

"Sniffed?" His imagination offered up a picture of palace clerks with their noses in the air.

His erstwhile friend's gaze remained bleak. "His Magnificence has some new servants. Certain among them possess an unusually acute sense of smell. I have seen two men so far named traitor by these blind sniffers and slain upon the steps before the Bladed Throne on accusation of having met with enemies of the Imperator. Accusation by sniff, mind you."

"Yet you come here?"

"I believe so long as I do not touch you nor sit in your accustomed chair, I will be as safe as I might ever be."

"Ah." Imago dreaded the next question. "What manner of man is it that has such a wonderful nose as to smell treason on another's sweat?"

"Truly you do not wish to know."

"I see." He walked across the room to the one piece of furniture he'd kept after taking this chamber over as his office—a good-sized liquor cabinet. Imago took down two large brandy snifters, which he proceeded to violate by pouring out generous helpings of Rose Downs rye. The stuff was the color of old urine, pungent enough to stun rats, and did not even begin to rank against the better distillates from the quarreling towns far to the north and west that were the old Highland Kingdoms. On the other hand it was strong and it tasted of the City Imperishable.

Home, whatever that meant amid the settling in of this killing winter.

"Here." Imago handed one of the snifters to Jason. He retreated to a drafting stool some feet away, to sit with a map of the sewer mains at his back.

Jason lifted the snifter and drained half the helping in one gulp. That had to burn his throat, Imago thought, but this was clearly a man lost to the milder forms of sensation. Imago watched his visitor gasp for breath in the wake of the harsh liquor, and waited for him to speak his piece.

After a minute or so of staring into the snifter, Jason looked up and met Imago's eyes again. "It's not him," he blurted.

"I presume you refer to our glorious overlord?"

"Yes. It's Ignatius, or something precisely like him. I mean, even the ear matches." Imago did not quite track that comment, but Jason carried on. "He's not the same man, though. He used to live under, well, covenants. As a philosophick doctor. They find their wisdom and power through careful bargaining with the noumenal world. It seems that he has come to have only power, without wisdom. My master seems to have forgotten his own bargains."

"He seems to have forgotten civil order in the process," said Imago. "Since I further presume it has not been you directing the Restorationist gangs running the streets."

"No. That would be Green Kelly, lately steward to my lord Second Counselor and now advisor to the Imperator. He has taken to his measure of authority with a glee that would be unseemly in a weasel loosed among new-hatched chicks. He is also a great believer in having people *sniffed*. He works to the will of the Imperator. As best as anyone can tell, at any rate."

Jason sounded defeated, but Imago did not miss the clue. "'As best as anyone can tell?' Is His Magnificence unclear of speech?"

"No... His Magnificence is all too clear of speech. Sometimes his words are bent strangely, as if he were talking around corners or through a mirror."

Imago shuddered. That description came perilously close to what Bijaz and Archer had described to him of their noumenal misadventures immediately after the Trial of Flowers. Bijaz had since vanished. His office-quarters on Bentpin Alley burned at the cost of the entire building and the deaths of three of those within, though no dwarf corpse was found. The dead child in the ashes was not of the family of cobblers who had lived below him, which was more than passing strange. No one had been able to locate the dwarf since. He had not come to the house on Fireside Street in the North Wall District where his befuddled wife still dwelt.

As for the godmonger, Archer declined to be party to the new city government. He took once more to the streets instead. Imago's City Men—his unfortunately rough answer to the Restorationists—brought occasional reports of the dwarf haranguing people in the markets, inciting them to rise against the Temple District.

He thought he understood where Archer's heart lay in the matter of the noumenal, but with the return of the Imperator the attacks had ceased. For that alone most citizens were more than pleased to bend their necks to the courtesy of the title. Relief about the City Imperishable was so great that folk paid little heed to the rantings of quondam madmen.

That His Magnificence's pronouncements of state should be, as Jason said, "bent strangely," was more than a little disturbing. Imago could not imagine that the labors inherent in ruling from the Limerock Palace were so much less than his own.

"What brings you here?" he asked. "Surely you cannot afford to simply bear tales, fascinating and horrifying as they may be." Rumors—Imago heard rumors by the bushel, but this was the first confirmation of any of them.

"We…" Jason took a smaller sip this time of the rye, then tried again. "We did not have time enough in the moments we met to forge any true friendship, my Lord Mayor. I would like to think we are not unfriends, either."

"Not at all." Imago twirled the stem of his own glass, watching the rye slop within the snifter and wondering why this man to whom he owed his life had become so fearful. Many possible reasons presented themselves, but which of them served to undermine Jason's fierce loyalty to Ignatius of Redtower, and in turn his loyalty to Ignatius' idea of the City Imperishable?

"As I said, he is not himself. He is something darker, stranger, twisted. He is all too clearly of this city. I first wondered if this was some bizarre prologue of the coming invasion. His Magnificence has never deigned to explain his disappearance, and it is not unreasonable to imagine Alates, or noumenal forces, in league with the Tokhari and their Yellow Mountain allies."

"Not in league with those who come, I think," said Imago.

Jason was disturbed from his channel of thought. "Why not?"

"What Bijaz and Archer the godmonger told me. Something I am willing to believe." He waved. "Continue. I shall explain another time if circumstances warrant."

"He sits upon the throne, and sometimes he drools. Ignatius of Redtower, drooling. The Imperator Restored, *drooling*. While maggots like Green Kelly and Prothro run to do his bidding, building up wealth and power and funds of terror by the day. This cannot be what was meant for us."

"What of Zaharias of Fallen Arch? And the rest of the Inner Chamber?"

"Zaharias marches his bailiffs and their new recruits about the gardens while avoiding the throne at all costs. I do not think the First Counselor cares over-much what the Provost is about, not now with all power concentrating at the Bladed Throne. His Magnificence does not seem to have noted the absence of his master of bailiffs. The others have variously fallen into line or found urgent business to keep them in their own quarters as much as possible."

That might explain why the bailiffs had not been much on the streets, Imago realized. "The Imperator allows the arms within the Limerock Palace to stay in the hands of the Provost's men, whom he does not trouble to oversee? That is rather difficult to believe."

"I think they are beyond caring. Zaharias has let it be known that he builds forces to meet the coming armies. His Magnificence has…other means…to meet the threat."

"The Old Gods," said Imago shortly.

Jason looked startled. "You know?"

"What I meant before, about the noumenal not being in league with our invaders. Bijaz and Archer worked it out, the day of the Trial. They believe our mummery before the palace's Riverward Gate might have been the sum-moning that brought Ignatius back to us."

"As may be. I am here, my Lord Mayor, to plead for your help in somehow stopping or redirecting what is to come. The sniffers are only the beginning, Imago. It becomes much worse inside the walls, and soon that horror will flow out into the streets."

"Where it becomes my problem," Imago said. He sighed, stood and turned to look out the window again. Snow was falling now, though the Limerock Palace was still dimly visible in the white haze. It was pretty from this height, a gingercake palace covered with sugar.

But there was blood baked within.

"I had hoped…" Imago leaned his forehead against the freezing glass. "I had hoped the babblings that drove Bijaz and Archer each to their madness were just that—babblings. The quiet in the noumenal world seemed to prove them wrong. Ignatius' return had settled that problem. I thought.

"I have set my efforts to strengthening the walls, righting the wrongs against our dwarfs and begging them to stay in place and call their cousins home. Wages for good clerks have tripled, did you know that? A Lord Mayor must be aware of these things. Too many with the skill of accounting have fled. This makes commerce more costly, and drives some to shutter their doors. In turn that means less coin for the city coffers, reducing our ability to pay for restoration of the walls, pay for your mercenaries—who are thankfully willing to answer to me now—pay, pay, pay. All a city does is pay."

Jason grunted. "All an Imperator does is take, it seems. His court pays. And the City will pay much, much more soon, if we do not stop him."

"Stop your master?" Imago laughed, though his throat seemed likely to close up. "Well, and it may even be that I agree with you. Your tale makes what the dwarfs told me all the more real. Not that I had truly thought they lied. I merely prayed for delusion." He turned to stare down at Jason. "The best thing you could do is stay where you are. Serve your master. Tell me of what may be coming next. I will seek out Bijaz and Archer, however they can be found, and see what might be set against the Old Gods. For you see, the secret they told me was that it is the threat of the Old Gods' return that draws our enemies toward us."

Jason nodded. "It makes too much sense, though it sickens me. That means every rite and spill of blood within the Limerock Palace only makes our danger worse."

"I will gather what power I can," Imago promised Jason.

The Second Counselor nodded, rose and wrapped himself in his cloak.

"Jason…" Imago said.

"Yes?"

"Send what word you can, but do not die for the task. Leave before it is too late."

"It is already far too late." For a moment, Jason's pisshole eyes had deepened to wells of endless darkness. "I thank you all the same."

Imago watched him go, and wished all he had to worry about were the municipal pumps.

BIJAZ THE DWARF

He shivered in a cloud of violet smoke. It was what the sellers called "crap dust"—the worst of the narcotic powder, scrapings from the grinding wheels and catchments of a violet cutting house, sold only in back alleys because no reputable trader would keep the stuff behind a counter where decent dwarfs might shop. Bijaz had long since passed through desperation to some trembling point of nihilistic humiliation. His arse still bled whenever he was forced to shit, so he ate as little as possible. Even crap dust cost money, so he cut the Sewn knots from his lips and sold himself suckling the cocks of farmers and drovers while he squatted before them in the nose-searing latrines of the city's markets. If he could, he would have turned the fig, but the continuing pain in his colon made that impossible.

There was nothing left of himself that he wanted, save the vague glimmer of peace that he found somewhere inside the violet smoke. Finally he understood the place to which his wife had long since retreated.

Sometimes, when the snow was not so deep and he'd managed a little soup or coffee, Bijaz thought about making his way to the townhouse on Fireside Street and apologizing to his wife. He wasn't sure she'd understand him though—the crap dust had begun to rot his teeth, getting in all too quickly through the breaks, and his tongue was always dry as leather and twice too big.

His one small thanks to luck and fate was that the sores he had lately developed were within his mouth. If they had festered on his lips, even the farmboys wouldn't have paid him for suck. As it was, pus on their cocks looked little different from their own pale come, and he never said a thing.

Most of the time the crap dust gave him muscle spasms, so severe on occasion that he'd once cracked two ribs, and something had been wrong with his left hand for days. If he fell asleep without the dust, eyeless children haunted his dreams. Young full-men dragging dead horses behind them while they bled from cheeks and guts and groins followed him, calling his name, begging for just a token of his mercy.

Bijaz had no mercy to give the dead, had surrendered that long ago, so he bought his own mercy in suck and smoke.

It was all he had.

This day he'd been lucky: a cartload of fieldhands from the downlands come in looking for winter work after the last slaughter, and willing to spend two orichalks apiece to start their day in style. Bijaz made enough in the first hour of the morning to get up off his knees and find some cat soup from one of the crusted pots set up among the crumbling buildings hard by the Green Market. Within some of those walls were little outposts of the Sudgate Districts' miserable poverty that he'd never realized existed this high up the hill.

He'd learned that even the well-off and their servants had needs that could not be met in ordinary ways. The dwarf pits where he had once pleasured himself at the sight of death were as ordinary as a baker's tray next to some of what took place in shadowed rooms here under watchful, gleaming eyes. It took the truly desperate to sell their bodies piece by bloody piece, and eventually their lives.

Bijaz knew that day would come soon enough for him.

Any of it, all of it, was better than those eyes in the river. The voice had told him to sacrifice a life, a limb, a love. He supposed he was doing that now, giving up whatever he cared for in the City Imperishable. That would be love. He knew he was burning his own life away, but the crap dust was better than the pain of memory.

Limbs were easy. He could make a handful of silver obols in some of the shadowed rooms by allowing himself to be cut. Of course, he would lack a hand to carry the coin after the third or fourth session.

Where the hells was his path, he wondered. Bijaz then realized he must have spoken his thoughts aloud, as the cat soup woman was glaring at him and brandishing her ladle.

" 'm sorry," he tried to say, but one of his teeth dropped into the cracked mug he'd rented to eat his soup.

"Fool!" she screeched. "Now I gots to wash that. You owes me another chalk-ie for lost rent and labor, you does. Get out, you fecking sot of a dwarf."

He was almost done anyway. Bijaz pushed away without paying her the last chalkie. She rewarded this with a shower of boiled-down bones. He did not bother to pluck them off.

It was time for more crap dust. Eleven farm boy cocks had brought him enough money for double a day's dose. He was having trouble with his feet, but there was a friendly wall to sag against.

Eyes in the river. And the eyeless dead.

The horror, the thing that had driven him from his offices on Bentpin Alley, would not leave his memory no matter how hard Bijaz tried to banish it. Bricks against his head, trash around his thighs, his sense of smell burned to cinders by the crap dust and the world he now moved through, Bijaz lived it once more, his crusted lips moving in a voiceless scream.

It did not matter. No one would come.

No one would ever come for him again, save for *them*.

He'd been sleeping, back when he could still do that. The bed was chilly enough to peeve him, as the gas line had developed a blockage he'd not found time to have fixed, while his little firebrick stove refused to work. The windows were shut against the cold.

It was two days after the Trial of Flowers. Imago was still being touched by silent hands everywhere he went—the cheering had gone out of the mob with the massacre at Terminus Plaza, but blame had fallen mostly on Bijaz and Archer for ruining the ceremony with some ill-gotten dwarfish magic. Thank the lords of all hells so few of the working men actually knew his name. The ones who believed in the Lord Mayor followed Imago, waiting for his blessing, while the rest camped and prayed in Terminus Plaza, begging for the Imperator Restored to show himself again.

Bijaz could not help wondering when his complicity would be found out.

Archer was becoming increasingly difficult to locate. Imago offered guards for his door, Winter Boys to stand over him or a place at the Lord Mayor's side in Ducôte's scriptorium, where the new government was first being assembled in feverish haste.

He'd refused. "I'm my own dwarf. How will it look among the Sewn if I hide behind full-men?" he'd said, with the last pride he'd ever known. He would scarcely admit he had no kidney at all for remaining close to the River Saltus day and night. Not with those children's eyes in the water.

Something disturbed him. A flutter of snow from the eaves of the cobblery over which he rented his offices. A noise out of place. Since the winch tower, Bijaz had been very well attuned to odd sounds. He awoke quickly, wondering if he had been sleeping or merely dreaming he was asleep.

Either way his arse burned like fire.

What was it?

A sniffle. An animal?

Then a footfall on his stair. Just one, the intruder stopping to listen for an alarm.

Bijaz wished then he owned a pistol, though he'd certainly just injure himself with one of the bailiffs' pepperboxes. He reached with slow care for the iron bar beneath his bed. He'd carried it home the day before as pilferage from a worksite down near the Little Bull River.

Another sniffle. Bijaz knew something was at his door. He slipped from the bedclothes as quietly as he could move, though his old bones were stiff with the cold, and cocked the bar high. There would only be one thief or assassin—had they come in a group, they would not have bothered with the stealth. He felt an echo of fear from the night of his rape—but how much damage could one man do?

The latch handle twitched as if pawed by a dog. They would have to break it down, for Bijaz had drawn the chain and turned the lock. Another sniff, another rattle of the latch.

The hair on his spine and neck stiffened as the little brass fitting of the lock twisted on its own. Bijaz's spine shivered. There was no key outside, he was certain. Had they a pick? The lock shuddered once more as the latch had done, then flipped with a quiet little snick.

When the chain began to move of its own accord, he knew he was undone. Bijaz stepped back from the door, dropping his bar with a rattle and bang that should have woken the monks down the street. He fumbled for his oil lamp, cursing the absence of his gas, wanting very badly in that moment to have light, heat, flame.

He turned with the wick fresh-lit and the glass chimney in his other hand as the door slid open. A girl child stood there, eyeless and naked, old blood crusted around the vacant sockets. His scream died in his throat as hot piss bloomed down his leg.

The Old Gods had sent one of the children for him.

In the flickering light of his lamp, Bijaz could see the girl had skin gray as rotten meat. She reeked of river water. For one moment of twisted hope, he saw she bore no weapons.

She raised her chin and sniffed like a hound. A tongue like no human had ever possessed flickered from her mouth, long as a leech, flat as a roach, edged with tiny, gleaming teeth.

He did scream, then, and hurled the lamp at her. Its globe shattered against her face and fire blossomed in a red flower down her naked chest. Bijaz threw the chimney after, then sought to flee.

She blocked the door, burning with the smell of pork roast and making no sound at all. He ran for his window with its view of the nearby walls and roofs, then turned as he reached it.

The girl, the sending, whatever she was, stood in the doorway, burning, that damned tongue flickering through the flames. The only noise he heard besides the crackle of oil fire as the conflagration spread to the carpet was the hiss of her trying to sniff even now.

She began to walk toward him.

He did not bother to open the window, just hurled himself through the shuttered glass and out into the street fifteen feet below.

"Bijaz."

There was a hand on his shoulder. Someone was disturbing his screaming.

Wait, he thought, he wasn't screaming. That was simply his breath.

A face swam before his eyes. Oddly colored skin, curious eyes, but eyes this one had.

"Not you," he said. "Not on fire."

"Sorry, don't understand that one," said the other. "You're drunk, or worse."

Bijaz made an effort to get the words out. It was important. "Much worse. Stay…stay away from me."

"Sorry. Not my choice." A pair of hands lifted him. "Dorgau take your eyes man, do you have the crab disease? You weigh nothing at all."

It was a dwarf, with no decent sutures on his lips. Not that Bijaz was Sewn either, not anymore. But he was fallen, a dead dwarf still breathing by accidental grace and nothing more. "Slashed bastard," he said, or tried to.

"That's more like it. I'm going to have to hire a cart for you, aren't I? No cab will take you in."

Onesiphorous, Bijaz realized. His new tormentor was Onesiphorous the Slashed. "Go...away... Stop...rescuing...me..." He tried to push at the other dwarf, but there was no strength in his arms and he had no leverage anyway.

"Imago has need of you." Onesiphorous peered into Bijaz's eyes. "You do remember Imago?"

Bijaz nodded, or tried to. Onesiphorous appeared to get the point.

"Good. Because you know more about the Old Gods than anyone but that forsaken godmonger. Believe you me, the Winter Boys are out hunting for Archer right now."

Archer. Ah, all his trouble come to nothing. Bijaz realized he should have just cast himself in the river that night. He'd been too afraid of what waited for him in the water. And too much the coward to simply take a knife, though that would have been much easier. "No. Lemme die by myself."

"We're all dying together, dwarf, or we all die alone. Be glad the City Men didn't find you first. They'd not have been half so gentle as I."

"Dead...dead...all dead..." Bijaz couldn't find any more words after that, so he let the Slashed dwarf drag him in search of some conveyance. A tiny malicious remnant of his self-respect hoped that no drover would be crazed enough to take his addled, stinking corpse down to the waterfront.

It would not be that easy, he knew. He would give anything for a quick blade now. Anything that kept eyeless, sniffing horror away.

The worst part was, dozens more remained where the last one had come from.

JASON THE FACTOR

He had not needed the guide of the severed ear to find his old master once more. In that, at least, there was some small favor. Little else, to be sure.

It had pleased the Imperator Ignatius that his new Second Counselor occupy the Acanthus Wing apartments that His Magnificence previously inhabited while serving as Second Counselor in his own time. During the weeks since, Jason had not found the nerve to climb the winding iron stair in the back room. Indeed, he strongly preferred to avoid it completely, and the strange shadow that capped the spiral. He lived in the one front room, which was still better quarters than his tiny, neglected apartment above the office down on Sturgeon Quay.

He would give anything to be back along the docks, with his office and his secret playroom, somehow returned to the days prior to Ignatius' disappearance. Jason could not decide which was worse—seeing what his old master had become, or living in the hell the unthinking Imperator made all around him. Prothro schemed and twisted, rigging agendas with abandon, while Green Kelly simply moved with the winds. Imago had been of little use, for all that Jason tried to attend to the ever decreasing mumblings of the Imperator. No one else told him anything. It was clear he survived largely on sufferance, some flicker of loyalty still within the dim shadows of Ignatius' soul.

He'd lost his father to a sudden fall from grace that began in the courts and ended beneath the feet of a shrieking mob in Delator Square. This…decay, this collapse, was sickening. Like watching wood rot. As he imagined the faces to be rotting in the room of wood that Ignatius had not once visited since his return.

It was that, as much as anything, which told Jason his old master was well and truly dead, in heart and head if not in limb and voice. The Ignatius of old would not have abandoned his books, his philosophick works, as the Imperator Restored had done.

And it was not just His Magnificence who was dead. People died now in the Great Hall. Rent by black dogs, or slain on the silent accusation of the sniffers, or joints smashed by Green Kelly's Restorationists and left to cry their thirst beneath the benches while the Burgesses sat in nervous session above the feeble fingers. It was dangerous to be anyone, anything, within the Limerock Palace now.

He wondered why the noumenal forces arrayed around the Imperator had not ridden out to make short work of Imago and the other doubters of the City Imperishable. Perhaps they awaited the approaching armies, which like winter itself were closing ever tighter on the city.

So Jason spent most of his time in shadows, and avoided company wherever possible, and lost the heart to even make plans. To move against Ignatius would be like rising against his own father. Not to move against Ignatius was like watching his father be snatched down to Dorgau's deepest hell.

Love was a trap that grasped him by the heart.

The Provost found Jason sitting in his front room. "My lord Second Counselor," said Zaharias. His sad-eyed face had aged of late, growing more lines than a camel's neck.

"Provost." Jason felt tired. He'd been working out ways to pass word to Imago, though in the days since their meeting nothing of political importance occurred in the Limerock Palace. The Imperator chose to withdraw from his throne to be closeted with his First and Third Counselors. That idiot Almandine, Secretary of the Inner Chamber, flitted back and forth like a bat on a thread between the Imperator's meetings and the frightened Burgesses in the Great Hall. Green Kelly trailed the Secretary everywhere like a particularly irritable haint.

They were crafting a new Act, Almandine proudly told everyone, his face gleaming with excitement. An Act that would remedy the errors of precedence and statute, which had accrued since the departure of the late, great Imperator Terminus.

At least they were at the business of state, though the executions went on as well.

Jason finally gave up on the muddled business of the Burgesses, who between the interruptions of terror had gotten themselves hopelessly tangled in debate over a bill authorizing the re-formation of the Imperatorial Armies. He sat here in shadow, wondering how to send news he did not have to give from a place where the walls had, if not ears, at least noses.

The Provost studied him awhile. "Come to the Inner Gardens with me. There is a curious chestnut tree I wish to show you."

"Arboriculture." Jason stood, gathered his cloak. "One must have one's hobbies."

It was snowing again, and the Inner Gardens were rather better supplied with drifts than the streets of the city, for the stuff had nowhere to go. As they moved down a path, Jason marked a number of men on the rooftops with rifled muskets, silhouettes amid the pale curtains of the weather. An unusual number of bailiffs wandered in the gardens, so he presumed the watchers were the Provost's men.

"Your long face is quickly stretching your neck toward a hangman's rope," said the Provost so quietly Jason almost could not make out the words. The man barely moved his lips, and did not allow his breath to puff out.

Jason made the fingertalk for BIRDS SHARE THE SAME BUSH IN WINTER, which was a way of inquiring about the other's skill with the signs. Zaharias just shook his head. "I do not have the silent speech, more pity."

"Apologies," Jason said, trying to control his breath and voice as the Provost was doing. "We are driving toward madness."

"Well past the border already, I'd say."

Their footsteps crunched on snow. The air was heavy with the damp tin smell of the weather, but nothing more. No scent of fire or evil. The Provost's chestnut tree would be nothing but a giant sicle of ice.

"So I die soon. Most will."

"No." The Provost paused, touched Jason's arm. "Some…Astaretto for one…" He took a breath, slowed and quieted the passion that began to emerge within his voice. "Astaretto, and Almandine, they had planned this. Not for a return of the Imperator, though. That was almost certainly unlooked for in their plotting. A mistake."

With a shudder, Jason had to agree. It was another tiny betrayal, this turning away from Ignatius even for the space of a conversation. He cast about for other blame. "The rest of it, though. The horrid magic. They intended all this?"

"This city is the oldest place in the world. When we were great, our gods were great. But they are very old, and dark. Astaretto and Almandine have called back the Old Gods. They want the empire restored, not just the Imperator. They desire to rule mountains and seas, not merely a waterfront and the flow of coin. Not horror, but power. As long as the power grows, the gods are fed."

The problem was clear enough when framed in that manner. "Which is why they need this war."

"Yes, though I do not see how they provoked the Tokhari these months past. The timing is strangely neat."

"With gods on one's side…this is what Ignatius always fought against." Ignatius as he used to be. "The coming of the gods."

"Chthonic. From below our feet." Zaharias leaned forward. "Both my brothers are priests. They have schooled me in secret history. There is blood far beneath our stones."

"There is blood upon the surface of our stones, as well."

"Fair enough. For now, to give us some chance, I would ask a favor of you."

Jason's tiny smile crooked, shedding the tiny flakes of ice that his breath had formed upon his lips. "An assignment, you mean?"

"Yes. I will be blunt." Zaharias glanced around, his eyes taking in the bailiffs. The threat was clear enough. Jason must answer well, or spend the rest of the winter beneath a snowbank. "If my forces can repel the invasion, without some damned hell-dogs erupting from the earth but rather by sheer dint of arms, I might have leverage among the Burgesses and on the street to move against our Imperator. A bullet is a miracle that can shatter even the most god-haunted skull. This old magic…it is a thing spun from ideas. Bad ideas, to be sure, but still nothing more than evil thought. Nonetheless, I cannot simply kill him."

A way out. The betrayal would not be his. It was a path. In a rush of panicked, guilty hope, Jason grabbed the fur trim of Zaharias' coat. Around him bailiffs shifted suddenly. "If you have the power, do it now. We can work to save the consequences. I think it quite likely he will find a way to turn a bullet, if he has not already. Or Green Kelly's lot will get you before you make your move. The sniffers man. Do it now, for the love of the City!"

"I take it you are ready to set your course against your master." Zaharias gave Jason another long look. "You were his man well before any of the rest of us joined him, save that idiot Green Kelly."

"Shoot *him* while you're about the business," muttered Jason, avoiding the question of where his course was set. Could he but support Zaharias to do what must be done, perhaps his own heart would not fail for grief.

"Indeed I shall squash that dreadful little crab of a man. But all of this must be done well, with an eye to politics and practicality, or you and I will be next against the wall."

"I would go gladly before a firing squad to stop what goes on within these palace walls."

"You, maybe," snapped Zaharias, forgetting all stealth for a moment. "As for me, I still love my life, and the comforts of power, if I can manage to retain them both."

Jason sighed. This offer on the part of the Provost was of sufficient importance that he must find a way to send or carry the information back to Imago. The Lord Mayor had questioned why the Provost was allowed to keep what was, in effect, a private army within the walls of the Limerock Palace. His Mayor's suspicions were obviously well-founded. "What do you ask of me, my lord Provost?"

"Two things in one stroke. In both you are the very man to do the deed."

As a betrayer twice over, first abandoning Imago, now turning from Ignatius, Jason seriously doubted that he was the man for anything. "I shall probably die poorly, if that tells you anything."

"Your death does not interest me half so much as it seems to interest you. Despair will slay us all, my lord Second Counselor."

"If the Old Gods don't kill us first." Jason softly clapped some of the cold from his hands, edging slightly away from the Provost to give the bailiffs a clear shot at himself should Zaharias call for it.

"Cease playing the child. Here is what I need you to do. First, go to the Lord Mayor and make him speak to you." Good, thought Jason, at least the Provost didn't know about his last visit.

The other went on. "Carry my offer to combine the forces of my bailiffs and new recruits with his Winter Boys and the City Men. We will have to kill most or all of Green Kelly's Restorationists, but then we will be together as the defense of the City Imperishable, and can stand atop the walls and gates as our attack arrives."

"A decent enough idea," said Jason, "and one with more than a little sense, if trust can be established. I suppose I see why you want me to carry the message—a letter would be disregarded as a trap."

"Yes. But there is another, more important errand that you and only you can do." Zaharias began walking again, forcing Jason to move, too. He cast his voice so low that Jason had to bend close as if to receive a kiss. "The Tokhari approach from the south. The Yellow Mountain tribes from the north and west along the River Saltus. Those lands are not empty, in either direction.

Farms are reived for food and fodder, but they are not slaying and burning. The armies move too quickly.

"From their progress, word has come to my ears. They ask after Jason the Factor. Someone in those armies wants you to come to them. Whoever they are, I want you to go. Tell them to make a set-piece battle before the walls, but not to fight me in earnest. If my men drive them back, I will be the hero of the street and the Burgesses alike. I can best aim my shot against the Imperator in that moment."

Jason did not even need to think on that. "You are as mad as everyone else," he said flatly, keeping his voice low. "To think that Imago would turn his forces over to you on simple trust. To imagine the Tokhari and their allies are the least interested in some deal. They are here to stop our ascendancy, to rend our gods to dust before we summon armies from the earth."

Yet, he thought, the plan fit. Not necessarily in the details, but within the wider scope of what Imago had laid out for him. He might be able to convince the Tokhari they could stop the rise of the Old Gods without the cost of an entire assault—it would not be a siege, to be sure, the City Imperishable was too large and too poorly defended for static warfare, but the assault against the walls would still go bloody, as many within would pick up a butcher knife or a dropped pistol and set to a defense. If the Provost took his shot, and power fell to the Burgesses, the Old Gods could be laid down once more, and some new, more powerful binding could be set in place against them.

But the Tokhari had no reason to listen to pleas from the City Imperishable. Save possibly for whoever among their highest ranks had been asking after him.

Jason had a sick feeling he knew who that might be. On the sundering of his family over the affair of the soul bottles so long before, his father had been slain by the mob after being broken by the bailiffs for a debtor, and he taken into Bijaz's service. His sister Kalliope sold herself to a Tokhari rug merchant.

His trade was by water. Few of the Tokhari took ship directly, so his name would not be known from the docks. Somehow Jason had no trouble imagining his sister remembering him well.

Likely enough with no fondness at all.

It might be she simply wanted to be sure of having his head on the correct pike before shattering the gates.

If it was her, after all these years. If she rode with the army in a position of power, and not as a concubine or slave. If, if, if.

"Despite your words, you are thinking long," the Provost said. "I suggest you be about your way. Their van is three days, four at the most, from the walls. Their fellows ride from the north no more slowly."

"It is finally come," Jason whispered.

"Indeed. You and I might manage to stop it. I cannot think of any better plan, though I have some alternatives if you fail."

"You hang your hopes from a slim thread, my lord Provost."

"Let us trust your thread does not choke my hopes to death."

"I go," Jason said. "As soon as I can find an excuse, and a horse to ride it on."

"Luck." Zaharias grabbed his arms. "We have never been friends and are scarce allies, but it may be that we can save this city together."

"I still say you would be best advised to shoot first and plot politics later," Jason told him.

"That is why I have made my life in politics and you have not. Always plot before you act. Now go, Jason."

"Good luck," he said, for all the good it would do either of them.

As Jason trudged through the snow, feet cold as old iron, he reflected that he had never heard the Provost utter his name before. Was that a warning, or a blessing? He was too tired, down into his soul, to look for the traps that lay within the trap.

He did not even want to think upon what Kalliope might have to say to him.

IMAGO OF LOCKWOOD

The godmonger was brought into his office dangling between two of the City Men, glowering as if he could burst into flame through sheer anger. Archer was dressed in the traditional muslin wrap of the dwarfs, but looked to have been dragged through the snow, and worse.

"Archer, my good friend," Imago began.

"Don't entreat me, you filthy cretin!" the dwarf shrieked. One of the City Men moved to backhand him across an ear already bloody, but Imago shook his head to make the man stop. Archer ignored everything to draw another breath. "You make a second way for the Old Gods to rise above the stones. Bibelot! We tried to warn you. You doom the city with every step."

"You will listen," Imago barked. He stomped across the office to grab Archer's chin. The dwarf tried to butt his head, but Imago had spent enough time in gutter brawls to know to turn away from that, setting a grip on the dwarf's neck.

"Listen to me. I have heard word of what grows within the palace walls. Trusted word. You were right. Both you and Bijaz. But even so, I cannot simply lay down my chain of office and surrender my arms. All will flow to the Limerock Palace, which is a greater danger than anything I might summon by accident." He let go of Archer's chin and neck. "I should have listened when you first tried to tell me, but other voices claimed my ears. Then the both of you ran away. Now, will you help me find a way to stop that madness? Or are you content to shout curses from the street corners and paint foolishness on the walls of temples?"

"True word?" Archer's voice was a dark muttering. "From inside the palace?"

"The Imperator keeps the Burgesses locked away, and the servants who do come out are scared beyond witless. Yes, true word has reached my ears."

Archer cast his eyes down. "Jason has turned his coat."

"Do not advance further theories, sir." Imago nodded to dismiss the City Men. Both looked as if they would just as soon slap the dwarf again, but they took their leave with a slam of the door. "Just believe that I believe."

Archer found a chair without being bidden, and collapsed in it to rub at his face. "No one listens, you know." His voice was muffled by his hands. "The trees no longer burn like midsummer firecandles, and there are no more torn corpses in the street. They may find little comfort in the Imperator Restored, but he has taken the monsters from their nights."

"Well, the monsters are returning. Already they roam the palace."

"What of Bijaz?"

"I sent Onesiphorous to find him. Whether he will succeed, I cannot say." Imago began to pace. "It's not enough to call for return to a vacant throne. We also need to find a way to lay the Old Gods back to rest. They need to sleep. Whatever binding Imperator Terminus worked upon the gods needs to be renewed, even strengthened. Very soon, for our enemies approach our doorstep. Their outriders have been seen from the walls, and the foreguards of both columns are mere days away. If we do not bind the gods, and soon, thousands of screaming horsemen and their stonecallers will do it for us."

"Every hedge wizard, priest and miracle worker in the City Imperishable working together could not reseal the tombs of the Old Gods."

"Then make new seals. Find some sacrifice, some bacchanal or ceremony. What I know of magic and gods you could write on a flax seed. Yet I have learned this much: everything has a price, and everything contains its own opposite. It was one of Jason's lessons from his old master, when Ignatius' mind and spirit were whole. If there is a summoning, there is also a closing of the door."

"Sacrifice," said Archer. He slumped lower in the chair, which creaked at the pressure. "Whatever Old God spoke to us at the winch tower…it said to sacrifice a life, a love, a limb. There is a price they will accept. Truthfully, I think they might even prefer it. Gods no more like to be called to someone's beck than men do."

"In that case, find their ceremonies." Imago grabbed a pencil from his desk, began twisting it in his hands as if the necks of all his enemies were hidden somewhere within. "Re-create their sacrifices."

"Not so simple." Archer sat up once more, began twisting his arms to stretch his back and shoulders. Imago hoped that meant the godmonger was thinking rather than simply despairing. "Terminus had their prayer tablets broken, their altars cast into the River Saltus and their temples pulled down. All that so they would not be called back by fearful prayer." He looked agonized. "We do not even know the Old Gods' names anymore."

"Were you and Bijaz not babbling to me about blood-soaked shepherd's caves beneath the city?"

Archer stared open mouthed for a moment. "Have you ever gone beneath the streets?"

"Why would I?"

"Well, I wouldn't, let's put it that way. You think the sharks and leeches in the River Saltus are bad? Ask your lead dunny diver. Last time I heard, he was a dwarf named Saltfingers. Works for your Water Captain."

The Water Captain Imago knew. They had been deep in conversation concerning the municipal pumps several times in the previous two weeks. "I suppose the dunny diver does something necessary somewhere down within the sewers?"

"Dives 'em," said Archer succinctly. "Knows underground better than anyone else. I've been told he worked some seasons down in Bas Gronegrim, learning the Raw Trade, as they call it. I know I've heard him say the blessing and power of the City Imperishable is that it's built on hills, else we'd all be rotting in shit."

"You find him." Imago stabbed a finger. "All I can do is stand around and look official. That and signing my name are the sum of this job, save for all the worry and fear. You go find Saltfingers, you have him lead you down through the sewers—" That phrase made Imago shudder. "—and you find where it is the Old Gods lie. For the love of the City Imperishable, set them to rest."

"I might," said Archer. "But you must swear to me to unseat this Imperator. The City needs the mild incompetence of the Burgesses. We need the quieter pace of life. Or else we shall be driven down and sown with salt by our enemies in their fear of our resurgence. And rightly so."

"I'll do anything to stop this madness with the Old Gods and our invaders."

"Swear it." Archer stood, took an old leather sack from beneath his muslin. "This is a fingerbone of the High Priest Nayyaam, who died on the steps of the Great Temple when the Imperator Terminus pulled it down. Some among the godmongers carry them, to remind us of our purpose in checking the rise of gods and politicians alike." He tugged the cord over his neck and stepped forward to place the sack in Imago's hands.

The Lord Mayor closed his fist and stared at the dangling cord. Frayed silk, that might once have been red but was now the color of melonflesh going off. "Such a simple thing. Has it any power?"

"What is power? If I believe it, and you believe it, it has power." Archer clasped Imago's fist, his voice slipping into a street preacher's depth and cadence. "Do you join with me now, Lord Mayor Imago of Lockwood?"

"I…I do join with you," Imago said after a lost beat.

"Swear before me on this relic that you will do as you have said."

"I do so swear."

"You will unseat the Imperator. You will restore the Burgesses. You will melt your own chain of office."

"I do so swear."

"Oh, very good, sir." It was Onesiphorous, at the door. "My friend of the Sewn was bad enough, but now we have a dwarf leading prayer here."

"Prayer is what is needed," said Archer mildly.

Irritated, Imago dropped the pouch back into the godmonger's hands. "It is for the best, Onesiphorous. Did you find Bijaz?"

"Yes. For all the good it will do. He's a raving addict in the last stages of degradation. I had no idea a man could fall so fast in a month. All he'll talk about is blind children and the dwarf pits."

Archer started at the words, Imago noted. "Something from your experience in the winch tower?" he asked the godmonger.

"Yes. I must see to him. Where is he?"

Onesiphorous waved Archer out of the office. "Ask Marelle." When the godmonger had slipped away, Onesiphorous closed the door. "What are you going to do with Bijaz, sir? He is truly wretched, and near death."

Imago shrugged. "Have Archer drag him down beneath the city to chase the tombs of gods. He'll do no one good up here. Armies are on our doorstep. The Imperator raises ancient wrath. Bijaz…well, only Bijaz can answer for himself in these times."

The dwarf crossed his arms. "And you?"

"I must treat with my good captain Enero, and see what we may do to break this assault. Now that it is upon us, we're done for if we don't arrange a truce."

"A surrender, you mean."

"I think it might be worthwhile, to protect the City Imperishable."

"Let them march on the Limerock Palace and confront His Magnificence directly?" the dwarf asked.

"Yes." Imago glanced out his window at the frost-rime and the snow beyond. "Though I have no doubt that I'd be hanged from a bridge as a traitor by the very syndics whose lives and homes I spared in doing such a thing."

"My suggestion is that you go meet with Enero, then. The man has his uses, sir. It would be very much worth your while to apply them."

"Indeed." Imago gathered his wool topcoat and checked the shine on his shoes. "I do not find myself overburdened with optimism."

"Then at least die well," the dwarf said philosophically.

"If I am given the choice."

Imago left the little man standing in his office and found his way to the street outside, where a riding squad of Winter Boys would escort him to Enero's headquarters near the eastern wall.

Even though he was Lord Mayor, Imago went to Enero because the freerider had maps and charts and tables covered with small pieces meant to represent this army or that. Imago understood very little about these tools for scrying out a battle, but he appreciated that Enero had need of them. Out of respect for that need, he took an extra measure of his precious time to sit with the captain.

Enero's company was settled into a decaying hotel that had once served the Wall Street area back when people and business still lived at the eastern marges of the City Imperishable. They cleaned out the derelicts and desperate poor to stable their horses in the kitchens and set out their maps and charts in the ballroom. The Winter Boys worked out their room assignments on some basis known only to them, save for the mummers on their camelopards who moved about the city among various temporary quarters until the recent appeal to the Lord Mayor.

The exterior was a rather shabby example of the architecture of two centuries earlier, when the finer points of ironwork were first understood. The roof was something of a fancy, with peaks and domes and little pleasaunces that only a steeplejack could reach, while once-delicate gargoyles looked down the face of the hotel. They were carved from too soft a stone, and time had reduced the poor beasts to so many sheeted ghosts, with an occasional ear or claw just barely visible in a protected nook.

The Winter Boys had mined the ruins near the eastern wall to build brick and timber hoardings around the hotel at street level, so that any visitor must apply to a small gate that was presumably well-guarded. Their other gates they left sealed save when they wished to ride out, insofar as Imago knew. All of which would do them little good against a determined enemy armed with gunpowder and massed forces, but the armies approaching fought with more of a raider's tactics. Thus, such a place might stand.

The makeshift wall carried the incidental benefit of keeping Restorationist troublemakers out of the mercenaries' quarters. Not to mention petty thieves and burglars.

The Lord Mayor, of course, was marched directly in. He followed his escort past the guttering chandeliers and rotten maroon carpets of the grand lobby and into the ballroom. Enero sat there atop a rolling ladder of the sort used by archivists or librarians, staring down at a large, flat table covered with sand. Hills had been sculpted into it, and two watercourses. After a few moments, Imago realized it was the territory of the City Imperishable, without any of the structures—he was looking at the rivers Saltus and Little Bull, with Nannyback Hill and the New Hill rising near the riverbank, with Heliograph Hill a bit further east amid the upward sloping ground where the city moved to meet the Rose Downs.

"I am wondering why a man would be naming a hill as new," said Enero to Imago, as if resuming a conversation just recently interrupted.

Though he'd lived in the City Imperishable all his life, Imago had never thought about that. "Perhaps because most of the buildings in that area were built about the same time some centuries ago, and there are none older upon that height. I believe it had been swept by fire."

"As may to be." Enero hopped down in one leap, dropping almost seven feet with his coat flying behind him. As always, he was neatly dressed, with a red silk smoking jacket and a white silk shirt beneath, over black wool trousers and narrow, checked shoes.

Imago thought this man looked less like a solider than anyone he'd ever met. "I am told we have three days, no more, until they come before our walls."

"My men are killing two scouts in the Green Market this morning." He took out a cigarette and lit it, though the smoke was foul and sweet.

Herbs, then. "They just rode into the city?"

"On a drover's cart. They were to be wearing farmer's rags. We are to be assuming there are a dozen more we have been missing, yes?"

"Yes." The thought of closing the gates sickened Imago. "Once I seal the City, we will starve quickly. Far too much of the harvest is stored outside the walls."

"No, we will not to be starving. We are to be either dead or victorious. There is not being a siege here, my lord friend." Enero grinned. "A simple problem, this is being."

"How will we attain victory?"

"To be fighting within the city. We are not having enough men to be controlling the walls. In truth, all the folk of this city might not be being enough men for that. So to let the enemy in, and to be killing them street by street. I am to be planning barricades and stampedes of the oxen and riots of the poor, yes?"

"That will kill many. What if I stand aside and leave the gates open?"

"You are being a fool." Enero looked him over carefully. "They are being no sort for listening to your reasons. If they are not taking our city, they are to be starving. And to be dying in the snow besides, to be sure. Horsemen are being too far from their winter pasture. Tokhari camels all the worse. Even if you are making nice, they are taking what is needful. I would be doing no less if I were to be their commander."

"We let them in, and we kill each other off?"

Enero grinned, hugely. "Until we can be feeding who is to be left, at least, yes? Do not fear, my good man. More help will be found."

"Within three days?" Imago asked.

"Within three days," said Jason, stalking into the ballroom trailed by Winter Boys and City Men with drawn pistols and bare blades.

"He, he was insisting to come in," a serjeant began. "Our orders were being—"

Enero waved the man off. "This is to be the friend of our Lord Mayor's bosom. We are to be talking to him now. Out, everyone else is to be out."

Moments later the ballroom was empty save for Enero, Imago and Jason.

"Your head seems to still be attached to your shoulders," said Imago.

"Much to my surprise. One of your patrols, Captain Enero, saved me from a small mob of Restorationists."

"To be a counselor of the Inner Chamber is not of any protection?"

"Not on pain of treason, I suppose." Jason dusted some snow off his cloak. "I do not have long. Please, listen to me, then let me go."

Imago dragged up a stool from the sand table's edge and sat. His feet were tired. "Listen to you what?"

"Zaharias of Fallen Arch, Provost of the Assemblage of Burgesses, has advanced a plan to our mutual benefit." Jason laid out word for word, as close as he could, the offer the Provost had made. It took a few minutes, and when he was done, silence followed.

Imago drew in a deep breath. Horseshit and blood—what else would one catch the smell of in mercenary quarters. His life had been nothing but blood of late. "I do not miss the tenor of the Provost's words, if you report them truly. He leads, he claims credit, he brings the new order about."

Jason shrugged. "Do you have the barrels of firearms the Provost does? His bailiffs and their new recruits number almost six hundred, nearly twice what you can field with the Winter Boys and the City Men. A thousand men fighting on the same side are much better than a force divided."

Enero stirred. "Are you to be endorsing this offer?"

He shrugged again. "I am to be endorsing nothing."

"No. You are to be having another errand, outside the walls, yes?"

Jason eyed Enero with a mixture of resentment and suspicion. "Yes, as it happens. How do you know?"

"I am knowing much the same way you are knowing, with no doubt to it, yes? They are to be asking after you."

Imago broke in. "What?"

"Someone in the Tokhari army is spreading the word that they wish to treat with me," said Jason.

"Who?"

"My sister, I suspect."

"You don't have a sister," Imago protested. "I've checked up on you."

"It is not to be doubting a man who is knowing his own mother's whelps."

"Two, actually," Jason admitted. He didn't even bother to glare at Enero. "We are a good fifteen years on since I have seen either of them. I am certain Ariadne is long dead, but Kalliope sold herself to a Tokhari rug merchant in our youth. Old betrayals, of my father's plotting for the most part. Though I don't suppose she remembers me with any goodwill either."

"And you are seeing her?" said Enero expansively. "Help within and without the walls. All is to be better even now."

Imago favored the Winter Boy with a long glare. "You knew the Tokhari were asking for him, didn't you? That's why you haven't been in a panic. There must be a way out of this war or they wouldn't bother. Why didn't you tell me?"

"What is to be done? The man is coming out of the Limerock Palace or he is not. We are not having the force to be plucking him forth amid bailiffs and sniffers and black dogs from the nine hells. I am hearing many rumors. Would you like to be knowing them all?"

"You can argue," said Jason. "I have delivered my message. I am leaving the city by the Sunrise Gate."

"The Sudgate is being too dangerous, too close to the Limerock Palace," Enero observed.

"Go," said Imago, irritated. "That the Provost will turn his coat and shoot His Magnificence is great news again. You might be able to persuade our camel riding friends to do the same."

"It would be my fondest wish, my Lord Mayor." Jason made a short bow, dropping more snow off his brittle hair and the collar of his cloak. "I am away."

"Jason." Imago stepped after him. "Good luck. This is not your day to die, either."

Jason nodded, then left. Imago wondered if the sacrifice of love that Archer had spoken of was between Jason and his sister.

There wasn't much love lost within the City Imperishable right now.

"Show me the disposition of the forces," he told Enero. "At least I will know who is dying where, when the horns sound across the wall."

"At the first I am to be assuming the current situation is continuing," Enero began.

They were there for some hours.

BIJAZ THE DWARF

He found his way out of a haze of pain and brilliance to see Archer looking down at him. Bijaz's mouth felt as if insects had been nesting within, so it took him a moment to unstick his lips. It was as if his Sewn knots had returned, for a moment.

"I thought you were—" Bijaz began, then stopped. Some of his teeth were missing. The rest were...soft.

He nearly retched.

"Ssh," said Archer. "Onesiphorous is busy elsewhere. I have told the Lord Mayor I will not take his next assignment save that I have you at my side."

"No," Bijaz said. "I am to die."

"I could certainly arrange that whilst on our errand. We have been charged with searching for the tombs of the Old Gods somewhere beneath the city. I have sent for Saltfingers, my Lord Mayor's dunny diver."

Bijaz settled back into the edges of what haze remained to him. "I will not go beneath the stones. There is blood there."

The godmonger made a rough, exasperated sigh. "Bijaz, you walked out of a fire and took yourself off to die. At least make your death mean something."

"No." Certainty stole into Bijaz from some unknown source. It was like a dream remembered for the first time. "I have another purpose. The Lord Mayor himself should go beneath the stones with you."

Archer made a visible effort to control his irritation. "I hold faith in signs and portents, my friend, but I cannot compel the Lord Mayor to spit in the street, let alone follow me down where none should go. What is this purpose you have discovered within yourself?"

"You told me I was touched by the noumenal. Why I'd survived several attacks. Then that voice spoke to me, in the winch tower."

Archer pulled his fetish bag from beneath his muslin. "Yes...?"

"I think the...eyes...in the river. The sniffers. Those weren't the voice. I was mistaken. The voice was another."

"The sniffers?" Archer's tone was sharp. "I've heard the word. What do you know of the sniffers?"

Bijaz felt himself stiffen in panic, tried to control the reaction and wound up shivering wildly. Archer glanced around, then threw more blankets atop him before turning up the little gas fire.

After ten minutes, Bijaz settled down. "Do not ask," he managed to gasp out.

"Hmm." Archer's face promised further inquiries. "So tell me of your mistake."

Bijaz explored the thought that was unfolding. Reappearing, from wherever it had been hidden. "I need to go to Cork Street," he said.

"What? To place a wager? You are an addled drunkard, my friend. My faith in you has been misplaced." Archer stood, paced around the small chamber.

Bijaz noted it was overwarm and close-walled, with an odd blunted wedge shape. There was a little shelf and a writing desk. He was stretched on a settee, wrapped in the blankets. From the shape of the chair, it was the office of some dwarf. There was little clue around him to the identity of the owner.

Onesiphorous?

"Addled, perhaps, but not by drink. I have been taking crap powder as if it were sugarwater." Bijaz extracted a hand from beneath the covers. He was shocked at how thin it was, how the spidery fingers shook. "This has broken much within me."

"Are you claiming revelation, or have you felt a calling? Some testament from the gutter?" Despite his obvious irritation, Archer gently took Bijaz's hand. "Addicts see angels and demons the way other folk see baker's boys and hansom cabs."

"No, not that," Bijaz protested stubbornly. The vision, if that's what it was, continued to unfold within his head. "Cork Street. The Numbers Men. Who are they?"

"Something like the Tribade. A gang. They control the gaming parlors, the flow of money from that portion of the city's economy."

Bijaz struggled for the truth at the heart of this. "The Tribade is everywhere. Have you ever met one of the Numbers Men?"

"Well, they—" Archer stopped himself. "Enforcers, floor managers, yes. But no...not the men themselves. Not that I have known."

"A thousand people have met Biggest Sister. As well as the other leaders of the Tribade. All you have to do is ask."

"Not all have returned from their meetings."

"It doesn't matter," Bijaz said, stubborn now. "The Numbers Men are something else. Hiding behind their name. They protected me, they lent me luck when I should have died, more than once, in the noumenal attacks."

"Luck?" Archer nearly exploded. "Your arse got reamed to bloody meat. You nearly died of it, in that alley just off Cork Street. That's their protection? Save me from the Numbers Men. The Tribade does a better job."

Bloody legs dropping from the sky jarred Bijaz's memory. "No, it does not. Listen. I have been a part of blood sacrifices for years. The dwarf pits. I am one of those who go down to the blood."

Archer recoiled, looking sick. "No. They are vile…"

Bijaz had his thread now. "Vile? No more so than half of what goes on in this city. But yes, I'll give you vile. Sacrifices. Summonings. The Tribade is tied in to them, my contact always through the dark sisters, but something else was being fed besides my lust. Something that kept me alive."

"The Old Gods?"

"The Numbers Men. Old Gods who were not laid to rest. The ones Imperator Terminus did not exorcise from the life of the City Imperishable. The Old Gods who stayed to swim supple in the rivers of money instead of blood. They are worshipped every time a gaming wheel spins or a card turns. They get what blood they yet need from a horse-headed dwarf dancing in a pit deep beneath the stones of the city, cutting flesh from a writhing full-man."

"You are cracked and more than cracked, my friend," Archer said sadly. "I must take my leave of you. Time grows short, and I need to go beneath the stones."

"Archer." Bijaz's mind felt clear now, sharp to the point of brittle, but more focused than he had been since before the Trial of Flowers. "This isn't about Sewn and Slashed, but it is very much about what we are as dwarfs. Who we are. I don't know how or why, yet, but the dwarf pits, terrible as they are, cut to the heart of it. My rape was my punishment. From the Old Gods. To awaken me. As for my certainty…I know you think me a deluded fraud right now. Still, I beg you. Take Imago with you when you go down into the earth. He must stand for the city and its people. It is part of what his office means. Please."

"Good-bye, Bijaz." A tiny smile flickered across Archer's face. "I don't suppose we'll see each other again. Die well if the war comes over the walls. Live well if it does not."

With that, the godmonger was gone, shutting the door behind him, leaving Bijaz to the hissing of the gas fire and the silence of an empty room.

He would go to Cork Street soon, he promised himself, but not until he'd rested awhile longer. Besides which, his mouth was bleeding inside from the trouble of talking so much.

When had talking ever made him bleed?

Later, after stealing ordinary clothes—nothing in the traditional muslin, he noted bitterly—and half-boots from a chest in the office where he had rested, Bijaz stumbled out of the oddly shaped room to find himself on a round balcony facing a shaft. There were ten or twelve doors about the circumference. A tower? Bijaz grabbed a rail and leaned over to look up. It was tall, with more levels above. The Rugmaker's Cupola, though he could not recall the tolling of the iron bells since he had been in the little room.

Stairs spiraled around the circumference, graceful wrought-iron things with vines worked in among the banisters. Their landings were cut out from where the balcony met the well, two on each level, so that the iron twinings formed a double helix joining the stones below to the bells above.

People moved back and forth, coming out doors with stacks of paper, but other than a few incurious glances, no one paid him any mind.

He headed downward. Wherever Cork Street was from here, it was not to be found inside the tower amid the quiet, busy people.

His feet cooperated better now than they had before, though his mouth seemed stuffed with straw. It took Bijaz an unconscionably long time to make his way down three flights to the ground, but he did. The floor at the bottom was covered in rugs, dozens of them thrown one over the other by the look of things, and braziers spaced about the room sheltered eye-bright oil flames.

There were guards here, too, burly men in street clothes as well as those gray-leathered mercenaries who had ridden into the City Imperishable before the Trial of Flowers. One of the grays pointed him out, and out of nowhere that Bijaz could see, a white-faced mummer in fool's motley caught him up.

"You are to be having an errand, little man, yes?" the clown whispered in his ear. There was a bare knife glittering in the stranger's hand, Bijaz noted.

"Cork Street," he croaked, trusting in the Numbers Men.

"We were to be laying odds of that." The clown gathered Bijaz up like a child or an animal, and carried him into an evening street so cold the fire in his mouth turned to burning ice. As he was loaded into a windowless carriage to lie on a familiar leather bench, the iron bells began to toll high above his head.

"Evening," Bijaz said.

"They are to be crying for the coming of the dark. You should be to cry much the same." The clown kissed him on the forehead, then placed a coin on each of Bijaz's eyes. "To be resting well, little man."

The door clicked shut, a whip cracked and the wheels clattered as Bijaz was driven off into the night.

He was standing on a kerb of Cork Street, knee deep in slush and feeling as cold as he had ever been. Bijaz looked down to find two gold obols in his hand. His memory was fracturing, a thousand pieces like mirror shards each broken off from a different scene.

But he was here, to find someone.

The Numbers Men.

"Be helping you along, guv?" said a sharp voice with no friendship in it at all.

Bijaz looked up into the dark, glinting eyes of a man he'd never met before and found he knew the name. "Three-Widows," he said. "I've come to place my final bet." He showed his gold.

"Ah." The voice was suddenly much different. "One o' them special customers." Three-Widows doffed his small, round hat, and bowed. He was dressed in a ruffled shirt, like a croupier, and tight wool pants over polished leather brogans. He was a very small man, not much taller than a boxed dwarf, but there was something of the steel spring about him. Or perhaps the bloody knife. "My mistake, sir, and we'll just be heading on to the White Table, shall we?"

"The White Table," said Bijaz firmly, with what he was being offered.

They walked a block along Cork Street, past two of the largest casinos, to a small white door with no handle or latch. It opened at a single rap from Three-Widows, and Bijaz was led upward, somewhat to his surprise. He'd rather expected to be going down beneath the stones here on Nannyback Hill.

Three-Widows took him by the hand. "Begging your pardon for the familiarity, your lordship, but when that door shuts these stairs are darker than the inside of a dog, and I knows the tricks and traps. To be sure you want to follow close and not let go of my hand, no matter what you sees and hears."

"Yes," mumbled Bijaz, whose mouth had found whole new ways to pain him.

They climbed in the dark. Tendrils or leaves brushed his arms and legs, then fingers trailed along his face. Voices laughed, shrieked, called his name. Once he heard the echoing shouts of the horse-headed dwarf from the pits. Smells, too: milk from a woman's breast, the hot blood of those severed legs in the street, the rot of the River Saltus that night he'd seen the eyes; it all washed over him. Violet smoke, as well, the best kind and crap smoke mixed together. Rose Downs rye. Bright wine from the Sunward Sea. The sharp, salty honey of a woman's cunt flexed open for the cock. His own fear-sweat. His name, called again. And again.

Through all of it, Three-Widows seemed to possess a most mutable hand, by turns a giant, slick claw, then a furred flipper, then something like noodles that twisted of their own, the fleshy gobbets clinging to bone.

After a time so long he couldn't measure how short it was, or possibly the opposite, another door opened. Bijaz stood in a glaring light with Three-Widows. The man's clothes were all white now, even his shoes, and his eyes had no color either. A table sat before them, with a gaming wheel mounted in the middle—a large, finely crafted wheel of white-stained oak with silver bands around the outer rim.

He walked over and looked. Every slot for the ball was white, with no numbers or colors. Every square on the table was just as blank.

"Place your bets," whispered Three-Widows. Even his voice was somehow lighter, brighter, whiter.

Bijaz opened his hand to find the two gold obols still solid as ever. He looked at the table.

He placed one at each end of the white felt, where the black would have been and where the red would have been. Let the wheel spin. He was already done.

"All in." Three-Widows gave the heavy wheel the lightest flick. The bearings within were so well balanced that it began to spin. He snapped his fingers and pulled a gleaming silver ball out of the air, winked at Bijaz with one white eye and launched the ball to race around and around against the clicking rotation of the wheel.

JASON THE FACTOR

He pulled the horse to a stop with a minimum of serious discomfort to his developing saddle sores. Jason had always at best enjoyed an indifferent relationship with the animals. He worked the docks after all, not the markets where goods arrived by wagon. However, given that his last mount had been one of Enero's rather bizarre camelopards, this creature was a welcome change. As far as he was concerned, horses were too tall, too smelly and too bloody-minded for their own or anyone else's good.

At least he had some experience in the saddle, a legacy of the moneyed days of his youth. Ancient history, that, brought back by the musky reek of a damp horse on a cold day, and the scent of saddle leather. Cold it was, night-cold now, with the City Imperishable only a vague glow of electricks and gaslight when he turned to look past his shoulder. Despite the continuing snowfall and low clouds, there was still a faint sheen of light upon the land—a gleam from the white ground cover. Haystacks, or possibly manure piles, steamed in the darkness. This was the beginning of the Rose Downs farm country: source of an endless stream of produce, grain, horses, cattle and farm boys not much brighter than what they hauled into the city.

As for the City Imperishable itself, the walls were a shadow line dropped between the gleam of lights and the glitter of snow. From his vantage up the eastern road, those walls were a trench dividing the work of man from the work of nature.

Somehow that thought seemed morbid to him.

He turned his attention to the horse. The beast had leaned over to crop at something in the snow. His legs were wet with the horse's sweat, a damp heat that threatened an instant shift to clinging ice. Jason had no idea what his mount's name was. He'd simply ordered the stable boy to bring him a horse. It had borne him before Green Kelly's men well enough, though on the city streets he'd only lost them with help from the Winter Boys. The poor beast now bore him into another wall of swords.

He hoped the horse enjoyed a better fate than his camelopard had on the day of the Trial of Flowers.

"I don't know you, boy," he said, awkwardly patting at the horse's neck. "You don't know me. Carry me true and somebody kindly will steal you and keep you safe with a hot bag of turnips." Or whatever it was horses ate when they weren't nibbling frozen grass.

He turned the beast south, following a muddy wagon trail away from the eastern road and toward the Tokhari column. Jason wasn't sure how far away an army had to be in order to be considered three days' distant—if they moved anything like a work gang, that could be five or ten miles.

At any rate, he aimed to be found by scouts soon enough. He would stay on the ridgelines where possible. By doing so, with luck he wouldn't be mistaken for a skulker. So long as they didn't vent his wind with a few precautionary bullets or crossbow quarrels first, Jason figured that all he had to do was state his name. Then he would be led on to whoever among the advancing army had passed his name to the people of the Rose Downs.

"Led" wasn't exactly the term for his current situation. Jason had no idea that camels could even move in snow. The Tokhari brought their caravans to the City Imperishable during the late spring through midsummer, while the few of the evil-tempered beasts that lived in the city year-round were stabled out of sight during the winters.

This one moved in snow, with Jason slung face-down over a strangely formed saddle braced atop the hump. He had shouted his name before the riders sliced him open. The little squad vented their frustration upon his poor horse before binding and gagging Jason, and tossing him atop one of their remounts.

In the hours since, there was little else for him to do save study the animal. His head had been jammed against its flanks and tied into place. He had now gone some miles with a mouth full of sweat-drenched fur. His nose-well was on the way to being permanently stunned by a rank smell more fit to some tide-dwelling monster than any decent land animal. Riding his horse had been tedious, the camel was torture. Its notion of a gait consisted of an irregular shamble with independent and uncoordinated control of each of the four feet. The digestive processes within the creature were reminiscent of a bad day in an alchemist's laboratory.

His ears were sufficiently free to enjoy the frequent clatter of blades and the snick of a whetstone as the Tokhari chattered away in their own tongue. Though he could puzzle out bills of lading, Jason's spoken command of that language was limited. He could tell people he didn't speak it, as well as several terms of varying impoliteness. He did recognize a few of those last in the gabble of his captors. They certainly made no effort at stealth, which suggested he was beyond the range of Enero's patrols.

The one advantage of being slung on the camel's back was that the beast's profuse sweating warmed his front. His back was unfortunately freezing. Literally.

Jason amused himself by trying to calculate the miles and hours from an estimate of the length of the camel's stride. Though he doubted he would die out here, he seriously wondered if he would ever see home again. That his first time outside the City Imperishable should come to this was a jest of fate.

Eventually the Tokhari cut him down and propped him against a tree while they set about tending their camels and building a fire. Jason was pretty sure one of them had ridden on. At any rate, the patrol seemed to have lost a member. The others continued to chatter and laugh, with occasional sly glances at him. They correctly assumed he'd be far too stiff to mount any form of escape or resistance.

Where would he go?

These were a traditional bunch, judging by their clothes and equipment. While every man around him was wrapped in some looted blanket or drapery or fur against the damp and cold, beneath that they all wore rawhide leather dyed the same color tan. Of one clan, then. Copper skin, brown eyes, long moustaches: these boys had ridden straight off the sand to come here. Nothing like the Tokhari drovers and tradesmen who had settled in the City Imperishable, diluting their traditional customs and costumes.

Jason turned his attention from his captors to his prison. He thought this might be an oak grove, but he was not so sure of trees in the wild. Lumber was easier to identify when it had been decently milled to be crafted into furniture or ships. He could recognize some of those species that grew in the City Imperishable amid tended patches of grass or indifferent packed-down dirt. Out here the trees were unkempt, ragged and far too close together. They had lost most of their leaves, and revealed a now cloudless sky with a late moon sulking among dagger-sharp stars.

It looked so different away from the city. He tried to remember when he'd last seen the heavens.

The Tokhari got their fire blazing. The stars faded to the usual smudges, while the unfamiliar trees grew shadows like capering demons. The Tokhari produced two haunches of meat that he realized must have come from his late horse and set them to sizzling. They played a game of fists and counting to find who should walk perimeter, then the rest settled down to pass a wineskin.

Jason was quite surprised when the skin came his way after a few rounds. He took it with trembling arms, raised the horn tip and squirted into his mouth as he'd seen the others do.

They were obviously expecting a show, but he'd been played this trick more than a few times, drinking with captains from Sunward ports. The stream hit the back of his throat, though he could barely keep from gagging on the taste.

It reminded him of liquid cheese, gone rancid and mixed with the raunchiest product of a Sudgate gin mill.

He gulped it down. Some ferment of camel's milk. He'd had worse. Jason forced a grin, then passed back the skin.

After that, they were a bit friendlier. When the meat came off the fire, the perimeter guard walked in from the cold for the first share while another stepped away. The others delighted in telling the story of Jason's drink, and he was forced to repeat his feat. This go-round he was rewarded with a hot, burnt strip of horseflesh.

He couldn't recall the last time he'd eaten—some fruit, maybe, before the Provost had rousted him from his apartments that morning. The previous morning, now, judging by the moon. Jason could swear that fear and the cold had shrunk his appetite, but the hot grease of the meat woke his own gut to burbling as bad as the camel's.

Eventually, full of meat and camel's milk brew, he sang along with their songs, making them laugh with his horrible efforts at imitating their words, teaching them city favorites like "The Fat Man's Bone" and "Maidens Three Upon My Knee." Both of those lent themselves to a certain amount of pantomime, in which he indulged.

Somewhere at the back of his exhausted, drunken thoughts, Jason kept the very clear idea that laughing enemies were marginally less likely to slit his throat for the pleasure of testing the color of his blood.

He awoke to yet more scent of camel, and a vague awareness of light. His head throbbed to distant drums. Some of them were not so distant.

It took Jason a few minutes to puzzle out that he was wrapped in a saddle blanket. His arse was hot because he was lying against the ashes of last night's bonfire. Someone was poking him very gently with something sharp.

"*Il-mezzi manit*," Jason said. He had no real idea what it meant, but the scouts had laughed themselves silly teaching him to say it the night before.

"Your accent is terrible," a woman replied. "Besides which, I seriously doubt that's true."

"Put the blade away, please." He found the corner of the blanket and looked up into the sunburned face of an old woman who might once have been his sister. "Hello, Kalliope."

Her mouth was set, unmoving, but familiar as the one in his mirror. The lines of her cheek and chin were different, but he recognized the storm-gray eyes and the pale hair colored like old straw. Though she squatted next to him as he lay beneath the blanket, Jason would guess her taller than he, which surprised him. That ran counter to his memory. Her face was tattooed with inward-turning spirals on each cheek, with three tears inked descending from her left eye and two from her right. A pattern of red and white dots encircled her lips.

Only the most traditional, or senior, Tokhari were so marked. He'd known the race for years in the City Imperishable, more as drinkers and street fighters than as traders, but there were Tokhari children whose parents and grand-parents had lived and died there that still kept to their own language. The camel people were scattered all through the city. Did they fear or welcome this army?

"So you do live," she said. "We had some correspondence for a while after father was killed. Since then I have seen your name from time to time over the years, but could never be certain of your fate." There was an odd quality to her voice, not quite a Tokhari accent, as if she were only now remembering the tongue of their youth.

"We both live, it seems. I cannot speak for Ariadne, or our lady mother."

"I can."

He waited a moment, but Kalliope did not seem inclined to elaborate. "I must break the courtesy of guests and ask you something."

She stared awhile, as the scouts moved about, readying their camels. None of them would look at her, or him, this morning, Jason realized. Did this mean he was about to be killed?

"I have been long among my people," she finally said. "We take time and time again to come to the quick of a question. *Maroush na-dja*, as we say. Now I must speak differently, though you will understand. You are still and always a man of the Stonesource."

"Stonesource?"

"What we call the City Imperishable, in the lands to the righteous side of the Redrock River."

"There are stones everywhere in the world, sister mine."

"You might wish to consider that the name assumes a different sense in our tongue."

They studied one another awhile, not in preparation for battle, but more as if each looked for some sign of the past in the other. Mindful of her rebuke, Jason kept his tongue this time.

"I would offer you coffee," she finally said, "but if I must slay you, I do not wish to violate the guesting law."

Jason grasped at the implied straw. "Your men fed me last night."

"Indeed. Which is why they will not kill you today." She spared a small smile. He saw that her teeth were stained blue, something he had not noticed before. "The men were quite upset with you. The only people they are allowed to kill are armed men, and here you came ahorse like a Stonesource scout, but without the decency to carry a fighting blade or pistol."

"They took out their frustrations on my poor mount."

"Meat does not go to waste." She glanced around at the frozen forest, the pearly sky of dawn slowly heading toward a pale winter blue above her head.

He realized that he'd not heard the bells of morning. Jason didn't think he'd ever been away from those bells, not in his life. He shivered, cold to the core despite the nearby fire.

"A horse," she continued, "must needs be fed. We are far and far away from our canal plantations."

"What are you doing here?" Jason asked softly.

"You know. Else you would not have ridden out from the Stonesource in answer to my call."

"I know what your army does here. Some dread bird hatches from the egg that is the City Imperishable. You seek to stop a larger war, a new empire before it can be fully born. Our ends are not so far apart in this, else, as you say, I would not have ridden out. No, I meant to ask what is my sister Kalliope doing here?"

"Your sister Kalliope died years and years ago," she answered. "I am a…well, you might say sandwalker. You know the stonecallers of the Yellow Mountains?"

He nodded.

"We have our spirits in the Sand Sea. It is not…magic, not as you know that word. Just a part of the land, like a sulfur spring or a tar pit, or a vein of gold running beneath an old man's hut."

"There is little sand in these countries where you have strayed, sister."

"Indeed. My feet are cold, and my heart is empty. Yet someone must sing down your gates and strike three times at your walls and tell the men of muscle and purpose where to swing their blades."

"Do you lead?"

"No one leads the Tokhari when they ride to war. Some give counsel, and the counsel of some is followed by all."

Jason had to laugh. "You are as bad as those old women in the Assemblage of Burgesses."

"Have you learned nothing, brother? Power draws power. At least in the oldest places. We have cities of red stone in our deserts that stand ten days' ride from the nearest wellspring. They are tall enough that a man might see from their towers horizons farther than the wings of the *rukh* of the sun can spread. No weed nor mouse has grown within their walls for a thousand years. The altars are still sticky with blood the color of the rock.

"Old places, Jason. Like your City Imperishable. We know the price of power, and would not see those wages be paid again."

"Hear me," he said, sitting up to better meet her eyes. "It will not surprise you that within the city we fight one another, as rats will when trapped in a brewer's barrel."

"Does the sun rise?"

It took Jason a moment to follow that. "Well, yes. Exactly. Certain factions seek to ally to the same purpose that your armies are pursuing. I was asked to propose cooperation with your forces."

"Ah…brother mine." Her eyes drew down, sad. For a moment he could see the sister he recalled from his youth somewhere inside this hard desert mage. "What purpose to cooperate? Even if we league with one or another of you, the truth has come out. In a handful of years some other fools with more ambition than sense will decide they know how to overcome the mistakes of this regime, and call the Old Gods once more. No, we ride to the Stonesource, and we shall reduce the city to mud and rock before we depart. No one wants to play your game of empire once again."

"I cannot let you do that," said Jason.

She sighed. He felt a bloom of sharp pain as her knife slid through the blanket into his gut. "You have no power here."

He moved his hands to staunch the flow, but the blanket tangled his arms and the blade held the wound open. "You…" The words flickered in his mouth. His sister, he thought. Slain by his sister, here in the cold woods.

The Old Gods must be laughing now, but the sky was already turning black despite the brave, brave sun.

IMAGO OF LOCKWOOD

The night was half-gone when Imago and his guards took a coach back to the Rugmaker's Cupola. He felt no wiser than before, but he trusted Enero's plans more fully. Enero had laid out all the lines of possibility—what would happen if the Provost held back within the palace walls, what would happen if he joined forces with the city's, what would happen if the Provost came out fighting. The same analyses had already been made for the likely behaviors of the Tokhari and the Yellow Mountain tribes. The freerider also possessed charts showing the numbers and usual disposition of forces: Green Kelly's Restorationists, Imago's City Men and the groups of citizens who would likely come out fighting, such as longshoremen, butchers and so forth.

He even knew how many farmhands were at winter labor within the walls, something Imago would never have thought to wonder upon. Those were stout lads who could swing a flail or sickle quite well, as Enero pointed out.

It was a dizzying array of information. Imago wondered very seriously how the commander of a small company so far from the busy wars of the Sunward Sea had the skills to put all that together.

There was an element of discomfort, that this man understood Imago's city in some important ways better than the Lord Mayor himself did.

The coach rattled over the cobbles and bricks lining the approach to the Bridge of Chances. Imago reflected upon the fact that though he was still ignorant of far too much, he was already fully committed. After the battles to come, there would be time for questions.

If there was an after.

One small blessing—the snow had stopped. At the Rugmaker's Cupola Imago alit from the coach under an open sky. The stars were brittle-bright, unusual here in the overlit city, and the cold made his chest hurt simply for the breath he took, but still and all he was glad to see the back of that last storm.

He nodded to the guards at the door. At this hour they were Winter Boys. The City Men didn't like to work the late, cold shifts and simply took themselves off-duty to some tavern or another. Imago stepped into the short hall leading into the echoing room that was the base and center of the tower. The Worshipful Guild of Rugmakers retained the use of the rest of their immense hilltop mansion for their own purposes, but Imago controlled a substantial amount of space for the work of his city government.

The view was much better than that from within the Limerock Palace, he thought with a grin.

He nearly tripped over Archer slumped on the base of the upward staircase. Imago leaned down and shook the dwarf's shoulder. "Why are you not away on the errand I sent you? Or at least resting."

Archer blinked away sleep, looking up at the Lord Mayor. "Bijaz is lost to us." Tears stood in his eyes. "I tried to cozen him from his bed. He refused me. I left angry. I returned later to find him gone. The guards had no orders to keep him, so he walked out, climbed into a coach and has not been seen since."

"A hire coach, or whose?"

"They could not tell me." His hand strayed to his wrappings, tugging nervously at a little bag hung around his neck. "No one thought to note it carefully. I know he had the Numbers Men very much on his mind. Also, when we spoke, he was very insistent that you go beneath with me. I thought he would do himself an injury, he was so nearly violent in stating that requirement."

"Why me?" Imago wondered.

"He said you must stand for the City and its people. That your office obliged you to that step."

"My office obliges me to crawl in subterranean filth looking for ancient caves?" As soon as the words left his tongue, Imago knew that was but foolish protest.

Archer gave him a sour look. "You would send me to shut the doors of time. I am just a pair of hands, a message with feet. It is your will, on behalf of all the City Imperishable, which must move down beneath the earth."

Imago tried to decline the logic. "The same could be said of Enero and his swords, or indeed anyone who labors on my behalf."

"This is not delegation, or bureaucracy," hissed the godmonger. "You stand in the noumenal world in the place of the people who elevated you to office. You picked this fight, Imago of Lockwood, by seeking the golden chain of your current estate and staging an ancient rite unawares. One seat of power has opened the tombs of the Old Gods. You are the other seat of power, here high on the hill. It is to you to close those tombs. You are the last person privileged to say, 'Let another do this thing.'"

Imago sank to the steps beside Archer. The dwarf was right, Dorgau take his slanted brown eyes. The end, or at least a terrible breakpoint, had arrived. Mischief certainly brewed in the Limerock Palace. The Provost was at the point of revolt against his master. Thousands of armed riders were nearly at the outer walls, where Imago could wield no spear in defense.

Was this what it meant to be Lord Mayor? To be, in some small way, a kind of king? That he was obliged in turn to lay himself out as sacrifice to save the life of the City Imperishable and all who dwelt within?

He did not want to do this thing. He did not want to crawl beneath the earth looking for blood-soaked stones and broken doors on ancient temple-tombs. The very thought made his mouth curdled and dry.

"I should throw off my robes and run away. What I should have done in the first place, instead of hatching a plan to attain this office." He squinted through peppered eyes. "I just wanted to avoid debtor's prison."

"You took on other obligations," said a new voice.

Imago looked up to see Biggest Sister standing before him. It was the first time he'd come face to face with her since his ascension, for all that her little missives often nudged him toward some policy or action. She was accompanied by Ducôte, whom Imago had also seen little of since the old dwarf had declined to move up the hill with Imago and his government.

"Yes, fool," Ducôte said. The old dwarf looked worn as the rest of them, his face more lined, his lenses spattered with grime he had not taken time to wipe off. "I warned you, did I not?"

"I sent for them," Archer admitted. "To talk sense to you."

Biggest Sister looked him up and down. Despite the weather she was dressed in nothing but her usual leathers. "You're the Lord Mayor now. Fine clothes on a man I found wet from the River Saltus not long ago. Well, if you are willing to remember the Tribade and what you owe, know this: we cannot tolerate that madman in the Limerock Palace."

Ducôte nodded. "Bijaz has gone to ground, for good I think. Onesiphorous has chosen to serve you directly. It remains to me to speak for the dwarfs, Sewn and Slashed alike. We stand with Biggest Sister in this. Even if the armies without were to vanish like morning mist, ill deeds go too far within. The palace is melting into hell. At the center of our city."

"They fear the resurrected empire of the Old Gods," said Archer. "I fear the terror in the streets. Whatever you fear, you must come with me if you have a hope of setting to rights once more."

"I pay my debts," said Imago. He raised a hand to forestall their objections. "In my own time and in my own way. I know how much I already owe you both. Everything, perhaps. However, in this I also have a price. Come upstairs with me. I shall write you out brevets to sit with Onesiphorous as a Little Council. My answer to the Inner Chamber. While I am off on my errand with Archer, you will speak for the City—to Enero, to the Provost, to anyone that comes calling with words or swords or spells. If I return, we will discuss what comes next. If I do not return, do as you see fit."

"The Tribade does not work with open power that way," Biggest Sister said flatly. "We had an understanding. Let it hold or fail at your wisdom, and your peril."

"You wish to stop the course of empire?" Imago felt his anger rising. "I will go and see what rocks I may get myself crushed beneath to that end. You ask much of me, which I will give, however great my reluctance. No, my cowardice. Let's call it what it is. I have always plied words, not blades or miracles. If I'm not too afraid to crawl beneath the earth, surely you are not too afraid to climb the stairs to my office?"

"Enough," said Ducôte. He turned and bowed to Biggest Sister. "I have neither power nor wish to compel you, Dark Mother."

Mother? thought Imago. Oh-ho. Mother's rules indeed.

The old dwarf continued. "This is a stranger moment in our history than any time since the Imperator Terminus marched away. It could not hurt the Tribade to have some part to play in what comes next."

"If anything comes next," Biggest Sister said sourly.

Imago took that for assent. "We may all break upon this rock. We can at least perish bravely in the attempt." He turned to walk up the stairs, trusting the others to follow.

The Lord Mayor decreed some small rest for the wicked, for he saw no point in going to fight the gods on an empty stomach and tired eyes. Imago and Archer met Saltfingers the dunny diver just after first light on the north end of the Bridge of Chances. The morning bells were just dying away. In dressing for the expedition, Imago had donned his formal chain of office. It felt ridiculous to be wearing that over layers of wool and leather, but the office was the point of the whole exercise.

Saltfingers turned out to be a curiosity indeed. Imago could see how the dwarf had gotten his name. He was albino, for one, and had a disease scaling his skin that made his hands pebbled and almost shiny.

"Killed me nose years on," Saltfingers said when he saw Imago looking at his hands in the dawn gloaming. "A real benefit in my line of work, you might imagine."

"Indeed," said Imago faintly.

"Though not so good as steam!"

"Steam?"

"Aye. I been walking the tunnels since I was popped of my box these sixty-four years past. The big steam plants didn't come in until I'd been down ten, fifteen winters. Burning all that highland coal."

Steam? What steam? Imago didn't even understand the water system yet. Who the hell ever thought Lord Mayor was a job for a sane man?

"Runs the big factories on both sides of the Little Bull," Saltfingers added. "You'd be knowing that, your worship."

Imago seized on honesty as a working policy for this man. "Actually, I wouldn't be knowing that. Ah…you do understand what we're about here?"

Out of the corner of his eye, he saw Archer smirking.

"Oh yes. Setting out to break down some temple and kill some gods, you are." Saltfingers grinned. His mouth was blood-red as the rest of him was colorless. "I seen strange things down these tunnels over the years, your worship. What's a god or two to me atop of the freshwater squid infestations, or the year the Heliograph Hill Hacker was putting the heads of the posh nobs down the storm drains faster than we could clear them out? Don't even get me going on the gangrene toads. No, a nice, clean bit of god-killing, now that would be a rare treat."

The man was a lunatic, Imago realized. Six decades working in and beneath the sewers had stripped him of reason and common sense alike. But Archer was certain the dunny diver knew his way around, and there was nowhere else to turn now. Not with the armies almost at the gates.

He had to ask: "What about the steam?"

"Oh!" Saltfingers laughed. "I don't care what manner of daft great bugger you've got crawling up out of the curst underworld. You turn a four-hundred-pound steam feed on 'em, they're smoked waterweed. How do you think me and the boys stop them freshwater squid crawling up drainpipes anyway?"

"There's steam all over the city?" Imago saw potential for serious mayhem here.

"Mostly along the Little Bull. There's a run over to the Limerock Palace, of course. Him was Provost thirty years ago, Alettino, had that one laid. Cut the heating costs on the old pile something fierce. They ran 'er on to the Sudgate, but gave up before they finished that extension."

"So…" Imago did a little mental mapmaking. "That last bit of line would run under Terminus Plaza?"

"Well, and yes. Strapped up high in Old Number Six sewer main, except the route-around for the Oakroot Cistern."

That was something worth knowing, if it came to the bloody ends of things over the next few days. Whatever a four-hundred-pound steam feed was, it wouldn't be good for a bunch of Tokhari camel bangers storming the Limerock Palace. Or a bunch of whatever nasty surprises the Imperator Restored and his crackpot court had cooked up storming *out* of the palace.

"Where are we going to find the temples?" he asked.

Archer finally broke in. "The Lord Mayor doesn't mean the rebuilds up on the Melisande Main, Saltfingers. Nor the family stuff here and there."

"You'll be wanting the old stuff. With the nasty carvings on the walls."

"Well, maybe…" said Imago.

"What's been moving down here since last summer?" Archer asked.

"Ah. That old stuff. Let me show you a thing or two."

Saltfingers led them down a mossy stair on the north bank to just above the Little Bull's usual waterline. There was a locked gate set into the retaining wall lining the river's course. Here within the boundaries of the city, the tributary river had been channeled and built over until the bed was a sluice, with intakes for the municipal pumps, outflows for the sewers and various private and commercial pipes. All of which, Imago noted, were at or above the current level of reduced flow. He hoped that whatever ice dam was holding the river in place upstream would not break so suddenly and cause the Little Bull to jump its banks.

If anyone was going to fix that problem, it would of course be him. Imago vaguely recalled a discussion of floodgates where the Little Bull passed underneath the eastern wall, but that conversation was primarily concerned with scrapping large quantities of brass and iron out of the damned things.

Saltfingers opened the gate, which was slimed and corroded both. He waved Imago and Archer in—Imago had to bend, though he was not the tallest of men. He could immediately see why someone had thought boxed dwarfs were a good idea for this work.

A few steps inward, standing in a greenish half-light, Saltfingers opened a locked cabinet hung high on the wall. "There's them that pilfers," the dwarf said. "I won't die in a pipe just coz someone needed another round of gin." He handed Imago a helmet with a tiny lamp attached. It looked much like a miniature of one of the gaslights that lined many of the city's streets. "This here's a carbide lamp. I've got plenty more of the gas rocks what feeds it. Don't go sniffing at it, it'll give you a headache worse than a two-chalkie hooker."

There was a certain amount of fussing with equipment, which resulted in Imago wearing a hissing, glowing lamp upon his head and carrying something rather like a boathook, along with several water skins slung over his shoulder.

"Come on, then," said Saltfingers, who was rather more heavily laden than either Imago or Archer. "One last thing, though. 'Tis the dunnyman's weird. You must each give me two coppers."

"Why?" asked Imago, curious. He had brought no purse, but there was some small coin loose in the pocket of his leather workpants. He sorted out a pair of chalkies as Archer did the same with a sidelong glance.

Saltfingers waited until he'd been given the coin before answering. "Then I owes them back to you. Pays your way beneath, and draws you up to the light once again. Now we're off."

"To say the least," said Imago. He was going to shut a temple door with a boathook? Or perhaps his native wit, charm and the power of his office. He hoped like hell the godmonger had brought along some holy seals or whatever one used for such occasions.

Saltfingers' voice floated back from his bright-limned silhouette just ahead of Imago. "It's dark as a miner's arse crack in here, so mind your step. Try to walk just exactly where I walks. My rope ain't long enough for some of these holes." He added reflectively: "Not that you'd have any need of rope you fell in that deep."

BIJAZ THE DWARF

"White, white," Three-Widows said after the ball had rattled to a stop. "The bet is white." He made a show of looking at the coins on the table's white felt mat. "Why, you've taken both at two-to-one odds."

"That makes no sense," Bijaz protested. "I came to wager my life and you give me a table which cannot be lost."

Three-Widows smiled, his eyes and teeth glinting like ground glass. "Would you prefer an unwinnable game? We can go to the Black Table if milord desires. There is no limit to the stakes, either here or there. Lay down your life if it suits you, sir."

Bijaz was frustrated. This was not what he expected.

"Oh no? Did you think to sit before solemn judges on thrones of skulls? We have those rooms as well. Though your taste runs more to horses and blades, as I believe I recall."

"I did not speak!" Bijaz wanted to deny the dwarf pits, but they were part of him.

" 'We'll find you a good trick.' " Three-Widows said the horribly familiar words in a horribly familiar voice. " 'Not one of these monkeys. Just you let me get rid of this one, all right?' " He leaned close. "Did you learn nothing, little man?"

"The Old Gods," Bijaz said. "I have learned to fear them."

"Then you learned the wrong lesson." Three-Widows picked up the gold obols and began walking them back and forth across the fingers of his right hand. "Everything has a price," he said, and snapped closed his fist. He opened the hand, and the coins were gone. "Everything carries the seeds of its own opposition, in equal measure. Have you ever toppled a wall?"

"A wall?" Bijaz was thoroughly confused.

"Certainly. You know, stones piled high." Three-Widows tapped Bijaz's hands. Bijaz turned them over to find the coins resting one in each palm. "You must press as much as it takes to move the stones. They react as they are pushed. What people care to call magic works the same way. No one calls lightning from the summer sky without burning a hole in something, somewhere."

He snapped the coins out of Bijaz's hands, flipped them both spinning high in the air. "Luck is much the same," he said. "The center always wins." The coins landed on their sides on the floor, rattling in circles around Bijaz as if possessed. "In terms of numbers, that is. Every toss of the dice is different, but I can tell you in the morning what they will add up to at the end of the day." Three-Widows smiled. "Well, I can tell you with each toss. But I would wager that you take my meaning."

"You are one of the Numbers Men," Bijaz said.

"Maybe." Three-Widows pulled a chair out of nowhere, a ladderback with a cane seat and offered it to Bijaz. The dwarf sat, and so did Three-Widows, on another chair that wasn't there until he needed it. Both pieces of furniture were as white as the rest of the room, and Three-Widows' was turned so that he leaned upon the back. "Chances are that I am one of the Numbers Men. *What did you learn?*"

"I learned…" Bijaz stopped, thought. "I learned fear. And pain."

"Better. You might do, in time." Three-Widows tilted the chair forward, holding it in place with his feet. "If everything holds its own opposite, what opposes fear? And pain?"

"Hope," said Bijaz without thinking.

"Yes. You might do." Three-Widows hopped up, tilted the chair on one leg and spun it til it vanished. "You're dead, you know. You died that night, legs spread bloody on a pile of rubble with the juices of a dozen men leaking out of your torn-open arse. We jiggered the numbers to make you something more, but there was opposition of course. All our numbers merely run in the face of far larger pushes. History has its own weight."

"Why did you save me, then?"

"Opposition. You are one of our seeds. Most are scattered unknowing, answering to luck. Everyone has choices, we merely make chances. Sometimes we must needs speak in words, rather than let the rattle of dice and twist of coin tell our tale. Tell me, did you truly mean to lay your life at stake tonight?"

"I have counted myself dead this month and more," said Bijaz. "I lacked only the courage to step into a blade and make an end of it."

Three-Widows examined something on one fingernail, then leered slyly at Bijaz. "You were doing quite the job of hustling yourself into the grave, from what I've heard." He licked his lips with a lascivious slurp.

Shame bloomed on Bijaz's cheeks. "Yes, well, I did what I did. I also meant to lay me down here, if the Numbers Men would have me. I finally understood what Cork Street was."

"A giant temple to the gods of chance?"

"Yes."

"Think of these gaming halls as prayer wheels, building us up and moving us forward in time."

Despite his misery and dejection, Bijaz's curiosity still prickled. "What do you *do* with that power?"

Three-Widows shrugged. "Run gaming halls. It's a much better line of work than following armies around building an empire."

"And what of me?"

"Lay down your life and find out, little man. Or walk away. It's a long stairwell, though, I'll warn you."

"I'm beyond being frightened of parlor tricks," said Bijaz.

"Ah, he gets his color back."

"Will we all die soon?"

"We will all die. How soon? Each has his own mischance to reckon with."

Bijaz snorted. This was degenerating into cheap philosophy. "Thousands of screaming camel riders would seem to be a substantial helping of mischance."

"Indeed." Three-Widows' eyes gleamed again. "We cannot save the City Imperishable. We made our bargains long ago. Unlike some, we keep them. Who could trust a crooked house, after all?"

"But…" Bijaz said slowly. "There is always a 'but' hiding behind such a statement."

"Action and opposition." The coins appeared between Three-Widows' fingers again. "We cannot save the City, but, we can throw the luck around a bit. Make some large things go well in exchange for a thousand dropped pots of water on the boil, a hundred scalded cats, a dozen children horridly burned. But a city unfired and whole."

"And this luck will give us…?"

Three-Widows shrugged. "Something lucky, I would imagine. We are the lords of chance, not fortune tellers."

"I have wrought fear in the dwarf pits. I have known fear beneath the straining cocks of ruffians. I will choose your hope."

"I should like to think you will share it as widely as possible. Now you must lay down your life."

"How?"

Hands spread, Three-Widows smiled. "It's your life, you tell me."

Stakes, thought Bijaz. Everything came down to the stakes being played. The clown had shown him that, back at the Rugmaker's Cupola. He reached out, plucked the coins from Three-Widows' hands and went to climb on the table. The dwarf arranged himself across the betting mat, then placed the gold obols upon his eyes.

"I am ready."

"Place your bets," Three-Widows said in the barking voice of a sideshow tout. "All in, all in."

Bijaz waited.

He heard the wheel begin to spin, moving with that rhythmic click of bearings. The ball hit, rolled round and round with a metal growl.

Eventually there was a clatter. "The bet is white. White, the bet is white. You have wagered your life at two to one odds, sir. The first you have won back from the house. What shall you do with the second?"

The dwarf considered that a moment. "I am the City's luck now, and so will trust in myself. Give it to him among my friends who most has need of it."

"Very well." Bijaz felt breath hot in his ear, smelled garlic and pork. "Aren't you glad we did not stand to the Black Table, sir?"

He sat up as the coins tumbled from his eyes to discover he was on the park bench where he and Onesiphorous had argued about truth, and what constituted the real source of the City's problems. They had been like boys chattering of troublesome schoolwork just before the wall of floodwater claimed them.

Three-Widows stood nearby, picking his teeth with a dagger, restored to normal color. The man's indifferent eyes passed over Bijaz without a hint of recognition. Bijaz went to pocket the coins when he realized they weighed strangely in his hand.

Both were foil, and far too light to be gold. He picked at the foil.

Candy. They were candy coins—one a pale white cocoa butter, the other bitter dark chocolate.

White and black. Bijaz wondered what would happen if he'd flipped them. Instead, being of a practical bent, he ate them. He then set about the serious business of thinking how to share his hope, and his luck, as widely as possible.

JASON THE FACTOR

Breath hurt. His mouth was wrong. Packed with wool? He tasted something very much like pickling vinegar. He would have coughed, had he more air in his lungs. Any air. There was only darkness in his eyes.

"Help me." The words weren't really there, just a flexing of the lips, but he thought he heard whistling.

Jason felt, quite frighteningly, nothing at all.

"Silence," said a woman's voice. "You are dead. Pass on into the next world like a good brother."

He felt nothing, but not *that* sort of nothing. More an absence of feeling than a feeling of absence. Maybe this was what it meant to be dead.

Cool fingers touched his face. No, it was his face that was cool. Something snagged on his eyes. "Strange…" she said.

Kalliope. His sister. Jason's mind had begun to reassert itself. He tried his lips again. "Help. Blind."

"Jason?" Her voice pitched up, tense.

"Ka…Ka…Kalliope."

She began shouting then, a torrent of Tokhari. More voices came, male, and rough hands that shifted him amid a chatter of the camel drovers' tongue. He had been *in* something. Now it flowed off his body like rough silk.

No. Not silk.

Sand.

He'd been buried in sand.

Buried?

"Careful, do not flinch," she said softly in his language. Something went snick close to his face, twice, then a thick liquid told him where his eyes were.

It ran down along his nose, then the scent of honey began to compete with the sour taste of the vinegar choking his mouth. Fingers pried his jaw open and he almost vomited at their touch, but they pulled cloth from between his teeth. Yards of it, by the feel.

A golden gleam reached his sight now, as if his eyes were peering from the bottom of a long jar of that honey.

"Ka...ka..." He tried again, but a shivering took him and he could not say the name.

She gathered him in her arms, shouting some more in Tokhari. There was grumbling, and shadows moved across his vision. He felt his face cradled against his sister's shoulder, then they were on a rug, lying in tight embrace next to a bright-burning brazier that he could actually *see*.

Or at least there were flames he could see, dancing in the golden haze.

"Jason." Her voice was soft, close to his ear. "You were dead."

"Y...you..." The shivering made his tongue thick as wood. The cloth that had crammed his throat left behind a scaly dryness that threatened to choke him. Nonetheless, he tried. The memory of blood blooming in his side was too strong of a sudden, a river of heat that left his body never to return. "You...you...ki...killed me."

"Yes," she said simply, and held him close.

It hurt to live. He tried to cry awhile, but his eyes were clogged with honey. Kalliope stroked his head, crooned some Tokhari love song or lullaby, and rocked them both while she bathed him in her own tears.

When he awoke once more, it was a more normal return to consciousness. There had been dreams of dark coins and the moon rising perfectly round, but he found his face pressed against the rough skin of his sister's breasts. She had enclosed him with her arms and legs, a cage of flesh. They were both naked. To his shame, Jason felt a stir in his own groin.

Her breathing was deep and even, but as soon as he tried to pull back, she awoke. "Do not," she told him. "You have no business living, so I make a loan of my own life to hold you here."

"How?" he asked, his head now full of death once more.

"Miracles come even amid the ice. Outside it snows to bring down the heavens, and there are a thousand spearmen circled around this tent. You are *sula ma-jieni na-dja*. The dead man of winter. They wait to see what you will do next."

"A thousand men...to kill me again?" A dry laugh trickled from the ruins of his throat. "It took only one...sister this last time." Sharks and eels, the words were difficult. What *happened* to him?

"A thousand men to see what will come next. Listen, brother." She slipped a pale nipple into his mouth to silence him. Jason took it, not to suck for he had no spit to make his lips flex, but just to be close to her beating heart, though that made his cock swell further. He could not feel his own pulse, and that frightened him more than lust.

She went on: "They tell stories, around their fires between squirts of *al-rakhi*. Among my people, stories are like boys in the ring. They fight and press and push until one stands tall among his groaning fellows. When the stories are done telling, the men will know what they believe."

He pulled his head away, his sister's flat breast sagging down across his chin as he did. "What are my…stories?"

"The dead man of winter has come to lead them into the Stonesource by secret ways. The dead man of winter has come to curse their loins that all their children will be born white and cold. The dead man of winter is the first of the Old Gods to return. The dead man of winter will suck the breath from their lips one by one. They go on. Morbid, hopeful, frightened. The cold takes the heart from our army faster than any wounds ever could."

"No one campaigns in winter," Jason mumbled. He'd recently heard it said in disbelief time and again within the Limerock Palace.

She laughed lightly and held him close again. "*Sula ma-jieni na-dja* does."

"Tell me." His voice was muffled now by the skin on the yoke of her chest, stretched tight over her collarbones and smelling of leather and salt. "Why did you take my life?"

"For love," she answered simply. "For fear. Because you came to give orders to an army that marches with sand in its boots. All of those things. Most of all because you were my brother."

"Were?"

"You are something else now, Jason. Whatever debt our blood might have held over me is broken by death. Our laws say that. Our spirits say that."

"You killed me for my blood. Our blood."

"Of course." He could feel a shift of muscles as she smiled—the motion stretched down her neck. "I ate your liver, to take your strength, and carved your heart into stewmeat for the army."

That her voice was so sweet when she said those words frightened him. Jason pulled away. "Then what is inside my gut now?"

"Last I looked, straw and silk and sand. I meant to take you home with me to rest well under the brass-bright sun, my former brother."

His hands slipped down to his belly. There was a line of stitches there, large and rough as any of the needlework he'd ever done in his playroom beneath the warehouse. The skin was loose and cold.

"I don't understand," Jason said.

"You *are* the dead man of winter. Your gods have brought you back."

"Why are you so damned pleased!" He was surprised to find himself shouting as he rolled completely away to sit up by the fire.

"Because you are alive once more." Her eyes glimmered in the firelight. "Because I now know what to do. Because I have already done the best of things."

Jason drew his knees close, shivering more deeply. "Just don't kill me again."

"No. You will ride with me at the head of the army. We will enter the Stonesource together, and see if your Provost is a man of his word."

"All this, from my death?"

"You would not have been sent back, here amid my camp, without a powerful reason, oh son of my mother."

"Jason," he said. "My name is Jason."

Eventually he realized he only breathed in when he meant to speak.

He could not choke down even a little water, and food was beyond question. The cold would not leave Jason either, so after she had clothed herself his sister helped him dress in the leather and wool of a Tokhari trader, stuffing the depths of the tucked-in robe with wads of silk that lay scattered around the large box of sand he did not want to look at. The rest of the tent was round and close, rich in rugs and otherwise sparse in furniture. Everything was woolen or woven, and meant to fold away. Of course, this entire army traveled by camel pack.

Eventually he was bundled tight. Little warmer, to be sure, but Jason did not know what else to do save perhaps set himself on fire.

"Let us go see what my story has become," he told Kalliope.

She threw back the tiny orange-painted door set in the wall of the tent and stepped out. He followed her.

They were atop a bluff, in some forest little different from the one where he had died. Snow fell thick as he had ever seen it, but even through the white murk he could tell that men were arrayed in arcs before the tent. Jason looked around—they were at each side as well, surrounding the bluff in expanding circles, little fires between some of them. The horses and camels were elsewhere—these were warriors in their sand-colored leather and their looted wool blankets, shivering under plumes of breath, so many that their numbers faded into the bright gloom of the snow.

Every face was pointed toward him, and each had a spear planted in the snow, tilted backward to point away from him.

He and Kalliope stood at the center of some great, metal-toothed star of muscle and lethal attentiveness.

"They do not kill you today," she said.

The men swallowed their breath as one, almost a wind to compete with the hellish cold weather. "*Sula ma-jieni na-dja*," they said in unison.

As quickly as that, the men wandered away. A few scrambled up the bluff, but most headed for business in the snow-shadowed trees.

There was a long jabber of Tokhari between Kalliope and an old man in a pointed helmet rimmed with some fur Jason did not recognize. Two younger men with him nodded enthusiastically, staring at Jason. When the youngest winked, he recognized one of his captors from the day before. It was so easy to see only the copper-tan skin and the deep brown eyes and lose count of which was whom, he thought. If their tongue had been more than jabber to him, he might have gotten a handle on a name, or if they were not all wrapped in the same shapeless, greasy furs and pillaged blankets.

After a discussion in rapid Tokhari that sounded rancorous if not on the verge of argument, Kalliope turned to him. "This is the story that they have taken as their truth. You are the dead man of winter, come to lead them to an easy victory and feasting in the hall of the Imperator. I believe it to be the worst of wishful thinking myself, but the Tokhari have spoken."

"I think they might simply hope to be quit of this awful snow," Jason said. "It is uncommonly thick for the end of Novembres, when we should yet have only frost and a scum of ice on the fountains."

"Indeed." She turned for another short burst of Tokhari, then back to Jason. "We ride. How are you atop a camel?"

"I survived my last trip." He realized as soon as the words left his lips that his remark was not exactly truthful.

Riding atop a camel was a noticeable improvement over riding athwart a camel, Jason decided, but still far worse than the meanest screw for hire in a dockside stable. The gait remained untenable, and the stench almost bizarre—his mount seemed afflicted with some terrible flatulence that kept his escort laughing into their silken face scarves.

The creature was not built for snow, certainly, but the barrel of its belly was high and the trail had been broken by men on horses. They moved slowly, no faster than he could have walked in decent weather, but the army readied itself all the same.

Tents had been left behind, along with old men and young boys to guard the camp and supplies, and butcher those horses and camels too sick to march. The Tokhari column carried only weapons and some food with them now. Kalliope obviously meant her men to sleep within stone walls within a day or two.

The thought did not encourage.

He had not seen his sister since she handed him over to his erstwhile captor. The young man was pleasant enough, spurring Jason to say "*Il-mezzi manit*" for the sport of it, but Jason's heart was not in the game. His heart wasn't even in his chest, come to think of it. He shied away from that line of reasoning—it chilled him with a cold altogether different from winter's icy grip.

The worst was the continuing rawness in his thighs and groin. By the nine brass hells, if he was going to be dead, he could at the least be free from saddle sores!

They rode for hours at this walking pace, into deepening gloom, stopping only to water and feed the camels, and for the men to release hot streams of piss that crackled like little fires in the icy bushes. Somewhere in the snowfall the column passed out of the woods. They were out upon the Rose Downs now, he supposed, near where his poor horse had been slain.

Shortly after a remount stop, he thought he heard the distant tolling of iron bells.

The evening bells of the City Imperishable. They would be before the walls by morning. He could not decide what he hoped for now, save to be warm once again, and feel his pulse once more.

Jason, who had never bothered with gods or temples or worship, began to pray to the hissing of the snow, counting each flake that whipped against him as a rebuke from the heavens. He prayed for the Sunrise Gate to be open, he prayed for the gate to be shut, he prayed for Enero to have his forces handily arrayed, he prayed for empty streets.

The one thing he prayed for without surcease or confusion was that Ignatius of Redtower might find his rest. In his current condition Jason was finally coming to understand the madness that had been visited upon the Imperator Restored since his return from the realm of the noumenal.

It was not a journey he would have wished on any man. Even his greatest enemy.

IMAGO OF LOCKWOOD

Many men had spent their lives down here, the Lord Mayor realized. The sewers were a monstrous agglomeration of architecture, engineering and lost art. Each of their three lights swayed and darted in differing directions as they walked. He would spy one part of a thing without ever quite knowing what it was or why, then another corner of something else.

There was a pillar, in the middle of a channel of stinking slop, carved in the semblance of a vine-wrapped tree.

Then, in another stab of light, a flaking portrait painted on a wall of a sad-eyed dwarfess holding a baby wrapped in a blanket. As the beam moved on,

Imago realized the child's face was limned as a skull.

All through this hypogeal warren was more of the same: stairways rising to blank ceilings; runs of carved railings replacing narrow, slime-covered walks; a large wooden trout mostly decayed but still recognizable lodged in the upper reach of a double arch.

As they went, heading uphill, Saltfingers counted off each shaft and tunnel in a soft voice. "Nannyback south number thirteen." "Artemis Street overflow." "Panface's Folly." "The false nine."

The old dwarf had a map in his head. Imago wondered if anyone had such a map on paper, somewhere in the archives. It would stand the City Imperishable in good stead.

Steam pipes were bolted to the ceilings of the mains. Imago found this inconvenience of installation strange at first, until he reflected that the designers probably intended to minimize the degree of their submersion. Insofar as he could tell, the pipes were black iron.

Every fifty paces or so, a large copper fixture was mounted on a brass collar ringing the pipe.

"What are those?" he asked, when they happened to take a brief break near such a one, half an hour into the darkness. He had no idea how far they'd come, but the going was so slow and treacherous, with several doublings around and odd circuits he didn't understand, that the distance could not have been half a mile.

"Hah!" said Saltfingers. "Let's hope you won't be learning. Steam relief valve." He fished something rather like a pistol from one of his packs. It had a coiled hose behind it, canvas coated with gutta-percha and enclosed in a wire mesh. "I clips this in, opens the cock on the valve up there, and I've got good, honest steam. The dunny diver's friend."

"Why so slow?" Archer asked, the first words he'd spoken since they'd descended. The godmonger seemed bothered by the darkness. Frightened, Imago wondered, or were the spirits he followed whispering in his ears all too loudly down here? He kept noticing Archer tugging at that fetish bag of his.

"Some ways are better'n others," Saltfingers muttered. "You don't want to step through the Nannyback Fall crossover, on account of the bricks is gone from the bottom of the tunnel and there's a mud trap there'd suck down an elephant. We worked our way around that through the old Winemaker's Guild inspection shaft. The narrow bit, with the strange bricks shaped like a woman's hand? And such forth. Besides, his worship over there is hunting gods and monsters. It don't do to walk in a straight line when you approaches one of them sort. Helps their aim, you might say."

Imago snorted. "My worship is wondering what I'm doing down here. But here we all are, and following your pace, my good man."

"Listen here." The old dunny driver stretched as if to touch his own shadow on the tunnel roof. "Man can come down this way, spend an hour and come out to find three days have passed. It's like the stories they tell the nurse-babies, if you take my meaning. More flows in than ever comes out, and the holes go ever deeper. So we walks slow and careful, and minds our manners. Else you could have took a cab about town and gone knocking on basement floors, I reckon."

"Archer?" Imago said. "What do you think?"

"Some priests walk a labyrinth to find their way closer to their god. Our good Saltfingers seems to have found the same secret here beneath the city streets." The godmonger shrugged. "He is also a priest of sorts, I suppose."

"Nah." The old dwarf cackled. "Me? Fat and full of robes and incense? Give me good, honest slopwater and a mossy stone to set on. Yes, things are different down here. You can hear the city sleeping."

Imago was certain Saltfingers did not mean the snores of servants in the basements above their heads.

The day went on, slow as treacle in a late winter barrel. Saltfingers took them first to a chamber most of the way up the hill, judging from the slope of the tunnels and the paths they followed. It was large as a good-sized carriage house, with niches carved out of the walls long enough for a man to sleep in curled tight.

There was no ornament that Imago could see, just a rough floor with a firepit lacking a chimney, and a ceiling scorched black with old soot out of which little pebbled daggers of stone had grown.

It smelled of dead rock and nothing else. No sacrifices, no sweat nor prayer, had passed here in more seasons than he could truly imagine.

Archer said as much. "A dormitory, or some other gathering place. There have been no noumena here in time and time."

Imago ran a hand along the stone of one of the little ledges. Some ghostly mold grew in a shape which hinted that straw had once been found there. "Why a dormitory down here?"

"Builders, maybe." Archer's light rippled as he shrugged. "Working on some tunnel or shaft."

"Aye," said Saltfingers. "And those who toil beneath the stone wants nothing more than to pass their nights as well as their days beneath a roof of earth."

"Do you have a better idea?"

"Peace, you two." Imago noted that in the course of their morning the godmonger's earlier silence transformed to a brittle edginess. "We do not know what we are searching for, so we shall have to keep looking."

"Here," said Saltfingers after a quiet, tense moment. He handed out little hunks of something pale and slimy. "Dunnyman's cheese, from our own molds. Just the thing for a hungry walker beneath the stones."

They moved on through the day, never taking a straight path for more than a hundred paces or two, crossing and scrambling along different byways, though Imago was certain they came back to the same tunnels time and again. For one, he kept seeing the steam pipe, which was either the same line over and over, or far more extensively routed than Saltfingers said.

Nonetheless, they found three more sites over the next span of hours. One had been a temple of sorts, to be sure, a squared-off room with a deep, burbling channel flowing through the middle. There was a low altar carved with drains for blood, and a brazier for burning the offerings that still remained in place, though largely as a lacework for verdigris. There had once been paintings on the walls. Mold and time had claimed them, so even Archer's careful study revealed no more than an elbow and one gleaming green eye that somehow survived.

"I do not know," he finally said. "There are scores of gods in the Temple Districts who require blood or flesh, and dozens of green-eyed statues, but neither serves to tell us who this was. Not one of the Old Gods, though. I can hear whispers here, but this was some cult of quiet, angry people from the alleys on the surface. There will be stairs up, somewhere near here."

"Syndic Marron's Alley," Saltfingers said. "Runs south from Filigree Avenue. Stairs was closed off by rubble when the old threadworks burned, a hundred years or so back."

Another locale they visited contained only candle stubs and some rotten fruit. It had the jagged look of a natural cave, broken into during some tunneling of the past. The street was close enough, for the sewer here was built with a high, vaulted roof that rumbled as heavy carts rolled by overhead. This place was more the work of children, or softheaded dreamers after the divine. Even Imago could see that from the childish offerings of beads and dolls and silver figurines that were scattered among the stinking, misshapen fruit.

Archer could put no name to that one, either, but he appeared to share Imago's opinion. "This one might grow to a god," he said, his voice less surly now, "if it had a prophet. At this time it is just a persistent memory lurking in the stone. Perhaps someone died here some while ago."

Saltfingers shrugged. "There's hardly a place in this city where somebody ain't died, now is there?"

"Ever counted the gods in the Temple District?" Archer said.

"Don't rightly need to. They all winds up down here in the end."

Imago finally called a halt after three more false leads found old holes with little meaning. "I've no more idea of the time than I do of the weather," he said, "but the City is due to fall and we're down here wandering from trashpit to trashpit in the same square mile. Something's not right."

"The Old—" Archer stopped himself. "The ones we seek…they come from beneath. Imperator Terminus sealed their temples even as he led their priests and power away."

"Under Nannyback Hill?" Imago sighed, rubbing his face with hands that stank of mold and stone. "How do we know that?"

"We don't," said Archer. "But time is short, and Ignatius grows ever greater with every step any of us take."

Imago felt a red rush in his head. "Having me wander around down here keeps me from being about the streets, accruing more of the power that makes the Old Gods dance, right?"

"Peace," said Saltfingers. "You're stone-crazy. Mayhaps this is the right place and mayhaps not. You're looking for the oldest, yes?"

"*Yes!*" shouted Imago, his word echoing in fading whispers as soon as it passed his lips. "Yes. The oldest, some blood-soaked goatherd's cave far beneath the heart of the city. Surely the sewers don't run that deep?"

"Not all of this is a sewer, your worship. Some is old basements, or storage rooms down where the temperature ain't changing much. Lower parts of town, off the hills, it's buildings under the buildings, old pavers. Down by Water Street there's the iron ribs of a bloody huge ship, saving the truth. There's shafts and stairs and rooms where men in masks meet to kiss old skulls then pretend to lie about their wives and tell the truth about their lovers. There's long-lost armories, a room beneath the Sudgate with a bronze chariot the stone's flowed around. Everything that ever was is down here, your worship."

"Much like the Sudgate," Imago said. "If that horrible old pile is the cellar of the City Imperishable, this is its foundation. We're lost in the foundation." He whirled on the other dwarf. "Where's the gods, Archer?"

The godmonger snarled through clenched teeth. "I. Don't. Know."

"Eat more cheese," said Saltfingers. "It'll stick to your chompers, and the chewing'll help you think."

They ate cheese.

The crazy old dwarf was right. The dunnyman's cheese did make you think. Not everything you *wanted* to think about, but something Enero had said nudged from memory back into thought.

"I am wondering why a man would be naming a hill as new," the freerider had asked him.

Imago had responded with some chance remark about the fires that had swept the New Hill some centuries ago. Everybody knew that. But now he realized that the important question was *when?* "The New Hill. How long ago was it rebuilt?"

"They builded it," Saltfingers replied. "Not rebuild. 'Tis all rubble and river dredgings up there, with pipe run through it for the water. The Water Captain ain't never going to get steam lines run up that way. They'd have to dig the place out to lay the iron in. No sewer tunnels, you see."

"When were the fires?"

"No idea, me." Saltfingers grinned and licked the cheese scum off his scaly hands. "I works below the stones."

"What would you trouble to build an entire hill to bury?" asked Archer slowly.

"Something old," said Imago. "And all too close to the Limerock Palace in the bargain. But you said your sewers don't run under that hill."

Saltfingers shook his head. "Oh, they runs *under* the New Hill. Just not up into it. Number two south main cuts right beneath it to join the Melisande by-flow. Old Number Two, that's one of the most ancient tunnels yet open. Them as lives up there has carts hauling their slops, or drop-runs sometimes."

"That's the other side of town," Imago said. "Across the Little Bull River. We'll have to go up to get there." He was relieved, actually.

"Up?" Saltfingers seemed surprised. "We're on a holy mission, your worship. Stay beneath the stones, we're safer. 'Sides, it's snowing wagonloads on the street."

"How do you know that?"

Saltfingers waved at a little channel busy with slushy water. "Look what's running away. We're warm down here, we're safe down here, we've got us some good steam. And we've already paid our way. You wants me to lead, you follows my lead."

He needed to go back to the surface, to send to Enero for word of Jason, to check in with his Little Council to see what new treachery had been threatened from the Limerock Palace. He needed to do so much besides creep around beneath the streets like an overtall cockroach.

Archer's face, in deep shadow beneath the dwarf's carbide lamp, glowed with the wrath of a small demon.

Imago realized that the godmonger was mortally afraid they would give up the search. The Lord Mayor pulled his gold chain of office out from beneath his clothing. "We are both crazed," he told Archer, "but I will follow this at least to the New Hill. If we find nothing by then, it will be too close to battle. I shall need to be above."

"Fair enough." Archer spat the words as if they were foul.

After a moment of searching for any peace in that glowering shadow, Imago turned back to Saltfingers. "I must ask. If we are to continue with your slimy labyrinth, how will we get across the Little Bull River while staying within the sewers?"

Saltfingers grinned. "Well, you see, the river, here in the City it runs on *top* of the ground, while we here are more in what you might say was *under* the ground, if you take my meaning."

Somewhere back in the main shaft down to the river, they followed a mossy ledge about a foot wide. There was no railing at all. The wall to Imago's right curved inward below the level of his shoulder, while the iron steam pipe sweated hot just at the height of his forehead. He walked off balance with every step. The dwarfs had it easier, but not much.

He already hated this place, the earlier beauty he'd seen swallowed by the filth and danger and sheer, dank darkness.

Amid Imago's smoldering thoughts, Archer plucked at his sleeve. He turned to look, but the godmonger laid a finger across his lips. Imago glanced forward at Saltfingers, but the dunny diver had stopped with his head cocked. The old dwarf reached up and twirled the knob on his lamp until the hiss died to a faint spit, and the light became little more than an orange coal.

Imago took the hint and did the same, as did Archer. All three were reduced to dim-edged shadows.

They all listened.

Darkness, especially beneath the earth, has a noise of its own. Something between the sound of distant water and the slow breath of stones. The slushy flow below the ledge where they stood slid and gurgled like a mountain stream. Straining his ears, Imago could hear occasional faint scrapes, as if stone settled. There was an odd echo from some distant drainpipe.

Nearby, someone...something...sniffed.

Could there be a dog down here?

"Them," said Saltfingers so quietly his voice was barely louder than his breath. The old dwarf crept up to Imago, pushed him back against the wall and carefully stepped around him. He did the same to Archer, then moved a few paces further on until he was beneath one of the steam relief valves.

Saltfingers eased his brass pistol from his pack, then stretched to the tip of his toes to clip the hose to the copper nozzle. He stayed stretched, one finger on the little cock handle of the steam relief valve.

Another sniff, then a slipping noise, of someone stepping too quick on moss. Saltfingers twisted the stopcock open, which produced a rising, rattling hiss as he turned the flame on his helmet back to its brightest setting. In the beam from his lamp Imago could see a naked boy with bloody eye sockets and a long, protruding tongue, standing not two feet from the old dwarf.

Sniffers!

Archer shrieked and tried to flee by running past Imago, sending them both toppling into the icy water that flowed quickly down the slope. Even as Imago fell, he saw Saltfingers send a blast of screaming steam right into the face of the eyeless boy. Imago found himself under the water, his head bumping on stones, fighting not to take the freezing filth into his mouth. The long, hooked pole he'd carried all day snagged on something, so he dragged himself along it to find stinking, terrible, breathable air.

"Coming your way!" bellowed Saltfingers.

Imago scrambled for footing, looking around wildly. His own lamp was out—no, his helmet was gone altogether—and he had no idea where Archer had got to. The old dunny diver had his own beam aimed at something pale that thrashed in the water and keened like a dying gull.

The current swept their attacker straight toward Imago, who braced his thighs against some obstruction beneath the surface.

He swung the hook ahead and jabbed it at the face of the crying horror. The metal slid off the gaping mouth but caught the sniffer in the neck. A long, black tongue darted out, serrated teeth glinting along its sides, and began wrapping its way up the shaft like some crazed snake in the bobbing, dashing light.

Saltfingers was jumping around, and the dip and weave of his helmet lamp was in serious danger of blinding Imago even while that impossible tongue unreeled toward his hands. He pushed the boathook a little farther away, but if the sniffer broke loose, the current was going to carry the thing right into Imago, face first.

"Looks like they found us!" Saltfingers shouted.

BIJAZ THE DWARF

He'd spent the short balance of that night wandering the Temple District, looking at the gods. Bijaz was infused with a certain energy he had not felt in a long time, his body moving with purpose alien to his recent experience. Though he still ached, he was stronger than he had been. Many of his hurts were gone, and the ones that remained seemed less overwhelming. He was, if not well, at least in health for the first time since his rape. Though his arse still burned—a reminder from the Numbers Men of their lesson. Nonetheless, winning back his life paid a bit more than the stakes of the bet.

Bijaz walked, breathing air that was stinging cold with a brassy taste foretelling snow. The wind worried at the spires and towers of the temples, setting prayer wheels to rattling and shaking bells all over that part of the City Imperishable. No one slept.

Not here.

Every dark-shadowed doorway, every glittery golden portal, every high window with red silk whipping in the breeze, everywhere in the district, they were praying, chanting, dancing. Others stood in ritual poses, offered burnt corn cakes and old ale, whipped themselves and their children, were chained beneath the bellies of bleeding bulls. All the rites of the one hundred seventy-eight temples and the uncounted gods they served were called upon this night.

Bijaz passed among them, frowning faintly. None of these small spirits could stand against what was coming, but perhaps the prayers of their faithful would provide a shield for some strong arm. The Old Gods, this was about the Old Gods, not the new.

He had been told, unmistakably, that the Old Gods were not of some single mind. The Numbers Men, those of the Old Gods who hid behind a collective name and the glare of their gaming lamps, made that clear enough. This frenzy of prayer—cymbals clanging, incense blown through the freezing city in multicolored clouds thick enough to dim the gas lamps of Upper Melisande Avenue and the surrounding cross-streets—might serve to call down some faint current of favor. But something older and stronger than these divinities would be required to break the back of the Imperator Restored and his coterie of sniffers, black dogs and worse.

Bacchanal, he thought.

The old summonings. He and Archer had gotten it half right, in that last frenzied hour before the Trial of Flowers and the return of Ignatius as Imperator.

The realization bloomed like dawn within his head. The bacchanals weren't meant to keep the Old Gods resting in some mockery of summoning. They were meant to keep the balance between the various of the Old Gods. Some of the bacchanals were dark, but some were not.

They had mistaken the Trial of Flowers completely.

And the morrow was the Festival of Winter Drownings, the one feast day of the year where the bacchanals were not marched. With that thought, Bijaz knew what would be required. As the morning bells rang across the City Imperishable, he hurried toward the Sudgate. The ragged, informal krewes among the most dreadfully poor would count double, something told him—the sniffers walked in the corpses of their beggar children after all. If he could get them moving, then he would work his way to the north end of the city and rouse the larger krewes.

He meant to force the greatest bacchanal ever seen in the City Imperishable into the streets on the next day. Fight winter shadows with the memory of golden days. But flowers only for the Winter Drownings. Rites of spring and sunlight. No black dogs or dancing skeletons. He would cause blossoms in the snows of winter.

Maybe that would balance the dread powers that moved within the Limerock Palace. Bringing the people back into the streets might shame the advancing armies. He hoped to call the City's luck from where it quivered within his soul like rising bread.

It was all he could think to try. At least he did more than simply cower in prayer.

Bijaz headed toward the south end of the city.

The people ebbed and flowed in the mean little alley markets around the Sudgate like spawning eels crowding a stream. The snow-edge in the air sent them out with their hoarded chalkies to buy turnips or catmeat for that night's stew before the weather came upon them.

He tried among the stalls first. "Excuse me," Bijaz asked a one-eyed woman selling soup bones and strips of bloody hide. "I want to find the bacchanals. Where are your krewes?"

"Buy 'un or g'er'off."

"Ma'am."

He moved on, slipping on cobbles slimed with old moss and filth crushed too slick for even beggars to salvage. The press of bodies was thick, reeking of sweat and fear and a certain urgency. Bijaz tried his query at other stalls, asking of a man with a rack of old bootlaces beneath a tattered awning, then two children offering quartered fruit guaranteed to have the garbage scent washed off, a crippled dwarf, bent and shivering from misboxing, who sold hair ribbons with bits of the previous owners' hair still clinging to them. Some were blank-eyed and indifferent to his questions, pushing their wares at him as if blind. The crippled dwarf chased him away with curses and a well-flung rock that raised a cut on Bijaz's forehead.

He was patient—he was the city's luck after all—but the snow was coming and Bijaz wanted to be away to the other end of town while the streets were still clear. Luck was not immunity from weather, after all.

Pressing on, he looked for young men with knives strapped to their thighs and an air of too much time about them. Instead he found a brown-leathered Tribade enforcer sitting on the lip of a cast-iron fountain filled with trash. She was a young woman with her hair shorn to yellow fuzz, eating a pear stored long enough to rot as she watched the movements on the street.

"Please, ma'am," Bijaz said.

"I know you." Another bite, her mouth moving briefly before she swallowed. "Some were looking for you."

"Some found me." He smiled, not so conscious of his broken and missing teeth as he had been.

"Biggest Sister said you weren't dead." Another bite.

"Her attention flatters me. Might I petition a great favor of the Tribade, who have been my sometime friends of late?"

"Might. I ain't no Big Sister to give an answer, though."

"Perhaps not. Yet you might help." He drew a breath. This was the time to make sense of his intuition, frame it into words that would stir people to action. Otherwise he was just another lost, crazed denizen of the City Imperishable, wandering the streets in search of something no one else could see or hear. "If you know me, you know where I was the day of the Trial of Flowers."

The Tribadist nodded. She wasn't watching the crowd now, just him. Trying to sort how dangerous he might be, Bijaz supposed. Let her sort. He went on: "I saw everything. I tell you, the Trial was a mistake. It summoned the Imperator Restored, and helped open the path for the Old Gods." A path—a life, a limb, a love, the voice over the River Saltus had told him. "The City is its people. The people need to mount a great bacchanal tomorrow on the Festival of Winter Drownings. Raise the light, bring only flowers and bright things. Leave our black dogs at home, the real ones are already loose. Can you help me raise the krewes of the Sudgate?"

Another bite of the pear, then the fruit was gone. "You are crazed, dwarf," she said, spitting seeds. "Nonetheless, I was told to watch for you, in case you returned from wherever. There are no bacchanals on Winter Drownings Day, though. We celebrate the cold dead by quiet visits and time before the fire."

"The cold dead are among us. Think how many died at the Trial of Flowers. What of the sniffers who walk even now? They are as cold and dead as you might want. Would you celebrate them?"

He warmed to his rhetoric, just as he had once worked salons full of the well-heeled Sewn. A small crowd gathered around him, an eddy in the hurried movements of the street. "We need a new Trial of Flowers," Bijaz proclaimed, pitching his voice to reach past the Tribadist and to the ears passing by him. He used cadences borrowed from Imago, meant to move listeners to action. "We need a Trial of Flowers done right. A bacchanal where all the flowers ride out at once. If we do not do it on the morrow, armies will sweep our city and we may never march a bacchanal again."

" 'Em as died that day might say different," someone shouted.

"They might!" Bijaz found thunder in his voice. "I, for one, tried to stop what overcame us all. But I was too late. I do not aim to be too late again. Can't you feel it?" As he spoke he climbed up onto the lip of the iron fountain, took an unsteady footing that put him a bit above the gathering crowd's eye level. "The end is close. You are here in the market at morning, instead of about whatever work it is you do. Snow comes calling like a white demon on the wing, and there are riders bound here to topple our walls. What will you do? Hide and wait to die, burned out in the snow?"

"Fight 'em," another voice called.

Perfect, thought Bijaz. "Then why not be in the streets? Why not be on the march? Why not call some light back into the growing darkness the Imperator Restored has visited upon us all? Raise the bacchanal and bring back the light!"

"'Bring back the light,'" said the Tribadist with a note of respect in her voice. "You'll go far with that one."

"Light," a woman standing near him said. Bijaz realized she was the one-eyed catmeat seller. "All what us had is gone to blood and darkness. 'Tis worse now than ever was beneath the Burgesses, Dorgau take their fat eyes."

"Sniffers," a man added. "I hear sniffers in the night."

Bijaz picked up that comment. "Sniffers. Creatures of this darkness that afflicts us, which will roll over us all soon. They were once children of the Sudgate, too. Pity them their pain. When we march upon the Limerock Palace with flowers and all things bright, we shall claim back the sniffers from His Magnificence, and at last bury them as our children." He spread his arms, half-boots slipping on the lip of the fountain as he opened his hands wide in invitation—not to mention to keep his balance. "Bring back the light!"

"Bring back the light," answered the catmeat woman.

Others joined in, voices rising in a ragged chorus that grew louder with each repetition. *Bring back the light. Bring back the light! Bring back the light!*

Bijaz waited until the chanting ran out. All pretenses at busyness had failed, and the street around the fountain was crowded with gawkers.

"March at the morning bells," he said into the silence that opened at the dying of the shout. "Flowers, fish, bright things only, but carry your gods and monsters into the street tomorrow for the Festival of Winter Drownings. March and meet at Terminus Plaza. We will lay claim to the stones that held our dead."

"Bring back the light!"

It was the better part of an hour before he could slip away and make his way north along Water Street, and the first fat flakes of snow had already begun to fall.

The Tribadist, long shut of her pear, walked beside him. Not close enough to be his companion, but unmistakably a shadow tagged upon him.

Bijaz made a stop at Ducôte's scriptorium. The press was silent, the steam engine idle, few of the clerks and printers even about as best as he could tell. The woman at the front desk told him the old dwarf was not there. She kept a nervous eye on the Tribadist, who had followed him in and had begun cleaning her fingernails with a long, narrow knife.

"Where is he then?" Bijaz glanced around, as if Ducôte might be hiding somewhere nearby. "I would spread the word of a festival tomorrow."

"You don't need our services for that," the woman said. "The Winter Drownings are hardly unknown. As for the master, he is away at his own business."

"There will be a grand bacchanal on the morrow. The Trial of Flowers restaged and done right. For that, I need your services, to send people to Terminus Plaza in the first hours after the morning bells. We will stand before the Imperator Restored and demand peace of the spirit, and we will fill the streets before the armies that come and demand peace of the sword."

"At which point we'll all die in the gutter," the Tribadist added. "Killed by black dogs or Tokhari swords." She produced another manky pear from a pouch at her waist. "You can print that if you want."

The woman shook her head with a half-smile. "Strange days in the City Imperishable. I shall send a note to master Ducôte and tell him of your message."

He could see the easy lie in her voice, meant to send him off. "Be sure to tell that worthless old inkspiller who these words came from. I am Bijaz the dwarf, late of the Sewn and now simply of the City Imperishable. The Lord Mayor owes me his very office."

"Ah." Comprehension lit her face. "I will send my letter soon. Where shall he find you, my lord dwarf?"

"I am no one's lord. I will be by the River Gate rousing the krewes that they might march tomorrow."

"There's no krewe that will march on one day's notice. It's two weeks work to move the big floats."

"We will have no more than this day," Bijaz said. "The last act of the Lord Mayor's Trial is about to play out." He glanced at the Tribadist. "Possibly on sword's point, possibly beneath the jaws of the black dogs and worse. Our choices have been made or stripped from us already. Tell old Ducôte that, as well. Good day, ma'am."

He stepped out onto Water Street, where the snow was falling even more heavily, followed by his leather shadow.

The krewe kings were easier to find than the folk of the Sudgate had been, but rather more difficult to convince. Bijaz heard arguing as he trudged through the slush of Three Asp Way. He stopped and looked to follow the sound, until he found a discrete brass plate screwed to a warehouse wall announcing it to be the house of Blackeyes Krewe.

A sullen guard stepped out of the door and nudged Bijaz, trying to move him off. The dwarf glanced at his Tribadist. She grinned and produced a dark-bladed stiletto, falling into a knife-fighter's crouch with the blade held close to her body.

"Hey, hey," said the guard, who was armed only with a cudgel,

Bijaz took advantage of the man's distraction to slip through the door. Inside was a high space filled with dangling heads and looming wagon beds. The krewe kings were gathered a ways inward, sitting in a pool of light cast down from above.

He approached, shouting for attention. "I come to call the krewes to meet the fate of the City Imperishable!" It was overdone, but then everything about the krewes was overdone.

The krewe kings broke off their babble to stare at him. One stood with a hand on his sword hilt, but another raised a hand. "We are not a criminal enterprise here, nor are we unduly fashed for time. I wish to hear what this foolhardy dwarf has to say to us."

Bijaz babbled his tale of bacchanals, flowers and the Old Gods, as they listened in grinning disbelief. Bijaz felt better than he had in a month, practically sizzling with energy.

"You're mad, dwarf," said the only woman among the ten men within. In her way, she was the strangest of the eleven kings. Sitting cross-legged in the palm of an enormous hand with red fingernails, she was thin as a vine stalk, with the complexion of old parchment, piercing blue eyes and huge white braids reaching her calves. He knew she must be the Queen of the Lost Brides, thinking on a lifetime of watching bacchanal processions. "There's none loves a good story so much as a krewe, and we are the Krewe of Kings here, 'tis true. Our purpose is to guard our houses and try to see that the flow of battle passes by."

"These aren't siege armies coming," said a fat man in a red velvet suit of very old-fashioned cut, trimmed with gold lace. He was sprawled sideways across a throne with enough gilt and paste gems to give a magpie a headache. "They'll burst the gates and ride for the Limerock Palace. They don't have time enough or equipment to scale the walls, particularly not in this weather, and they don't give a fig for the likes of us. We'll be safe enough. Off with you, before your safety is in doubt."

Bijaz tried to frame an answer that would reach them. "You aren't just parade marshals. Your bacchanals are ancient rites of the City Imperishable. You are the priests of those rites. If we do not call the light now, put flowers against the evils that stir among us, none of this will matter for aught."

"Mad," repeated the woman.

"Mad. Hardly!" Anger stirred within Bijaz, along with a glittering determination. He knew what to do next. "If I can prove the divine is afoot, will you call in the krewes and march with the morning bells?"

"We know the divine is afoot." This from a flame-haired man in a dark suit that would have passed muster within any bank on Heliograph Hill. He stood on bare concrete, avoiding the bright gauds around him. "Only a fool would think otherwise."

"The divine speaks in me," Bijaz stated flatly. "Surely one among you has dice?"

Just behind him the Tribadist stirred, muttered something and moved to stand so close to him that the dwarf could feel the warmth of her.

"I do," the fat man in red said. "Will you roll bones and tell me the Old Gods made you do it?"

They all laughed.

"I will bet my littlest finger against yours, red man, that I can best each of the dozen of you in a throw. One by one. Twelve throws. I will take them all."

Bijaz did not know if that would be true, but he prayed the Numbers Men had left some of their favor with him. He had, after all, won back his life at the White Table. Three-Widows made him the City's luck. Or something very like it.

The audacity of the bet certainly caught their imagination. There was more laughter. "What use have I for your finger?" the red man said, pitching his voice to boom loud.

"Take my hand, then," Bijaz answered, rising to the challenge. "You could use it to stroke your cock on a cold night."

More laughter, mostly aimed at the red man this time. "He has you there, Card King," said the woman.

"I will take your hand." The Card King grinned, coldly. "Just to teach you a proper lesson. Then you'll serve me in the holding of our krewe houses against the armies. I know who you are. Your word might even have some standing." He struggled from his throne with a hard gasp of breath and reached in his breast pocket for a suede pouch the color of his suit. "Here's my dice. We shall throw, beginning from my left, each of us. When first you lose, my knife comes out as well."

"If I prevail, you will take that as a sign of favor?"

The Card King shrugged, the movement rippling through the red velvet of his suit. "What else?"

"Then you march in the Festival of Winter Drownings. Come snow or war or wrath of the Old Gods. Now, we roll for the high number."

The flame-haired man took the bones first and bent to throw them in the circle that had formed around the concrete where he stood. Doubled ones, snake-eyes. Someone chuckled softly, saying, "An easy win for the mad dwarf."

Bijaz gathered the dice. They sat cold and hard in his hands, more stones than bones, but he made himself think of the two coins upon his eyes. I am at the White Table, he thought. Show me, Numbers Men. Keep your luck alive a little longer.

The dice rang like pebbles on brass when he threw them, spun whirring and settled to a doubled six.

"Hmm," said the red man. Bijaz looked up to see the woman staring strangely at him.

The next roll went to a stout fellow wrapped in brocade like an enormous cushion. He threw a three. Bijaz threw another clangorous twelve.

So it went, the next throwing a four, Bijaz a twelve. When the Queen of the Lost Brides lost her five to his twelve, she announced, "I am convinced."

"As am I," said the flame-haired man.

The Card King shook his head. "We play out the bet. My stakes, my dice."

Around they went, six, then seven, then eight, then nine, then ten, all losing to Bijaz's unvarying twelve.

The last man to throw before the Card King, a gangrel in baker's whites, looked at his fellow. "Are you certain?"

"Throw," said the red man. His voice was flint now, hard and sharp.

The Baker King threw an eleven.

Bijaz gathered the bones and threw another twelve.

The Card King retrieved the dice and closed a meaty fist about them. He stood, staring at his fingers, then met Bijaz's eyes. "If I throw a twelve, and you throw a twelve, none will have the high roll. The bet will be tied. We made no stakes for a tie, friend Bijaz."

"Why would you play for a tie?" Bijaz asked softly.

"To prove that no god owns me." The Card King shook his dice within cupped hands.

"So I ask your krewes to march tomorrow, to prove that no god owns you."

The Card King's arm shuddered. With a swift motion he cocked his hand far back and hurled the dice up into the air. They flew, sparking and whistling, to explode in two tiny bursts of blue-white fire. "I cede the bet."

Bijaz sagged with relief, the Tribadist touching his shoulder. "And I cede you back your littlest finger, if you will hold your word to march with the morning bells."

"He palmed them in a fast sleeve drop," the Tribadist whispered.

No miracle at all, Bijaz thought. Surely the krewe kings knew what they had seen.

"Well enough," said the Card King. "There is much work to be done. Some of it could use a small man's help."

Bijaz thought of the snow outside. It would soon be difficult for a dwarf alone, or even in the company of one, to travel all the way back down to the Sudgate. Furthermore, this far across town he might not have to see sniffers until their moment came on the morrow, selfish as that thought seemed. He knew he should seek out Imago, visit the walls, carry the luck of the Numbers Men everywhere, but a cold warehouse with suspicious krewe folk seemed far the better opportunity than a slog through weather and damp.

"My labor is yours." Bijaz bowed.

"He is his own krewe, I think," the Queen of Lost Brides said.

"Mayhap," Bijaz answered, "but I am king of nothing. I serve all now."

"Serve, then," the Card King told him. "There is work to be done throughout the krewe houses this night."

Honest labor for a change, Bijaz thought. When he turned to the Tribadist to ask if she would stay, he found she was already gone.

Good. Biggest Sister would know soon enough.

JASON THE FACTOR

Dawn came on the sound of bells. The rising sun swept the night's snow clouds before it, but the lands here east of the City Imperishable were hip-deep in snow. Jason was crusted to his camel by a coat of slushy ice clinging to his legs. The beast moaned and burbled with a species of gastric misery that seemed even deeper than his own suffering. A terrible knifing wind came with the touch of sunlight, worse than the snowfall it replaced.

He was as cold as he had ever been.

The camel riders certainly were. Dozens had fallen in the night, even hundreds, mounts and riders alike dropped by the killing chill. Some of the bodies had steamed in the cold as he passed, others already covered up as the snow kept tumbling from the sky as if shoveled from on high.

There had been no chattering on this ride, just a grim determination locked into place by a sheath of icy death.

The Tokhari army was drawn up in a loose column that had its head a quarter mile short of the bronze doors of the Sunrise Gate. Sometime in the late hours of the night a runner came for Jason, tugged him alongside the line of march through frozen mud and over sprawled bodies until he rode with Kalliope and some of the oldest men of this group. They were dusted white, bundled tight, until they rode like so many refugees from the darkness at the top of the world.

He sat on his mount next to Kalliope's white camel and three old men brown as their own beasts, all of them staring at the wall. Drifts had piled the snow higher against the stones, so that it seemed as if a man might ride on upward to the crumbled battlements. A few soldiers stood there, lit blood red by the dawn behind Jason's shoulder, but no banners waved. He didn't see any lines of riflemen, either.

Today was the Festival of Winter Drownings, he realized. In an ordinary

Novembres there wouldn't be more than a dusting of snow on icy streets, while the recently bereaved would be wandering door to door with corpse candles and old bones wrapped in wet silk. But this snow…was it a sending to protect the City, or a sending to bedevil it? The weather was no friend to the Tokhari, of that he was certain.

On the north side of the city, the Yellow Mountain tribes should be gathered. Awaiting whatever signal for which Kalliope also held back her armies.

Oddly, the roadway leading to the gate had been shoveled and swept. They stopped at the edge of the cleared pavement. Relatively cleared—snow had not stopped falling til after the city's now-vanished work crew had called off their labors, but it was a nominal ankle-deep churn there, a mere placeholder for the banks piled to each side.

Jason tried to find his breath, but it failed to satisfy. He could draw it in, but if he did not speak, the air simply leaked out with a faint, slow squeak that tickled his throat. It was as if he were the Drowned Man of the day's festival, drowned in blood and sand instead of foul, honest river water. *Ma-jieni na-dja*. The dead man of winter.

He certainly was not the Tokhari's luck. Their story had lied to them. Even if the fighting was easy, the victory was already killing-hard for far too many of them.

The Sunrise Gate squealed open. Snow shuddered from the gate house as the bronze doors moved, and he glimpsed a dozen men putting their backs into the effort. Even with the clearing of the snow, there was sufficient heavy, wet slush to make work of that.

He was baffled, but held his tongue. It would have been harder to speak, in truth, for the Tokhari had been silent as their frozen dead these last two hours.

A man rode out on a shaggy pony. He was not a large man, wrapped in pale blue silks. The rider did not seem to be armed.

Enero, Jason realized, recognizing the build and stance. Traitor was his next thought. But that wasn't true either, or rather, even if it were true, the epithet was stale. For one, the foreign freerider had been taking his coin from the Lord Mayor since Jason re-entered the service of Imperator Ignatius. That betrayal was a month in the past already. As for what happened now, Jason knew too little to draw worthy judgment yet.

Time to hold his thoughts tight as his tongue, Jason told himself, and see what developed. He noted with great interest that Kalliope and her escorts seemed unsurprised. As if they had waited for this man at this moment.

The little pony picked its way with care, staring myopically at the path in search of icy patches as it walked. Enero appeared unworried, riding with his hands laid on the pony's neck and letting the mount find its own way. Even from a hundred yards, Jason could see the amused glint in the mercenary commander's eyes.

Enero stopped a dozen feet before the row of miserable, whuffling camels. Where the Tokhari beasts strained for warmth and seemed stricken by the snow and cold, the mercenary's pony stamped and puffed a bit of steamy breath that was immediately snatched by the whip of the wind. The little animal appeared quite at its ease. Its rider was at his ease, too, for all that he was forced to look up in order to meet the eyes of the enemy leaders. That their army was sworn to lay his defenses to waste bothered him not at all.

"Well and I am seeing they are to be finding you, Jason," Enero called. Though only his eyes and part of his nose were visible in the scarves that wrapped Enero's face, Jason still saw the smile.

He took a shuddering breath. "My sister has lost more than she has found."

What Jason was able to see of Enero's expression grew close. "Ah. My friend of old. I am also to be seeing what it is that has been done to you." He touched the quilted hat, about where his forehead was beneath the layered cloth. "I am regretting you are coming to this pass. My condolences on your dying."

Jason wasn't quite sure what to say. He had played the only card he held in announcing his relationship to Kalliope, but Enero did not strike at the bait. He glanced sidelong at his sister, who opened her scarves to let her face meet the weather—something reasonable only because the wind was at her back and thus could not freeze her lips or steal the breath from her nose.

"We are here," she said succinctly. This from a woman backed by more than a mile's worth of mounted warriors. What a woman she had become. Kalliope went on: "What news?"

That startled Jason even in his cold-numbed state of decedence.

Enero nodded, focused entirely on Kalliope with that strange intensity Jason had seen before in the freerider. "I am believing we are being able to take them at the source."

It was obviously a continuation of an old conversation. His sister knew the commander of the city's defenses. How?

Kalliope frowned, closed her eyes a moment. "So the cancer is still rooted in the Limerock Palace. You believe it has not spread?"

"Strangeness is to be afoot. But since the Imperator is to be returning, no. They are to be hiding behind palace walls. The Lord Mayor is to be doing much right." He shrugged. "Luck, inspiration, good advisors. Since the Trial of Flowers the power-seekers are not to be spreading out so much. To be digging deeper into the noumenal, I am thinking."

"What counsel do the Arlecchini offer?"

Enero shrugged. "Paolino is to be saying much the same, though in fairness

I am seeing him much listening at gutters and walls. Today is to be a festival, so he is also thinking there will to be an opening of the way from the darkness. Much power, and the Old Gods are most likely to be dancing."

"The weather leaves us no choice," Kalliope said. "We cannot even pretend to invest the walls."

One of the old men rattled a string of Tokhari at her, but she cut him off with a few sharp words. Jason interrupted the silence that followed. "How…how is it you know each other so well?"

Enero looked at him once more with another shrug. "I am much to be sorry, my friend Jason. There are to be pretenses both good and false between us. Enough to be saying fear of your Old Gods is to be making bedfellows of strange people."

"He is a general from Bas Luccia, on the Sunward Sea," said Kalliope with some distaste. "No friend of my desert-dwellers, but no enemy either. Those cities fear your Stonesource gods as much as we do. Memories would seem to be longer the further one goes from the City Imperishable, brother mine."

The freerider—no, the general—bowed slightly in his saddle. "I was not to be thinking to say so much to you, Jason, but your sister is to be spilling truth like last night's wine. Winter Boys are to be from the Sunward Sea." He gave a short, humorless laugh. "It was to be too close to obvious, I am to be fearing, but no one is ever asking. Where are you thinking any northdweller is to be finding camelopards, yes? Creatures of the grass seas which lap at the desert shores, they are being."

"The wind eats my army, Enero," Kalliope snapped. "Are we admitted to the gate, or must I draw them up in battle array?"

"You are to be coming in," he said. "Though now I am to be betraying the coin your brother was first giving me. It is being my head, perhaps."

"Your head has been poised on the block since you first rode north." She whistled, and the army began to move.

Jason expected Kalliope and her honor guard of old men to ride straight in, but she prodded her pale camel up onto the packed bank of snow that Enero's sweepers cleared from the road sometime in the night. Groaning and spitting, the escorts' camels followed, and so did Jason's. To his surprise, Enero turned his pony up onto the bank, next to Kalliope who was now on the far side of her old men from Jason.

He could not ask anything of the freerider. Not now.

Perched on the bank, Jason found himself higher into the wind, which he swore he could feel through the rough sutures in his gut. Kalliope, he realized, climbed up to show herself to her army and count them as they came. He supposed she must need to do so, after the dreadful night march.

The size of the Tokhari army had never been clear to Jason. City rumor had magnified it to a horde, but the Tokhari were not so numerous in the first place as to sweep the world like locusts, insofar as he knew. An enormous wave of men and mounts would have crashed across the lands to the south and east like a fleshly sea. No, he had seen a thousand or so men outside his sister's tent, and assumed four or five times that many.

The army passed in a review of misery. Many of the mounts—horses and camels both—were bleeding, chafing, with ice crusting their lips, their nostrils, their legs and bellies. Some riders had found blankets or the covers of tents in which to wrap their beasts, but Jason could not tell if that made a difference.

Watching them in clear sunlight, he saw that these warriors came from dozens of different Tokhari clans. Though all were bundled in fur, leather, wool and ice, one group of men had round silk hats in red the color of poppies. Another squad passed bearing unusually long spears with ornate copper heads that flashed in the morning sun. A third, on ponies, boasted ornate silverwork on their bridles. Each man rode and equipped himself as he would, that was clear enough, but each group had their tokens.

They were pretty, in a curious way, these men riding out of the dawn with their blades and shields gleaming. Possessed of a certain majesty even, if Jason ignored the bloody lips and the eyelids frozen closed and the number of men slumped or even tied into their saddles. And the stench, like the world's greatest wet dog. Camels only grew worse in the cold.

None of the warriors had brought their dead with them. Not a one. As far as he knew, Tokhari made a great show of honoring those who passed on. He'd seen more than a few Tokhari funeral feasts on the streets of the City Imperishable. They cut free the scalp of the departed and sent it back to the sand in a presentation box that was thought to carry the spirit as well. The quality of the container varied with the wealth and standing of the deceased. But they also celebrated the interring of the body.

He took a shuddering breath that he might find his voice. "Where are the fallen?"

Kalliope gave him a quick glance, leaning forward to speak past the old men and answer him. "This is a storm of war, not a caravan. We leave the bodies on such a cleansing ride to guard our path home. We will collect them again along our way as we return."

"Ah." Back to the sand, he thought.

"It is no great ill in the desert to give of your flesh to other creatures," she added. "A thing that took me a good long time to understand. The rocks of the Stonesource still pave my soul, brother. Now I must continue to count."

Count she did, while one of the old men made tallies on a looping frame the size of an embroidery hoop, from which horsehair dangled. He slid variously colored beads on and off in some complex calculation that went beyond a mere running total of the numbers that passed before them. Reckoning by clan?

When the last group of stumbling camels passed, the tallyman handed his frame to one of his fellows, who pulled a similar frame from a loop on his camel saddle and compared them.

A rapid exchange of Tokhari then, in which Jason heard more numbers. Kalliope made a response with the measured cadence of something formal. "We are one thousand, four hundreds and two tens," she translated. "Two thousands and eight crossed the Redrock River out of our lands." She spat into the snow. "Over five hundreds lost just to see these walls."

The old men spat in sympathy with her. The one closest to Jason turned to look at him with leering yellow eyes. *"Il-paj adani tuala, ma-jieni na-dja."*

"Perhaps you have opened the way," Kalliope said, then urged her camel down onto the roadway that had been swept almost clear by the passing of the army.

If they meant to raze the city, Jason thought, they must be relying on the Yellow Mountain tribes to bring far greater numbers. Yet here Enero was meeting them. Numbers were not the sole game afoot.

IMAGO OF LOCKWOOD

By the gods, he was going to die. Imago jabbed once more with the boathook, but that tongue kept coming, reeling out of the sniffer's mouth like some unholy asp. He had never seen anything so terrible. The razor-toothed edges caught his attention as surely as any bailiff's headclamp.

Cold water. Darkness. A crazed and elderly dwarfen dunny diver. This boathook. He was running short of assets.

"Dorgau take you to every hell!" Imago screamed. He was going to have to grab at that horrid tongue and lose some of his fingers.

Archer exploded upward from the frigid sewer water. The godmonger was screaming as he leapt, some incoherent outpouring of rage, butting the sniffer flat in the face with his own broad forehead. Imago, soaked in a glittering spray of icy water, saw Archer shove something into one of the sniffer's vacant eye sockets.

The sniffer screamed, a noise even worse than the shriek of horses trapped in a stable fire. Its tongue whipped backward along the shaft of the boathook as it tried to pull away from Archer, who stuffed his weapon of choice in the other eye socket.

Leeches, Imago realized. The godmonger was attacking the sniffer with leeches. He took advantage of the reduced pressure on the boathook to drop it between the sniffer's legs and yank up and back, hopefully snagging at the scrotum.

This thing might be a walking nightmare from the noumenal world, but Archer's attack showed that it could be hurt.

The sniffer's shrieking cut off with a muffled grunt as Imago's boathook caught firmly. Saltfingers took advantage of the distraction to lean out from the walkway edge of the sewer and jam the steam pistol in its ear. "Back!" the old dwarf shouted.

Imago let himself tumble over the submerged barrier against which he'd been braced, as Archer let go of the sniffer and dropped away. There was a violent hiss, and the creature's head exploded just as Imago fell beneath the surface, clutching his boathook in one hand and his chain of office in the other.

They reorganized themselves, and what they were able to find of their gear, at a little stone platform upon which set a tiny iron stove. The scuttle was empty, as was the coal box beneath it. The only light they had was from Saltfingers' helmet, which they propped atop the squat metal box.

Before collapsing into a torpid silence, Archer shivered violently and babbled briefly of dead men in the dark. Which wasn't precisely news to Imago, but the godmonger had also experienced a vision of snow-crusted faces that seemed both too obvious and to make little sense. Saltfingers stomped around, milling his arms. Imago almost asked the dunny diver to stop until he realized the old dwarf was simply warming himself up as best he could. The godmonger simply lay still as the dead.

"Archer may die of the cold," he said quietly when Saltfingers finally did settle a little.

"Cold?" A pale-toothed smile flashed gleaming in the dark. "Let him run out a bit. I'll take care of the cold." Saltfingers grabbed up his helmet and his steam pistol and stepped to the sweating iron pipe, where there was another copper valve.

"You're not going to blast him with that?" Imago was incredulous.

"No." Saltfingers was angry, Imago realized. Or frightened. The dwarf's voice trailed from the bobbing pool of light as he worked, his words thickened by emotion. "I'm going t' blast the blue hells out of yon coal stove. Then'll put his hands in't. Then'll put his feet in't. Then'll put his head in't. I'll be blasting it again, too, til the little bastard comes warm enough f'r'us to ask him what happened."

"What happened? That sniffer followed us down here, or found us. That's what happened."

"Not that." Saltfingers returned with the pistol, trailing his mesh-wrapped hose. "Get him to the edge of the platform, will ye? Consider this, your worship. Where'd he find them leeches? Little buggers don't live in fast-moving water what's a cat's whisker from being froze solid."

That was a good question. Imago tugged the shivering, whimpering Archer as far from the coal stove as he could get, all of six or seven feet, and waited out the whoosh of steam and the quick-cooling fog that followed.

It took a very long time to get warm. Like Saltfingers, Imago shivered and stamped until circulation returned, but the inert Archer didn't seem to improve. After the third or fourth blast, the dunny diver extinguished his carbide lamp, "To save on the rocks, y'see," he said. " 'T'will be well."

Oddly, it was. A faint gray gleam of light was visible in the hurrying sewer channel, presumably filtered down from some street drain a ways above them. Their platform was in a larger space that extended beyond the edges of the stone, though Imago did not remember passing such a room on the way in from the outside. He wasn't sure what lay past the edges of their resting place, except that it plopped and burbled occasionally, and the stink had a different quality here. More *green,* like a garden pond gone to rot, or a kitchen midden so old it was wet and growing.

Whatever was out there, it glowed. That took a while for Imago to notice, once Saltfingers had cut the lamp, but as his eyes grew to meet the darkness he saw a faint, numinous green that matched the ordure. In the vague light he could make out pillars and arches, characterized more by the darknesses where the glow did not reach than by any visible aspect of their own.

Ribbed, like a temple.

"Is this our place?" he finally asked, after studying it for a while.

"No." Saltfingers still sounded upset, but calmer. "Quiet now. I'm listening for sniffers."

Which made little enough sense, as every time the dunny diver fired off the steam pistol to warm the metal of the coal stove it produced an unholy racket. After which the two of them had to strain to lift Archer into a bit of the warmth, with all the grunting and puffing that naturally accompanies such an exercise conducted by clumsy, tired people in darkness.

After that, Imago's ears would regain their sense of the darkness, much as his eyes had found theirs. He heard the faint plops from the green glow, the chuckle of the sewer flow with the occasional hiss and rattle of slush moving down the channel. Deep groans once in a while, apparently coming from the very stones of the City Imperishable. At the least, they caused no alarm in Saltfingers, which led Imago to conclude these were ordinary noises of the underground.

After a time that might have been minutes or hours—for Imago could not track the passage of time down here at all—Saltfingers finally spoke, in a low voice. It took Imago a moment or two to realize he was being told a story. Or myth.

"There's always been places below the earth," the old dwarf said, "since first a man set spade to make a grave, or put his back into digging a latrine. They's one and the same, for the meat's the shit what's left behind when a life has passed on, while soil and stone are the arms of the world to fold them back in. There's always been places below the City Imperishable, since a man built a wall to shelter his goats and needed a place to shovel the scat and lay his children to rest.

"The first dunnyman was Lothar the Small, who opened the ways.

"The best of the dunnymen was Left-Hand Miscali, who raised the stones over the greatest graves.

"Whatever happens, the last dunnyman won't be me, because our work goes on so long as there's people to eat and drink and shit and die."

He fell silent again.

Imago thought through Saltfingers' words. Everyone had a purpose, everyone had pride, everyone had a price. He had thought the dunny diver something of a joke, when Archer first urged him to seek out this old dwarf. Even in this short space of time, Imago had come to see both the majesty and terror of the hidden regions below the City.

Something caught at his thoughts. The greatest graves. Quiet, Imago told himself. Don't shatter the moment. He pitched his voice low. "What did that mean, what Miscali did?"

"Left-Hand Miscali," Saltfingers said absently. "Young Miscali was dunnyman before him, and three generations after we had a Dyagene Miscali who was to have taken the lamp, but died in Garth's Raw Flood. We've had four other Miscalis besides them."

The sense of history settled on Imago like a cloak of prickleburrs, stirring his scalp and the skin of his back. "You know them all."

"Aye." Saltfingers' eyes gleamed in the almost-darkness. Between them, Archer snored, a more normal breathing than he'd had since they'd hauled the godmonger out of the freezing current. "Can't be no proper dunnyman without you know some of the history. Can't be dunny diver to the City Imperishable without you know it all. We learns the tunnels and channels and ways, that keeps us safe and saves our lives. We also has our chants and songs, that keeps us right in our ways and saves our souls. Lays of our tribe, oncet I got tole in a bar by a drunken poet from the Sunward Sea. He wanted to make a song of us, but a whore's minder killed the boy, I heard. Least I never saw 'im no more.

"So, yes, your worship, I knows them all. Someday soon my name will be on the song, too. Saltfingers what died beside the Lord Mayor, I expect they'll call me. Et by something with too many teeth and not near enough brains, I reckon."

"You think we're going to die in here?"

"There's sniffers down the sewers, man!" Saltfingers sounded incredulous. "They've opened too many ways in the Limerock Palace. You hurried them. Those armies on the march hurry them, too. So Astro and the Almond Man, they got to move faster. First, he moves along the current with the power, and the Imperator is no more restored to us than Left-Hand Miscali is. That poor old wight don't know he's dead yet is all."

Imago took a moment to work that through. The Almond Man was Michael Almandine, of course, Secretary to the Inner Chamber and now to the Imperator Restored. Astro was probably Astaretto, the Third Counselor. Which would mean that Saltfingers' "First" was the honorable syndic Arran Prothro, First Counselor.

Well, Saltfingers certainly had his touch on the pulse of politics in the Limerock Palace. Which should be no surprise given that the dunny diver went everywhere and apparently heard nearly everything. The serious men and women who sat in Imago's office in the Rugmaker's Cupola and gave him their assessments of this and that might have phrased things differently, but they would have said much the same.

The sniffers, however, were a surprise, both to Imago and apparently to Saltfingers. He wanted to take the conversation back to the greatest graves, but he needed to steer the dunny diver through the shoals of this mood to get there.

He tried to tack the conversation. "Why are you surprised at sniffers?"

Saltfingers sighed. "We got our monsters down here. I can show you claws long as your left leg, dangling in a room where Perry Corpsepants hung 'em after he and the Left Bank Boys beat back the Lambtown Wyrm. There's them freshwater squid what come up from somewheres time to time through the DerMeer springs under the old parade grounds. Gangrene toads and all manner of creatures that makes their homes in dark filth.

"But they protects us, too. From sendings and summonings and the glittery stuff that washes down drains from certain temples and guild halls and houses. Our monsters, they're *our* monsters. Our luck. The dunnymen, we're *their* luck, for all we goes to war on one another from time to time. These things, from the noumenal, they ain't for us. And they ain't come down here since Left-Hand Miscali closed up the greatest graves. It was sealed in the bargain what was made then."

Push now, thought Imago. Lightly, still he must push. "You've known this whole time where I wanted to go, haven't you?"

"Aye. Beneath the New Hill. You but had to ask the right questions." The dunny diver's voice slowly found its way from the fey mood back toward normal. "There's mysteries and great oaths sworn in my calling. A mere Lord Mayor ain't enough to set those aside for, begging your worship's pardon."

Imago had to laugh at that—softly, without mock. He felt rather mere himself, more often than not, since achieving this idiotic office. "You'd not be setting those oaths aside for me, my faithful dunny diver. You'd be setting them aside for the good of the City Imperishable."

"What good would I be to the City if I didn't hold my secrets?"

"Indeed. Yet what good would it be if the City died to keep your secrets?"

"And so here we are, your worship."

"So I see." Imago took a deep breath. "Have I asked the right questions?"

"Near enough. Time is short, and I'm feared of more than sniffers ere we're done."

"It's only been a few hours," Imago said.

"Your worship, we're well into the watches of night now. You've been down here a day, and halfway through the moon's walk."

Archer stirred at that, then pulled himself up on his elbows. "I was in a swamp," he said in a muzzy voice. "Have you anything to eat?"

Imago groaned as Saltfingers produced another wedge of that vile dunnyman's cheese. The stuff glowed faintly in the dark, almost the color of the stinking slop around them. Sausage came as well, which was more frightening, but Imago refused to speculate on its origin or composition. At least it had enough garlic in it to stun his tongue, which argued for a multitude of meaty sins lurking beneath that concealment.

"Eat," said Saltfingers, his voice completely ordinary now. "And have a bit more of your water. Though go easy on it. There's not much clean down here to refill the skins from. Then rest a bit, you and me, while Archer stands a watch. We'll need it now. We got to move on soon. Time is too short."

Imago didn't bother to make any argument for a return to the surface this time. Saltfingers' tale had convinced him this course was the best he could do for the City. Enero would fight, and the Little Council would watch and wait at least as well as Imago could.

He choked down the sausage and the slimy cheese and chased sleep awhile on the cold, cold stones.

Sleep must have found him, because Imago had the distinct desire to avoid awakening when Saltfingers began to shake his shoulder. The dunnyman stuffed another hunk of sausage into the Lord Mayor's hands and made urgent noises that might have been words had his ears been less fuzzed with sleep.

Soon enough they emptied their straining bladders into the running sewage, and were walking, though this time down a winding stair. This direction surprised Imago. It was carved out of raw stone, and did not appear to serve, like all the other passages they had been through, as some portion of the water or sewer systems of the City Imperishable.

When he inquired, Saltfingers said, "Sometimes we've built byways, just to get around a thing that must be got around. It's that a man has to go a bit deeper than the muck runs to get below the river, your worship."

Imago followed the bobbing glare of Saltfingers' lamp and tried not to snag the boathook on the close-curved spiral of the wall, and listened to Archer struggle along behind him.

"It was a swamp," Archer said after a while. He tugged at the bag around his neck. "You saw the leeches."

"Those rather upset our friend, I think," Imago replied in a low voice. Not that Saltfingers couldn't hear everything they said, but he didn't care to have his words echo up the spiral to the bristling ears of whatever might follow them. "I thought you were gone, killed by that thing or your fall, but I would swear before a judge that you were not there beneath the current."

"Swamp, I tell you." The godmonger fell silent.

Imago could not help needling him a little. "You of all people should know to expect miracles."

"No one should expect miracles," Archer said. "That is the surest way to banish the divine to the margins of imagination."

"So where did you go?"

"A swamp. I already told you." The godmonger's tone made it clear he was finished with the conversation.

Whatever else was real or illusion below the stones, it was certainly true that a dunnyman's life moved slow. Imago judged that it took them the better part of an hour to make a half-mile's distance, as the dog ran on the streets above. Very little in these passages and cracks and caverns had been made for the convenience of walking men. The lower levels, beneath the sewers, were much more raw—crude excavations connecting natural voids in the clay and stone that underlay the city, unfinished work where walls had been laid or baulks raised to save some threatened ceiling.

A mine, more than sewers. Unlike the levels above, here there was little ornament, and no real effort at beauty.

"What did they ever dig for here?" he asked, wondering if it truly had ever been a mine.

"Gods, for the most part," said Saltfingers. "Not all of this is dunnyman's work. You know the old Temple District stood where the New Hill rises now?"

That was the missing idea that helped this all make sense. The realization bloomed in Imago's head like fire in the night. "And so the Old Gods lie below the New Hill?"

"Yes. Our city was built on mysteries of soil and stone, your worship. All this stuff with Balnea and Dorgau and them women in swan chariots, that come a lot later."

"You speak of chthonic religions," said Archer, finally joining in. Imago was pleased that the godmonger sounded almost his usual self. "Soil takes blood well," Archer went on, "and is watered by it for next season's fruit, and any fool can see that stones are the bones of the world. Easy to find gods there, but they tend to be foreign to mercy or laughter or light."

The connection was obvious enough to Imago. "Old Gods."

"Yes," said the dwarfs together. Saltfingers added: "Soon. Sooner than you'll like."

Someone should have done this years ago, Imago thought. He realized someone *had* done this years ago. When Imperator Terminus broke the temples and the Empire in the same stroke, he could not have meant for the divine monsters to be summoned back.

The current Lord Mayor only wondered with a bitter fear how he and two half-mad dwarfs could accomplish now what had taken a former Imperator with an entire army to manage somewhere back in history.

"Here," said Saltfingers. They stood on paving stones—paving stones!—twenty fathoms beneath the surface, with timbers and pillars of stacked rock keeping a passage open before and behind them. "We're under the New Hill," the dwarf continued, "just about beneath Roncelvas Way. The Rebuilt Second East Main runs between us and the sunlight, though there's older tunnels below these pavers." He stamped his foot. "I wouldn't care to make my way down there. They ain't been walked or chanted or cleared since the New Hill was raised."

Imago looked around. The harsh spotlight of Saltfingers' headlamp showed mostly stones and clay and layers of tight-packed spill. What had been dumped here, then built upon. It must have taken the labor of years, he realized. Not much was left of what had stood before. "Here is where the old temples were?"

"I never thought to see this," Archer whispered. "We have our rumors, in my brotherhood, and we are sworn and set to stop the Old Gods from returning, but to find...this..."

"It's rocks and stones," Imago said.

"Rocks and stones where the priests of the Bloodless One walked." Saltfingers stared at his feet as he spoke, his light shining on a crack in the ancient pavers. "The Great Wolf had her processions. All of them, from the Black

Ox to the Bone Breaker to the Little Man."

"Do not call them!" snapped Archer.

Imago was confused. "I thought their names were lost."

"They are." Saltfingers looked past Imago at Archer, forcing the godmonger to squint and cover his eyes against the glare of the carbide lamp. "But a man must call a thing by some word or another. They grew new names, the Old Gods, down here in the darkness of their graves. Because sometimes a dunnyman sees a drawing scratched on a wall that he knows he must chisel away, and he needs a name to put to that so's to warn others. Or we hears things that move with a scrape, a click, a slither."

Archer was aghast. "To name a thing brings it into the world."

Saltfingers' response was flat. "They's already in the world, dwarf."

"They're in the City," Imago said. "I saw the black dogs and worse, the day of the Trial of Flowers. Those sniffers as well. But all I see here is dirt, rocks, old shadows. Where are these open graves?"

The dunny diver turned away. "The greatest graves." His light shone down the tunnel until the beam attenuated to vagueness amid swirling dust. "Why do you think this road is open?"

Imago shivered. The gold chain was heavy and chill on his neck. It all came back to power—to focus. What would he be giving now, sacrificing to try to reseal these broken doors? The old dwarf's words echoed within his thoughts: *Saltfingers what died beside the Lord Mayor.*

The dunny diver had cast no bones to tell the Lord Mayor's doom.

They walked on.

"Judgin' by what we seen in the city this last season, I think 'tis the Great Wolf and the Little Man they called back," said Saltfingers. "Maybe the Water-Bearer. Though it could be any of them, I reckon." He halted, forcing Imago and Archer to stop close behind him. "Look here."

His light showed a path, scuffed with footsteps. Saltfingers turned his head to follow it. The walkway issued from an iron door canted against the crazed wall of soil and scrap. With a dizzying turn, he looked farther down the tunnel. The path went on.

"Evidence enough," said Archer. "That door must lead up to the Limerock Palace."

"From the New Hill?" Imago said. "It's bit more than just a nip up the stairs from here."

"We'd have seen that, me and my boys." Saltfingers mused. "Must go up to one of the great houses on the hill. Chetlips, what is brother to Astro, he has a little gold palace tucked up there. Or so I hear tell."

Chetlips? Chelattini, Imago translated mentally. Intendant-General of the

Assemblage of Burgesses and until quite recently master of all coin that flowed in the city. "Therefore we know we're on the track we need."

"Quickly now," Archer said. "Can you feel it? The stones are beginning to speak."

Imago heard nothing, but Saltfingers stirred nervously. " 'Tis the Festival of Winter Drownings today. The dunnymen takes that for a feast day, on account of so many of us end our lives in water. Or least in that which flows. A bacchanal for the dead would be a day for the Old Gods to rise up into the sun."

"Then show me," Imago almost shouted.

They began to run.

The god-graves were strangely simple, when they found them. The mine-shaft street ended in a round-walled cavern, an enormous subterranean chamber that proved to be nearly a sphere. In the flickering glare of Saltfingers' headlamp, Imago saw that the sides of the room were built of architecture, as if some demon had swallowed a city then regurgitated it deep beneath the earth. The light passed over pillars broken and stacked like snapped sticks, a large corner of mortared brick, lintels and doorposts and windows and corbels and caryatids and iron gates covering only more stone.

Imago was dumbfounded. He could not truly imagine how such a place had come to be. It was as if the fill that was dumped to make the New Hill had grown a cancer—a void deep within that over time forced the fragments of stone and brick and metal outward like a tumor within the flesh of the City Imperishable.

Which quite possibly was the literal truth.

"Down," he whispered.

Saltfingers depressed the beam of his lamp. The room was a pit beneath them, though a path led down across the broken city bones. Eleven coffins lay beneath his feet, arranged in a circle so the foot of every one faced a center ring. Each was built much like the whole of this space, from fragments of larger-made things. Though where the walls were a riot of disjointed detail from a hundred different sources, the coffins were made from materials more consistent.

The broken ruins of each god's temple.

A detail popped into his memory, from one of the endless conferences in the Rugmaker's Cupola. Eleven krewes marched in the bacchanal processions. Here were eleven Old Gods. Gods supposedly long since laid to rest.

"See," said Saltfingers, playing his lamp around the circle. "Those slabs atop of 'em. Bluestone. Couple of tons for each grave. Not from anywhere around here. Imagine the cost, shipped down from the Yellow Mountains to cap these. That'n there is cracked." The light swept on. "That'n there is broken altogether. Your fine men of the Burgesses been playing at silly buggers with old darkness, to break those stones." He sighed. "And me without my steam down here."

Imago began to pick his way along the path, though he could barely see by the scattered glare from Saltfingers' light. The dwarf followed, so that Imago's shadow preceded them.

Down in the center of the tombs was a smaller pit, though this had seemingly natural sides and was more irregular. One end was sloped, the other overhung. A grotto. The remains of a little wall were tumbled before the grotto.

"A blood-soaked goatherder's cave," whispered Archer. He clutched his fetish bag as if it were a lifeline.

Imago's hair stood up from his scalp. He heard buzzing, like fields of locusts on the move, and the chain of his office was hot on his chest, even through his cold, damp leathers. He walked down the slope, approached the grotto, the dwarfs trailing each to one side of him.

A blue stone sat there, lumpy as old milk. It glowed. Blood was crusted on it, both ancient and fresh, and the remains of a fire were spread before the altar.

"Where the city began," the Lord Mayor whispered. He slipped the chain from his neck. It was almost too heavy to lift, and pulled him forward like one of the magnets that the electrickmen use in their plants.

"The Little Man?" he heard Archer ask Saltfingers.

"Who else, for us?"

"Well," said Archer, "that would go some way to explaining what became of Bijaz."

Imago fell to his knees before the blue stone, warm ashes flying around him. He bent his head and lay the gold chain on the altar. It clicked as it touched the bloody surface, and began to glow with the same faint light as the altar itself.

"What must I give?" he asked the shadows. Locusts buzzed closer, the walls breathed.

"You knows the Little Man?" Imago heard Saltfingers say to Archer.

Couldn't they tell what was happening? How the darkness had closed in around them?

"What do you imagine that we godmongers gossip about?" Archer said. "Gods, of course. Besides that, the subject of dwarf history is much of interest to me. The City Imperishable is the only city in the world where we box our children to grow them small and stunted."

Imago heard them as if through a curtain. Some great hand closed around him.

Saltfingers laughed. Nasty. "Sacrifice, always with the sacrifice. That's all we dwarfs ever are. Sacrifices to the good of the city or some family."

"Indeed." A pause, then: "I know what the Old Gods want of you, my Lord Mayor." Archer's voice was almost light.

The dunny diver sounded surprised. "You'll cut him? Down here?"

"Where else? It will call the Little Man back and maybe lay him back to rest. If the city has luck left in it, we will find a way to beard the other gods. Lose one, the rest will be weakened."

"Cut…" Imago moaned at the thought. It was rare that a grown man, usually younger than he, was put through surgeries to shape them as if they had been boxed in their youth. Though it did happen, he had never even met a cut dwarf that he knew of. "You would make me one of…one of…you?"

Saltfingers' light moved close, throwing Imago's shadow hard against the altar as if he were already splayed across it. "What is wrong with us?"

The great hand, shadowed and noumenal, closed around Imago, seeming to reach into his chest. That convinced him far more than any words of these two mad dwarfs. Something was afraid of him, wanted him to stop. "Then do it," he said. "Before my courage fails me, or my heart."

"Can you walk in the darkness?" Archer asked.

Saltfingers sounded surprised. "Of course."

"Leave me your helmet and spare rocks for the light. Go and find the Tribade, tell them to send Grayshadow. Their woman philosophick doctor. I will need her if our Lord Mayor is to live."

Imago was surprised he was expected to survive. He crept up onto the altar and lay himself down as Archer began to sharpen a long, curved blade Imago had never known the godmonger was carrying.

Saltfingers had left without a word to him.

BIJAZ THE DWARF

The night passed quickly in a rush of men and women. No dwarfs that he could see, save himself. Perhaps his folk were something of a krewe of their own, an endless procession of the ridiculous and the pain-wracked.

He stayed in the Blackeyes krewe house even as the other krewe kings went to rouse their own folk. What else was there to do? Following the Card King about through night's freezing darkness seemed more trouble than he could face. In any case, this place was an education in its own right.

For one, these people could have planned an invasion. They seemed to be aware of everything at once. As the weather continued to worsen, the Blackeyes king dispatched men to find or hire horse teams to keep the streets clear enough for them to set out in the morning. The king was one Alfaz who threw the seven against him in their betting round, clad in motley made of shimmering chains and paste gems that gave strain to Bijaz's eyes.

King Alfaz had boys greasing the axles and wheels of the wagons that would carry their stages, the floats that served as their rolling artwork. Women pulled down the riders' costumes and cleaned the spiders and dust from within the wickerwork frames. A small committee of older members of the krewe went from stage to stage deciding whether each one in particular should go out on the Festival of Winter Drownings. Bijaz stayed with them, as he knew nothing of the craft required to maintain the stages and riding costumes.

He was surprised that once the Card King threw in his stakes there had been no more challenges. Just questions of the most usual sort. Usual for the krewes, at any rate.

"Is it forbidden that we bear blades on the morrow?" they asked him.

As if Bijaz knew anything of that. All he could do was trust the Numbers Men who gave him the city's luck. He made the answer that seemed best to him. "Weapons are not carried on the Festival of Winter Drownings, for it celebrates those who died bloodless," he said. "If the worst comes, we will not be fit to fight charging armies in any case. Better our armor be the stages and costumes, and our weapons be our pride."

That answer caused them to send runners to the other krewe houses to pass the word, and so questions came back by runner, as well as more from the committee.

"We do not normally take processionals together. Is there an order to our march?"

"No," Bijaz told them. "Do as you see fit."

"The Card King asks if we may make mock of the Burgesses and the Imperator, or do you truly mean only the signs of spring to march?"

"Mock as you will."

"Is a ship above the clouds within your vision for us?"

"If it sails in peaceful sunlight, it is for us. But leave off the cannon."

So it went.

He learned more and more, though. How a clever arrangement of chains and a kingpin can articulate a wagon so that a long stage was able to move through the narrow, drunk-walking streets of the City Imperishable. Why some stages required that the krewe drovers harness horses three to a rig, and some by pairs, depending both on the beasts' gender and nature of the pull. That faces of those on the stages were painted to be seen from far away, but faces of costumed riders were painted for closer work.

So much effort to make a world that was real only for a few hours on a few days of the year.

Bijaz sat with King Alfaz and several other seniors of the Blackeyes Krewe on some overturned water butts on a balcony above the bustle of the krewe house. They chewed at a midnight meal of cold roast pigeon out of an ice chest which had been set here earlier, and honeyed peas from a great jar someone had brought up from a cellar below the main floor. The pigeon was tough and the peas were mealy, but he was glad to eat, glad of the sharp flavor of the spices in which the pigeon had soaked, glad of the cloying, tangy sweetness of the nearly rancid honey.

"You are unlucky," said Alfaz over the smack of lips and the grinding of jaws.

The eating stopped of a sudden as all ears pricked.

Bijaz found that statement almost amusing, given his recent time with the Numbers Men. "Me? Why am I unlucky?"

"Oh, not yourself, friend Bijaz. You are a nice enough fellow, and the luck is upon you. Else we would not all be here now, eh?"

"Indeed."

"It is dwarfs I speak of. No dwarfs in a krewe. Unlucky."

That directness stung. "Dwarfs are unwelcome in many places of this city, for all that we were made to serve here."

"Different." Alfaz tore at a tiny wing, swallowing the slivers of meat without pausing to chew. "We have our laws in the krewes. 'King' is not just a title of courtesy. When the krewe is met, I have the right to bind and to loose, to hear petitions and make judgments that are recognized in the courts of the Assemblage. Only with my own folk, and only in pursuit of the affairs of the krewe—should I meet Mariah there on the street, I could no more compel her to my will than I could make her grow wings. Here in the krewe house, though, she is my subject."

Mariah, raven-haired with streaks of gray and skin dark as a walnut, made mock bow with eyes a glittering.

Alfaz went on. "The power means little directly, now, save sometimes in dispute of petty debt at dice or cards, and in keeping discipline during the processional. No krewe king has had a player whipped in my lifetime or longer." He waved the stripped wing bone at Bijaz. "Still we carry it with us. An echo or mock of the powers that rule courtroom and guildhall and ship's deck, if you take my meaning."

"Where in this is the poor luck of dwarfs?" Bijaz asked politely.

"Our laws tell us you have your own power. A dwarf is never bound to a krewe king. Your word trumps mine at your will. That, truly, is why we first treated with you this past day instead of simply tossing you back in the street as we might have done with any other lout who broke into a council of the kings."

"We are unlucky because we are beyond your power." Bijaz laughed softly.

"Oh, that it would be so."

"Much is lost to us these days," Alfaz answered. "For the best, most like. You have your traditions, and we have ours. I will say only this much more: the krewes and their kings respect what the dwarfs once were."

Bijaz would have loved to question that, but Alfaz tossed his bone to a lazing mongrel, stood with a great yawn and bellowed at his folk—most of whom had never paused in their labors—to take their lazy hides back to work.

The morning bells saw the chosen stages drawn up in a snaking circle, ready to roll out the great doors. Those set aside for this day were already broken down and winched into the rafters of the great krewe house, or stacked along the walls, in order to make room for the marshalling of the processional.

Again, Bijaz was struck by the stark competence of these folk. He knew of caravan masters who could not arrange their mules half so well with an open field and a day to work at it. The wickerwork and timbers and rope lashes were put away in their places. All he saw now was the bacchanal procession coiled in on itself, a vast and lengthy chick of every color, just waiting to hatch from the stone-walled egg that was the krewe house.

It fair vibrated, like a shout amid meditating priests, or an ape set to romp among white-robed dancers.

An arrow of color and summoning, loosed at the Limerock Palace, he thought.

"Soon," said Alfaz. "We wait word from the others. We will arrange ourselves in the order the line of march passes by each krewe house, from the farthest forward that the others might fall in behind as the stages pass them by. That makes Blackeyes third in the processional. Would you ride forward to lead alongside the Card King and the Krewe of Faces?"

Bijaz had taken something of a liking to the glittering man with the gruff heart as the night went on, but there was also wisdom in Alfaz's request.

"I think you may have the right of it, sir, though I have enjoyed your company. And thank you for your hospitality, as well."

A smile quirked Alfaz's lips. "Well, old Pollis is here now, so you can speak of it yourself. I will leave you to your business." He nodded at the Card King, who was approaching through the colorful, stinking bustle of the final preparations. Somehow, though it was eighteen hours or more since they first met and Bijaz could not imagine that Pollis had found sleep to steal from the night's watches any more than he, the krewe king still looked fresh—bright red, gleaming, ready to erupt like a human volcano.

"I wish to show you something," the Card King said, extending his overlarge left fist.

Bijaz stared at the hand a moment, wondering if despite Alfaz's pronouncements on the dwarfs this were some not so obscure threat, when the fingers unfolded.

Within were two dice.

Blank.

He plucked them out of the field of pink flesh where they lay, and studied the cubes. "Yes?"

"They had pips when I went to throw them. Last night." Bijaz had immediately known what the Card King meant, but he nodded. "The bones moved in my hand like two live things, and they bit me. I know the feel of dice as well as I know the feel of my own teeth. That was when I chose to throw the flashbangs. I did not want to toss blank dice. Your wager was won in that moment."

The big red man held out his other hand, palm flat. An array of pips was embedded in the flesh, shallow black pits in the patterns of the face of a die. Two dice.

"Ah." Though he knew he should not be surprised, Bijaz still felt a certain relief that the Numbers Men attended him. As Three-Widows said, gaming was a form of prayer.

"There is another piece of business," the Card King said roughly. "The snow is deep and dreadful. We've had boys and horses out beating a route open for us, but none of the krewes can follow the traditional bacchanal processions. We are going to work our way down Orogene Avenue and across Lame Burgess Bridge, and thence to Short Street and Terminus Plaza. To open the side streets and hills to our stages will be to cry for disaster. In all this, I would have you ride with the Krewe of Faces, if you will do that."

"Alfaz said much the same. I would be honored."

"One more thing, sir dwarf. Your mask has been delivered." The red man snapped his fingers and two damp boys with sweat steaming off their clothes ran up carrying a horse's head. "I am told you are to wear this when we march."

Bijaz stared at the too-familiar thing, his gut knotting in a rush of bloody flux. It was the head from the dwarf pits. That the torturer always wore as he slew the youth. All the sense of well-being and goodwill that had settled on him since meeting the Numbers Men escaped like air from a dead man's lung. There was no erasing his guilt. Even the punishment he had suffered through could not atone. The Old Gods would have him dance as the knifeman at the head of the bacchanal, with all the blood that had been spilled behind this mask.

Blood he bought and paid for with gold, and stroked his cock to watch flowing.

He would have cried, then, who had not shed tears in four decades and more, but it was too cold. Besides, Bijaz was afraid if he surrendered to the return of the guilt and fear he would not stop. If he was going to die today, better it be underneath that dread mask than in some market gutter near the eastern wall.

Bijaz managed to choke a few words out. "I would say thank you, but…"

The Card King placed a hand upon his shoulder, gripped Bijaz briefly in a shiver of brotherhood. "We who wear the masks understand."

"Who…who told you?" he asked the Card King.

"If you do not know, it is not for me to say."

The Tribade, he thought. Though why they would do so, Bijaz could not reckon.

When he took it from the boys, the head weighed nothing, as if it were already part of his body.

He made his way to the Faces krewe house. It seemed that noise moved the krewes forward. With a whistle and a rattle of drums the great doors were thrown back. The Card King rode first, on a white stallion caparisoned with red and gold that matched his suit, carrying instead of a sword or spear a great pennon on a pole long as a lance.

Bijaz came beside him atop a black mule, a beast he had been introduced to moments before, which seemed terrified of him. This was not his usual experience of mules, and he was somewhat distracted by its tendency to dance too fast away at his touch. Quite the opposite of most of the creature's famously ornery similars.

Even though he wore the shame of the horse's head as his own riding costume—probably what frightened the mule, he realized—Bijaz could see well enough. It sat farther down on his chest than he expected, his head jammed up into the dome of the top of the horse-head shape. The eyes, which gleamed like oiled opals in the dwarf pits, gave him a clear but unorthodox view, acting as lenses that both widened and distorted what he could see. To Bijaz's irritation, whatever lay directly in front of him was hidden by the snout and the placement of the eyes, though he nearly crossed his own trying to see there.

The street was piled high with snow, though a path had been broken and smoothed down not much wider than the bodies of the stages. A few shivering boys stood atop the mounds that were shoveled aside, but the buildings beyond, mostly halls of commerce, warehouses and the sort of shabbier shops one found in a district such as this, were all shuttered.

The sky was blue as a baby's eye, with the pale distance of hard winter. Wind whipped along the street, cold as anything Bijaz could remember. The Card King paid it no mind, but sat tall with his pennon streaming nearly flat, then snapping with the gusts in a whipcrack.

The world smelled of ice, and though the air was clean as ever it was after a winter storm, Bijaz also scented death on the wind.

The bacchanal procession moved outward. The Card King's horse minced along sidestepping while he inspected the line. Bijaz's mule skittered after it, wiggling as if his weight burned the animal. He tried to ignore the poor behavior and look sidelong through the mask's eyes at what his will had wrought.

Flowers, as he had asked. But more. This was the Krewe of Faces, of course, so the stages featured cards from a divination deck set out in scenes, as well as figures out of history—many of those quickly repainted and dressed to match the mighty folk who had stood at the center of the city's affairs of late.

He saw Arran Prothro in front of a giant bed where two people wrestled in identical costumes of exaggerated nudity—the same in all respects save for the floursack breasts and long hair on one. The First Counselor seemed not to notice his wife and brother-in-law at their sport as he waved a huge book with the word "LAW" painted on the cover.

This was followed by a tableau showing the card known as Farmer Amid Stars, then another of a feathered snake with the head of Michael Almandine. He had watched that one being hastily assembled from some scene of jungle sacrifice, back in the small hours of the night.

Amid the faces and the mockery there were also gardens of flowers, trees in flower, flowers on horseback, flowers dancing on foot, flowers painted on wooden flanks and great muslin banners. The Card King nodded as the last stage rumbled out the krewe house doors, then gave Bijaz a hard look.

"We are away, friend dwarf. Would you come to the front with me?"

He came, mule balking all the way.

Riding at the front meant he saw none of the other ten bacchanal processions. Bijaz knew from the chatter overnight that each krewe's train of stages would be somewhat abbreviated. This was in order to honor his request to emphasize springtime and light, but also a limit imposed by the sheer exigencies of the weather and street conditions. All he saw was open doors as they passed and the bulking, colorful shadows within waiting to follow.

Somehow he knew that it would be enough for whatever they accomplished this day.

Riding at the head of the processional right into the teeth of the wind was more than he wanted. There was nothing for it but to accept the ice that crusted inside his mask, the chill in his joints, the glare of sun on snow.

The Card King rode in silence with his lance high and his banner snapping ever to the right, moving with the east wind that cut across the city toward the river. As they made their way down Orogene Avenue, crowds began to gather despite the weather. People stood knee-deep in snow, hip-deep or more where the wind had pushed drifts, and began to ring bells and bang pots to toll their coming.

Some grabbed plants from conservatories within their homes, or waved broomsticks with lengths of green cloth affixed, and ran to join the processional. Others scuttled ahead to make sure the streets were passable, clearing the route and calling to their friends. Bijaz knew perfectly well from years of watching the bacchanal processions that the krewes worked vigorously to keep people off their stages and out of the line of march, but on this day the Card King merely waved his free hand and continued to ride.

They might allow the folk of the city to join their stream of flowers, but the processional would not slow.

By the time they crossed the Lame Burgess Bridge to head south toward the Limerock Palace and Terminus Plaza, bells across the City Imperishable tolled furiously. Not with the assonance of the morning bells, but more like metal-tongued shouting.

Had the invasion come? Or did the bells ring for them? Bijaz had no way to know. He reached up to touch the muzzle of the horse's head. It felt warm, almost real.

This was a day for the Old Gods to dance along with the drowned men, and for magic to walk the streets. He who had gamed at the White Table should expect no less.

Numbers always balance, Bijaz thought. Every dwarf knew that. Terminus Plaza might prove to be his Black Table. Now would be the moment of his luck, when he carried whatever the Numbers Men had given him and laid the stakes for the entire City Imperishable.

Hopefully today's snow and blood would wash away the guilt with which he had stained his years.

As they passed the shoulder of the New Hill and could see the Limerock Palace down the line of the street, a half-mile or more yet, a terrible racket rose across the city.

Howling. The black dogs from the Trial of Flowers were baying to be let loose.

The Card King continued to wave and carry his banner high, not allowing his horse to hesitate, showing no question or fear in the seat he kept. Bijaz, knowing he looked the squat and dour mock on his mule next to the great man on the fine white horse, could do no less, though the noise of the black dogs struck a fear of great teeth and flowing blood deep within him.

JASON THE FACTOR

Jason's camel trailed the others into the City Imperishable. He was preceded by his shadow on the stones, already shortening as the sun rose higher. As he passed through the arch of the gate, the bells of the city began to ring. Not the rippling call of the morning and evening bells, nor even the peal of bacchanal days, but a clangor like the signals for fire or flood, as if each ringer had caught a whiff of panic and meant to set his own tempo and pattern.

A rain of metal sound then, rippling out over the city.

He wasn't sure what that meant, save that it was not likely to be much to his taste. The Festival of Winter Drownings, indeed. Perhaps the rest of the dead men of winter had begun climbing from the freezing banks of the River Saltus. Much like those damned sniffers.

Inside the gate, the Tokhari army moved down into the Green Market. The snow was too deep for them to spread among the ruined city blocks of the Wall Street area, which was nothing more than a gently hummocked white plain as high as his knees were he dismounted. Ahead, awaiting the army, he saw Enero's forces drawn up on horseback, and even those camelopards from the grass sea, each with its mummer mount.

The Arlecchini. Whoever or whatever they really were.

The bells continued their trembling cacophony as Jason followed as his captors' lonely rearguard. The tolling was bad enough, harbingers of what the day would soon bring. The howling that erupted to drown out the bells was even worse. It sounded as if the very stones of the City Imperishable had been given voice to express their anguish.

Jason knew full well what that noise meant. Ignatius had finally let loose the black dogs that had been penned since the massacre in Terminus Plaza.

"Now we are to be going!" Enero shouted, and with no more ceremony than that, the Winter Boys and the Tokhari began to gather speed as they moved down Upper Melisande Avenue, throwing a glittering fog of snow in their haste. Kalliope cursed and prodded her camel to race forward, trying to gain the head of the column. Jason made his best effort to follow.

He was already dead, which somehow made him fear what was to come all the more. He was denied even the escape of mortality from the erstwhile master whom he had so thoroughly betrayed.

The snow-fog whipped through the air, shimmering with tiny rainbows thrown by the sun as he passed. Cobbles pounded beneath the slush, the wind was at his back and it might have been a good day to be alive.

Dead or alive, he took comfort from being in his city once more.

The camelopards took quickly to the head of the charge, their long legs carrying them better through the snow. The Tokhari camels were making it harder work, but the sunlight and open streets set them on their course, with much sliding and slipping in the unfamiliar snow. Enero's men ahorse mixed with the squads of like-mounted Tokhari, turning the street to a churning stampede.

It was more a race than an assault, the armies glad to be out of the storm and in good sunlight, however miserable the cold, however portentous the howling of the black dogs. The snow-fog continued to hang over them all as Kalliope and her followers, including Jason, pushed farther ahead.

They came into the Temple District, racing along Upper Melisande Avenue, where the first of the black dogs leapt from an alley and launched itself into a group of Tokhari packed close together. The dog was at least as big as Jason remembered from the day of the Trial of Flowers, the size of a camel, and its sheer mass foundered three horses when it sprang.

Kalliope swore and pushed her camel up onto a sidewalk, ducking beneath the winter-dead branches of the lindens planted there. All Jason could do was follow. The tree threatened to tear at his face, and he was not enough of a camelman to turn his head and watch behind him to see the progress of the roaring, screaming fight that had erupted.

Priests and monks and acolytes were pushing onto their steps and balconies, some hurling fruit or other offerings. Jason wanted to tell them to go back in or join the charge. They needed to know that army raced to storm the Limerock Palace, not to lay waste to the City. Given that he could barely make himself heard to his sister, it was pure fantasy to think he might rally the Temple District.

He took a great jolt as his camel slipped on the kerb and bounced against a pair of Enero's men on ponies shaggy as their leader's mount. Jason caught a flash of a grin from one before another camel overran the Winter Boy's pony from behind and trampled him in a spray of pink froth.

It was a stampede, not a charge, but he understood well enough what Kalliope and Enero were about. They needed to quickly secure Terminus Plaza and storm the Limerock Palace. Otherwise they would be trapped fighting bailiffs, black dogs and worse monsters, street by street. Once that happened, the army would be bled to nothing for no gain at all.

Why had they all been so afraid of these Tokhari, he wondered? The City Imperishable could swallow the army's bones.

People ran toward them in the street, carrying poles and butcher knives and chair legs. The Arlecchini on their camelopards rode them down, or strode over them, firing crossbows as they went. The front line of camels and horses did not have it so easy, meeting the impromptu defense hard.

Again, a trampling, though more of the Tokhari went down. Still Kalliope pushed forward as if she would meet that opposition head-on. The people of the city should be fighting with them, not trying to defend their homes.

They poured into Delator Square, where a gang of drovers was trying to make a blockade of wagons. The defenders were too late, or the army too fast, and the mix of Tokhari and Winter Boys spread around and through the still-closing barricade. Jason could only fix on his sister's white camel and follow.

She had made him what he was now, she owned him, much as Ignatius had in earlier times. Would he betray her as well before the day was done?

The charge focused again down Melisande Avenue, though some of the riders found other streets heading the same way. The bells were still clanging for fire, invasion, fear. Alates flew snap-wingéd and low above the riders, though they dropped no rocks nor fired weapons on either rider or defender. More people were trampled, one of the camelopards went down with a sickening crunch, and Jason saw torches being thrown.

The houses would be on fire soon with that.

He could do nothing to stop it, any more than he could have stopped a flood rushing down the Little Bull River. People died and died, but the army hurtled on.

Too soon, it seemed, they cornered onto Roncelvas Way, then spilled into Terminus Plaza. An unbroken field of snow spread before the Limerock Palace. The camelopards, still leading, kicked up great clouds of the stuff as their leader—Paolino?—reined in to assess what stood against him.

Camels, horses, men and women, civilians, City Men, the entire mob poured out into the snow, which was knee-deep or more in this open space. The people followed the charge more than fighting it now, recognizing with the dim intelligence of a mob that the invaders in their midst were an arrow aimed at the Limerock Palace and the Imperator Restored.

Alates circled overhead like crows above a corpse yard, though Jason could not say at whose bidding they flew. At least a dozen black dogs were arrayed outside the Riverward Gate. Naked, dark-eyed figures rode on their shoulders or stood among them. Sniffers, of course, their bloody sockets not visible from this distance. Other creatures were present: a quivering tower of clear gel in which fish darted, a monstrous sending from the River Saltus no doubt. Also two great birds roosting on the wall with smoke issuing from their beaks, feathers a mixture of molder and brass. These noumenal forces were surrounded by Green Kelly's Restorationists in their dark coats, with cudgels, swords and pistols. Jason thought he even saw the steward himself, riding a large white lizard.

He did not see Zaharias' bailiffs, and that gave him hope. He took a shuddering breath of air so cold that it stung his lungs like crystal knives. In doing so, Jason realized that somewhere on the charge his heart had begun once more to beat.

"Alive," he said. "I am alive."

"Silence," Kalliope barked. "We only have moments."

The defenders stood aside as the Imperator Ignatius rode out on a skeletal black horse twice as tall as a man. His Magnificence was forced to duck to clear the arch, but still he came, and pulled himself short in front of his forces, a hundred yards distant across the virgin snow.

If I am come back to life, Jason thought, then it follows that my master may be brought back, too.

Ignatius raised his hand. Every bell in the city stopped at that moment, even those in midtone, leaving only a crackling silence. Jason spurred his camel forward, leaping out from the attackers' line to cross the field just as a great blare of horns erupted from Short Street.

He saw a fat man in a red suit riding next to a horse-headed dwarf, the two of them leading a bacchanal procession into Terminus Plaza. Neither army moved while both considered what this might portend. Jason seized the moment to prod his camel onward.

He had to get to Ignatius. He would bring his master out of the half-world where the Imperator now dwelled and pull him back among the living.

In the middle of the plaza, something stung Jason as a rifle cracked. He looked down to see blood blooming from his shoulder.

"No!" shrieked Kalliope behind him.

Another crack and his camel foundered, tossing Jason into the snow. He tried to pull himself up next to the dying beast, remembering this had happened the last time he rode into Terminus Plaza. Something was wrong with him again. He was unwinding, heading back to the sand grave his sister had made for him.

Jason looked up, his eyes blurring in and out of focus, to see the camelopards charging toward him in fountains of snow. The mummers on their backs had left their crossbows slung in favor of short poles or batons wrapped with ribbons and each tipped with a bright brass ball. Their tall mounts, knees ungainly, fur colored like broken rocks on sand, ran into the bullets without a call, just ruffling snorts and the faint jingle of their harnesses.

He saw the camel riders and horsemen break once more into a charge behind the camelopards, Kalliope's white mount leaping at the front. In that moment, he wished he'd known more of her to love her, simply as his sister. Too late, he supposed. Years and blades stood between them now, and only minutes remained.

He focused his thoughts again. The approaching charge moved in an eerie silence, breaching the snow on the square like an ocean to be conquered.

There was a beauty to it, he thought, these brave warriors who would die on the wings of bullets or be torn by the black dogs. It occurred to him that the entire charge would be riding him down in a few more seconds.

Hands grabbed him and hoisted him.

"By the fires, you weigh nothing," shouted a horse as it hauled him onto a black mule and kicked the panicked animal to move ahead of the charge.

That wasn't right. He tried to focus, but all Jason could think was that he once more found himself slung over an animal riding through cold snow to his death.

Was this his hell, to die over and over face-down against wet fur?

"They're coming to meet us," the horse said, and Jason recognized Bijaz's voice.

"Once again you save me, old dwarf," he tried to say, but the mule's sweating flank swallowed his words.

IMAGO OF LOCKWOOD

It was pain beyond anything he had experienced. Fire, shock, blades—all ran together as Archer sliced open the skin and muscles of Imago's left thigh.

"Do you imagine this hurts?" shouted the godmonger, whose face was nothing but black shadow beneath the burning eye in the center of his forehead.

Another slice. Imago would have screamed, but he seemed to have mislaid his voice. The blue stone altar steamed and bubbled beneath him. He felt its heat in the naked skin of his back.

"Try the pain of the box, full-man," Archer hissed in his ear. "Legs closed off to stunt short, gut so tight you can't shit for a week at a time, sitting in your own piss till they remember to come clean you."

A different kind of slicing this time, some rough-toothed knife cutting into bone. "I'll take you from the bottom up," the dwarf said. "That way you feel each leg twice. When a doctor makes a cut dwarf, it takes a month for all the operations, and six months more for the healing."

"Sacrifice," Imago squeaked.

"Yes, my Lord Mayor." Through some trick of reflection he glimpsed Archer's face twisted in a bloody knot of lust and hatred. "Sacrifice. The same that every dwarf of this city made all through their childhood."

The hacking took time. Though he felt nauseous and chilled as the stone, Imago never stopped hurting. He would have swallowed hot lead just to bring an end. A pistol to his jaw. Lowered his body into vile poison. Pain ran on flaming pain. The measure of his agony kept climbing, to heights he did not know existed.

With each cut, the altar continued to steam and warm. Blue light filled the grotto, an eldritch echo of an ancient dawn that illuminated the fierce concentration on Archer's face.

In a momentary flash of lucidity, Imago thought he would never have recognized the godmonger now.

The other leg then, more slicing. This was a butcher's job, not surgery—meat for the divine flame. Imago could not understand why he had not already bled out his life. The stone altar was drinking him in, keeping him alive and conscious long past any rational measure.

Around them the scrape of much larger, heavier stones began to echo.

"I'll take a fathom out of the ropes of your guts," Archer said. His voice had become almost normal. Though not Archer's voice, in truth. "I'll break your hips. Take a pair of ribs from each side. We'll make a city dwarf of you yet, my Lord Mayor."

Footfalls now, locusts buzzing loud as summer, that prickling dark taking him despite the blue light.

This was death, finally. Thank the gods, he thought as he screamed. No, no, not the gods! Not the Old Gods. Waves of red pulsed through his body, burning off the prickling dark like fire moving through dried cotton.

He opened his eyes to look at Archer. The dwarf had grown huge. His nose was a shattered stone. His hair gorse. His eyes glinting black coals. He was stumpy, with a misshapen body formed badly as any dwarf, but Archer creaked as he towered over Imago.

The Little Man, Imago realized. One of the Old Gods had come to Archer's call. To his own call.

"We are sacrifices, every day," Archer's voice said weakly from the god's mouth, but then it was drowned in laughter on a fire-hot breath that gusted with the reek of blood and smoke as Imago's left leg was twisted away at the kneecap, then at the hip.

He would have fainted if he could, but the pain was too great. It kept him awake, burning.

Stone creaked again. A black dog loomed up behind the Little Man. The Great Wolf. Its eyes were yellow moons, each hanging half-spent in the starry skies behind the Old God's face.

"I am the City Imperishable," Imago managed to gasp through the waves of his pain. "I come to lay you back...within your graves with...respect...and regret."

YOU LAY NOTHING the Little Man said in a voice that buzzed within the bones of Imago's skull.

Clicking, then, and a damp scent as something with the smell of a woman passed close. NONE OF THE OTHERS HAD THE COURAGE TO OFFER THEMSELVES

Her voice was every orgasm Imago had ever experienced, the sound of water on stones. Had not Saltfingers named one of them the Water-Bearer?

The Great Wolf only growled. The Little Man laughed, a sound like a building falling.

THIS IS NOT COURAGE...JUST FAITH MISPLACED IN DESTINY

"I am yours," Imago said.

YOU WERE ALWAYS OURS said the Water-Bearer. Her tone was not unkind.

"As…is…the…City," he gasped. "Yours. But we must…go…onward."

The Great Wolf growled again, snapping at the Little Man. Shapes moved in the shadows. ENOUGH said the Water-Bearer. THE FORMS HAVE BEEN SERVED…WE ALSO OWE OUR PART

The Little Man grumbled. NEVER ENOUGH

He finished his tearing and jammed Imago's knees back onto the stumps of his thighs. With fingernails like shovels, he tore into Imago's gut and chest. NONETHELESS IT WILL BE DONE WELL

THIS IS JUST the Water-Bearer said. THEY ABOVE ALSO GIVE OF THEMSELVES

Imago heard a clattering of bones, or perhaps dice, as his ribs were torn from his chest, one by one.

Bijaz the Dwarf

He carried Jason right into the teeth of the black dogs, knowing there was nowhere else to go. The bacchanal procession had brought flowers to Terminus Plaza, but the swords were here first.

Bijaz tried not to think about the bullets flying past him, the wingéd men skimming overhead. His eyes were only on Ignatius, though he had to cock his masked head thus and so to keep his target in sight. No wonder horses were such great ninnies.

He hoped Jason would still be alive when they dismounted in a few more seconds. The rebel Second Counselor had bled the snow red as spring roses by the time Bijaz had grabbed him up for this last ride. If he was the City's luck, then Jason was Ignatius' luck, or something so close as to never mind the difference.

The City Imperishable needed Bijaz to bring Jason and the Imperator together.

Just as he passed the black dogs bounding the other way, the monsters cut loose with a howl in perfect unison, then folded themselves into dark whirlwinds of coal dust and dried filth that threatened to fill his lungs. The sniffers astride their backs tumbled loose-limbed into the snow, their fellows on foot tripping and falling silent. The naked youthful bodies were immediately blue with cold.

In a moment, the battlefield had changed. Archer must have found some way down to the tombs of the Old Gods. Bijaz made a prayer of thanks to the Numbers Men—this was the City's luck.

The collapse of Ignatius' skeletal horse and all his monsters was accompanied by shouts of dismay from the Restorationists. Almost as quickly, they began falling alongside their erstwhile allies. Bullets hit the snow with a series of muffled thwops while the noise of the shots rang from the top of the wall.

The bailiffs were up there, some fighting hand to hand with Restorationists around Arran Prothro, while others fired down on their own lines in the snow. Alates, he saw, were dropping on the Imperator's forces as well, to snatch at firearms and hurl people from the wall.

This travesty was almost over.

The mule balked to throw Bijaz and Jason both right into the pile of bones where Ignatius sprawled like a small child, legs wide and arms splayed behind his back. He looked lost in the great gold and black Imperator's robes, and the crown had tumbled from his head to lie glittering in the snow.

Jason sat up, swaying, to vomit blood on his old master's lap.

"My ear…" Ignatius looked confused. His hand rose to the freshly oozing stub at the left side of his head.

"Every thing contains its own opposite," Jason said quite clearly, and pulled the Imperator into a bloody-mouthed kiss.

JASON THE FACTOR

Life, Jason thought, I will give him my life that he might live in my stead.

No pulse beat in the neck he held. He heard the screaming clear enough behind him. Battle had been joined.

Jason held Ignatius close. "Live, by Dorgau's nine hells," he whispered in the torn ear hole. He wished he'd somehow fetched the ear from his old quarters, though that miserable scrap must be long lost to rot. At the least he could have made his master whole.

"Too much…" The Imperator shuddered.

His old master was the true *ma-jieni na-dja*. The City Imperishable's dead man of winter.

"Where did you go, Master? Who took you there?"

"Beyond."

Beyond? Jason looked up at the sound of a bubbling hiss, fearing some revived devilment. He saw only mist and steam, Bijaz with his horse's head a strange silhouette. Clouds of pale vapor rushed into the air as water trickled all across Terminus Plaza.

The snow was melting with unnatural haste.

Still cradling Ignatius, Jason watched as patches of damp, clear stone appeared. Tiny green shoots pushed up through the cracks between the pavers of the gate arch and out on the plaza itself. Fingers of spring, reaching back through the course of time into this too-early iron winter. Or the very soil, perhaps, fertilized by blood and fighting back with its only weapon.

He watched, fascinated as he held his master close.

The shoots expanded to vines, to stalks, to young trees arrowing skyward with a noise like the crackling of pork fat in the pan. Flowers peeped from the green with the same bizarre velocity, erupting like firesparks on this storm of growth. The pink of peonies, the maroon of wine cups, the yellow-white of daisies and more—every varietal that ever bloomed in the City Imperishable seemed to have sent its ambassadors to this invasion. Above the blooms, new-formed trees exploded into leaf. Green arrived on a storm of sap and vine, to overtake both the snows of winter and the armies that invested the city in the same swift stroke.

Ignatius mewled and pressed himself closer into Jason like a blind pup. "I was made to take too much," the Imperator gasped.

Questing vines had wrapped both their thighs, Jason saw. Where the plants only lay across his limbs, binding him without killing him, they stabbed into the Imperator's cold flesh.

"Please…" Ignatius said in a child's voice.

"I love you, Master," Jason replied. His eyes stung. Giving the only gift that remained to him, he twisted the Imperator's neck til it snapped.

IMAGO OF LOCKWOOD

Imago looked up to see a strange woman staring down at him. Gray-haired, with tiny spectacles that glimmered in the light of a number of lamps. She frowned. "You were not a dwarf when last I caught sight of you."

"I am not a dwarf at all."

Her frown deepened. "I am a doctor, both philosophick and medical. I believe I know a dwarf when I see one. I studied long to find such wisdom, I assure you."

Saltfingers' strange, pale face loomed next to the doctor. "You live. I would not have bet a dried groat on you. She is very good."

"I am…alive," Imago said.

The doctor's frown slid into a grin of asperity. "You're most welcome, my Lord Mayor."

He felt strange. More accurately, the *way* he felt was strange. Imago's memory was crowded with booming voices, impossibilities. The sound of stone scraping figured prominently.

Imago tried to sit up. Everything was wrong, as if he wore someone else's body. He was lying in that underground street.

Memory began flooding back to him, recollection wrapped in pain. The mere echo of it made him curl tight to vomit, his body rejecting the violations that had been committed upon it.

"You will quickly forget," the doctor said distantly.

"Where is he?" demanded a new voice.

Saltfingers answered. "A moment, your worship."

Imago realized the dwarf hadn't meant him this time. Saltfingers and the doctor propped him up and wiped his chest, then wrapped him in a blood-stained leather coat that had belonged to a much larger man. To him, in fact.

Too much light shone in his eyes, from lanterns held by a dolorous collection of pale men and dwarfs that had to be more of Saltfingers' dunnymen. Biggest Sister stood, arms cocked on her hips.

"Not so handsome now, are you, lover boy?"

"Hello," Imago managed.

"You succeeded." Biggest Sister shook her head. "We'll all be a long time sorting it out, but you laid enough meat on the altar to draw the Old Gods down to their holes. Whatever you and that godmonger did, it was enough."

"Archer?" Imago tried to jump to his feet, torn between terrified anger and angry terror. What that hellish dwarf had done to him! He succeeded only in falling back on his arse. "Where is he?"

It was Saltfingers who answered, after looking at a few of his dunnymen. "Spent. Enough to say he served us all well."

"As did you, my Lord Mayor," said Biggest Sister. "You told me that when you saw the City you saw its people, and you have proved that on your own body. The Tribade considers all your debts to be fully cleared."

"And this…" Imago reached down to rub the stumpy legs, touch his hideously sore, warm belly. "A god touched me. Several gods." He looked around. "I think I understand. One of the Old Gods, maybe the first of them, is a dwarf. Boxing is not a torture, or bondage. It is a sacrament, that…" Imago struggled to follow the idea. "That once made priests, perhaps. Who held the Old Gods in check. Even…even after the Old Gods were cast down, their graves were sealed on the pain of the dwarfs. Year after year, generation after generation. When the Inner Chamber grew too strong, and the ambitious came below the earth seeking chthonic power, and the dwarfs were forced from the city, all this at once…the god-graves began to open."

"Now you know the bargain," said Biggest Sister. "With as much certainty as any of us. Better, I think. You should not speak overmuch of this. What you should do is get to the surface and show your face. Great deeds are afoot in Terminus Plaza."

"One more thing," Saltfingers said as Imago started to rise. "The mysteries below the stones should stay below the stones. I shall keep your coppers lest I need to call you back."

"Why should you call me back," Imago said, "when I am already home?" He looked around. "Where is my chain of office?"

BIJAZ THE DWARF

Bijaz stared at the teeming field of flowers that Terminus Plaza had become. His mask proved impossible to remove, and so he perforce looked wall-eyed, turning his head this way and that to see. The surviving camelopards cropped at copses of tall lindens and oaks. Horses and camels roamed among children screaming at their play. Snow still glimmered on the streets leading out of the plaza, but the sun was as gentle-bright as the unnatural flowers within. Wingéd men circled watchful in the springlike air. Bailiffs, Tokhari riders and Winter Boys idled along the verges of the grass, just within the warm zone, their hands on their weapons and their eyes on each other.

As far as summoning the spring, he was successful beyond his expectation. The true Trial of Flowers had bloomed, and found the City Imperishable innocent. Sentence reprieved. The new verdancy had taken up the bodies of the fallen as it grew, which somehow only seemed fitting.

I am the City's luck, Bijaz told himself, though he had no idea how long this meadow would stand against the hard reality of winter. For now, it was enough.

A council was taking place now before the Riverward Gate, though it was being held with a strange mixture of informality and intensity. Someone had dragged a trestle table out from a nearby tavern, as the combatants refused to leave the field until a settlement was agreed upon. All the members of the Inner Chamber save the Provost and the Second Counselor had been summarily hanged from the gatehouse in a show of what might be considered to be both vengeance and good faith. Their creaking ropes punctuated the deliberations. Green Kelly the Steward dangled with them, his own execution provoking the loudest cheers even as he screeched threats until the snapping of his neck.

Jason, looking quite ill, sat at one end with Zaharias of Fallen Arch at his left, though they were clearly much at odds with one another. Kalliope of the Tokhari, equally at odds, sat to her brother's right, with Enero beside her and the mummer-priest Paolino in turn next to the Sunward officer. The Card King was next to Zaharias, to speak for the people of the City Imperishable, and Bijaz next to him for the dwarfs, Sewn and Slashed alike. This put him across from Paolino, who seemed most amused by casting hooded glances at Bijaz and picking at his nails with a long dagger not much thicker than a needle, sometimes making a horsey noise with his lips.

The chair at the far end was left empty, against the Lord Mayor's return.

Discussion ranged back and forth, with verbal violence though no hands went to weapons. How to prove the Old Gods were laid down. What sureties the City Imperishable would post against future uprisings of this sort. Why not tear it stone from stone? Death-geld for the fallen Tokhari and Winter Boys. Damages to the streets and structures affected by the charge.

It was endless and irritating. All refreshingly normal bureaucratic muddle in full fly.

Bijaz's nose flicked open, scenting something coming. A series of muddled thumps echoed from the ground before a fountain of steam tore patches of the new-grown turf away, sending dirt and grass and flower petals flying, along with several good pavers.

Imago of Lockwood climbed up out of the ground a very different man. A dwarf, to be precise. Much paler than he had been before, his hair a brittle, wiry white shock instead of his dark curls.

All fell silent, and Bijaz understood. A life, a limb, a love. He had given his life at the White Table, and the stakes had been doubled by Jason's murder of Ignatius. His love for Jason, in the name of Jason's father, had been betrayed. Jason had in turn doubled those stakes in betraying his own love for Ignatius of Redtower who had finally taken Jason's father's place. Now Bijaz saw that limbs were given by Imago, who appeared to have surrendered half of each leg in closing the tombs of the Old Gods.

That the Lord Mayor was a dwarf promised much turmoil for the future.

As Imago stumbled to his seat, a runner came—one of the Winter Boys, trailed by a man in an outrageous krewe costume.

"To beg your pardons," he said, out of breath and on one knee as the krewe man nodded vigorously beside him. "There is being a great lot of horsemen waist-deep in snow at the River Gate along the north wall. We are telling them the Tokhari have taken the city, but an ancient stonecaller is wanting to see a Tokhari up on the wall too fast or they are soon to be attacking."

Argument immediately broke out all over again, even as Enero and the Provost both began signaling their troops. Imago bellowed for silence. He climbed up on the table to be taller—something Bijaz understood quite well—cupped his hands and shouted: "We will open the gates, we will bring them here where there is warmth and pasture for their horses and we will show them that their fears are no more!"

"Who are you to say that?" demanded Kalliope.

"I am—" Imago stopped and looked around a moment. Something strange crossed his face, a complex of thought and emotion and challenge. He climbed down off the table and took his seat. "I am a dwarf of the City Imperishable," he told her quietly. "Who are you to say differently?"

"A Tokhari who has business at the River Gate, I think," she said, almost sweetly. "This city is impossible, you know."

"The city is," Jason said from the head of the table, meeting Imago's eye.

Imago nodded. "The city is."

Night Shade Books Is an Independent Publisher of Quality SF, Fantasy and Horror

ISBN-10: 1-59780-049-X
Trade Paper; $14.95

From Alexander C. Irvine, Locus Award-winning author of A Scattering of Jades, The Narrows, and One King, One Soldier, comes Pictures from an Expedition, an astonishing new collection of thirteen fascinating fantasy and science fiction stories, including the World Fantasy Award-nominated "Gus Dreams of Biting the Mailman" and the all-new tale of identity crisis and uncertainty, "Clownfish." Alexander C. Irvine's crisp, startling, genre-bending prose makes Pictures from an Expedition a captivating, compelling read that, once started, is impossible to put down.

"Scene by scene and setting by setting, Alexander Irvine has rapidly emerged as one of the most accomplished new fantasists of the last several years."

— Gary K. Wolfe, *Locus Magazine*

ISBN-10: 1-59780-048-1
Trade Paper; $14.95

Elizabeth Bear's science fiction trilogy (Hammered, Scardown and Worldwired) have received widespread popular acclaim, but it is her short fiction which has really been turning heads. Routinely defying genre boundaries and exhilarating her readers, Elizabeth Bear's short fiction demonstrates why she is one of the most exciting young writers in the genre.

Whether the inspiration is Ragnorok, Stagger Lee, Elizabethan Drama, John Lennon, or matters even further a field, Bear proves to be up to the task of taking recognizable icons and settings, and making them her own. The stories in The Chains We Refuse range from recognizable SF and fantasy, to contemporary-fantastic stories, to forms not quite so easily described. The twenty-two tales in this collection are sure to please.

Find these Night Shade titles and many others online at http://www.nightshadebooks.com or wherever books are sold.

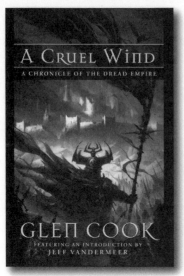

Night Shade Books Is an Independent Publisher of Quality SF, Fantasy and Horror

Seconded to a military-religious order he's barely heard of—part of the baroque hierarchy of the Mercatoria, the latest galactic hegemony—Fassin Taak has to travel again amongst the Dwellers. He is in search of a secret hidden for half a billion years.

But with each day that passes a war draws closer—a war that threatens to overwhelm everything and everyone he's ever known. As complex, turbulent, flamboyant and spectacular as the gas giant on which it is set, the new science fiction novel from Iain M. Banks is space opera on a truly epic scale.

ISBN-10: 1-59780-044-9
Trade Paper; $14.95

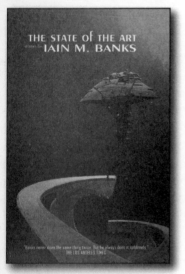

The State of the Art is the first collection from the author of *Look to Windward* and *The Algebraist*. The title story is a Culture novella that features characters from other Banks novels, but is set on Earth in 1977. An additional Culture story is included in this collection, as well as several other non-Culture stories that demonstrate Banks' tremendous range and skill.

This U.S. edition of *The State of the Art* Contains the essay "A Few Notes On the Culture" which is not part of the british edition of this collection, and has not been previously collected.

ISBN-10: 1-59780-074-0
Trade Paper; $14.95

Find these Night Shade titles and many others online at http://www.nightshadebooks.com or wherever books are sold.

Night Shade Books Is an Independent Publisher of Quality SF, Fantasy and Horror

ISBN-10: 1-59780-058-9
Hardcover; $26.95

Zima Blue is Alastair Reynolds's first collection; It spans almost the whole of his career, ranging from "Enola" (which appeared in 1991, only his third sale) right up to recent work such as "Understanding Space and Time," a novella written in 2005, and "Signal to Noise," a new piece written specially for this book. It is the perfect showcase for the evolution of his writing and themes over the last sixteen years, and features extensive story notes.

ISBN-10: 1-59780-022-8
Hardcover; $29.00

War Stories collects together two novels, several short stories and two long poems that deals explicitly with Haldeman's Vietnam, and post Vietnam experiences. The novel *War Year* was one of the first books written by Haledman upon his return from Vietnam, and the novel *1968* (which chronicles time in country, as well as a soldiers return "home") was not published until 1994. These two novels form compelling bookends to a career's worth of writing that has been passionately engaged with the questions raised by the Vietnam War.

Find these Night Shade titles and many others online at http://www.nightshadebooks.com or wherever books are sold.

Night Shade Books Is an Independent Publisher of Quality SF, Fantasy and Horror

ISBN-10: 1-59780-051-1
Hardcover; $26.95

Dark Mondays features five never-before-published stories including the forty-one-thousand-word pirate novel, "The Maid on the Shore," which chronicles the lesser known aspects of Captain Henry Morgan's infamous sacking of Panama City.

"Ms. Baker is the best thing to happen to modern science fiction since Connie Willis or Dan Simmons." — The Dallas Morning News

"Baker Possesses a unique voice—wry and witty but still compassionate. She specializes in detailing the interior lies of the people whom others miss or ignore." — *The San Francisco Chronicle*

ISBN-10: 1-59780-057-0
Trade Paper; $14.95

Hugo and Nebula Award-nominee Kage Baker, creator of The Company series and the fantasy novel *Anvil of the World*, delivers a spectacular collection that includes stories set in both universes, as well as several stand-alone pieces that demonstrate why she is one the most talked-about writers in the sf/fantasy genre.

From contemporary settings to a not-so-innocent America of the 50s and 60s, to the roaring 20s, to Victorian England and to imaginary realms beyond, Kage Baker's fiction delivers layers of historical and social detail that become the stage on which her instantly recognizable characters perform. Her insightful portraits of humanity create an immediacy that is undeniable and compelling.

Find these Night Shade titles and many others online at http://www.nightshadebooks.com or wherever books are sold.

Night Shade Books Is an Independent Publisher of Quality SF, Fantasy and Horror

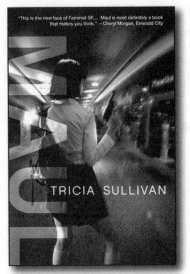

蛇警探

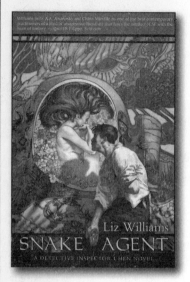
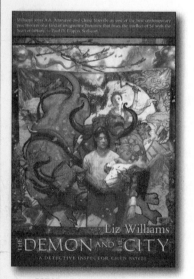